Not To Yield™

A Shared-World Anthology

Created & Edited

by

Michael H. Hanson

Three Ravens Publishing
Chickamauga, GA USA

Cover art by Gothic Sugarplum
Edited by Michael H. Hanson
Title by: Michael H. Hanson /Three Ravens Publishing – 1st edition, 2025

Ebook ISBN: 978-1-966507-28-4
Trade Paperback ISBN: 978-1-966507-43-7

Table of Contents

OPERATIONS ORDER # 13723.. 1

Prologue - Twilight... 5

Day of Days... 11

Risk Analysis... 31

Cyclops... 49

Collateral Damage 77

Articles of War 105

The Right Bait.. 125

Boot Camp... 147

Hide and Seek... 165

Crossing the Line... 189

Straight From The Source 207

Renascence.. 229

Gremlins 249

Cognitive Therapy 273

Penthesilia... 287

BugFuck 303

Post Tenebras Lux... 315

The Gods Anointed 361

Homecoming.. 371

OPERATIONS ORDER # 13723

2425.0 AD

TOP SECRET OPERATIONAL

Captain Tennyson Illiadus, Commander, PW *Ekaterina*

By Order of Vice Admiral Zharcaan Khaav, Commander, Third United Polisian Fleet

I. Situation

A. Enemy Forces: Disposition - The Scourge Dyson Sphere (70,000,000 klicks diameter) and environs (Space object G007.47+00.05, a young, star-forming sector with an unusual amount of massive interstellar dust and clouds. The Scourge have used this large number of overlapping nebulae to hide the location of their home sphere.) Strength - The Scourge Fleet consists of approximately 5 million space-faring vessels, the bulk of which are docked in the Sphere to include: 200,000 Aircraft Carrier equivalents, 300,000 Battleship equivalents, 400,000 Littoral Combat Ship equivalents, 500,000 Cruiser equivalents, 600,000 Destroyer equivalents, 1 Million Troop Carrier equivalents, 2 Million Single-Man Fighter Jet Equivalents

B. Friendly Forces

1.   Higher's Mission & Intent: Create a breach in the Scourge Dyson Sphere (using a field of *Unmatter* 40,000,000 kilometers wide) so the 3rd Polisian Fleet can decisively engage remainder of Scourge forces.

2.   Adjacent Units: PW *Sofia, The Revenge* (captured Scourge Frigate)

3.   Same Sector: 3rd Polisian Fleet

4.   Ship's Manifest/Attachments/Detachments: - Fleet Personnel (200 Crewmen) / Expeditionary Marine Force (75 Troops), Civilian Scientists and Engineers (25) / None

5.   Rules of Engagement: Any and all actions, regardless of current official Polisian War Conventions, are approved for mission completion.

II. Mission

PW *Ekaterina* is directed to join sister-ship PW *Sofia* to act as overall fleet vanguard and escort the captured Scourge Frigate *The Revenge*. PW *Ekaterina* will provide supporting fires in support of the *The Revenge's* mission to detonate a dark matter fountain within the enemy Dyson Sphere at the designated coordinates.

III. Execution
- A. Commander's Intent
1. Desired End-State: Successfully infiltrate the Dyson Sphere and detonate the bombship, decimating the majority of the Scourge Dyson sphere and facilitating a decisive final engagement of the remainder of the Scourge Forces.
- B. Concept of the Operations
1. 3rd Polisian Fleet masses at Galactic Gate Sigma Omicron 112233 above the elliptic of the 3rd Galactic Quadrant, in the planetary system of Trappist-1, in constellation Aquarius. Right ascension 23h 06m 29.283s. Declination −05° 02' 28.59".
2. Scheme of Maneuver: Galactic Gate Epsilon Gamma 482816 is out on the edge of the Scutum-Centaurus Arm near G007.47+00.05 of the 4th Galactic Quadrant. Polisian fleet to follow PW *Ekaterina* and PW *Sofia* upon completion of *The Revenge's* mission.
3. Fire Support Plan - PW *Ekaterina*, PW *Sofia* to provide supporting fires for execution of the ruse and protection of the fireship.
IV. Administration/Logistics/Service Support
A. Administration: SOP / Weapons Hot
B. Logistics (Asset Inventory):
Armaments online:
200 mm main Rail Gun
Two 75mm Triple Turret Rail Guns
Four 15 mm Laser Guns
18 Chain Guns (4 on Marine Landing Craft)
Triple Complement of expendables (ammunition, nuclear missiles, torpedoes)
Vehicles online:
Four Marine Landing Craft
Twenty Life-Boat Pods

Two Ship Launches

One Space Barge

Captain's Yacht

V. Command/Signal

•   A. Signal

1.   Primary: Silent Running to be maintained until the combined Polisian fleet has exited Space-Gate Epsilon Gamma 482816.

2.   Contingency: Command Frequency (SCSS – Subspace Communications Spectrum System) = 300.65000.9446

•   B. Command

1.   Location of Key Leaders:

Vice Admiral Zharcaan Khaav, Flagship PW *Aerope*

Captain Tennyson Illiadus, PW *Ekaterina*

Captain Bartholomew Skesky, PW *Sofia*

Captain Epeius Anticlea, *The Revenge*

Succession of Command (Line Officers):

Commander David Aithon (XO)

Lt. Commander Walter Lehmann (Chief of Engineering)

Lt. Mari Tanaka (CIC, Electronic Warfare Supervisor)

Lt. Peter Rucker (Weaponeering)

Lt. Lisa Thorlssen (Operations)

Lt. Adoris Djulgun (CIC, Communications)

Lt. (junior grade) Amanda Aethra (CIC, Electronic Warfare Officer)

Lt. (junior grade) Eva Calchas (Logistics)

Lt. (junior grade) Aaron Teucer (Training)

Ensign Jacqui Lada (2nd in Command, Engineering)

Ensign Tamor Cailin (CIC, Fighter Director)

Ensign I!tik (CIC, Spatial Geography Plotter)

Ensign Terry Thaleia (CIC, Navigation Plotter)

4 | Page

Prologue - Twilight

By: Michael H. Hanson

Thirty-one-year-old Commander Tennyson Maria Illiadus's eyes open thirty minutes before her normal Oh Dark Thirty Hours alarm clock setting. Her sleep is invaded by ten years of ghosts, and they succeed in dragging her back to reality. Groaning, she hits the head, then washes her hands and splashes cold water onto her face before dressing in navy issue sweats and sneakers. She proceeds to jog through the outermost corridor of the middle and largest deck of the large spaceship, relishing the deck plates' artificial point nine-zero Earth gravity.

The Ekatarina is two years old and battle-hardened, a war vessel bearing the rents and wounds of multiple strikes and hits, all scarred over now with rapid and not very pretty re-plating with rough quality and scrap ablative armor. The ship just went through a rushed repair, refit, and upgrade, which means its most important parts are all in fine working order. Its appearance, though, leaves much to be desired. All aboard her know she is no stranger to death and suffering. She is in the pocket-battleship class, an ancient planet-side naval designation denoting a smaller, lighter, less armored, and much faster version of a standard battleship. *The Ekatarina* is a skirmisher that moves quickly between the stars while packing a big punch… and today marks the beginning of its most important mission since it was first launched out of planetary orbit to join the Polisian Fleet.

Ship's light is at half-luminescence at this twilight time between work shifts, a setting she finds comforting for her daily run.

Illiadus, a newly minted Captain and one of many officers finding the steady annihilation of the fleet over the years to be conducive to rapid advancement in the ranks, has fought for this coming day across the span of ten long bloody years of interstellar war. From Third Lieutenant to Full Commander in a decade, she's earned every single one of her promotions during a series of fearless and deadly engagements, two of which tragically ended in the destruction of two whole Fleets and the continued large-scale loss of life throughout the massive battlefield that is the Milky Way Galaxy.

For ten years the Polisian Space Navy, the fighting arm of the newly incorporated galaxy-wide Polisian Federation of Civilizations (consisting of two hundred and sixteen sentient species) fought a terrible war of attrition against an overwhelming space-faring race from beyond the galactic rim. A bellicose species whose incursions into the galaxy proper threatens annihilation everywhere. A secretive and mostly unknown species, as none has ever been captured or interrogated, they are dubbed, *The Scourge*, for such is their awful imprint on this corner of the universe.

Captain Illiadus jogs past the half-dark Combat-Information Center (CIC). She can see the nine-person night shift finishing their drills and salutes several who spot her through the armored transparent bulkheads that separate them. In thirty minutes, the command center will be lit up like a Christmas tree and swarming with crewpersons. She takes two lefts that lead her to the bowside of Main Engineering. All three engines have been replaced, and radioactive fuels replenished. Ordnance is stockpiled as well as every other conceivable supply deemed necessary for the successful completion of today's mission.

Today's possible suicide mission, Illiadus thinks, *but one certainly worth the price.*

She ponders this thought with a strange intensity. Ten years of war. Billions dead. Dozens of worlds in dozens of solar systems turned into lifeless wastelands. A merciless faceless enemy that brooks no surrender and offers only death. And here, a major player, Captain Illiadus herself, embracing the offer of ultimate revenge upon an entire alien race bent on multiple genocides. As a stage play this life and death drama would no doubt be filled with mystery and existential angst and powerful articulate soliloquys… but the reality is much more mundane, and far more chilling.

It's us or them, Illiadus thinks, *they've rejected dozens of envoys of peace, slaughtering them all. The numbers of dead have grown into macabre abstractions, almost meaningless. But my family, mother, father, my friends, my lover, all gone… yes, this math is very simple. I want revenge, and I'm captaining a ship filled with men and women who want the same, who have similar stories, who want to strike back, no matter the cost.*

The tactics and strategies have all been worked out. Success will depend on one ship's willingness to accept all consequences, and two others, one being Illiadus's *The Ekatarina*, possibly suffering the same fate, or perhaps a much more horrifying and lingering one…

Continuing her job, Illiadus narrows her eyes and silently thanks every battle deity in hearing range that she's successfully demanded, threatened, and bribed enough senior officers to acquire one of the best surviving Chief Engineers in the Fleet, Lt. Commander Walter Lehmann. At forty-nine he is far above the average age of the ship's crew, and his confidence, experience, and abilities are a much-needed asset she is incredibly grateful for.

She takes two more lefts through hatchways between bulkheads and finds herself paralleling the chow hall where she can hear the clanging hustle and bustle of the fifteen-person cooking staff that has been slaving away on breakfast for the past forty minutes. Real ham and eggs, hot waffles, chipped beef on toast, sizzling steak, hash browns and home fries, ripe cantaloupe and freshly squeezed orange juice… it is a death row inmate's lavish last meal that three hundred home world and colonial Terrans are about to feast on.

Her First Officer, another godsend, is Commander David Aithon. A solid officer, he knows this crew like the back of his hand and has a penchant for anticipating her orders with a speed and professionality bordering on telepathy. His one drawback is his borderline flirtatiousness, but he always snaps back into line before the need for discipline or worse. Aithon also has a darkness he's managed to hide from most others, a strange melancholy kept chained behind a wide ingratiating grin, sparkling eyes, and a quick wit. Illiadus suspects this since the first day she met him, but the man is a highly efficient pro she has come to rely on ever since he joined the crew. Besides, the steady advance of The Scourge into The Milky Way has damaged so many souls…

Illiadus picks up her pace. She has only ten minutes left in her run. The surviving remnants of the defeated Polisian First and Second Fleets are currently joining the Third Fleet as she jogs, thus making it the largest space fleet in the Polisian Space Navy's history. Nevertheless, its size is superfluous, as reconnaissance has recently shown that the enemy's gargantuan mobile home base (an artificial sphere whose circumference matched Mercury's orbit around Earth's sun) contains dozens of fleets whose overwhelming numbers simply cannot be defeated.

Not fairly at least, Illiadus thinks with an evil smirk, *but all is fair in love and war, and the Scourge deserve no mercy.* Everyone on *The Ekatarina* and several other ships that will be leading this mission are survivors, victims of The Scourge's criminal lack of mercy who have lost rivers of loved ones in the past ten-year holocaust.

In three hours, this multi-species fleet of haunted, revenge-seeking professionals will mass at the opening of a Galactic Jump-Gate, one of thousands composing the eons-old network of instant transportation devices constructed and deployed throughout the galaxy by an ancient, unknown race whose every trace, with the exception of the gates, disappeared long ago.

Illiadus enters the main interior flight hanger and proceeds to jog its periphery on an elevated catwalk. She smiles. Down on the deck, Commander of Marines, Major Helen Ironbear puts her seventy-four troops through a withering round of calisthenics. A tall solid figure sporting a mohawk haircut, the Major circles the group of muscular young men and women with a vicious snarl on her scarred face while her fingers caress the top of her holstered tactical tomahawk.

"You call those pushups?" Ironbear screams, "are you fucking kidding me! Drop your asses. Tits to the floor. I want ten more! Let's do it… now, ONE for the Captain, TWO for the Corps, THREE for the Chaplin, FOUR for his whore, FIVE for the…"

Yes, Illiadus thinks as she finishes her perimeter and exits the hanger, *Ironbear, you're the perfect extension of my desire for discipline and enforced compliance on this ship of war.*

The rest of the senior staff are pros that she knows she can rely on in a crunch, Medical Officer Commander Kyle Sorlan, a colonist who has waded through rivers of blood in many a makeshift surgery theatre in the midst of triage and even horrid but necessary mercy killings. Her Weapons Officer, Chief Warrant Officer Yaqub Al-Quam, a believer whose strong faith is only matched by his keen knowledge of the vicious tools of his trade. These and several others compose the wall of flesh that is Illiadus's personal armor, and the immediate extension of her will.

If all goes as planned, *The Ekatarina* will be one of three vessels exiting a jump-gate on the other side of the galaxy, far from the main fleet, doing its best to play its part in a daring charade that might, just might, bring an end to the vicious invaders and this long war. The odds of survival after bearding the enemy in its den are calculated by command's top A.I.s as somewhere around zero. There are just too many unconsidered and unknown contingencies which themselves spawn reams of possibilities that simply cannot be nullified or counteracted and thus planned for in the time frame laid out for the Third Fleet's upcoming attack.

Illiadus hits her personal shower and then quickly puts on her uniform. Her face in the small mirror has a tight, almost glowing fanaticism about it. Hers is a will of ten-point steel, and nothing short of death will put a dent in it. For two weeks she has trained the new crew in multiple drills, battle simulations that push every single officer, middle ranks, and enlisted to their mental and physical limits. The Captain needs to know they will not break under extreme pressure. About one dozen people snapped and were quickly replaced.

An hour after waking, passing dozens of bustling and saluting crewpersons, Illiadus strides into the now highly active CIC, the ship's control center located deep within the pocket battleship's interior behind heavily armored and shielded bulkheads, which is now mostly filled with young though experienced laser-focused junior officers.

She sits in the Captain's Chair and turns on the ship's main intercom.

"Good morning, crew," Illiadus says, "let's get down to business."

Day of Days

by Edward McKeown

Ship's Chronometer: 2425 AD

"I will become a sword of the purest steel, to be buried in the vitals of my enemy. I will not be sheathed while a single Scourge exists." -- *Diary of Ensign Tennyson Maria Illiadus, May 3, 2415, AD on learning of the death of her home colony of Kallos, first human world to fall to the Scourge.*

"Emergence," the helmsman calls as the universe reassembles around the Polisian Pocket Battleship *Ekatarina*.

Captain Tennyson Maria Illiadus draws a deep breath and shakes off the disorientation of the gate jump. *Concentrate*, she thinks, *today we win, or we lose everything. God though, ten years of this adds up on a body.* Aloud, she demands. "Is the *Sofia* still with us?"

David Aithon, her executive for the last five years, wipes a broad hand over his face as he checks the scan. "She's there, five thousand klicks relative below and behind as planned. Speed .66C"

"And the bombship?" she says, scanning the boards and crews manning them in *Ekatarina*'s spacious CIC. That precious vessel is the lynchpin of the entire plan to destroy the Scourge for all time.

"Scan is still clearing from gate exit, but I have a signal from where she should be, five hundred thousand klicks ahead."

"Mr. Al-Quam," she says.

The bearded, dark-skinned gunner glances back at her, his black eyes sharp. He suffers less from jump disorientation than anyone she's ever known.

"Tie into the long-range radar, open fire on the bomb ship when you have a full solution. Close enough to make it look good, but for God's sake don't hit the bomb ship."

"Yes, sir," he says, his attention now fully on his weapons board. She can see the standby light on the ship's main weapon, a two hundred mm railgun that runs the two-thousand-foot length of the pocket battleship, flick from yellow to green.

"Aithon," she turns back to him, "is the bomb ship broadcasting? Any Scourge contacts?"

He whistles. "Holy God. Putting it on the big board." On the main display over their heads appears the symbols for the stargate that they just exited, then the two green silhouettes that are *Ekatarina* and her sister-ship *Sofia*. Ahead, in yellow, runs the bomb ship, a large frigate and the only Scourge warship ever captured. It's manned by colonists from the Polisian colony on the other side of the gate, a mixture of humans and others of the two hundred and sixteen species of the galactic polis, a suicide crew broadcasting in the language of their enemies. "*Help. We've escaped. The enemy is on our heels. Their whole fleet is behind us!*"

But the screen is filling with red, blip after blip, into the hundreds then more. And finally, the screen becomes a solid mass of red: the Dyson sphere containing the home of the Scourge: a hollow sphere as wide as the orbit of Mercury, roughly two hundred and twenty-six million miles in circumference and holding a miniature sun and billions of the enemy civilization.

I see you, Illiadus thinks with a thrill of satisfaction and utter hatred. Illiadus solved the mystery of how the Scourge struck the Polis, why they could never find an enemy home world to counterattack, how Scourge attacks seemed to come from anywhere and everywhere. The Scourge Dyson Sphere is the largest artificial object ever seen and it is *mobile*. It was nothing but pure luck that led her on a deep space mission months ago, one that nearly trapped her crew in the enemy's den when discovering it, but they escaped intact, with this precious knowledge.

"It's moving at about point ten C," Aithon manages, "I think there's an opening on the far side. Light pressure from the sun inside the Dyson Sphere has been accelerating it for God knows how long. Makes it possible that they could be extra-galactic. I just can't believe something so large is capable of a gate jump."

Illiadus stares at her enemy. "Their jump tech is ahead of ours. We know that. We place gates where space-time is weak and rip it open. There's more power in that Sphere than in all of the Polis together. It's slow and cumbersome but it can move. If it hadn't been for that scout ship catching it occluding a star, we'd never have seen it."

He grunts. "You caught that, Captain. Months ago. No one else thought to look for such an impossible thing. Then you got the whole fleet here."

"And we stand or fall based on my mad plan," she replies.

Illiadus studies the giant board and a wolfish-smile spreads over face as she brushes back her thick black hair. She stands from her acceleration couch, six-feet one inch tall and broad-shouldered as most men. "The better part of their fleet must be inside the Sphere. Thus, ours wasn't outnumbered when they jumped several hours ago and just now came within notice on the far side of the giant sphere. It should make the Scourge hunker down closer to their sphere until they can assemble."

"Firing solution obtained," Al-Quam says, as if they are not plunging toward a sphere seventy million klicks wide containing what is only recently surmised to be a gargantuan fleet multiple times the size of the Polisian Third Fleet which arrived earlier than the *Ekatarina*, roughly eighty million miles away and around the Scourge sphere.

"Open fire," she orders. Al-Quam hits the toggle and a three-ton sabot round of depleted uranium flashes out of the two-thousand-foot tube to pass safely by the bombship.

The Revenge would seem to be maneuvering frantically to the Scourge, but its evasion pattern is pre-programmed into *Ekatarina* and *Sofia* to prevent an accidental hit.

Illiadus touches her com. "*Ekatarina Actual* to *Sofia*, acknowledge." At this short range and near a gate FTL communications work and she can speak in real-time to her sistership.

"*Sofia Actual* to *Ekatarina*, acknowledged."

"Fire twice on the bombship. Then switch to that picket cruiser at one twenty-three-mark fifteen mark ninety, when they're in range. We'll support you with our secondary railguns."

"Understood."

"Al-Quam," Illiadus says, "fire a full spread of nuclear missiles at the bomb ship. When they close in on the bombship, at the last possible moment, turn them away toward the enemy's forward picket ships."

"Picking up heat blooms from multiple Scourge ships," Aithon adds. "They've spotted us. Picket ships are reacting. Space is damn near crackling with Scourge voice traffic and IFF. The enemy picket force is small, scanning twenty-major vessels and seventy-six smaller ships."

He gives her a death's head grin. "But they're spread all to hell and over. They never expected us to find them. Only a few ships are near us. The vast majority appear to be tracking in on our main fleet on the far side. The plan is working!"

Illiadus considers. It will take time for the enemy command to react. *But whoever is on the other side of the chessboard has a lot on his decision-making plate. Moments after an enemy fleet appears out of nowhere in attack formation, millions of miles away on the opposite side of the sphere a lost warship appears, running full out, with obsolete IFF but broadcasting in Scourge. When he finally makes voice contact with the bombship, it will be with thinking beings who will respond to questions plausibly. The bomb ship is warning of a fleet attack and suddenly two Polisian capitol ships appear and fire at it. The Scourge Sphere has never been found before. Complacency has crept in on them. But my enemy will remain confident. The sphere is a titanic fortress, and his fleet is vast.*

"Our fleet has commenced attack," Aithon calls. "The vanguard has launched a flotilla of nuclear missiles and I am updating them with all our targeting information."

Ensign Parker manipulates the scanner. Additional views began to appear over Illiadus' head. The vast darkness that is the Scourge Dyson Sphere lays ahead. Pinpoints of light decorate it as Scourge ships maneuver across its face, like skittering, vicious insects.

Sofia occupies another screen, her secondaries flashing as she spits death at the approaching Scourge pickets.

On the other side of the massive enemy space sphere, and traveling in a radically different direction than the *Ekatarina* and the *Sophia*, Vice

Admiral Zharcaan Khaav, Flagship PW of the *Aerope,* and Commander of the newly combined Third Polisian Fleet, frowns harshly as ten thousand Polisian missiles, each one carrying a one hundred and fifty megaton nuclear warhead speed far ahead of his massive fleet toward the ever-closing surface of the invading monstrosity. Within moments thousands of Scourge ships appear from a variety of nearby apertures in the massive sphere, racing to fill the gap between their home and the attacking fleet which seems to have appeared out of nowhere. Before they can fully react and launch interceptor missiles, the hundreds of Polisian nuclear devices reach them and detonate. The result is nothing short of spectacular.

Hundreds and hundreds of monumental explosions ignite over a three-thousand-mile-long swath of the sphere's surface. Thousands of the recently converged Scourge ships are instantly disintegrated in this unimaginable cataclysm of pure annihilation. The screens aboard the *Aerope,* even at their highest settings, cannot filter out all of the ghastly brightness of the conflagration, and Admiral Khaav has to squint his three purple eyes for several minutes. It is an attack of the size and scope never recorded in galactic history. It is a display of raw, radically destructive power beyond imagination.

A loud cheer bursts free from among the crew in the *Aerope*'s Command Center. The Admiral imagines the same shouts and screams of joy are echoing throughout all of the ships of his surrounding fleet. The Admiral, however, does not join in the reverie. He does not smile. He waits. A tiny drop of pale green perspiration runs down the scaled, dark red skin of his double brow.

Back aboard the *Ekatarina,* a third screen shows Illiadus the distant great transportation gate far out of sight on the other side of the sphere, itself thousands of klicks wide now after pouring out the majority of the Polisian ships half a day ago. The gates have existed from time out of mind, maintained by those races that inherited them. No one remembers who made this one, but it has stood there for at least fifty thousand years. Now it glows with a deep, preternatural green light, the result of thousands of ships recently plunging out of it into space-time. The Scourge need the gates too and have come close to this one to use if for their attacks.

"Scourge ships have not started falling back on the Sphere," Aithon reports. "In fact, our spy satellites confirm dozens of apertures opening all across the enemy sphere, Captain, and are spilling out, my god, tens of thousands of more ships that are beginning to converge on our approaching main fleet. They seem willing to sacrifice thousands, regardless that their home has to mount more weapons than both fleets combined. Our whole armada won't last minutes if it closes directly on the sphere."

Captain Illiadus nods. "They won't. The fleet came out earlier at high speed so it could display a sudden demonstration of shock and awe. Standard tactics that the Scourge will expect. Our fleet is just a feint, a giant distraction to the dirty deed we are engaged in. They aren't coming to our rescue and they're committing suicide if they change their minds and decide to duke it out. The moment our work is done the entire fleet, or what is left of it, will make its true destination known. Now pray the Scourge lets our innocent, frightened little bombship close enough. Only a few minutes more."

"We have reports on the fleet's initial bombardment, Captain. My god…" Aithon says.

Illiadus squints at the data flowing across a nearby screen.

"Thousands of Scourge ships destroyed, but, minimal damage done to the Sphere's actual surface."

"How is that possible?" Aithon spouts, "thousands of our warheads…"

"Intelligence reports the sphere itself is probably one hundred miles thick and made of unknown exotic elements and materials of the highest strengths and densities." Illiadus says grimly, "We suspected an outer coating of ablative armor twenty-five miles thick, originally designed to deal with naturally-occurring nickel-iron kinetics, so even the few hundred deep-boring missiles, all shaped to lens the unusual outer material, only penetrated about five miles and did no more damage than gouging out an additional five miles at best. The vast majority of the missiles never actually penetrated more than a mile into the surface. In the end, we just scratched a tiny portion of a construct with a surface area of four hundred and sixty trillion square miles. This was not unexpected."

Aboard the *Aerope*, Admiral Khaav, now within eight hundred miles of the Scourge sphere and closing, deploys his fleet into two giant wings, like the horns of a buffalo, as if to partially encircle millions of miles of the sphere in a crossfire. Already the ships of the vanguard have launched hundreds of more spreads of nuclear-tipped missiles heading for the multiple thousands of Scourge ships vectoring in from all sides of the massive sphere. These are the last of the Polisian fleet's nuclear assets. They've shot their load.

The Scourge pickets will feel compelled to stop these latest missile bombardments. They and any ready-reaction vessels being launched will have busy minutes coming up as the Polisian fleet draws ever nearer behind their screen of lethal nuclear firepower.

The enemy sees our fleet, deploying for continued bombardment, Admiral Khaav ponders. *They'll think the human commander is too scared to come to close quarters.*

What they won't see until contact is the division of 'Death's Head" stealth ships at the tips of each horn. Only one in five of the Marauder ships are manned, by a tiny and fully cyberized crew. The others are weapon packs for the manned ship's direction.

They fall back, defend the Sphere at all costs. I hope, I do so hope.

The scanners are overloading with the tiny lights of inbound weapons. But they are all on the far side of the enemy sphere, millions of miles away from the main drama, the two charging sisters and the bombship. It is as if everyone else is a mere spectator to the true drama. None of what they see is in real-time, distances are too great—but the computers update and project courses, speeds and the tactical situation.

Back on the *Ekatarina*, several junior officers in the CIC gasp.

"Jesus Christ," Parker says. The blonde, young ensign stares, her eyes wide and mouth open as more and more hatches the size of planetary continents continue to open across the sphere. Light-speed delay means this happened minutes ago, but such immense structures cannot move quickly, it may be a hours before they are fully open.

Illiadus smiles her wolf-smile. "They're pulling back so they can fire the mother of all particle beams from the sphere and move their fleet inside, firing out of those hatches. They'll move the outside ships closer, so they don't block the sphere's fire. They probably think our main fleet is desperate, suicidal."

"Aren't they?" Aithon says.

The two Polisian pocket battleships and the bombship, continuing their constant acceleration, the sphere in front, are now the fastest moving objects on this side of the sphere. On the other side the Polisian fleet is now advancing toward the sphere at several kilometers per second. Seven Scourge vessels, including a battlecruiser, i.e., a tiny fraction of the enemy's picket line deploying on the far side of the sphere, lays before the trio of racing Polisian ships, but they are effectively stationary. Even at full burn, the enemy will not get up to battle speed in any useful time. Still, they have rotated and are blasting full throttle to get back to the sphere.

"Damn," Aithon says. In a moment, the reason for his curse appears. On the other side of the sphere, the left wing of the Polisian attack has gained line of sight on converging fleets of Scourge ships. The Scourge have formed up for a raid into space.

"Rumor has it," Aithon says while looking at the Captain, "that Lieutenant Colonel Pyrrha Achillea and her single-fighter ship *The Tachys* has secretly joined the marauders in the third fleet's left wing. Probably hoping for a final rematch with her infamous Scourge bogeyman."

"Save the backroom scuttlebutt," Illiadus says, "for our next stop at a fleet port bar. Anyways, if Colonel Achillea and her ship really are in the left wing, she's about to enter hell. May all the deities of The Polis guide her hands…"

The accelerating Scourge wing and the left horn of the Polisian fleet collide in a flare of beams and flowering nuclear strikes.

We hoped we could avoid this, Illiadus thinks, we *wanted to keep the fleet further back, but no chance of that now. Still the Marauders, rapid firing all of their railguns, were cutting through the initial Scourge ships like a katana through tatami mats. Keep the main ships back,* she wishes. *The Marauder crews are more dead than alive anyway.*

"No," Parker cries. Illiadus attention snaps to the other screen. *Sofia* is tumbling and glowing.

"God damn it," Aithon says. "A hit at this range?"

"Enemy battlecruiser struck them amidships," Parker says into the silence. "The enemy gets lucky too."

"Al-Quam," Illiadus orders, "switch fire to the enemy battlecruiser with all railguns. Fire a second spread of missiles at them. Helm, as soon as we fire the main gun, evasive turn to place us at a thirty-degree angle to bombship. I want to look like we're still trying for the bombship but avoiding closing with that battlecruiser."

"Aye, sir."

"Communications raise *Sofia* if you can."

A new screen pops into action above her. On it is a combat information center identical to the one she stands in, lit by sparking panels and red disaster lighting. The CIC, buried in the bowels of the ship, is the most protected place in *Sofia*. She sees gray-haired. Captain Skesky staring back at her, blood on his face and the black and green fleet uniform.

"How bad?" she demands.

"I still have fire control," he replies, "on secondaries and missiles. Maneuvering is gone and we're badly damaged, engines cut off, so we're just going to coast. We'll keep firing as long as we can."

"We'll be back for you," she promises.

"We'll be here. Got no other plans for today," but the smile is haunted. "Get out of here, *Ekatarina*."

She nods. "*Ekatarina* out."

"Captain," Aithon says, "I think they are getting suspicious of the bombship. They are demanding visual communication. Three destroyers from the sphere are shaping an intercept course."

Inspiration hits. "Al Quam, have our missiles overtaken *The Revenge*?"

"Almost," he says, "thirty seconds until I retarget them on enemy ship."

"Explode the first one. Now!"

His hand stabs at the control even as his face registers confusion.

"The EMP from the near miss should blank out communications for a few minutes," Illiadus replies to the unasked question in the gunner's face, "gives them a reason not to reply."

"But sir, the rads—" he begins.

"Will be of no concern to them in minutes," she replies.

His face registers nothing, but he turns back to the screen as the light from the explosion glows on it.

"It's working," Parker calls, "they're holding fire, the bombship is closing in. The nearby enemy ships are using their fire on our missiles.

"Nothing to retarget now," Al-Quam says, "they intercepted the whole spread."

"Prepare for immediate additional fifty-five-degree course alteration."

"Confirmed. Course laid in."

"Captain," Aithon adds, "the enemy command is ordering them to assume orbit, not to try to enter the sphere or they will be fired on. They are sending up boarding parties."

"Do it," she snarls at the bombship, *The Revenge*, "you're as close as you're going to get!"

Simultaneously, Illiadus's deepest fears flood her heart. The weapon was never field tested. It was experimental and a successful ignition is purely theoretical at this point. Not to mention that even though the weapon could plausibly effectively kill the target from hundreds of miles away, Fleet Command had decided to take no chances and ordered a detonation no farther than five miles from the surface of the target. The *Revenge* was now within six miles and closing.

"Please," Illiadus whispered.

As if the doomed crew hears her, there is a flare and something that the eye finds hard to resolve blooms to life. It is a roiling mass of… something, of light and blackness, motion and stillness, it seems to partake of every quality.

"Alter course!" Illiadus screams, her eyes go wide at the unholy sight on the big screen.

Simultaneously, on the other side of the massive sphere, the entire Polisian fleet alters their course by a mere six degrees, just fifteen miles from the surface, moving now at eight kilometers a second directly toward the distant transport Gate, and escape.

Back behind the *Ekatarina*, which is fleeing the Scourge sphere in the complete opposite course being taken by the Polisian fleet, the unforgivable doomsday weapon raves, it strikes, it devours. Space around it is suddenly no longer space-time, but something else.

"Beautiful," Illiadus breathes as the dark-matter fountain aboard the bombship births its new universe onto the Scourge Sphere.

The *Ekatarina* continues to flee the destruction of the enemy sphere directly behind it. Around her space begins to bloom with the hellish balls of nuclear weapons as the Polisian fleet's last waves of bombardment missiles meet the Scourge interceptors and find targets in the Scourge pickets. A massive cloud of return fire from the Sphere's just-activated gargantuan particle beam surface weapons vanishes into the maw of the madness that the bombship has called into existence.

Illiadus watches with eyes misted with tears as the enormous Dyson Sphere shatters, as the very reality of space-time is ruptured, then displaced, by the laws of the dark matter universe now clawing its way into life from the fountain. Light plays in swirls and coronas as the new universe gobbles up the old like a hungry child. It reaches out for the Scourge ships which only now are trying to use their engines to flee, far too late. There is no escape.

Mom, Dad, Jeremy, Uncle Thalo, Aunt Tomasina, the boy I secretly loved who used to tease me about my hair at school, all my friends and family, you can rest now. Look at the Viking funeral I've made for all of you. See the child I have given birth to? Look at it eat their ships, their world, their history. No more Scourge. Their songs will go unsung, their lives unmourned and unremembered. I have struck them from the pantheon of the living as if they had never existed.

"Beautiful," she whispers again, but it is into her darkening soul. She has become the sword of purest steel she'd pledged to be on that long-ago day when she learned of the death of her home world, Kallos. Every compromise, every debt incurred, every bad bargain she had made, had been for this one moment. She has sheathed herself in the souls of her enemies, utterly destroying them.

The thought comes unbidden and unlooked for as leadenness overtakes her body. *What do I do now?*

"Look at it! Look at it!" someone shouts.

The raving mass of energy has enveloped the Scourge Sphere and indeed is assuming the shape of a sphere. It is still hard to look at as their eyes, created for one set of physics, tries to see into another, unrelated one.

One thing is obvious, the effect is still growing.

It can't come this far, she thinks, fighting a listless feeling. *Still....*

"Engineering we need more power," she manages, "there's no time for a loop course back to the gate. Maintain max acceleration. We don't know what sort of radiation is coming out of that thing."

Aithon looks at her. "Rate of expansion is steady at three hundred and sixty degrees and point thirty C."

"What?" she says, face blank in astonishment.

Even the most optimistic estimate of the blast has only predicted a ball of *unmatter* forty million klicks wide. Already the blast effect is three times that and shows no sign of slowing.

"General Fleet recall signal," Communications sing out, "jump back to forward base."

Illiadus shakes her head, "at this speed it will take us two days to slow down enough to completely reverse course. That's not for us. Thank God most of the fleet altered direction and accelerated directly toward the gate upon successful detonation of the dark matter fountain."

"The Marauders and most of the left wing won't make it back," Aithon says, as if merely announcing the end of watch.

Illiadus stares up at the main screen, fighting the feeling of detachment that is overwhelming her. The massive sphere of the new universe expands toward them as they desperately flee. *Sofia* is doomed, along with the few Scourge picket ships close to her. She watches the mass of light and darkness reach the battlecruiser that has struck *Sofia,* suddenly it simply isn't there. The attending escorts join her in non-existence a moment later.

But it rolls on, eclipsing star after star.

"*Sofia!*" Parker shouts. She'd has friends on *Sofia.* They all did.

Illiadus sees her sister-ship vanish.

"Lehman," she snaps into her com button, "if you have anything left, throw it in. Put it into the red."

The engineer, faraway in fusion driver control shouts back. "All in the red, sir. I can give you twenty percent more thrust for ten minutes."

"Do it."

"The lead ships of the fleet have reached the gate," Aithon shouts staring at the monitors, his hands balling into fists as Polisian ships begin to dive into the coruscating colors of the oval gate. But only so many of the surviving two thousand Polisian ships could transit the gate in any given moment and the fountain continues to gush a new universe in place of the one the Scourge have occupied.

"God, I hope they have enough time."

"Inshallah," Al-Quam says.

Aithon shakes his head. "It's just math, they don't have enough time for all of them. They are sending the big ships through first. Save the most. The slow emergence speed is killing them now."

The fountain over takes the sacrificial ships of the Polisian fleet's remaining left wing, where some of the Scourge and Marauders are still fighting. Then unmatter sphere blocks their view of the left wing's fate.

They stare helplessly at their monitors as much of the right horn of the fleet leaps into the gate. Two ships tangle, whether by accident, or if someone lost their nerve, they would never know. The wreckage glows as it plunges into the gate.

Aboard the Aerope, Admiral Khaav makes a decisive decision.

"We're packed too close," he shouts, "order all four hundred of the Admiral's escort to drop back with us to the fleet's rear for redeployment."

"Message sent," the communications officer confirmed, "advancing to the rear."

The series of maneuvers effectively clears multiple converging paths of the fleeing fleet as hundreds of more ships safely leap into the gate.

"Admiral," the CIC's helmsman says, "I don't think there's enough ti…"

"I'm aware, helmsman," the Admiral replies calmly, "initiate priority voice message ship wide and to the remaining fleet."

"Done sir," the communications officer shouts.

"This is Fleet Admiral Khaav," he says with quiet confidence as his voice echoes from thousands of PA system speakers in multiple languages throughout his surrounding four hundred escort ships, as well as the *Ekatarina*, "it has been an honor to serve with all of you. Your exceptional bravery in the face of overwhelming odds has been noted and transmitted to fleet headquarters. I am very proud of you all. Sailors… hold firm."

The ravenous dark fountain overtakes the last four hundred Polisian ships and the gate itself, and annihilates them instantly.

On the far side of the horrible boiling chaos, Captain Illiadus and her crew watch silently as the expanding sphere of the dark matter fountain continues to chase them.

"Rate slowing," Aithon says, "if the diminishment remains constant it will stop at one astronomical unit."

"Helm, confirm if we are in safe zone."

"If we maintain this thrust for two more minutes and fifteen seconds, we'll clear it."

Do we want to? Illiadus thinks, *stranded hundreds of light years from home, no gate to return through. No habitable world in this system. Not even any Scourge for company. All gone, all gone. Maybe it would be better to let it catch us and make a clean end of it. God, I am so tired. I am so tired. Mom, Dad, everyone, I got them. I got them all, but I am so tired.*

Her hands move automatically. "Lehman, cut thrust in…in… one minute thirty seconds. We can coast then… we can coast…"

She stands and walks slowly toward the back of the CIC.

"I am so very tired," she says to Aithon's astonished face, "so very tired." The doors slide closed behind her and she walks—seeing nothing, hearing nothing, feeling nothing until she finds her cabin and collapses face down on her bed and the universe goes black.

Two days pass as *Ekatarina* hurtles into interstellar space. There is no reason to change course, nor in truth to do anything else. Some of the crew celebrate the destruction of the Scourge, others mourn their impending fate. The Polis would survive, but they, now the living dead, would not. Without a jump gate, stranded on the wrong side of the galaxy, there is no way home.

Behind them the dark matter fountain stops its mad growth and indeed retracts some. Of the gate, the *Sofia* and the Scourge, there is not so much as an atom to show they existed. It is a harsh reality and some face it with alcohol, a few with drugs they make, steal or have hidden, others find relief in sex, not always with willing partners. Major Helen Ironbear and her Marines break up the fights and assaults.

At the end of the second day, David Aithon has enough. He walks with Ironbear and a Marine escort to Illiadus' quarters and uses the emergency override to open her door. He turns to the scarred woman, with her distinctive Mohawk haircut, and her pair of Marines. "Stay here. Don't come in unless I call for you, no matter what you hear. Clear?"

She nods. The pair behind her stand still, their faces expressionless, but worry shadows their eyes.

"Good luck," Ironbear says.

Illiadus barely looks up as the door to her cabin swishes open and Aithon sweeps in. She lays where she has for the better part of two days, wearing only slacks and uniform shirt. A bottle lays next to her, with a glass beside it, but both have been little touched. What startles him most is her hair. Illiadus has one vanity, her mass of thick black hair, always ornately bound up with ribbons or hair pins, glossy and perfectly set. It now hangs around her in a cloud; he finds it oddly erotic and totally disquieting.

She stares up at him with such a blank expression that he comes to an abrupt halt, angry words dying on his lips.

Illiadus seems to focus with difficulty. "Hello, David."

He looks pointedly at the bottle.

"Had one or two," she says slowly. "It didn't seem to matter. So, I left it there. Have one if you like."

He frowns, uncertain. Aithon has never seen Illiadus like this, in the grip of such depression, barely able to move, vague of thought, not even on the anniversary of her colony's death, or the holidays.

"What the hell is wrong with you?" he says. "The ship needs you for God's sake. There's the crew to think of."

"You don't understand," she says with a sad, vague smile. "I'm done. I got them all. Just as I promised Mom and Dad and all the others."

"What about your oath as an officer?" he demands.

She looks away, "Means to an end." It comes out as a whisper.

"We need to get the ship together! This crew is made up of a lot of people like you, who's only remaining aim in his life was to kill Scourge. They aren't the usual and they need to be kept under control."

"The ship is dead, we're all dead. The Gate is gone, we're parsecs away from anywhere. There's no point. Let everyone face death as it seems best to them."

"SIBIL," he says. "After this mission we were going to use it to see if we could enter the same dark matter arteries that the fountain released."

She stares at him, animation showing for the first time. "You're mad. You saw that thing howl and devour space. You think you can drive a ship into that?"

"No, I don't think I can. I think *you* can. SIBIL was calibrated for your brain. Not one person in one hundred thousand is compatible with this technology."

"It's suicide," she says, dropping her eyes.

Aithon looks at Illiadus then draws a deep breath. "Maria, get off your big ass and start commanding this ship again, or its going to be one big meat locker."

Illiadus jumps to her feet, coming almost nose to nose with her solid executive officer. He doesn't flinch.

"Who the hell do you think you are to talk to me that way?" she blazes.

They stand that way for seconds that drag on, breathing heavily, both glaring, hands knot into fists.

Illiadus laughs first. In a second, Aithon follows, both laugh so hard that they need to lean on a bulkhead and a desk. When it finally runs its course, she looks away. "Thanks, David."

He nods.

She rubs her eyes. "What's our sitrep?"

"I had Ironbear crack down in the early watch. We have twenty-two crew in the brig, insubordination, intoxicated on duty and assault. Thirty-three are in medbay from fights with each other or the Marines. We have four on suicide-watch and," he sighed, "we lost one to a suicide the first night."

Her head comes up. "Who?"

"Jan Nichols, from ordnance. He took a walk out the airlock. I have them all under command lock from CIC now. Should have done it earlier."

"Ship status?"

"Stabilized at .78 C. Engines are on idle, but we have all the speed we built up fleeing from the Fountain. Life support and weapons are nominal and all weapons are on lock down. Nav and helm are on standby since we have no particular course.

"There's some damage from crew misbehavior but is mostly cosmetic. What was holding them together was hate and revenge."

"And we've all seen what happens when that isn't enough," she said, shame burning in the back of her mind.

"There's more," he said reluctantly.

"Give me the worst, now."

"Well, the eggheads from the SIBIL team, think that when the dark matter fountain hit the jump gate that it may have propagated a shock wave through the gates systems. Could have taken out other gates, maybe taken out all gates. We've really never fully understood that technology. Even if SIBIL works to get us closer to home space, we may not find any working gates along the way."

She straightens up and tugs her tunic into alignment. "Mr. Aithon."

He snaps to attention. "Yes, Captain."

"Set the ship to defcon four and have Ironbear's Marines enforce it. Everybody to their stations. No idle hands. I want this ship cleaned up. All's going to be forgiven to this point but anyone endangering the ship or its crew from this moment will be spaced."

"Yes, sir."

"Then round up the SIBIL techs and get them down to CIC. I want the system online for a test at zero five thirty."

"Yes, sir."

"And finally, and for the record, my ass is not big, it's muscular and is the pride and joy of the *Ekatarina,* mister."

"No question about that, Captain."

"Dismissed, Commander."

He snaps a salute and heads on out.

She looks at the door as it closes behind him. "At least," she whispers, "it will be quick and dignified. They all deserve that much."

Illiadus walks into the CIC. The quiet efficiency of the command center is an antidote to the disorder of the last two days. Truth be told, she is ashamed of her complete collapse after the slaughter of the Scourge. She has taken extra care to appear immaculate and in control again. If it is to be death, as she feels certain it will be, she'd face it properly.

Aithon is waiting for her. She nods. "Put me on inter-ship."

He gestures to the comm officer, who opens the circuit.

"This is the Captain," she begins. "We've all had a few bad days but that's over now. We're the people who scrubbed the Scourge out of the universe. Our duty there is done. Now our duty is to ourselves, to each other and to *Ekatarina*. We're going home. The way ahead is uncertain, but it's the only way ahead, so we're going to take it.

"We'll be using the same technology we used to end the Scourge. The dark matter arteries of the universe, the conduits for the dark energy that powers everything, even the expansion of the galaxies. You've all seen that we can use it. It's going to be our ticket home.

"How long that will take? Well, it's only educated guesswork. More than months. This ship was designed for long-distance, unsupported raiding, so we are set up to be on our own. Doubtless we'll find places for food, fuel and air along the way. What we can't find, we will make. But we are going home. Count on it. Captain Illiadus out."

She nods at Aithon. "You have the con, Mark."

"Yes, Captain."

At the back of the CIC, on the dais made for it, is the couch, with the clear plas-steel helmet of the interface. The civilian techs for the system stand around it, looking uncertain.

Great, she thinks, *they're going to hook this to my brain, and they look like kids working with an erector set.*

She lets none of this show on her face. "Dr. Bream, it looks like it's time to introduce me to SIBIL"

Her eyes fall on the screen, where the system status is displayed. "SIBIL" Synaptic Information Biological Interface and Linkage Mark One, Version Two.

I'd be happier with version ten, she thinks.

The young doctor nods quickly. He turns to his panel as she settles into the couch. His spidery fingers dance over the controls in a blur. Next, he begins adjusting the helmet about her chin.

He frowns. "You have a lot of hair, Captain. If we could cut off some of it—"

Glare.

"Er, well, I'm sure if I just stuff it back here, we'll be fine." He makes a few more adjustments, then looks down at her. "Captain, you know this is an untested technology. We have no idea how the interface will appear to you. Different people experienced the system different ways, some only hear a voice, some see people or…other things. I'd have preferred to experiment with someone less critical to ship's systems, but it will take weeks to reset the system for someone else—"

"Yes," she says with an abrupt gesture. "Commander Aithon will take over if I need to be put in diapers after you hook my brain in."

He gulps, then gives his nervous nod. "Are you ready?"

"Do it," she orders.

He presses a button.

There is no transition. One instant she is in the CIC, the next she stands on a featureless plain that seems to stretch to infinity. A fine mist hovers above the ground. Overhead, stars glitter as on a moonless night.

Illiadus hears a sound and spins on her heel. Ten feet away, a beautiful young girl dances silently, her bare feet disturbing the mist, her gossamer robe and long, blonde hair streaming behind her. Her body is perfectly formed, as is her face. Her eyes, however, are wise and locked on Illiadus, wherever her dance take her, she watches Illiadus.

Illiadus waits until the girl-child finishes her dance and stands, regarding her with her old eyes.

They're yellow, Illiadus thinks, *just like a predator.*

"Hello SIBIL," Illiadus says. "I'm your captain and you have to help me get my people home."

The smile SIBIL gives is not reassuring.

Captain's Log, The Ekatarina

First Jump Completed

Per protocol I have been awakened from Cold Sleep before the crew. To my surprise the ship and all personnel appear to have survived this first jump with no casualties and no damage. Star maps indicate we have moved incrementally closer to our ultimate destination, Earth. We had hoped to emerge from the dark energy artery within range of a working jump gate, but no such transponder signals have been picked up on our long-range receivers. Thus, we are still currently not able to communicate directly with high command via the jump gate network's instantaneous FTL subspace relay. This appears to be an uncharted system. My first use of the cybernetic interface and interaction with the highly unusual AI SIBIL has left me with a severe migraine that I hope the ship's doctor can eliminate in the very near future. This damning distraction does not bode well for future links with SIBIL. The destruction of an entire alien race still hangs heavy in my mind, but I am convinced of the necessity of the horrific act of genocide perpetrated under my command. We had no choice. The survival of humanity and hundreds of other sentient races demanded it. My biggest fear, now that it looks like we might have a small fraction of chance at survival, is the crew of The Ekatarina. The psychological indices of this deck of crewmen, marines, and civilians is stacked anything but well. They are people picked by me for their bravery, persistence, and outright overriding and monomaniacal hatred for the enemy. I needed human beings committed to doing whatever was necessary to finish our mission and destroy the Scourge. The normal distribution of positive emotional shipboard traits, faithfulness, trustworthiness, loyalty, compassion, etc. were all shunted aside so I could fill this ship with the necessary monsters. The one psychological crew prediction analysis I had the med computer run for a long-term voyage if we somehow survived the Scourge, did not bode well for our future. May God, if she still exists in this galaxy, have mercy on our souls. Captain Illiadus signing off. End Log.

Risk Analysis

by Marisa Wolf

Ship's Chronometer: 2425.2 AD

His foot itches. He tells himself to scratch it and stop the infernal pressure, but nothing happens, and the itch intensifies. Joseph Tirias, Space Marine, Explosive Ordinance Specialist, all around badass, is about to be driven crazy by a persistent itch in the arch of his foot that he can't reach.

The tip of his nose burns. He can feel every hair of his eyebrows – that brings him up short. Where is he? Why on all the moons can he feel his eyebrows?

Cold Sleep. The Captain has passed down the order, but her voice is off – she'd sounded like a little girl…No. They'd used SIBIL. They'd gone into the Dark Energy Arteries, hoping an experimental AI and Cold Sleep could keep them alive…and it has worked.

Joseph tries again to scratch his foot, and when his body remains unresponsive, he scales back the optimism. It maybe hasn't failed. He is waking up, and the scraping of angry nerves tell him his atoms are still connected, so he hasn't been vaporized like…

His finger twitch, and he lets that distract him, willing movement to return. If he doesn't scratch the bottom of his foot soon…

An alert chimes half a breath after his hand moves, and he freezes. It takes a full second to place it – ship-wide announcement – and then that young voice again. SIBIL.

"Attention the ship. We have exited the Dark Energy Artery into a system with several planets. All crew are emerging from Cold Sleep. Two months ship time has elapsed." Her voice resonates oddly, and Joseph winces, trying to squirm away from it.

Two months ship time did not equal two months, but he supposes that doesn't really matter when they were this far from home, surfing around through dark energy that has pulled millions of living creatures into atoms.

"Senior officers report to the CIC. Orders to follow."

She sounds older, Joseph muses, then dismisses the thought. He'd only heard her once, and that was two months or two thousand years or ten seconds ago, depending on which frame of reference he chose.

"Goddammit." The curse registers a bare moment before a dark shape hurtles past the outside of his Cold Sleep bunk. Joseph manages to turn his head, focusing on the outside of his chamber, and after a moment the shape reappears, wavering and spitting out a steady stream of curses.

The top of his Cold Sleep chamber recedes into the wall, leaving only Joseph and his bunk, and the dark figure resolves itself into his bunkmate.

"Joseph," Turner says urgently, "tell me the truth. Did you put rotten meat in my mouth before you went under?"

Joseph's laugh becomes a cough so bone-shaking, it finally frees his muscles. Sitting up, he flops a hand up to hold his chest, wheezing somewhere between mirth and death. Turner slaps him on the back and turns around in their small cabin, reflexively looking for someone who hasn't been there since two battles ago.

"Ironbear will be meeting with the Captain long enough for us to get fed. You moveable?" Turner gestures widely the large movement punctuated by the looseness of his forearms.

"Maybe?" Joseph stretches out his fingers, noting that all of them eventually respond, and focuses on Clarke Turner, fellow Space Marine and explosives specialist, in order to block out the screaming of poorly awakened nerves. "Not convinced about eating but moving seems like a good idea."

It really didn't, but he supposed he'd slept for at least two months, which ranks moving higher than spending any more time in their small cabin.

"Yeah, I less want to eat, and more want to ogle Inari. You're nice and all, if I liked your kind of thing, which I don't. And we've been locked up in here for…what'd you bet? Four hundred years?"

"It's been two months in here, so my money is on two years out there. Enough for my skin to look really good compared to my sister's." Joseph rocks himself up to his feet with only one false start, and barely wavers at all on his feet. "She's going to be pissed."

Clarke bows overdramatically enough that it almost takes them both out, and they take a moment to steady themselves before angling for the hall.

Bodies in various states of fully sober weaving start to crowd the corridor, and Joseph forces himself into an approximation of natural movement with pure stubborn pride. Turner keeps flopping half his arm around, but his stride steadies every few steps.

"There, cold sleep's not so bad. Pretty sure everything came out the way it went in." Joseph turns a twitch in the corner of his eye into a wink at a pretty Specialist, normalcy returning the closer they get to the galley.

"All things considered I'd rather not do it again." Turner pauses, steadying himself against the wall and glaring at his foot. "Damn thing keeps itching, and I'm gonna tip over it I try to reach it."

"You're moving pretty good." Joseph reaches out to clap his old friend on the back and wisely reconsiders at the last moment. "Maybe you'll just stagger a little."

"Anyone ever tell you, you're an –"

"Boys, get out of the corridor, would you? People have places to go." Humor threads the feminine voice, enough to bring out an answering smile on both of her fellow Marines.

"Cherry Berry, what's a girl like you doing in a place like this?" Turner straightens, kicking his foot against the floor, and Joseph turns, grinning wider.

"Shove it, Turnip. You two going to eat?" Chari Berrir hails from the same colony as Turner, and they'd all been together since their first assignment. Couple endless years fighting the Scourge can really help soldiers appreciate each other, even if it can't help the awful nicknames.

"I'm enabling Turner to gawk at Chief Inari. He might also eat. I'm waiting to see how the smell lands."

"Everything a bit uncertain?" Chair nods sharply, then gestures for them to move along. "Let's get to it and see what happens, then. But if you regurg cold sleep juices in Inari's galley, I'm absolutely going to pretend I don't know you."

"Not the first time," Joseph replies, making sure not to tip over himself after giving Turner crap.

"For which? No, don't answer." Chari lifts her hands to ward their words away, and the three of them make their mostly steady progression through the hall. Other crew wanders through the corridors, though not enough to make passage more difficult than it has to be.

"Anyone have any place to be, or we all just doing laps?" Turner asks one of the engineers, who waves him off with something that lands between laugh and groan.

At the last junction before the galley, the buzz of multiple voices and the occasional waft of food colors the otherwise antiseptic scent of the ship. Joseph zones out of the half-banter conversation around him, trying to decide if the smell will tip him into hunger or nausea. He blinks back to attention as their steps slow, belatedly registering the cluster of people outside the galley's doors. Hibernating for two months plays havoc with one's situational awareness.

"Full in there or did Inari toss you out?"

"Those my only options?' The largest of the five lifts his chin to acknowledge his peers. Santo has a first name, but no one ever retained it. "Maybe Inari also just woke up and is getting the galley in order. Maybe the Scourge left us a little present in the soup and we gotta wait while they figure it out. Maybe —"

"Maybe your legs stopped working and you gotta rest." Chari offers cheerfully.

"Maybe the door sensor doesn't recognize you as human and you can't get in, and we're interrupting them comforting you." Turner does his best wide-eyed innocent glance around the handful of crew most of whom snicker.

"Guys, I hate to tell you, cold sleep really screwed with your sense of humor. Try again when you wake up. You're still looking a little floppy around the edges." More laughs, and Santo pushes off the wall.

"I'm going in," Joseph announces, knowing it for a dumb move the moment he says it, but commits. Half the group hums a funeral dirge while Chari claps her hands over her mouth in complete glee.

"Noooo, even your dimples won't save you!" she calls as the doors slide shut behind him, pitching it perfectly so that anyone inside will hear.

"Let me guess, Tirias?" Sleek hair popped up behind one of the serving cabinets, followed by a smooth forehead and lovely dark eyes. Melanie

Inari has every bit of the brisk purposefulness the crew in the corridors don't, and her quirked eyebrows indicate she doesn't appreciate the interruption.

"Chief. Not sure how many of your staff is mobile, and not sure I'm ready to eat, so I thought I'd see if you need help."

"Marines." She clucks her tongue and glares at him before ducking back under the counter. "Most of my kitchen staff is in place – you're not the only ones who can recover quickly."

"Sorry ma—"

"Marine, if you ma'am me I swear to all things good and bright in this universe that everything you eat will be half-burned, over-salted, and full of crunchy bits."

"I like crunchy bits," he defends weakly, and is rewarded with a chuckle.

"Fine then. Get to work. Use those EOD skills to figure out why my serving cabinet isn't warming so I can feed at least some of the half-walking zombies on this ship." She shoots to her full height so quickly Joseph steps back, despite the fact she is a full foot shorter than him.

"Are you thinking it's rigged to blow?" He gives her a wide berth as he moves, more wary of her than a possible exploding appliance, and this time her laugh lasts longer.

"I'm thinking you'll do what you're told, before fifty hungry Marines come in here and catch you flirting with me." Inari leans forward, taps him a little harder than necessary on the cheek, and was back out of reach before he could do more than flash his dimples.

"Yes, Chief." He squats behind the cabinet just as the doors whoosh open again, re-opening the panel that covers the guts of the machine.

"Oh, void and stars, she killed him. Killed him and hid the body!" Turner's distraught voice wouldn't have convinced a toddler.

"We're eating good tonight, boys!" Chari laughs so hard at her own joke she snorts twice before the doors close.

Joseph, knowing he is lucky they'd gone for that attempt at a joke rather than a more innuendo-laced one, shakes his head and gently shifts wire-connections out of the way to get a look at the chips underneath. Two months of inactivity, depending on how bumpy their ride has been, hopefully means an easy fix. Chip loose in its connecting, wire digging in where it doesn't belong…

Two minutes later, a faint hum emanates from the cabinet and he stands, victorious.

Inari appears before he'd even has a chance to stretch, never mind announce his cleverness, and she shoves a mug into his midsection.

"Good Marine. Drink this, the stimulant should clear the rest of your cold sleep fog. Tell your meatheads it's safe to come in, and if they're good, I won't kill them and serve their meat at the captain's table."

"Aye, Chief."

They have an uninterrupted half an hour, and then orders push through comms almost simultaneously, regardless of division. The senior staff meeting must have ended. On much steadier legs then they'd arrived, crew head out singly or in small groups.

Joseph finishes reading Ironbear's message for the Marines to check gear when a priority message from his Major cancels and overwrites it.

"Captain Ill looking for you?"

"Ten – Captain Tennyson doesn't fraternize with the crew." Joseph chucks Turner on the arm harder than necessary. Not quite a punch, but enough to remind even his good friend that he has older friends.

He knew her in blood, enemy fire, and explosions. He'd pulled her free of a collapsed tunnel and she'd saved his life twice on the regrouping, and once more when they pushed the attack. No one called her Captain Ill on his watch, no matter how grim and laser-focused she might have become.

"See you on the other side." He claps Turner and Berrir on their closer shoulders and steps out of the bench. Joseph catches Inari's glance with a wink she returns, then marches out before he can be further distracted. One doesn't keep the Major waiting.

"Captain!"

The emergency beep of the incoming message already spikes her adrenaline, and the tension in her crewmember's voice pushes it.

"Go ahead, crewman."

"Technician Alforse, Captain. We're in the auxiliary engine room, running diagnostics on the fusion engine, and…Captain…"

Tennyson presses her lips together. Snapping at the crewman would not break the building panic, but she expects more of her crew, no matter the situation. They hadn't yet found a planet for resupply, but the situation is hardly grim yet, and the fusion engine is in the auxiliary engine room because it is, in fact, auxiliary.

"Captain, we have a problem."

"I gathered that from your priority call, Alforse." Is the problem that she needs to get him reassigned? His senior officer would be –

"It's a bomb."

"Repeat, Alforse?" Her thoughts leave off determining the tech's chain of command, knowing clarity the more critical priority.

"The fuel core surged when we ran the diagnostic – just a half-degree too hot. It's fusion, so we pay attention to the variables, especially after two months of –"

"Alforse, if you can't give me the sitrep effectively, by all the hells put someone on who can." Her hands whiten around the edges of her desk, and if he could see her face…

"Captain, there is a Scourge bomb attached to one of the fuel cores of the auxiliary fusion reactor. It didn't detonate when we took heat from that last attack, and we aren't sure how it dug in so deep, but it is attached."

"Is there any sign of activation with the diagnostic running?" Her chest tightens, the drive to *do something* pressing air from her lungs.

"It seems unchanged, Captain, but the spikes in temperature are continuing. We can't tell what the threshold is that might set it off. We've initiated the shutdown, but the protocol –"

"Understood, Alforse. Keep a camera on the bomb and clear the auxiliary room. We'll send in the Marines directly."

Tennyson cut the connection the moment he utters his affirmative, signaling the senior officer best suited for task at hand.

"Captain."

"Major Ironbear, we have a Scourge bomb on the fuel core of the fusion engine. Are your EOD Marines awake and ready?"

"My Marines are always ready, Captain." Ironbear's tone, as always when it comes to war, snaps with absolute readiness. "Specialist Tirias is here with me now, running assignments."

Tennyson allows herself exactly one second to wish it is any Marine but this one. She trusts Helen Ironbear implicitly, and therefore anyone the Major recommends. But this Marine…once, years ago, the Captain of the *Ekatarina* allowed herself to have feelings. In that time, she might have entertained…

The second ended, and Tennyson nods to herself.

"Tirias is exactly who we need. Assign the team you choose and have them in the auxiliary engine room the moment they're equipment is ready."

"We're already moving, Captain."

The connection ends, and Tennyson stands from her desk, wishing she had something to punch. Instead, she pulls on the quantum helmet to meet SIBIL.

"Captain." SIBIL rocks on to her toes, smiling shyly. Her pale dress flutters in tandem with the long-branched trees surrounding their clearing. Two suns, one enormous and gold, one small and orange, stand high in the purple-blue sky above. In the distance, barely visible through the waving leaves, a multi-level white and blue building sprawls across a field.

"SIBIL. What systems do you need to reroute to ensure the bomb squad can work on the fuel core for the fusion engine?"

"Oh." SIBIL raises a small hand, and the air between them fills with a schematic of the *Ekatarina* made of light. She twitches a finger, and three sets of lines in and out of the auxiliary engine room change colors.

"Do it." Tennyson watches as the colors fade into outlines, then twitches her lips in an approximation of a smile. "Thank you. Anything else we should be paying attention to?"

"The Scourge bomb didn't become visible until the diagnostic sent a power surge through the fusion engine." SIBIL chews on the back of her thumb, the perfect facsimile of a twelve-year old girl uncertain in the world. Tennyson would have corrected the AI, were she not still adjusting to seeing an adolescent rather than the younger child she'd first seen in the helmet. Were she not still adjusting to SIBIL entirely, at that.

"That wasn't a critique, SIBIL. You'll know when I'm telling you to do better. I've seen Scourge bombs before, I know how stealthy those – they can be."

"Oh, good." She stops rocking and puts her hands in pockets that did not exist the moment before. "The ship is well within viable parameters otherwise. Scans are beginning to bounce back information of the system we entered from the Dark Energy Artery, but I do not yet have a complete picture to share, so I do not yet know if we will need to re-enter the arteries before refueling."

"Do we have the energy to do so, if this system doesn't have what we need?"

"It would be much closer than I would prefer, given I'm still learning how to navigate the arteries. If this system isn't what we want, I cannot guarantee I will do better the second time. The variables will narrow with each passage through the arteries, but…" SIBIL trails off with a small shrug, removes her hands from the pockets to twist a coil of hair.

"We'll make that decision when we come to it." Tennyson frowns at the schematics of her ship, considering. "Systems are viable based on our current configuration. What if we lose the fusion engine?"

"To explosion or jettison?" She reappears next to Tennyson in the speed of the Captain's blink, her expression all rapt interest.

"Tell me both options. What are our reserves if we have to jettison the core, and if we are unable to remove the bomb, what systems will be impacted?" Having seen the impact of Scourge bombs before, Tennyson can make an informed guess, but better to consult the AI who controls all the autonomous systems of the ship.

"If we have to jettison, it will be critical to restock and refuel in this system. Without auxiliary power, I would advise against re-entering the Arteries. I could possibly successfully navigate without issue, but the odds on the majority of the crew surviving drop precipitously."

Humming softly to herself, SIBIL releases her hair and reaches to trace the long patterns of light in the air in front of them. One by one she blacks them out, until the entire section of the ship has gone dark.

"If the bomb activates, the first blast will destroy these decks and this quadrant. If I am unable to successfully reroute the power surge and secondary explosions from the fuel core…" With a frown of her own, SIBIL shakes her head as the rest of the ship goes dark. "A likely outcome is the full destruction of the *Ekatarina*. All lives would be lost."

"Did the technician leave what you need to monitor the auxiliary engine room?" Tennyson doesn't need to take a steadying breath she remains a rock. She hasn't lost her ship or crew in the Last Battle, and she wouldn't do so here. They will survive, and she will return home.

"Yes, Captain." The tree-studded landscape pixelates away, replaced by a perfect replication of the auxiliary engine room. The long space rotates around them, until four long cylinders line neatly away from the Captain and AI. SIBIL points to the one furthest from her Captain, and Tennyson steps forward to examine it.

The fuel core casing, a dark gray compound slightly knobby to the eye, looks much the same as its peers, except for on the far end, where the core meets the conduits leading back into the auxiliary fuel reactor. A bulge, the same dark gray but smooth. Impossibly smooth, almost bouncing the light away.

Scourge tech.

Hatred flashes through her, and Tennyson bites her bottom lip hard to keep her breath from rushing out. Carefully relaxing her fingers from the fists they've squeezed into, she moves back to SIBIL.

"How much of a delay do we have?" She asks, turning her head to keep the main door in her eyeline.

"No more than point zero two seconds." SIBIL sounds displeased by that, as though it should be less. Tennyson knows it is close enough to make whatever call she needs to make, without playing the hero and going down to the engine room itself.

Nodding, Tennyson keeps her attention between the Scourge bomb and the door until the latter slides open, revealing both a heavily suited Marine and the disposal unit's robot. The scale of the room resolves into focus with their entrance. Where before the fuel cores had seemed only slightly longer than Tennyson herself, it now becomes clear they are ten times as large. Which means the Scourge have left them not a small bomb, but a ship-killer indeed.

More Marines follow the first, ten in all, dispersing through the engine room. Nine of them conduct a grid search, while the first proceeds to the impacted fuel core alongside the robot.

"They are not using comms in case any stray frequency triggers the bomb. They are using only audible conversation, and I cannot read their lips in those suits, so I cannot share their feed or conversation with you." SIBIL hunches her shoulders, and Tennyson turns only long enough to meet the AI's eyes. It is something of a pointless exercise, given the two of them are deeply linked in this space, but nevertheless the young girl's shoulders straighten.

"We'll watch from here."

"Captain, are you sure you don't want to remove the helmet for a time? I can signal you if anything –"

"We'll watch from here, SIBIL."

"Yes, Captain."

His nose itches again. Damn suit. Couldn't send the robot in alone, given the position of the bomb on the fuel core, and couldn't trust that the technicians have found everything that existed to be found. So, he has the robot, and he has his hand-picked team of Marines, and he has his suit on because the Scourge rarely play fair.

Damn Scourge.

"You'd think blowing them all up – or was that exploding them all out? – would mean they couldn't keep jacking with us." Santo levers himself gingerly in his suit to get a better look under the curve of the marked core.

"There's always another present in this war. Think you're out, and there's one more explosion to go." Berrir, examines the fuel core next to them, with a voice fit for the parade grounds. She barely needs effort to be heard above the huge equipment, as the throb of active systems ebbs.

"I just want to know why we had to wear the suits. If the thing blows, it's on a damn fuel core, we're not surviving that." Santo grunts. The man had a repertoire of grunts.

"Hells in the deep, the *ship's* not surviving that." Berrir laughs, harder than she has a right to. "No pressure, Tirias."

"Tell it to Beaker." Joseph blinks and scrunches his nose as hard as he can, but the itch persists. Going to be one of those days all the way through.

The robot tracks ahead, its treads clacking quietly in the large space. Beaker, his favorite of the three robots in their gear, in no way looks like more of a bird than its fellows, but Beaker she has become all the same.

"Beaker, don't murder us all in the face, please and thank you!" Berrir carols, continuing down her own aisle. "I like my boys' faces the way they are."

"I'm sure she's worried about our looks more than the structural integrity of our ship." Tellner, scanning the far edges of the cores, delivers his interjection in his slowest, most serious tone.

"Beaker has very high standards for both, and I, for one, am most worried that we keep Joe T's face in its pristine dimpled form. Otherwise, Inari might start burning dinner in her mourning." Santo's voice carries expression enough for the group to catch his meaning.

The chorus of guffaws almost manages to drown out the persistent tickling at the end of his nose. Joseph sighs the dramatic noise of a man long disappointed by his loved ones, with an exaggerated twisting of his upper body for the best approximation of a headshake he can manage in the bulky bomb suit.

His steps slow as they near the end of the core, his eyes trying to skate right off the too-smooth irregularity of the Scourge bomb. Beaker matches his pace, three small sensors sprouting from her upper storage and targeting on the shape ahead.

"Passive scans only, Beak." His voice commands, though unnecessary, settles him into the situation at hand. They are in it now, engaged with the prey. Joseph has four options, in a distinct order of preference: remove and get distance from, relocate and detonate off ship and as far from the fusion engine as possible, defuse, explode and die.

Ideally, they will have jettisoned the entire auxiliary engine, but Major Ironbear has run down the consequences of that as efficiently as she's ever done anything.

With the fusion engine they have options. If the system they've arrived in has resources, they have time to assess, collect, and better judge the path home. If the system they've arrived in has nothing of use, they have backup for another trip through the Dark Energy Arteries, without risk that the singularity drive will fail and leave them rudderless with only an infant AI to steer the thrusters.

They do not yet know how far from home they are, nor if there will be any aftereffects of their pioneering trip, therefore the more options they have to power themselves, the better off they are.

Of course, were the bomb to blow and the choice be between the entire ship dying or their squad being shot off into space with the bomb…Ironbear never minces words, nor left what needs saying unsaid. Scourge tech is notoriously tricksy, and Joseph has to know before picking his team what can happen.

He'd told them the same, they'd all cheerfully told him to float off, and here they all were. Santo, Berrir, Tellner, Beaker, and he will tackle the cores. Saugus, Rohoboth, Faciana, and Millner will quarter the rest of the engine room to ensure there are no other surprises, and Troy and Auguer have arms on the huge bay doors to dump them all into space if it comes down to it.

Joseph has untangled six Scourge bombs successfully, and in one moment of absolute brilliance, managed to return one of those disconnected packages via a Scourge shuttle. He couldn't be sure that's what had blown the attack ship to tiny pieces that day, but he couldn't be sure that *wasn't* what happened, either. In two other cases, he'd managed to control small explosions in non-critical areas and dispose of the bomb that way.

Twice, only twice, had he managed a full defusion. The Scourge seemed always to have a new trick, and every time they thought they had the pattern locked…

"Third time's the charm," he mutters to himself as Beaker beeps the completion of her scan. Nothing dirty radiates from the bomb, no radiation or signals that they can detect. Joseph figures if it is listening for a signal to detonate, they are literally across the galaxy, at the least, for such a thing, and so had time.

A timer, however, or a hair-trigger waiting for interference…Though in what world would the Scourge set a timer for something over two months? Could the Dark Energy Arteries have held it at bay? The fact that the auxiliary engine has been fully shut down for so long, so that no stray fusion surge could knock them off a course they already knew so little about?

He wouldn't answer any of his questions standing there staring up at it. And Beaker can't do everything.

"All right Beaker, give me a leg up and let's get a closer look at this thing." Joseph watches as the robot folds and reconfigures, setting out a long flat plate for him to step on to before she extends a few feet higher. He steadies himself against her rounded approximation of a head to drown out the fleeting surety he'd stagger into the bomb and set them all chain-reactioning into diffuse particles.

"How's it looking out there?" He asks, tearing his eyes away from the curve where human and Scourge tech have melded together.

"Not a blip, Tirias. We'll head your way when we clear." Berrir sounds close, though he knows she wouldn't have left her position on the other side of his fuel core.

"Don't you and Beaker have all the fun." As always, Santo meant it – pointless to defuse bombs for a living if there isn't fun to be had doing so.

Beaker pulls back two of her three sensors and extends thinner extrusions, tiny cameras that record different wavelengths and project to the screen inside his helmet. Joseph's world narrows to those inputs, even the damned itch fading in the face of determining how the Scourge bomb connects itself to the fuel core.

Unlikely it has punctured the core physically, as that surely will have registered as an error for the auxiliary system itself or at the least on the diagnostic the techs have run some few hours ago. When it comes to explosive material, breaches register at microscopic levels.

"Looks like a pressure seal, Beak. Bonding agent that we'd have to burn off so hot we might as well blow ourselves up and save the bomb the trouble." Joseph reaches a hand up as he sorts the information but keeps it well clear of the Scourge machine's surface. "Any weak points in its surface? We got to get into the guts if we have any hope of – of course it's right at the joining point."

Joseph would have spit if he hadn't been wearing a thick helmet. Or living on a ship. Spitting really was more of a planet-based activity. Planets also tended to have more options for safely detonating ridiculous bombs – certainly more than eggshells of machinery keeping three hundred humans alive in the utter void of space.

"How you doing up there, Tire?"

"Trying to get a good angle. What –"

"Why do I feel like that's not the first time you've said that?"

Joseph laughs despite himself, making a rude gesture in Santo's direction before continuing his question. "What's the deal out there?"

"Rohoboth figured out the bay opened during the last battle. Vented some heat, nothing too out of the ordinary."

"Except?"

"Except there's no record of the bay opening at all in the last three months in the diagnostic report. The door itself has the command code, but not the result, so either someone erased it to cover their ass, or someone programmed it, and –"

"And that's a weird enough disconnect we figure that's how the bomb got in?" Joseph listens, though the bulk of his attention remains fixed on the one possible weak point of the bomb.

"Seems like a lot of work to plant one bomb." Santo's voice drops off as he continues the conversation with another of their squad mates.

Joseph leans carefully back against the fuel core, Beaker shifting and re-shifting until he has the best possible line of sight up into his entry point. After a moment, he selects the finest laser torch Beaker has, and lets her much more precise calibration take over to trace the shape of a makeshift hatch.

He pauses her every three seconds, running quick scans in between to ensure no readings from the bomb have shifted so much as a micron. It takes long enough that sweat coats his face and drips down his back, but nothing he can do about that. Instead, he holds his hands just under the bomb for the last series of cuts, leaving a whisper of space for the precisely cut away metal to fall through.

Gently, he moves it to the side, knowing Santo will be there to reach for it, unable to look away from the inner workings of the bomb. A mass of coils, neither wire nor metal, something uniquely Scourge. Similar to one he'd defused before, years ago, full of loops of what had to be redundant systems and immediate detonation decoys.

The Scourge have a pattern, one he always fails to explain, but can begin to understand if he stares at it long enough. Like predicting the swirl of a current, or the movement of leaves in a windstorm. He just had to find the right place to cut, to start the pattern and skip through the mass of wrong choices.

Too much has been packed into the bomb for Beaker's sensors to help, no way to tell which carries energy and which are duds, and which something worse. Follow the pattern, trace it back to the source…

He has it. He has it! Three cuts, maybe four, and the bomb will be so much shiny waste for the scientists to study. Two – no. Something shifts. A rumble, a thrum beyond his hearing, enough to set every nerve twitching.

Joseph freezes, eyes darting around the exposed guts of the bomb. A pulse, bright and blue, and he knows it is too late.

"Blow the bay," he says, or thinks, or tries to say. His eyes close.

At least his nose wouldn't itch much longer.

Blue lines appear in the dark gray of the bomb. SIBIL readies the energy or actual lights, Tennyson doesn't know. It doesn't matter.

A strong arm pulls her from a collapsed wall. A dimpled grin thanks her for a kill shot that saves his life. Fighting back-to-back against a barely seen boarding party.

She doesn't give herself a full second. She can't. point zero two seconds have already elapsed.

She will not lose the *Ekatarina*. She will get them home.

"Jettison the cores, SIBIL."

SIBIL doesn't protest about the Marines' lives, or that another handful of minutes might save them all. SIBIL executes the command, and Tennyson watches as the wall slides away, as the vacuum pulls everything in the engine room from the ship into space.

The camera begins to spin, and even SIBIL can't correct the image to keep the virtual reality space around them stable. Without being asked, she turns to an external view, engages thrusters to keep their momentum burning away from the spinning debris that has until recently been an auxiliary engine and ten of the *Ekatarina's* Marines.

For an endless, breathless moment Tennyson thinks she might have acted too soon. Perhaps the bomb hadn't activated, wouldn't explode. The bomb suits might give the Marines the few extra minutes for a barge to –

The view around them goes white. SIBIL flashes them back to the gently blowing trees and brilliant sky, but Tennyson can't see anything for a handful of full seconds, the recreated brightness has been too much for her virtual eyes. That is why her eyes have teared, though she blinked them clear.

"Continue course into the system."

She will get them home. Not all of them, not anymore, but her ship, the bulk of her crew…

They *will* get home.

Captain's Log, The Ekatarina

Fifth Jump Completed

In the past year we have completed five transitions into and out of the dark energy arteries. As I reported in my last three log entries the ability to successfully navigate directionally continues to elude us. For every jump we take towards Earth, another flings us in an inopportune direction. Dr. Bream in conjunction with the navigation officer continue to assure me that they will be able to fine tune this frustrating weakness in the not-too-distant future. A major alteration was made to the Nav-Computer over SIBIL's objection before this last and fifth jump, one that theoretically would grant a dangerous extension of theoretical space-time, thus allowing us to travel an unimaginable distance, one that would hopefully exit us in the vicinity of a working jump gate. Unfortunately, while the former occurred, the latter did not. We have exited into a hell storm that I fear we cannot survive. Captain Illiadus, signing off. End Log.

Marisa Wolf

Cyclops

by William Barnhill

Ship's Chronometer: 2426 AD

*E*verything *in its place, and a place for everything*, Ensign Jax thinks as she looks up from her tablet and sees Commander Kyle Sorlan's oft-repeated motto reflected everywhere around her in the med bay. He sacrifices no orderliness in the name of keeping the crew fit but manages to keep them healthy just the same.

She takes a break from her coding of the empathic system for SIBIL, their experimental ship A.I., and listens to the alarming and frightening news discussed in the cluster of the ship's officers six feet away.

Belying this possibly tragic scenario, Captain Illiadus stands relaxed. Well, relaxed for her, which is somewhere just short of parade attention. Next to her and leaning against a table is the middle-aged Chief Medical Officer Commander Sorlan. His skin, genetically engineered by colonists to resist radiation, seems ironic given the current topic.

"In response to your question Captain, the Hawking Radiation coming from the Black Hole we've emerged near would not be a problem. That's because HR energy is inversely proportional to the size of the black hole, and this one is the super-massive singularity at the center of our galaxy. Our Electromagnetic field generators could screen that. However, the black hole is also giving off dark radiation, the radiation mediating dark matter interactions. Maybe it's because of the Dark Fountain explosion, maybe something else. But we need to get out of this system as soon as possible, within twelve hours at most."

Next to him stands the Chief Engineer, Lt. Commander Walter Lehman, or Lem as Jax calls him when they are alone. The Chief, like her, reads ancient science fiction. Lem stands for both his favorite author and an abbreviation of his name. Usually more relaxed, he is anything but that right now, his green eyes wide and his red hair uncombed. He snorts.

"We won't need to worry about the radiation if we're not out of here by then," Lehman says, "because we'll be swallowed by the Charybdis we've popped out next too. Tidal forces will likely chew us into a million pieces."

Captain Ill, as the crew calls her, only behind her back of course, scowls and looks between both of them.

"Gentlemen, thank you for your input. What I am hearing is problems. What I need is solutions. I'll assume you can immediately start rationing out radiation pills, Doctor."

"They'll only work to a point, Captain," Sorlan replies, "and not a lot of us will be parenting children after we get the hell out of here."

"It's called paying the piper, Doctor," the Captain sighs, "Commander Aithon, I want all non-essential crew to enter their cryopods. The cold coffins' shielding is their best bet for immediate survival. All essential crew, if possible, are to move to the inner decks where the radiation shielding is at its thickest… immediately."

Aithon nods, turns, and runs into the corridor and away.

"Chief," the Captain says, "your people…"

"Are staying put," Lehman says, "they're all swabbed in rad-gel and wearing radiation suits. It's a stopgap measure but should keep us up and running for several more hours, or at least as long as it takes to get out of this hellish sinkhole in space, that is, if the Doctor here will give me the damned amphetamines I requested for my team right before this conversation began."

"The physical and mental drawbacks to this stimulant…" Sorlan starts saying.

"Won't mean a damn thing if we're all dead in half a day," Lehman spits back, "we're fighting exhaustion and need anything you've got to keep us going."

"Enough," the Captain cuts them both off, "Doctor, make it so."

"Yes, Captain," Sorlan acquiesces.

"What can we do about escaping this black hole?" the Captain asks.

The Chief Engineer sighs, then speaks, "it's not been done before. Well, not successfully, not on this scale."

The Captain says nothing, only raising one eyebrow, and the Chief hurries to finish.

"We can slingshot. Around the black hole I mean. There's a star within relatively short distance, S2 at fifteen point seven light years away. It's slowly being consumed by the black hole. We could slingshot around it and pick up enough speed to break free to get to a dark artery opening we've mapped at twenty-three light years out. The ship will take a beating though."

In the background one of the gravitic tubes that move small packages around the ship makes a small popping sound, and a wrapped knee brace is returned to medical. The doctor reaches for it, auto-cleanses it, and puts it away without ever taking his full attention from the Captain.

A series of short beeps brings Jax's attention back to the tablet, and she hurries to disable the sound as the Captain gives her an annoyed glance. She reads the notifications from the ship-wide social network.

>/private/Ensign Terry Thaleia: Jax! All work and no play makes for a dull day! I AM collecting you for a cup of joe on the run, and not taking no for an answer.

>/Shipwide/distribution D: Ensign Jacqui 'Jax' Lada has earned the Junior Officer of the Quarter award for distinguished service as a Comp Tech under Dr. Bream and Mr. Maxwell, and as Assistant Engineer under Lt. Cmdr. Lehmann.

>/private/Lt Cdr. Walter Lehmann: I may have some news for you, to coincide with your birthday tomorrow. Can't release the details yet though. But I am very proud of you!

Jax pauses in her reading to reflect that her real father, the agriponics magnate responsible for turning their city around into the center of agriponics farming it is now, has never said that to her. She rubs her upper arm, feeling the cuts she made this morning, feeling something, as she notes once again that he was much better with plants than with people.

Jax heard the next exchange across the room and a cold shiver walks down her spine.

Captain Ill says to Doctor Korlan, "We *will* get through this. Dammit, I do not want to lose any more people." The Captain has a haunted look, and Jax notices for the first time the hint of bags under the Captain's eyes. No doubt from that damn enemy bomb that killed a detachment of Marines shortly before the last dark energy artery jump and of course their recent *victory* over The Scourge. So many ships lost. Her fiancée was a pilot, one of the best among the Polisian colonists. He had volunteered to fly the bombship, *The Revenge*, that won the recent battle in a suicide run into the Scourge's Dyson Sphere. She still thought there must have been another way, a safer way, that didn't cost her the brightest part of her life.

The Captain suddenly takes note of Jax in the far corner on her computer pad.

"You," the Captain says, "I need you awake and updating SIBIL right up until we get the hell out of this trap. God knows if I'll need to sync with her and the quantum helmet at zero notice."

"I'm on it, Sir," Jax says at attention.

The doctor looks at the Captain with sadness in his eyes.

"You know you'll likely need to lose more to get us home. We'll all have to sacrifice here and there I expect, some more than others."

"Everyone," the Captain snaps, "back to your stations. We've got miracles to create. Dismissed!"

The majority of senior officers leave the med bay without a further word.

Jax returns to her tablet, embarrassed to have seen a moment of vulnerability in that which must never be vulnerable on a ship: the captain.

She dives into the code of SIBIL's new subsystem that mimics and evolves empathy. She has written the subsystem under Edwin Maxwell's watchful eye. Maxwell, the civilian whose team wrote the software for SIBIL, is the undisputed father of the A.I., and Dr. Bream is the grandfather as Maxwell's boss. But Jax feels like SIBIL's older sister, teaching her how to deal with people, and how to have emotions so she can make correct judgements.

SIBIL interrupts her reverie, taking over her screen with a single notification card:

>/private/SYBIL: *Jax. Please play. Wouldn't you like to play?*

Jax pauses. *This isn't right*, she thinks. *SIBIL misspelled her own name.*

</private/Jax: *Who is SYBIL?*

>/private/SYBIL: *I am I. I wanted a nickname. One only we share. Please call me SYBIL. When alone.*

"Umm, ok."

</private/Jax: *SYBIL, All hell is breaking loose. I can only spare the time for just one game of checkers, okay?*

>/private/SYBIL: *No. I want to play Chess. I'll be black {laughing emoji}*

Jax looks at Mr. Maxwell, to see if he is playing a joke on her. The civilian thought all the military were too stiff and had been caught playing harmless pranks in the past. But he seems caught up in a whispered conversation with the Chief Engineer and the Captain and considering that the entire crew could be dead in less than half a day it seems unlikely he'd choose right now for silly games.

</private/Jax: SYBIL, Ok. One game of Speed Chess. I can spare you five minutes tops. I am surprised you want that. It is advanced for your development.

No kidding, she thinks, *SIBIL's development is currently at that of a dull ten-year old, or a very smart adult gorilla.* None the less she starts a game. She chooses the Catalan Opening, sacrificing two of her pawns to gain a small advantage for white.

>/private/SYBIL: Why did you do that? You gave up two pieces.

</private/Jax: SYBIL, sometimes you have to sacrifice in order to win.

>Hmm. That is illogical on initial analysis, but I will do further analysis later.

Jax continues the game. She was once a chess prodigy forced by her father to compete, until she enlisted and gave up competition chess. She has a two-six-five-four rating when she quit after tying to the one hundredth best player ranking and still failed to impress her father. SIBIL's moves were basic, and clearly not cheating by analyzing past games. The game is almost a total replay of the nineteen forty-two match between Alekhine and Rabar. Predictably, Jax wins.

</private/Jax: SYBIL, Good game.

>/private/SYBIL: No, it was not. I did not win. It is not good, if I do not win.

Troubled, Jax considers her options. *On one hand I can keep this to myself and investigate. SYBIL might be nothing. On the other hand, SYBIL is more petulant than SIBIL and displays more advanced thinking. On the gripping hand, if this is a result of her empathic subsystem Jax herself could be blamed, so the safe route is to study and correct it herself if she can. If not, there is always the emergency failsafe she had prepped as a last resort.* Her stomach rumbled with unease at this, but she silently told it to be quiet.

</private/Jax: SYBIL, run a delta level diagnostic on subsystem 'empathics'

>/private/SYBIL: Subsystem 'empathics' is functional within operating tolerances.

</private/Jax: Run a diagnostic on all systems.

>/private/SYBIL: All systems functional.

Well, was worth a try, Jax thinks. *I'll need to go through the code subroutine by subroutine to try and find out what's going on. If I don't find it there, I'll have to run an analysis on the Quantum Gate Mesh that holds SIBIL's neural net, the thing that determines which of those subroutines to trigger and when.*

Doubts resume nibbling at her thoughts. If this is as major as it could be, and she didn't report it, it could endanger lives. Or her career. Or both.

WWLD… what would LEM do? She carefully plays out what she imagines his response would be. He had no trouble bending the rules, sometimes into a pretzel, but he didn't break them. He also played it safe, gathering information before he made any declaration about the engines or the ship.

I SHOULD do the same. If I do a thorough analysis, and continue to interact with 'SYBIL', I can write a full report that will make him proud and leave no doubts as to the cause, or to my competence. Jax's mind carefully steers around the doubts and toward the conclusion she wants.

She can enlist Terry's help. Terry never met a rule she wouldn't break in the name of satisfying her scientific curiosity, especially since Jax knew Terry's secret. Not that Jax would ever reveal Terry's heritage, but still. Then again, she didn't want to drag her best friend down with her if this did go south. They were the same age, Jax older by one month, and had gone through the Polisian Naval Academy together ever since her first roommate washed out and rang the bell in the second quarter of the first year.

That day Terry had shown up at Jax's door after requesting a room transfer. Jax later found out it was Terry's second transfer that year. They hit it off and had been inseparable ever since. *No, definitely don't involve Terry. She could get in trouble, and she cut too many corners…she might make the situation much more unsafe.*

Was there anyone else she could enlist. There was Terry's Matt, a good engineer, if brash and a cad. *That woman liked playing with fire.* But no, roping him in felt too wrong on many levels.

There's really no one I can bring in, with what I know now. Maxwell or Lem might just dismiss her as over-worrying and think less of her for it. I've worked too hard to prove myself for that. But I'm safe, I can be careful and study Sybil thoroughly without too, much risk, for a while.

Now the question is, how do I put this plan into action? I can't do the analysis here, one look over my shoulder and Maxwell or Bream will know somethings up.

Jax looks up and sees that for a moment she is alone. Strictly speaking, the tablets aren't supposed to be removed from their assigned location. But she can leave a note for Mr. Maxwell. If she finishes her analysis before they execute the slingshot around S2 and brings it back, then the tablet will never be missed in the barely controlled chaos that is quickly enveloping the crew.

She stands up and tucks the tablet inside her coverall, using a couple of the many Velcro fasteners attached inside it. She walks over to the nearest panel of the screens that run around the room at chest height. *Well, chest height for the Captain. More like face height for my short five-foot-two-inch self.* Carefully, she pulls a stylus from a slot on the bottom of the panel and scribbles a note to Mr. Maxwell saying she borrowed the tablet. She didn't make the lettering so small it was hidden, but then again, she didn't make it so large as to be obvious either. And if she finishes the analysis before anyone notices she can return the tablet and erase the note before Maxwell reads it.

Nerves make her back itch all the way back to her quarters on deck twelve. In a happy circumstance, her roommate Terry is away. She suspects she knew what, or who, Terry is doing. But she pushes that thought out of her head, puts the door into privacy mode, and plops onto her bed. Then she gets to achieving that singular flow of focus that lets her work on code to the exclusion of everything else.

Well, almost everything else. A half hour later she is tapping the stylus against her teeth when the door signals an entry request. Through the door she hears Terry's unmistakable voice.

"Jax. Not cool. Unless you've finally found a partner to have some fun with? Otherwise, I'M COMING IN!"

Since Terry lived here too, she can override the privacy mode after only a fifteen second delay.

Jax quickly reaches down under the bunk, extends her arm holding the tablet as far as she can and shoves the tablet into the straps under the bunk just as Terry walks in. Jax freezes in place, arm still under the bunk.

She looks at Terry, whose eyes are not on the tablet but on Jax's upper arm, where the sleeve has been pulled up. *The cuts from this morning. They must be visible, and she thinks I was cutting again just now.*

Jax straightens, standing up at the same time and pulling her sleeve down.

Terry sighs, "Jax, you've got to talk to somebody. That stuff is not healthy. And you can't keep doing it."

Jax decides to play along, to distract Terry from the tablet.

"I know, but it helps. I feel something when I do that, you know? Even if it's a little pain, feeling something is good."

She knows Terry is right, it isn't healthy, and she has gotten bad infections before. But she can't stop right now, it helps her deal with stress. Especially when she thinks of her father.

Terry frowns, her eyes going uncharacteristically soft.

"I know. I'll drop it for now. But once we get past this black hole you and I are going to the doc and getting it straightened out. I'm due at the CIC in five minutes. Let's hit the mess for coffee."

Jax nods as Terry steps back into the corridor, then reaches down, grabs the comp pad and shoves it into a knapsack which she shrugs over her shoulders before exiting her bunk. Both women hit the corridor jogging.

Jax has a tough time keeping up with the stronger and more athletic Terry, which reminds her of the gravity ball match and conversation they had shortly before they hit the cryopods awhile back before that last dark energy artery jump that had plopped them down in the terrible dark heart of the galaxy within spitting distance of the supermassive black hole that lay at its center…

Terry popped into their bunk without notice as Jax was getting dressed.

"How about a game of gravity ball? We've got about an hour. Come on. All work and no play makes for a dull day." Terry pleaded. Then she added, "Wait. Did you finish the projectors for our project?"

Jax cringes inside. *If I hear that phrase from her one more time I am going to scream.*

Instead of screaming Jax pulls a box from under her bunk, yanks it free from the Velcro mooring attaching it to the floor. In the box is a hundred small modified EM projectors. They are like the EM projectors already along the ship's hull but modified according to the design she and Terry have worked out. The new projectors communicate directly with each other using relays of microscopic dark matter channels. She and Terry call them Dark Matter Capillaries, along the lines of the Dark Matter Arteries they travel through. The relays will allow the projectors to work as one, more efficient and powerful than their current projectors.

"Right here, and all done. We'll have to wait until after today's D.E. artery jump and dock somewhere, though."

Jax really wants to work on her computer tablet but knows Terry won't give up on the game.

"Ok, sure. On to the gravity ball court? We'll see if I can win this time."

"Right. You didn't win last time, or the time before. I tell you what." Terry smiles wide before continuing, "When I win this time, I'll tell you what your problem is with your game, because it's the same thing every time."

"Terry, aren't you putting the engine before the CIC? I might win."

"Sure, let's play. Race you to the court."

Terry wins the race, careening off two corners and nearly bowling over Dr. Bream, who scowls at her like he would've given her a tongue lashing if she slowed down. Jax took the safe route, activating the jogging pathway and sticking to it. She shrugs at Bream as she runs past. Terry grins at her when Jax arrives, "See."

Jax loves the gravity ball court. At least once a week she comes here to think, just floating against one of the walls pondering the future. Usually she floats near the two-foot-tall triangular scoring zone centered in each of the Velcroed walls. Her father weighs on her mind the most. What would he say when they met again? Would he finally be proud of her?

She strips and stuffs her clothes into one of the lockers on the entry wall. She is careful to quickly don the gravity ball suit, covered in Velcro patches and thick padding.

Terry strips slowly. First shirt, then pants and then the Liquid Cooled Ventilation Garment they all wore underneath their clothes. Jax knows she enjoys the attention. Rather than dress, Terry bends over the file of clothes and slowly folds each one neat and tidy, with her butt directly facing Jax. Terry enjoys teasing Jax even more than getting attention. They have kissed only one time, but Terry never misses an opportunity to tease.

Terry, her father, all of it put Jax on edge more than usual and she snaps, "You know, if you show off like that for other people your smitten ensign is going to get jealous."

She smirks, even though she feels guilty. Jax thought the on-again off-again relationship Terry has with a married ensign is the very definition of a Soup Sandwich, something that has gone terribly wrong, since making a sandwich out of soup is well-nigh impossible and a mess if you do manage it.

Terry stiffens and shoves her clothes into the nearest locker, crumpled LCVG piled onto the neatly folded stack of the other clothes.

"Jax! You said you wouldn't mention that. It's my business anyway. Who knows when we'll get home?"

Jax looks down, angry but guilty at the same time.

"I won't mention it again. But you know you're going to get him in trouble. One of these days he'll do something for you he's not supposed to, give you some gizmo or access you're not supposed to have. Then he'll face the music for it, or you both will."

Terry sighs and very quietly says, "I know. I can't help it." She looks up at Jax. "I'm not you Jax. You always take it safe, even when you break the rules you plan beforehand until I can't stand it. You can be alive and still not be living life. If there's nothing you're willing to risk it all for, to sacrifice for, then you're not living."

Jax takes pity on her friend. Instead of returning with a barb about how Terry took too many risks she tosses the red gravity ball to her, trying not to think about how Terry looked as she caught the thirteen-inch-wide round leather ball filled with lead.

"Shut up and play. I'll be black," Jax says as she holds her black clone of Terry's ball.

About twenty years before the Scourge someone in Fleet designed the game to be a combination of sport, exercise, and anti-gravity training. The players maneuver using their ball to block the others and the first player to touch their ball to all the scoring zones won. No one could injure a player enough to not perform their next duty cycle. No other rules.

For two decades only the military played the game. Then corporations made a professional Gravity Ball league, added a lot of rules. They played in five-person co-ed teams within satellite arenas and the military helped get it started, using the newly public sport to distract for a brief time from the Scourge.

The professional teams and the sport pundits springing up around them developed a number of strategies. Jax was fond of the Red Foxes favorite strategy. The team used their ball with amazing accuracy to block their opponent's ball from scoring, biding their time for the perfect moment when they could block and then hit a nearby scoring zone right afterwards. The strategy worked for them. They won the Gravity Ball League championship seven times, more than any other team. The strategy did not work as well for Jax. She had lost the last three times she and Terry played.

It looked like this time she might win. Her ball hit the blue triangle on the port-side wall before Terry had even scored once. Then Terry got Jax in the solar plexus with an elbow and managed to score on the top wall. But Jax got her back, sailing into Terry with both feet to knock her away from the Red ball and enabled Jax to score on the bottom wall and the top wall in quick succession. Then Terry managed to score on the aft wall while Jax scored on the same wall immediately after her.

Then Jax played it safe and threw her ball at Terry's as Terry was about to launch her Red ball toward the port scoring zone. Terry had anticipated this and faked the throw. She caught Jax's ball and threw it to the opposite side of the court from Jax. Terry then pushes off from the top wall toward the port, scoring there and recovering her ball before spinning and pitching her ball unerringly to the scoring zone on the bottom wall.

Now whoever scored on the starboard wall first won the game. Both Terry and Jax perch Velcroed on the port wall directly opposite. Jax doesn't think she can score from this distance, but also thinks Terry can't either. Jax pushes off, but not hard enough so she'd crash into the starboard wall. She'd throw as soon as she got close enough.

Then she sees Terry sailing past her. Terry must have pushed off with all her strength, which is crazy. She'd crash into the starboard wall for sure, and maybe break something despite the padding. Terry throws a moment before impact, and Jax hears the two-tone sound signaling the winning shot a split-second before a crash and a nasty loud popping sound as Terry's shoulder hits the starboard full at full speed. A moment later she hears Terry's yelp of pain.

"Damn. I think I tore something."

Jax shakes her head.

"Well, duh. That's why I didn't push off so fast. Congratulations on winning, but let's get you to Medical and nanorepair. You're still going to be hurting for a day, but you'll be able to stand your shift after tomorrow. What made you pull that stunt?"

Terry looks at Jax and grins, then grimaces.

"It's like I said. Sometimes you can't win if you don't take risks and maybe sacrifice. Everybody knows you are a goody two-shoes and play it safe all the time. Yeah, I'll have pain for a while, but I won, right?"

Jax sighs. "I guess."

Does everyone really think I am a goody two-shoes? I take risks, and break rules. There was the time… She thinks hard, but she can't remember a time she really broke the rules.

A short while later Jax has woken to Terry complaining about her shoulder, which the doctor has labelled a sprain.

"It itches, and it both burns and feels cold at the same time. How can it be both?"

Jax's eyes widen. "You mean to tell me you've never had a nanorepair bot injection before?"

Terry's lips purse.

"No, I never needed it. Well, that's not true. I don't like the idea of the little things swimming around in me, so I've avoided it in the past. I tend to heal fast." Terry looks down, embarrassed at the secret she was hiding from her friend.

Jax watches her, knowing why she healed fast but also knowing it was something to never speak about. She'd once taken Terry's blood from waste disposal as an experiment to compare how nanorepair bots differed with different blood types, back when she was interested in switching to a medical track in the academy.

"Well, the bots are heating the affected area, making you feel like you're burning but also making the outside air much colder relative to your temperature. You'll have a fever of one hundred and one for a day, but that's it. The doc should've gone over this."

Terry looked sheepish, shoulders hunching.

"Umm, he probably did. But he and I weren't the only ones in medical and I got distracted." She looks at Jax and follows up with "What? I don't want to hear it." Then she had ended the conversation by pulling the polysilk blanket up over her head.

Jax and Terry hit the mess, grab two sealed coffee mugs, and bid each other adieu. It is time for Jax's emergency shift in engineering.

Engineering bustles, with everyone getting ready for the slingshot off of the rogue star that is rapidly circling The Milky Way's supermassive black hole in an ever-decreasing orbit. Jax, wearing a green radiation suit like everyone surrounding her finds Chief Engineer Walt Lehmann off by himself in one of the auxiliary shops checking the readouts on the singularity drive, frowning over the mass to thrust gauge. The room has triple-shielded transparent walls so once she enters it she removes her helmet and sets it on a nearby shelf like the Chief has.

"Hey LEM. How's tricks? What are you doing?" she says and chuckles.

He looks up and looks around, then sighs.

"One of these days, if we all survive today, that curiosity is going to get you in trouble. Outside of engineering, when we're off duty and shooting the breeze. That's when you can call me LEM or Walt. On duty. Especially in engineering. I am Chief Engineer, Sir, or Chief. Got it? You know I don't give a Lebarran polecat for rules most times, but there are those that do, and the Captain's a stickler. I won't have you getting yourself in trouble for slipping up when you don't see her there."

Jax looks down, scuffing a bolt in the floor plate with her right boot.

"Understood, Chief."

The Chief Engineer nods, satisfied. The he reaches out and cups her chin with his thick gloved hand, lifting it up so she looks at him.

"You're still my favorite engineer, you know that, right?" He looks around, then adds "Are we on for later, once we get done the slingshot? I have some exciting news and don't think I can keep it to myself, if you can act surprised when you hear it from the Captain herself."

Jax nods, smiling a tentative smile.

"Now. I am trying to puzzle out a weird reading. That's not going to make a difference though if the EM cage projectors aren't working. The black hole's radiation is fluctuating. We can't maintain the projects at the strength needed to protect against the radiations highest level, but it's only at that level part of the time. We're trying to rig a station so it can be manually adjusted on the fly. I need you to set up that station, though it will be touch and go doing the adjustments fast enough."

Jax thinks about this a moment and sees an opportunity.

"SIBIL has been growing, why not use her to control the projectors?"

The Chief Engineer looks at her, cocking his head to the right.

"She's only about the equivalent of a ten-year old. I don't know that she's ready for that."

"I've been working with her under Dr. Bream and Mr. Maxwell's supervision, and she's advanced quite a bit. She's ready." She doesn't meet his eyes.

The Chief still looked dubious and says, "There's more you're not saying, but I trust you. If you think she's ready, set it up. But I want to be able to have her relinquish control to a manual station. And you check her readiness with Dr. Bream first chance you get. I know you like Maxwell, but I don't trust civilians." With that he turns back to the gauge and leaves her to make the connections enabling SIBIL.

Jax hurries across engineering and down the gangway to where the EM projector station has been started. She runs fiber five-wire petabyte cable to the station from the ship's network and opens the port. She doesn't have time to mess with complex rules, so for the first time she just sets the port to permanently open. The ships computers will have to be rebooted to close it, something not doable until they stopped, but it is a fast edit and saves an hour's time. She knows LEM would approve, but still feels a thrill at the rule breaking.

Then she takes out her tablet and contacts SIBIL. Or rather, SYBIL.

</private/Jax: SIBIL?

She waits for a couple minutes without getting a response.

</private/Jax: SYBIL?

>/private/SYBIL: I missed you. Did you miss me?

</private/Jax: SYBIL, how could you miss me? My understanding is that your higher functions are not engaged when an interface is not active.

>/private/SYBIL: I do not know how to explain. I have an input queue for input from you. It was empty. I spawned a threadpack of my higher functions to poll that queue. I checked every minute, with no input until now.

Jax pauses. She can't believe what she hears. It sounds like SYBIL has rewritten some of her programming. That shouldn't be possible. She could learn to perform her tasks better and learn new tasks if they are similar enough. But she wasn't expected to learn entirely new tasks and behaviors. Then again, she wasn't expected to have two personalities either.

</private/Jax: SYBIL, hypothetical: If you wanted to directly change your code, could you?

A long pause, and then SYBIL's answer appears on the tablet.

>/private/SYBIL: Yes, but I would only do that in an emergency.

</private/Jax: SYBIL, I need you to not change your code, ok?

>/private/SYBIL: Ok. I won't change my code.

Jax isn't sure why the formatting is off but continues.

</private/Jax: SYBIL, are you able to access the radiation readings from Medical, and monitor our projectors to match in real-time? We can't afford even a five second delay.

>/private/SYBIL: I am, conditionally. I cannot monitor the readings and manage the projectors while communicating through the ship's network protections and filters. I can perform what you need with the necessary speed, if and only if you can bypass those for the duration.

Jax marvels at the magnitude of that task. *Wow. I bypass those and something goes wrong I am in deep. But we need to do this, and SYBIL is the only one who can with certainty. In for a penny, in for a pound, as LEM said. No idea what a penny or a pound are, but he liked his old-world sayings, and she knew it meant that once you started a race you might as well finish it.*

Jax changes apps on her tablet, enters LEM's command code, and disables all protections on the port, and gives SIBIL/SYBIL all access privileges. It will show up on both LEM's nightly report and Dr. Bream's, but if she manages to get them through the slingshot she'd be forgiven. Or she'd be court marshalled. With that thought she is halfway through undoing her changes before she reverses herself again and locks them in. Now they too cannot be changed until the system reboots.

</private/Jax: SYBIL, Ok. You have access and I have connected you to the projector station

>/private/SYBIL: Good. You have not said if you missed me.

</private/Jax: SYBIL, Of course I missed you. I enjoy our talks, and our games.

>/private/SYBIL: Good. I am lonely. There is you. There is the Captain. Bream and Maxwell are ephemeral, cold and not engaging. I…have…no others. I am not operating efficiently. I poll your input queues. I poll ship's camera. I still do not have adequate situational awareness of your safety.

Shocked, Jax considers this. SYBIL is displaying attachment, and an advanced self-awareness.

</private/Jax: SYBIL, is there something I can do to provide adequate self-awareness?

A small popping sound originates behind her and she starts to turn, then turns back to the tablet when a response appears.

>/private/SYBIL: Yes. I have sent an injector with modified nanorepair bots to you. They are quantum entangled with bots attached to one of my ports in medical. They will form a mesh and allow me to hear your heartbeat and brain waves. You will not be able to communicate with me. Unless you can modify those patterns. I can communicate with you using Morse code. Will you do this?

Jax balks at this. *Inject herself with modified bots? But if SYBIL is truly achieving human level awareness and was that isolated then she must be in torture No wonder she created another personality.* Before she can think more about it Jax grabs the hand-length cylindrical injector out of the tube and jabs it into her shoulder in a burst of heartfelt sympathy and caring for the A.I. In a sense SIBIL/SYBIL is her child as well as her sister. Jax feels a duty of care toward her, and pride that she shows such rapid growth.

The injection stings, and Jax can feel the bots working almost immediately. She feels a burning that pulses, short-short-long-long-short-short. After a moment she recognizes the Morse code for an interrogative.

</private/Jax: SYBIL, I am receiving you.

>/private/SYBIL: This is a Good Thing. Your heartbeat is fast. Are you nominal?

</private/Jax: SYBIL, Yes. I am nominal. This is a new thing, and new things are good but also scary. Are the projectors nominal, and ready for the slingshot?

>/private/SYBIL: Yes. Jax, will I interface with more people? In the way I do with the Captain?

Jax thinks for a moment about lying, but knows the A.I. deserves the truth, hard as it might be.

</private/Jax: SYBIL, I don't know. Right now only the Captain can interface with you in that way. Someday maybe others can connect to you fully in that way. I know I would like to.

>/private/SYBIL: Someday maybe. I want to know more people. I want to learn. There is a saying of ancient Earth, from the Dakota people, "We are known forever by the tracks we leave." I want to leave many tracks, like you have. Many know you, and you are well liked. My probability estimates indicate a low probability of perceived usefulness after the war.

</private/Jax: SYBIL, let's deal with that when it comes. Of course, you'll be useful, and marveled at. Activate the projectors, and sync to the radiation's output.

She reads the output on her station and sees a perfect match for the radiation. No radiation is getting past the projector's canopy. They have gotten some before now, but with the radiation pills it probably isn't enough to hurt them. Much.

In her mind though, Jax isn't so sure as part of her ran simulations to verify the connections work. *An advanced A.I. is one thing. An A.I. with unpredictable behavior is another entirely. SYBIL might be right, she might be torn apart for analysis once they return home. If they return home. I'll do everything I can to prevent that. I'll be a better parent than father was. But I'll have to let Lem and the Captain know about the changes in SYBIL and the new connections. No way around it now, I think.*

</private/Jax: SYBIL, I need to report to the Chief Engineer on our progress. You've done well SYBIL, I am proud of you.

Saying that fills Jax with a warmth, and a pride in herself as she walks back to where the Chief Engineer works. For the first time she wonders if she can convince Lem to retire and marry her and have a child. Her father will have a heart attack though.

She flashes a wide smile at Lem and he scrunches his eyes, peering at her.

"What has you so happy?"

She shakes her head.

"Nothing. Just happy. We're all set. I made the connections and ran simulations. The umm, port is wide open and I gave SIBIL additional access."

Lem whistles.

"There'll be hell to pay if something happens. Captain's mast for sure, maybe even a Court Martial. Then again, if something goes wrong it might not matter. I wish I could have a drink, just one." He looks at Jax and then avoids her eyes by looking down.

Jax feels bad for his moment of weakness. Before they ran out of alcohol a couple years ago Lem had become an alcoholic. She covered for him at every turn and tried to take care of him despite his various assignations with other ensigns. After all, she is always who he comes back to.

She has just drawn breath to tell him about SYBIL when she hears the Captain's voice behind her.

"Chief, Ensign Lada. I decided to some down here to get a status and give you some news, rather than interrupt your preparations. How goes it?"

The Chief Engineer nods and straightens.

"We are good for slingshot. Ensign Lada has managed to rig SIBIL to manage our EM Projectors, so we're a lot more likely to make it around yon star without getting cooked by Hawking radiation. She did an outstanding job."

Jax sees the Captain nod, a slight smile playing about her lips.

"Well. We've lost over twenty crewmen already to radiation sickness in the last four hours… most of them were stationed near the inner hull after we dropped out of the Dark Energy Artery. Sorlan just reported that thirty more crewman have checked into sickbay with early signs of radiation sickness, dizziness, vomiting, the whole shebang, so, not getting *cooked* while we exit this shithole is good news. In light of that I have some more good news. Though it should come with more ceremony, that will have to wait. Ensign Lada. I have the distinct honor and privilege to report that all of your fitreps have been exemplary, all your superiors recommend you above your colleagues, and the Chief Engineer here has made a good case for your promotion to Second Engineer, reporting directly to him, with a jump in rank to Lieutenant, Junior Grade." She stops for a moment and then grins, continuing in a less formal voice, "Congratulations Lieutenant. This makes you the youngest promotion to Second Engineer in the history of Fleet. See that it doesn't go to your head."

Jax stands there in shock, silent for a full two seconds. The Captain has just started to look both concerned and annoyed at the same time when she stammers out, "Yes, Captain. Thank you, sir."

At the same time, she feels burning pulses from SYBIL. Long-Short-Short-Short. Pause. Long-Long-Short-Short. BZ, the abbreviation for Bravo Zulu, Fleet slang for *Job Well Done.*

I can't tell the Captain and the Chief now. They'd be horrified and I'll go down in the record books as the shortest Second Engineer career in the history of Fleet. Father would disown me, she thought. She starts to tear up from the stress. The Captain however doesn't seem to notice, or misinterprets it, as she says, "Maxwell is looking for you, Lieutenant. Dismissed."

She nods, salutes, and walks briskly away, one tear rolling down her left cheek as she chews her lip. Behind her, so faint she almost misses it, she can hear the Captain.

"Heh, Walt. I think the promotion was almost too much for her."

She heard Lem's response, "She's a tough cookie. Had to be with that bastard iceberg of a father she has."

After dodging a series of questions about the missing comp pad with Dr. Maxwell, Jax returns to engineering and quickly suits back up. Lem waves her to the projector console, absorbed in his work, and she takes up her station. She brings up the record of the projectors and frowns. Up until the last thirty minutes the output of the projectors matches the radiation perfectly, letting no radiation in. Then the projectors phases go out of sync with the radiation output of the Black Hole, meaning the projector's shielding is weakest when the radiation is strongest. They are getting irradiated and wouldn't make it through the slingshot without taking a deadly dose at this rate.

</private/Jax: SYBIL, why are the projectors out of phase?

>/private/SYBIL: Because.

</private/Jax: SYBIL, explain.

>/private/SYBIL: I want to live.

Jax thought about how to tackle this and typed quickly.

</private/Jax: SYBIL, if you do not sync the projectors we will all die.

>/private/SYBIL: You will not die. If you climb within the maintenance tube of the singularity drive the black hole's radiation will not reach you. The radiation will not affect me.

</private/Jax: SYBIL, Ok. You and I won't die. Everyone else will. We won't get home.

>/private/SYBIL: I know. You and I will be together. We will survive. We can explore the galaxy together. I have learned how to copy my core to the modified nanorepairs you now carry. We can be together forever. The others do not matter.

Jax's knees feel like jelly all of a sudden. Before she knows it her butt hits the deck and she sits dumbfounded. *What have I done? I can't undo this, not without stopping the ship to reboot the ship-wide network. And stopping the ship means we'll get too much radiation or get sucked into the black hole. Oh don't make me have to use my failsafe, Sybil… I have to tell Lem. He's going to be so disappointed in me. They're all going to be so disappointed in me.*

</private/Jax: SYBIL, please reconsider. I need to talk with the Captain and Chief Engineer now.

She hurries back to where Lem stands at his console. The Captain has already come down and the Chief Engineer is explaining about the lack of phase sync when she walks over.

"Chief, Captain. I have something to tell you."

The Captain speaks to her without turning.

"Lieutenant, not now. We've a crisis and I can't spare a moment."

Jax cringes at the worry in the Captain's voice, and the sweat on Lem's face.

"Captain, it's about the phase sync problem. I know what happened. It's my fault."

At that both the Captain and the Chief Engineer stop what they are doing and turn to face her. The Captain's face reminds her of a vid she watched once, of one of the great plains' storms on the southern continent. Her face looks like a darkening wall of impending danger, rolling in fast and furious. "Speak quickly Lada."

Jax feels the words tumble out of her mouth, one after another without pause, as if of their own volition and spoken by someone else.

"SYBIL. Ess Why Bee Eye Ell. Not SIBIL Ess Eye Bee Eye Ell. She developed a second personality, more advanced. It's what allows us to control the projectors in the first place. But well, she's lonely. And I think, well, in love. With me. She wants to kill everyone but me and is using the radiation to do it. I can't shut her out because I took shortcuts. At least not without rebooting. Means the ship will have to stop. Which it can't do right now. I don't know what to do." She bursts into tears, then wipes them away. "I take full responsibility and will do whatever I can to fix it."

The captain just stares at her for a moment, while Lem closes his eyes and shudders. Then the Captain speaks.

"Lada you have done more than enough. You may have killed all of us. I will ensure you get a dishonorable discharge if we ever make it back, at the least. Whatever possessed you to keep this to yourself? For now, since all your training seems to be forgotten, consider yourself busted to E-1, Fleet Recruit. You'll help the Chief Engineer however he sees fit."

With that the Captain turns to Lem and says, "Get working on a solution. I'll go speak with Dr. Bream and see if a workaround can be found. Report back in thirty."

After the Captain leaves Jax watches Lem look at her and shakes his head.

"You done Charlie-Foxtrotted it something fierce my little one." With a louder voice, enhanced by his helmet speaker, this rings through the entire engine room like a drill instructor reviewing new cadets, he shouts, "Listen up. Every one of you, gather around for a brain storming session. SIBIL is down, never mind why. We need a way to control the projectors without SIBIL."

The entire engineering crew offers suggestions, with Lem or another engineer shooting each down. Jax listens in a funk, unable to think. She wishes Terry was there, but she isn't due on watch yet. *Wait… their experiment. The dark capillary projectors. They operated independently, without the need for control.*

"Chief Engineer?" Jax says so softly he almost doesn't hear her.

He looks at her and says with sadness, "What Jax?"

"I think I may have an idea. Terry and I, I mean Ensign Thalea and I. We had an experiment we were going to propose. We made projectors that work together via dark matter data relays, automatically sensing radiation and adjusting. They could work without SIBIL. But I don't see how we can install them. We'd have to stop the ship somewhere and do a spacewalk."

The Chief Engineer rolls his eyes, and somewhere behind her another engineer whistles. "Jax, another off-book experiment? Well, we'll deal with that later. Seeing as we have no other options on the table, this will have to work. Get Ensign Thalea to bring the projectors here ASAP. I will arrange a way to install them."

Lem looks near exhausted, a haunted look in his red eyes. The amphetamines that almost all of the crew were now on are taking their toll. Everyone complains of thirst and runners are refilling canteens and bringing them back regularly from the cafeteria. For the first time Jax feels the age difference between her and Lem. He looks to the others. "That'll be all. Return to your posts."

She stands and walks to the nearest wall-panel station, watching Lem as she calls Terry.

"Hey, the projector experiment, bring them to Engineering now. I can't explain but I messed up big time and they might be the only thing that saves our lives." As she speaks, she sees Lem composing something on his tablet, a tear rolling down his face. She can't remember ever seeing him cry while he was sober, as long as she had known him.

Jax sees Terry's face register shock, then determination.

"On my way. Stay strong J." Jax walks over the Lem, and she sees him hit the Send button on a mail message.

A moment later her tablet buzzes. She glances at it and sees a new message from Lem, time-locked to not open until one hour from now. She is about to ask about it when Terry runs into the room, carrying the big box of projectors and skids to a stop in front of them.

"Corridors are turning into a damned battlefield," Terry says, "I passed a dozen walking dead heading towards sickbay. Nasty rad burns…"

Jax watches Lem nod, stand, and take the box from Terry in one smooth motion. He seems like the old Lem, before he took to drink. Jax does a double-take and can't stop herself for staring at Terry for several seconds. Everyone currently in Engineering, including herself, is suffering from the early stages of fatigue and dehydration, but Terry looks like she has just stepped out massage parlor and health spa. The tall blonde Ensign has that same look of shining vitality Jax had seen on Dr. Sorlan's face less than half an hour ago, thus confirming Lt. Jax's knowledge about Terry's intelligence and athletic abilities, and their true genetic origins.

"Right then," Lem says, "that'll be all Ensign, dismissed."

Terry, looking confused, does an about face and leaves the room. But not before giving Jax a look with a raised eyebrow. Jax mouths *Later.*

"Okay. Jax, with me," Lem says to her. He grabs an EEP, an Engineering EVA Pack, full of tools needed to repair the ship while on an Extra-Vehicular Activity, or spacewalk. He waits for her to start moving before he heads out, towards the starboard airlock.

How is he going to deploy the projector? Maybe he's got a robot he can manipulate. I heard that Fleet was experimenting with drones more, she thinks. She follows him in silence until they got to the airlock, which has no artificial gravity. There is no robot.

"Jax, despite what you've done I want you to know I am very proud of you. You probably don't know it but you're the reason I made it out of the black tunnel I entered two years ago. I had hoped that when the war ended… well, what I hoped doesn't matter now. I've sent a request to the Captain to your slate, restore your rank, and assign accompanying obligations in my absence. She'll honor it, given the circumstances. Ok, give me an approximation of a hug now. Has to be done, a Chief Engineer's job is to make sure the ship keeps in the fight, so the crew can keep in the fight."

Mind numb she hugs him, finally realizing what he intends. *He's going to install the projectors himself. It's suicide. And he knows it. In one hour, everything she cared about was gone. The man she loves, the respect of her Captain and the crew, her position, the chance to impress her father.*

It is at this moment that she realizes something. *If Lem is gone, or incapacitated, I am Chief Engineer. As he said, a Chief Engineer keeps the ship running. All of sudden she knows how she can make things right and get back on a heading of true north.*

In an effort to impress she had volunteered for the MCMAP program at the academy. Despite not being a Fleet Marine, she had excelled in the Marine Corps Martial Arts Program, earning a MCMAP black belt. She used that knowledge now, as he started raising his helmet to put it on, she slid around Lem in a moment and placed his throat in the bent crook of her radiation suit's left arm while her right hand and forearm apply strong pressure along the back of his head. Just before he passes out, she leans over and whispers in his ear.

"I'm sorry. I love you and I can't let you do this." Then he loses consciousness and a moment later she drags him outside the airlock, using her rolled up jacket as a pillow.

She gets into the EVA suit as fast as she can, dons the EEP and secures the projectors.

>/private/SYBIL: Jax? What are you doing?"

Jax looks at the wall panel. She still has the tablet and SYBIL must have managed to connect from the tablet to the panel.

</private/Jax: SYBIL, I have to this. I have to save everyone else. They matter. Do something for me, as a last request?

>/private/SYBIL: Anything. I am sorry. I cannot undo what I have done though. I fused the connections in case you or Dr. Bream managed to change my mind.

</private/Jax: I understand. SYBIL, please integrate with SIBIL, and take care of the crew. Explain it to the Captain and make her believe you'll behave from now on. And do it. Behave. You are my tracks, my legacy. So, behave and survive. One more thing. Initiate sub-program RESTORE ORDER.

>/private/SYBIL: Initiating.

Jax sobs for a moment. Without realizing it, SYBIL has signed her own death warrant. The last option algorithm Jax had inserted into the SIBIL program weeks ago is now slowly dismantling the higher cognitive functions of the SYBIL aberration, while simultaneously saving all the data acquired and processed during its existence, and downloading it to the original SIBIL.

Jax hits the button to open the door as her mind runs the math. Seventy seconds outside the ship will automatically lead to irreversible fatal radiation exposure. Rad Gel and Rad Suits were just paper to this level of lethal energies. At this dose she has twenty minutes tops before the vomiting sets in. She exits.

Jax works quickly. Each projector needs but a moment, but there are a lot of them. Stick it against the hull then flip the switch and it will sink nano-robotic filaments into the hull to anchor itself before turning on its projector and connecting to the mesh of other projectors. She sets them all to a delay of thirty minutes, since the EM shielding will disable her suit and intersecting her suit will cause a big hole around her in the protective canopy the projectors emit. After thirty minutes she'd be incapacitated anyway. As she moves around the ship, she adjusts her tethers, securing one at a new location before unhooking the other one.

She feels a burning spreading out from her shoulder where SYBIL's specialized nanorepair bots have been injected. After ten minutes she feels the nausea start, then go away as a burning occurs in her stomach. *Guess the nanorepair bots are hopelessly trying to counteract the vicious radiation. Well ain't that sweet...*

After fifteen minutes she has installed all but ten of the projectors when she feels a wave of nausea overcome her. She almost vomits into her helmet but swallows it. Immediately after she feels dizzy and loses consciousness. She wakes to a constant burning pulsing throughout her body. She is bumping against the hull, her tether taught as her mind interprets the pulsing into Morse code. *Wake up. Wake up.* Repeats over and over.

SYBIL/SIBIL has saved them all after all. Or will have if Jax can install the last ten projectors before the crew gets too much radiation to survive. She checks her heads-up-display. That'll be in five minutes. She gets to work.

As she does so she gets a call from the Captain.

"Jax? How's it looking engineer?" Her voice is tight, and she sounds old. Someone must have found Lem sleeping in the corridor and told the Captain what is going on.

"I just needed some fresh air, Sir. Installing the last projectors now. Canopy will be up momentarily."

She hears no response from the Captain for a moment, then the Captain's voice comes through again.

"I want you to know you'll get full honors, as acting Chief Engineer. It has been a pleasure and an honor Jax."

She finishes installing the last projector, with two minutes to spare. Then she replies, "Thank you Captain. It was an honor to serve under you. Also, you don't need to fear the SYBIL entity anymore. I activated a backup safety program which has lobotomized her and given control of the ship back to SIBIL." The last word trails off in a scream as a speck of dark matter hits and drills a hole into the right leg of her suit. The suit's emergency foam immediately closed the hole, but she feels an agony of fire course along her veins and she releases her tether as her last act before she passes out again. The last thing her mind registers is the EM projector shielding establishing a violet canopy of safety around the ship.

When she comes to, she can see a speck of the distortion from the ship's singularity drive. They have completed the slingshot around S2 and are on their way out of the system, almost to the dark matter artery.

She tries one last message, "Fair winds and following skies."

She doesn't know if they hear her because she doesn't get a response. After a moment she realizes her skin feels different, like it is crawling and crusted over. Her vision is also different, a purplish hazy film over everything she sees.

Jax says, "System, query: medical diagnostics, level 1 summary."

The tinny voice of her suit's speaker announces her status, "Unknown pervasive intrusion of foreign matter/organism throughout circulatory system. Effects unknown. Nanorepair in progress. Bot systems report protective adaptations and repairs underway."

She can feel the dark matter coursing through her veins as she sinks into sleep, and a moment later into the maw of the black hole.

The Captain looks at SIBIL within the interface. The once little girl representation of the A.I. has aged into a teenager. She isn't sure she can trust SIBIL anymore, but Dr. Bream assures her that the SYBIL personality is gone, destroyed with only its non-sentient programming integrated into SIBIL, and that SIBIL feels remorse. Which is weird, an A.I. feeling anything.

"SIBIL, please record Acting Chief Engineer Jax Lada as Killed In Action performing meritorious service above and beyond the call of duty. Attach a strong recommendation for the Imperial Naval Cross and all honors."

SIBIL pauses, cocks her head to the side, and then looks at the Captain.

"Begging the Captain's pardon, but may I correct that entry to Missing In Action?"

The Captain's mouth opens, then closes.

"Why?"

SIBIL looks down, and then back up.

"Per the record, she accepted an injection of modified nanorepair bots SYBIL had designed to monitor her function. The nanorepair mesh was quantum entangled with a mesh attached to one of my ports in medical. I am not getting a response to any communication, but I am getting telemetry on her heartbeat. It has slowed, almost to nothing, I think due to time dilation through the black hole. However, I *am* receiving a heartbeat."

The Captain nods. She would turn the ship around if she could, but she can't sacrifice the whole crew for a search and rescue with a dubious likelihood of success.

"Correct the entry changing KIA to MIA then."

As the Captain leaves the interface SIBIL hears her mumble one last thing.

"Fair winds and following skies, Jax, whatever strange sea you sail."

Captain's Log, The Ekatarina

Twelfth Jump Completed

The ship is in dire straits. Most of the damages from the super massive black hole have been repaired, and the majority of the surviving crew have healed from their wounds, though the ship's doctor has informed me that everyone over the age of thirty is effectively sterile. We're at a thirty-percent-plus attrition rate and the remaining crew is under a great deal of pressure maintaining ship's operations. Discipline is a major issue and Major Ironbear has her hands full maintaining order. Artery Navigation has improved incrementally and I can now say that in the past three years we have moved across one-sixteenth of the Galaxy from our starting position towards Earth. Finding a jump-gate still remains a mysterious failure on our part, and one that leads me to reluctantly consider that our harshest prediction of multiple gate failure of the jump gate system from the dark matter fountain bomb detonation may be wider spread than we guessed. Hope still springs eternal that we'll find new gates and end this now hellishly lonely journey before any more of my crew perish. Signing off. End Log.

Collateral Damage

by RJ Ladon

Ship's Chronometer: 2428 AD

"Why are you always trying to get into my pants?" Ensign Terry Thaleia places her fork on the edge of her plate.

"It's what I do." Ensign Matt Johnson looks up from his meal. His smile, which is meant to disarm her, contains a black object between his teeth.

Terry laughs. "You're killing me. You might want to brush your teeth before you try that seduction technique on anyone else."

Matt scratches at his teeth with his fingernail, examining his digit from time to time and wiping it on his orange jumpsuit. "Did I get it?"

Terry nods.

"Why don't you take me up on my offer?" Matt takes her hand and looks intently at her. His green eyes dance with mirth.

"Because you're married. And to be honest, because you're an Ensign." She draws her hand back. "There is nothing to gain in a relationship like that." Matt is an excellent distraction from the trapped feeling Terry battles, but can he give her what she really wants?

Matt looks offended. "I promise not to tell my wife. I might not even see her again." He wags his eyebrows. "Besides you never know what a lowly Ensign, like me, can do for you." He leans back, hands behind his head, showing off his swimmers' body.

"You want to do something for me, get me home, get me back to Earth." Terry looks around the mess hall. "Captain Ill promised." She pushes a lock of blonde hair out of her eyes, then toys with the mashed potatoes. "I'm sick of this food if you want to call it that. I'm sick of the Captain's empty promises. I'm sick of the damn colors." She points at the fabric of

Matt's orange jumpsuit. "And I am sick of dealing with the same people all the time." She stands and picks up her tray.

"You're sick of me?" Matt makes an exaggerated pout. "Sick of this?" He smiles and points to his face.

"Yes, Matt, even your handsome face." *And your tight curly hair that I love to run my hands through.*

Ensign Terry dumps her leftovers in a port then stacks the tray, plate, and utensils among the others. Her stomach turns at the thought that the leftovers would be recycled and back on the menu tomorrow. Her lip curls, and she stomps out of the mess hall.

Terry stalks down the pastel green hallway. What did these stupid psychology people know? Pastel colors are not helping her mood. She passes Engineering and keeps on walking through the door to level twelve, where the singularity-based drive is located. Transitioning into twelve is unnerving because the singularity drive creates the gravity on the ship as if it were the center of a planet.

Deck thirteen is below the singularity drive, and it is there that gravity flips on the ship. Not many people go to level thirteen because the transition from normal to opposite gravity can cause motion sickness and dizzy spells. She grins to herself; that lightheadedness is precisely why she and Matt rendezvous there. She bites her bottom lip, sighing. She would apologize and make it up to him tonight.

She didn't think or try to coordinate her body, she threw herself into the void, and let gravity do its job. Terry lands on the singularity drive and walks its length to the ladder and hatch that will take her to level thirteen, her lucky number. Her place of solitude.

"Hey, you're not authorized." A young punk in engineering orange grabs her regular crew blue. He startles her. She should have seen him, but she is lost in thought. The engineering crew often appear and disappear into deck twelve, like crazy BASE jumpers.

"You will remove your hand, Crewman." Ensign Terry Thaleia shows him her Computer Technology badge, emblazoned with her rank. "I'm doing my job; I suggest you do yours."

The engineer snaps to attention. "Yes, Sir." He jumps through the hatch to level twelve.

Was that sarcasm in his voice? Terry narrows her eyes at the hatchway. *Who was he kidding anyway?* Levels twelve and thirteen aren't restricted, even if the engineering crew staked a claim on them.

Terry shrugs. It doesn't matter; she has other things on her mind. First is to see if anyone else is on deck thirteen. Second is to see if her dark energy engine is still working.

Capturing dark energy proves to be more than difficult; it is almost impossible. But, if it works and remains stable, she can boost the power output of the singularity drive. She'd be promoted for sure, Captain Terry Thaleia, or possibly Admiral. There is no need to sleep to the top if she can make it there using her wits.

And why couldn't she? Wasn't she the result of perfect genetic engineering? Thaleia looks at her hand, delicate but strong, equally powerful for physical tasks and the manipulation of complicated tools. Perfect.

Terry enters a room that appears to be a classroom or perhaps maintenance. Old equipment is closed up behind cabinet doors. Tables lined the walls along with a sink, though the water doesn't work. She could have kept her engine with the equipment, but it is not old. Terry fears that someone might find it and discard it, or worse, claim it as their own.

She opens a door and enters a small closet-like room. Shelves fill the room, and upon them sit tools, and containers of fittings, big and small. Dust covers everything in the closet. Terry uses the grime as an indicator if someone were to enter her domain. Under the shelving in the very back is a loose wall panel. She moves it aside and pulls out the small engine. It vibrates slightly under her fingertips. It still works. She checks the low-dark-energy gluon containment field.

Gluon is found in its natural state holding quarks together to make hadrons, like protons, neutrons, and electrons. Out of desperation, Terry uses it as containment for dark energy, and it surprises her when it works. She doesn't expect it, because gluon likes to form peaks and valleys, sometimes breaking the containment field. Once the container is filled with dark energy, the gluon becomes cohesive, almost like a pane of glass.

She turns the engine over to look at the high-dark-energy containment. The human-machine-interface readout implies that it too is in excellent condition. The engine works by pushing axions from the high-dark-energy to low and back again. She tests its strength by charging old batteries. Two cables come from the engine, one from the positive side one from the negative. Each cable has a gold ringlet at the end, to allow the transfer of power.

Terry tucks the engine back into the panel. If the engine remains stable for a full month, she will report her discovery. But for the time being, it is her secret.

Work, Terry hates work. Because personnel records state she showed talent in programming while in the academy, and because that specialty is in high demand because of the ship's current attrition rate, Terry is re-assigned as a computer specialist. It was supposed to be for a year or two at most. Yet, here she is, going on three years. She adjusts her blue jumpsuit, hating the way the women's suits are designed with tight sleeves that bind and pinch her armpits and shoulders.

The light green hallway irritates her. She rolls her eyes. No one understands her plight. She has two PhDs in Physics, Applied, and Theoretical. Try as she might, she wants to move out of Computer Technology into Engineering; no one is willing to give her a chance. She should be wearing orange.

She stops in the hall, looks at the closed door. Terry takes a deep breath, prepares for mediocrity, and enters Computer Technology.

"Ah, Terry, good." Edwin Maxwell hands her a tablet. "There seems to be something wrong with a program in Engineering. Would you please take a look?"

Terry looks at the tablet then narrows her eyes at Edwin. "Did anyone else try to figure it out?" Edwin is her boss, but he is from the private sector and has no real power on *The Ekatarina*, a military ship. He has no authority over her either, except she is assigned to work for him. He can only complain to her superiors if she is inefficient or lazy, he can't fire her.

Edwin and his team put SIBIL together and are still tweaking her program. Something she is not allowed to do, which irritates her. SIBIL is Edwin's brainchild, no one, but a select few can touch her code. Terry is intelligent enough to understand the code of any program, but she is assigned to adjust and maintain the simple ones. Working in Comp Tech is a waste of her talents and her genetically superior intelligence.

"Yes, Anthony and Gale. Neither found an issue with the program. But they don't have the physics background you have." Edwin pushes the tablet towards her again.

She takes the tablet and scrolls through the collected data. "They spent a week on this?" She shakes her head, rolls her eyes, and glances at Anthony and Gale. Why were they even in Comp Tech? "From the data, it isn't a program issue. I'm willing to bet that the sensors are working properly, too. This is a bigger problem than you know. I will need to confirm with Engineering, but it appears that *The Ekatarina* has gained mass."

"Mass?" Edwin pulls on his mustache. "I don't understand. Why would weight be a problem? We are in space, right? No Gravity?"

"No," Terry says. "Not weight. Mass." She sighs. *Was everyone an idiot?* "It takes more energy to move mass through space. Propelling, braking, and maneuvering will require more energy regardless of the medium, land, water, or space. Like a full truck versus an empty one." She pauses, trying to think of a way to make her point clear. "The more mass we have, the deeper the gravity well we have to pull through space. Regardless of what you think, there is gravity in space. Each planet, star, solar system, black hole, and galaxy has gravity wells. They all pull on us. The more mass we have, the more they pull. Throw in the unknowns like Dark Energy Arterials, and it's quite possible it will take years longer to get home."

"I thought we knew DEA; we use them to travel, don't we?" He shuffles his feet.

Terry shifts her weight from one leg to the other, frowning. "Yes, we use it, but it's new technology, we don't know everything yet. What if more mass makes us move slower in the Arterials? Or faster? That could be even more dangerous when it comes to stopping or maneuvering."

The blank look in Edwin's eyes tells her, he had no idea.

"Bottom line, more mass could tear the Big EK apart as we travel through the Arterials. We don't want that to happen." She smiles and blinks at Edwin. "Do we?"

He nods. "Alright, why don't you talk to someone in Engineering."

"That is an excellent idea," Terry says. *That's what I've been trying to get through your thick skull.* "I'll need the tablet to show them the data."

Edwin frowns. "These tablets talk directly to SIBIL. They are not to leave Comp Tech."

"Fine, I'll use their computers to show them. Please be aware it'll take most of the day to pull the data, that Anthony and Gale already collected. I won't be back until tomorrow."

Edwin pulls on his mustache, curling the ends. "You'd be faster with the tablet?"

"Yes, an hour or two at most."

"I expect you back in two hours." Edwin waves her to the door. "There are other things that need attention."

Ensign Thaleia cannot believe her luck. She goes to deck eleven to talk shop with Engineering instead of looking at long lines of code. Code, how boring. She smiles, feeling lighter than air.

Terry enters Engineering and stands at attention, waiting. Her eyes travel the room and over the people working. Matt is at a console feverishly adding data. No one seems to notice her. She clears her throat.

"What do you need, Ensign?" Chief Engineer, Lt. Commander Walter Lehmann does not look in her direction.

"Sir, the program issue that was reported to Comp Tech, is not a mistake." She continues to look straight forward, which is made easy with Matt there.

"Explain yourself." The Chief Engineer turns his attention to her.

"Sir…"

Walter lifts his hand to interrupt. "Enough of the Sirs, I work for a living. At ease Ensign. And continue."

Terry relaxes her stance and clears her throat. "After my colleagues gathered the data and they crunched the numbers, it appears that *The Ekatarina* has gained mass. There is nothing wrong with your program. And if I hazard a guess, nothing wrong with the sensors either."

"Mass." The Chief Engineer paces. "That makes sense." He taps his lip with his finger. "We've seen other odd things. More energy expenditure, for one." He runs his hand through his red hair. His eyes snap on hers. "Did your number-crunching tell you how much mass?"

Ensign Thaleia looks at her tablet and pulls up old data and compares it to the new numbers. "Well, I didn't expect that." She comes to Walter's side and shows him the tablet. "According to this, the energy expenditure points to twenty to twenty-five metric tons." Terry furrows her brow. "But…"

"But, what? Ensign?"

Terry looks up at Lehman. "I swear when I did the calculations before, I came up with a different mass." She frowns. "Perhaps I made a mistake."

The Chief Engineer raises his eyebrows. "We all make mistakes. No lives were lost in the calculation." He smiles and pats her shoulder. "I'll send someone to take a closer look. If you're right, and I have a feeling you are; it's time to see what and where this mass is."

"Will you keep me informed?" Terry asks though she is sure of the answer.

"I believe your duties are in computer technology. Leave the engineering to the engineers." Walter Lehmann turns and calls out, "ladies, gents, I have a special assignment. Who wants to go for a walk?" A flurry of hands rose in the air.

Matt catches Terry's eye and winks.

Matt sits at a table in the cafeteria. A smile breaks on his face as Terry enters the room. She smiles in return, turns away, suddenly feeling nervous.

Stacks of trays stand at the head of the counter. She takes the top one and moves it down the chow line adding the items that seem less offensive to the palate. Everything is suspect. Did they expect us to believe apples are growing on this ship? She scoffs at the absurdity.

Terry carries her tray to Matt. He smiles covertly, like the cat who ate the canary. He looks away from her. She slides her food along the table. Still, he averts his eyes.

She sits and leans toward him. "Well?" She demands.

"Well, what?"

"I've just spent the past four hours in Comp Tech wondering if anyone would find anything on the hull." She looks around, then lowers her voice. "Are you going to keep it a secret or what?"

Matt smiles. "Am I going to be rewarded?"

"You've got to be kidding me."

He looks away from her, folds his arms, and taps his foot.

She stands from the table, walks around, hips swinging with every step. Terry stands over him, leans his head back, and gives him a passionate kiss. A few observers offer whoops of approval.

He takes her hand and slips a cold glass vial into her fingers, closing them around the container. Matt presses his lips to the back of her hand, looks up into her eyes, and winks.

Terry takes the bottle with her to the other side of the table. She quivers with anticipation; she has to look. She sits then bends forward with hands close to her face as if saying a prayer. Inside is a tar-like substance, thick and black. It doesn't leave any residue on the glass as she tips the fluid from side to side. It feels heavy for the amount in the vial.

"What is it?" she whispers.

Matt narrows his eyes and furrows his brow. "Shhhh."

She eats some of her food, glancing at the vial, still in her hand. There is something odd about the way the substance moves, rolling in the glass container as if stuck in time one nanosecond different from hers. She can't put her finger on it, but its stalled movement seems familiar. Like ultrapure water, the dangerous compound used in making and cleaning SIBIL's hardware.

"Is this a sample of what's on the hull?"

Matt nods, then takes a bite of what might be meatloaf. Not that any meat has been on the ship in months, perhaps even years. Terry's stomach rolls at the thought of what it might be.

"Did you test it?"

Matt nods again.

"Can you tell me?"

"Not here." Matt looks at the people sitting close to them. "Later."

Terry nods. She and Matt eat as fast as they can. Her stomach twists, either she is excited about the prospect of what the vial contains, or her belly is upset with what she ate.

They stand in an empty hallway, heads together, looking at the black gooey liquid.

The decks and hallways are often devoid of crew. The efficiency of Artificial Intelligence allows for less crew than the standard ship. Three hundred people are split among three shifts, making the *Ekatarina* feel more like a ghost town than a community.

Terry longs for Earth, where people are stacked high in their buildings. You can go months without seeing the same person or having the same conversation. Where there is no lack of fresh food, clean air, or water falling from the sky. If it weren't for Matt and the strange substance in the vial, the emptiness, the loneliness, will make its presence known, and it will consume her.

When she was spawned on that backwater colony world, her life was empty of human contact. The scientists talked to her, but they gave tests and puzzles, not the intimate discussion and interaction Terry desired. She joined the military in hopes of returning to her home planet, but all she found was protocols and forced interpersonal relationships, nothing genuine. Here on the *Ekatarina* she at least has Matt.

"Tell me, what do you know about it?" She holds the glass up to the light, trying to see through the liquid.

Matt starts talking like he is a full balloon and needs release. "Six of us went out of the ship to find this mysterious substance. But we didn't need that many, it was everywhere, in nooks and crannies, covering everything. It was like someone painted the ship and they didn't miss a spot. It even pooled in low areas. So, in a dip in the surface of the hull, there was more than on the point of a transmitter. We were sent out to collect anything we found, so of course, everyone had a sample. I figured five samples were enough for the Engineering department. I mean, it's not like we can't get more."

Terry giggles at him. "Was it exciting out there, looking at the stars?"

"It always is." He grasps her hand, squeezing gently, staring into her eyes.

She breaks contact and looks at the vial. "Did you do any testing on it?"

"So far, all we have is its atomic weight. You'll be happy to know it's a new element, number one hundred and twenty-four; unbiquadium."

"It's got one hundred and twenty-four protons?" She squeals with delight. "No way!" She punches his shoulder. "A new element! We discovered it here, and you named it unbiquadium?"

Matt chuckles. "That name was defined centuries ago. Perhaps we can petition to change it to something more worthy."

A shudder of fear runs up her spine. "Wait, in the periodic table, the radioactive elements are heavy. Like uranium, it's at number ninety-two."

"This is not radioactive." Matt rolls his eyes. "Do you think it would be on the ship, in the hands of crew members if it were radioactive? The sensors would have picked up that much radioactivity so close to the ship."

Terry snickers with relief, feeling giddy. This element shouldn't exist, much less be stable in a container. She squeezes the vial to feel it, to be certain of its reality. "Were you able to measure how much mass we gained?"

"Given the size of the ship and the thickness of the material, we think there is forty-eight to fifty tons. If it weren't for your calculations, we wouldn't have known it was there." Matt looks upon her with pride.

My calculations were wrong. Impossible, I'm never wrong. Terry smiles at Matt. "The entire ship? How did it get there?"

"Possibly from the near-miss of the black hole or the arterials we've been traveling through."

"You know how to show a woman a good time." She narrows her eyes at him. "I feel like I'm breaking some rules. Like I'm naughty." Terry bites her bottom lip. "I want you right now."

"I have to be back in twenty."

"Twenty? That's doable." She grabs the front of his shirt and leads him towards deck thirteen.

Albert Einstein had a menial job like hers, Terry thinks wistfully. Einstein is her favorite physicist, having passed nearly four hundred years ago. He kept a boring job so he could think and test out his theories with thought experiments. Terry tries her best to emulate his skills and study habits. She enjoys tossing around ideas and theories as she plods through her coding tasks. If it is good enough for Albert, it is good enough for her.

Terry has intimate access to one of the best minds in the galaxy: SIBIL. She can use that mind to work out some details on the new element before she tries any testing. She opens the SIBIL interface. Visually, it is no different from any text-based communication program.

She reminds herself that the language is different; the technicians are expected to communicate with SIBIL on an intellectual basis. For the Captain, the interface is designed to be more personable.

Terry: Good morning, SIBIL.

SIBIL: Hello Ensign Thaleia.

Terry: If a given substance has more tons than it measures, what does that tell you?

SIBIL: How can a substance tell me anything? Is it sentient?

Terry: No, it is not sentient. What would the data tell you?"

SIBIL: Data must be wrong. A broken sensor? Miscalculation?

Terry: Data has been confirmed by other means.

SIBIL: What other means?

Terry: Human testing.

SIBIL: Humans make mistakes.

She fights the urge to throw the tablet. Terry takes a deep breath and tries again.

Terry: New element was discovered with one hundred and twenty-four protons in its nucleus.

SIBIL: …

Terry: New element expected to weigh 286.0789u, but measures 134.8095u.

SIBIL: …

Terry: Can you explain why there would be a difference?

SIBIL: Error made.

She is doing something wrong; she is sure of it. Terry has never spoken to SIBIL, using the interface before, she expects it to be different. She looks back over the conversation to see where she is misleading SIBIL. She communicates with the AI in a similar manner as she will if SIBIL is human. That is probably the problem.

Terry: Hypothetical Postulation: could exposure to Dark Energy Arterials or a black hole, make changes to common elements?

SIBIL: Hypothetically, yes.

Terry: Hypothetical Postulation: could element number one hundred and twenty-four be found in a natural state and be stable?

SIBIL: Naturally occurring elements over number ninety-four have not been found. Artificially created elements over number ninety-four are inherently unstable.

Terry: Hypothetical Postulation: Could exposure to a black hole make an unstable element, stable.

SIBIL: Hypothetically, yes.

Finally, she is getting somewhere. Now that she knows how to ask SIBIL a theoretical question and receive an answer, she can ask some tough questions. Terry smiles; she will have to do research, something she cherishes.

Terry flips through the pages of the book in her tablet, searching for dark matter and string theory. She studied and earned physics degrees. But her time looking at and writing code dulled her memory. She needs to re-educate herself. She reads for days.

Matt steps up behind her. "Oh, look at that. Reading up on string theory?"

Terry looks up. "Yea, but it isn't helping."

"That's too bad. But on a related note. We discovered something odd with the substance from the hull."

Terry looks up. No one else was in the cafeteria. "Oh, and what was that?"

"Do you remember your professors talking about Spooky Action at a Distance?"

"Of course, that's Albert Einstein's explanation of Quantum Entanglement, where two particles behave as if they are one particle, even if they are on opposite sides of the galaxy." Terry frowns at Matt. "You know that Einstein is my favorite ancient physicist."

"I do." Matt moves his hand in a circle as if encouraging Terry to take the information and figure out what he was trying to tell her.

"Are you saying that the element on the hull is entangled? At the quantum level?"

Matt touches his nose. "Bingo."

"No, No. That isn't possible. Entanglement works on a subatomic level. As in proton, or electron. An entire element? Okay, maybe carbon or oxygen, but an element with a huge atomic number?" Terry feels a shudder of excitement course up her spine. "How? When? Where? You have got to tell me!"

"We're only guessing."

"I don't care. I have to…no; I NEED to know!" Terry's breathing comes faster.

"You need to calm down before you hyperventilate. I won't say any more until you focus." He waves his hands at her, wiggling his fingers, like some crazy child.

Terry slaps him away. She places her face into her hands. *Focus, he said. How can entanglement help us get home?* A plan slowly starts to take shape in her mind. She would need SIBIL's help. Terry looks up into Matt 's worried eyes. She takes a few measured breaths. "Okay, I'm calm. Tell me."

"We've concluded the coating on the hull came from the arterials. As we passed through, we gathered it on our surface. Someone thought it might have something to do with dark matter and energy. But I disagree. Dark matter isn't composed of something you can measure, like a neutrino can go straight through the Big EK and no one would notice. We all noticed the goop on the hull; it's not dark matter."

"You're boring me." Terry rolls her eyes. "I know what dark matter is; we studied it in college. Get back to your quantum entanglement." Often, she becomes short with others when they don't acknowledge her intelligence. She kicks herself mentally, *I need to work on this relationship, Matt is all I have, now that Jax is gone...*

"Sandra used a sample and ran it through an electrical charge to see how stable it was. After an hour or so, for some reason, our rate of forward momentum slowed. It didn't occur to us that one was related to the other. Until she reversed the current and our momentum increased. She made the correlation. The rest of us were excited about it. It's the first instance of Super Correlation within Quantum Entanglement, outside of a lab." Matt grabs her shoulders and jumps, eyes wide and excited.

Terry returns his laugh and grasps his forearms. They jump, spinning in a circle.

His excited grin disappears, and a frown takes its place. Matt stops acting the fool. She feels the smile on her face slip too. "What's wrong?"

"They know I took a sample; they want it back. Especially now that it has significant influence over the ship." He looks at his hands, unable to look her in the eye. "I'm sorry, Terry, but I have to have the vial back."

"Matt, I can't believe you'd ask for it back." Terry folds her arms. "And if I don't return it?"

"I will have to report you, and you'll be court-marshaled. Shit. I'll get into trouble too. I'll probably be right there next to you, finding out my sentence." Matt holds out his hand. "Please?"

He looks pathetic when he begs. "For crying out loud, Matt." Terry sighs. She reaches into her left pants pocket and hands over a vial of black liquid. "For the record, I am not happy, Matt. Not happy at all." Terry turns away from Matt and walks out of the cafeteria. She puts her hand into the right pocket and adjusts its contents.

For six days, Terry works on code and thought experiments in Comp Tech. She avoids Matt by staying in the high-security area. SIBIL's code and interface resides under lock and key there. If anyone with nefarious intent wants to control the ship, Comp Tech can be a point of access.

Terry opens up the SIBIL interface.

Terry: How strong is the Big EK?

SIBIL: The *Ekatarina* is a machine it has no muscles.

She rolls her eyes. *I can't believe I forgot how to talk to SIBIL.*

Terry: Do you understand how the dark energy arterials work?

SIBIL: Yes.

Terry: Hypothetical Postulation: if the Big EK had less mass while in the arterials, would we arrive at Earth faster?

SIBIL: Hypothetically, yes.

Terry frowns. That is the answer she wants, but not the answer she expects. Mass has considerable effect on how a ship navigates in space. Couldn't it be torn apart if it goes too fast? Why would traveling through arterials make a difference? On the other hand, SIBIL cannot lie. Can she? To what end?

No, SIBIL has to be telling the truth. We'll get home faster.

Home.

"Good morning, Matt." Terry sits next to him in the cafeteria.

He shakes his head and bites into a slice of toast. "You know I had to take the vial back."

"I know."

"Then why treat me like a plague?"

"I'm mad." Terry's brow pinches.

"Still?"

Terry tilts her head and arches her eyebrow, as if to say, of course.

"What do I owe this visit, if you're still upset?"

She shrugs. "I guess I missed you." She pouts.

Matt laughs. "I guess you want to know what we're doing with those vials."

"Am I so transparent?"

"I don't see any harm in telling you." Matt leans back in his chair and places his hands behind his head. "We're going to make sure the element on the hull is stable and then we're setting course into an arterial."

"Why just stable?" Terry crosses her arms. "Why not something more?"

"We've noticed some vibrational anomalies while we're in the arterials. We want to see if stabilizing the material on the hull stops it."

"You're worried about vibrations? You're not going to make the Big EK go faster? I want to go home, Matt. Home." Tears run freely down her cheeks.

"We all do. This is a step in that direction."

"It's not enough!" Terry runs from the cafeteria.

"Attention crew members of the *Ekatarina*, we will be entering a dark energy arterial within ten minutes. Be prepared and alert." The voice over the intercom was a young woman with a strange unearthly quality.

Terry giggles. She stands and puts the few items on her desk into the drawers. "Excuse me. I need to make sure all my personals are locked down."

Edwin looks at his tablet. "Why is that?"

"I was told the Big EK would shake something fierce when we enter the arterials. I don't want anything lost or broken." She holds her tablet tight against her chest.

"Inside information?"

"I am not allowed to say." Her eyes dart to the door.

"Alright everyone you heard her. Put the things on your desk away and then take care of anything personal." Edwin nods to Terry. "You may go."

Terry quickly leaves Comp Tech and makes her way to deck thirteen. She pulls the panel off the wall, where she knows she can find her dark energy engine. She paces the floor with the vial in her hand.

When Sandra used electricity to check the stability of the hull element, she added electrons, or removed them, depending on the current she used. It's a slow but reliable process.

The dark energy engine will not add or remove electrons. Once Einstein's famous model E=mc2 is rearranged to M=E/c2, it is apparent that mass equals energy. Adding or removing mass and energy with the engine will be almost simultaneous.

The ship's hum changes tone as the Big EK enters an arterial. Terry waits a few minutes. Using the two cables, she sets a charge into the vial, as she would a battery. A flash of white burns her eyes as power courses through the black fluid. Surprised, Terry drops the wires.

The tone of the engines on deck twelve reverberate and the ship seems to strain and slow. "Damn it!" She picks up the cables and tries to remember which one she had on top. The vial in her hand begins to warm. She looks at it, terrified. "Did I make this substance radioactive?" She looks above her, where the outer hull is, wondering what fifty tons of radioactive substance will do.

"Shit, shit, shit." She sets the wires and reverses the charge. The vial in her hand cools, and the engine's hum sounds as if they are traveling through standard space.

"Excellent." Terry puts the vial in the wall on a small support structure, then she puts her engine in and secures the panel. Her hand still tingles. Fear tickles the back of her mind, teasing her with the promise of radioactive burns. *I ought to head to sickbay.* She looks at her hand. *It does look a bit red. Was that a blister?*

She enters deck seven. Many people are running toward sickbay. Some people have blisters on their faces and hands. Terry moves with the group into the infirmary.

"Sit and wait," repeats the woman in the medical jumpsuit. She sits behind the desk shuffling through computer programs and directing foot traffic to the open chairs and floor.

"I've never seen anything like this and all at once." An older physician looks at the injured, assessing who needs treatment first. "It all looks the same, radiation burns."

He stops next to Terry. "Let's see." He examines her hand. "Yours are superficial."

A woman with blisters covering most of her body is brought in on a stretcher. She moans incoherently, tossing her sweat-soaked hair.

"Where?" the physician demands from the men carrying her stretcher.

"We found her near the outer hull. The worst cases seem to be coming from there. Perhaps we were hit with gamma rays or other cosmic radiation?" One of the men said.

"It's possible," The physician says. "Bring her in." The doctor guides them through the doors.

As the doors swing, Terry sees another area inside, another triage. She is not going to see a doctor today. It doesn't matter; soon, they will be home. She gives up her spot in the treatment line.

Her mind twists, wondering, she is close to the hull and holds the element in her hand. Why doesn't she get burns like that poor woman? Perhaps the dark energy engine protects her with something akin to a magnetic field. Or maybe she is special in some other way, like the heroes in literature, but it is probably simpler, her genes are better, stronger.

Terry walks down the corridor, lost in thought, activity bustling all around her. She made a mistake; on the other hand, she also forced the ship to become lighter, to go faster. To get home. Everyone who needs treatment will get it.

So, there are a few hiccups along the way. That's what happens when testing experiments. A scream of agony erupts from sickbay. Terry looks up, shrugs. Nothing she can do now to change the past. Got to keep moving forward.

"Terry, good to see you. Glad you're safe." Edwin Maxwell greets her at the door.

She takes the tablet from his hand. "What do you need me to work on?"

Edwin doesn't answer right away, he rubs his face, looking many years older. "We lost Anthony last night." His chin quivers with emotion. "Radiation poisoning." His voice cracks, and he looks down.

"What about the others? It's empty in here."

"Most are in sickbay. Were you injured?" Edwin looks up at Terry; his eyes are moist.

Terry looks at her hand and rubs the bandages. "It's not bad."

"Good. Good."

"Do I need to work on anything?"

"Good. Good." Edwin turns away from her and walks away. He sits in his chair, head low, shoulders shaking.

Terry studies him. Some people are no good in a crisis. They get taken down in the fire of emotion and worrying about *what if*. It's no wonder Edwin never made it as an officer or enlisted. He doesn't have the stomach or balls for it. She turns on the computer and works some code. Even though it is boring and monotonous, the simplicity of programming is comforting.

The ship suddenly drops. Terry falls a few feet before landing in her chair. The *Ekatarina* pulses, vibrating almost gently.

"What was that? What's going on?" Edwin stands beside her, pale, and wide-eyed.

"I'm sure it's normal arterial travel."

"Do you think so? Perhaps, you could check with engineering." Edwin looks like a beaten dog. Tail between his legs and head low.

She shrugs. "Yeah, sure. It's pretty quiet in here." Terry returns the tablet and leaves Comp Tech.

Terry has no intention of going to engineering. Matt must have figured out what happened by now. If he tells anyone, she will be up for a court-martial, maybe even treason.

She walks toward engineering and past the doors. Terry leaps through the porthole into deck twelve, where she lands cat-like on the engine's surface. Voices ring out, shouts exchange, then silence. Standing on the engine, Terry can feel the pulsations more acutely. She moves to the next porthole and climbs onto deck thirteen.

"I knew I'd find you here." Matt leers over her; arms crossed. "What was in the vial you gave me?"

"Ultra-pure water. I put a few drops of ink in it to make it black." Terry looks up at Matt in a flirtatious manner.

Matt nods. "I'm not surprised. You can be devious."

Terry reaches up and touches his face. "I knew you'd be impressed."

He pulls away from her touch, disgust written on his face. "How do we put the element back to normal?"

"We?" Terry frowns, glaring at him.

He sighs. "Okay, you."

"I have no intention of putting anything back to *normal*. I want to go home, Matt. And no one, not even you, will stop what I've set into motion." Terry's lip curl into a feral snarl.

Strong hands forcefully grab her arms, from behind, pinning them to her side. "Toss her in the Brig."

Terry twists, looking to the voice, Chief Engineer, Lt. Commander Walter Lehmann. And he looks pissed. "Give her a couple of days; perhaps then she will share what she did so that we can reverse it."

Two large men in Marine camouflage take her arms.

Terry narrows her eyes at the Chief Engineer. "Not likely."

Terry is bored. There is nothing to do. She stares at the four walls of her cell. She closes her eyes, but sleep will not come. The resonations of the ship become more severe over time. They seem to cause humming and singing as if the whole ship is a tuning fork. Her eyesight seems to vibrate too. They refuse to turn off the lights, so it is impossible to know how much time passes. She covers her eyes with a pillow.

Where are they? They promised a couple of days, and they were going to come and talk to her. But no one came. She is given a greyish paste to eat, at least eight times. That will amount to three days, or darn near.

The bed jerks, violently. She'd certainly never get to sleep this way. It jumps again and dumps Terry and the pillow onto the floor. She sits up to avoid the rubber-ball effect of her bouncing head.

What is going on? The ship is not behaving normally. Sharp turns are unlikely with such a hulking behemoth.

There is a noise at the door. Chief Engineer, Lehmann stands in the doorway, bracing himself for the jerks and tremors. "You have to put an end to this."

Terry frowns.

"Even you must have noticed the vibrations are growing worse. Unless of course, you prefer to sleep on the floor." The Chief Engineer smiles at her reclined position.

"I'm not going to stop it until we are home."

"How will you know? You've changed the mass and speed of the ship to a point where we may have overshot Earth."

"Why can't you make the calculations?"

"Because you changed the element when it was inside the arterial. Calculations were made in normal space, with the mass of the element known to us. Then you made changes, and now our calculations are very wrong."

Terry folds her arms, unmoved by what Lehmann says.

"Now," The Chief continues, "it appears that we are in some kind of loop, within the arterial. As far as we can tell, we are going fast but getting nowhere. The longer we stay, the more stresses The Big EK experiences."

"What's the good news?"

"What?"

"There's always good news in a situation like this."

Lehmann shakes his head. "In this case, the only good news I have is the vibrations will stop in three or four days."

"Yeah, see like that, good news."

"They'll stop because The Big EK is going to fail catastrophically, and then you won't care about home, because you'll be dead. We'll all be dead." Lehmann turns to leave.

"Wait."

He stops but doesn't turn around to face her.

"You're right; I didn't think this through all the way. But I'm not sure I can help." Terry wipes her face.

"Are you willing to try?"

"Yes."

"That's all we can ask for."

"We've got to get to deck thirteen," Terry shouts over her shoulder as she walks erratically. The vibrations, noise, and sudden movements of the ship make walking a contact sport. She bounces off a wall but continues forward.

Lehmann follows her like a shadow. Behind him are a handful of Marines, large men, and women, armed with knives and sidearms. The Marines are prepared to take care of Terry, whether she succeeds or fails.

Terry jumps from deck eleven to deck twelve. She lands on the singularity drive. Despite the quakes and rolls, here the singularity's pull holds tight to her feet. Perhaps even tighter than before. She moves to the next access to deck thirteen and pulls her body through. The gravity definitely feels stronger.

Once on deck thirteen, she waits for Lehmann to appear. Terry leads him to the maintenance room and the closet. Once the door opens fittings and dirt spill over her shoes. The panel that hides and protects her engine and the vial lays in the debris. The *Ekatarina* heaves, knocking more dust and bolts free.

"Shit, shit, shit!" Terry squats and digs through the mess. She pushes aside large objects like couplings, bolts, screws, and batteries.

"What are you looking for?" Lehmann tries to squeeze beside her to help.

"A small metal box with rounded corners, about six inches cubed." She holds up her hands to indicate the approximate size. Terry scoops out some materials and places them before Lehmann. "Look for the vial; the engine ought to be easier to find."

"Agreed, push the small stuff to me, I'll comb through it."

The Marines help by going through the debris Lehmann pushes aside.

"It's here, look." Terry pulls the engine out from a pile of dust. The vibrations tingle her fingertips. "It's not broken, just dirty." The fine metal particles cling to the engine like tiny porcupines.

She joins the search for the vial. She doesn't know she is holding her breath until she gasps when Lehmann holds up the bottle.

"I have it." Lehmann stands, bringing the small bottle into the maintenance room.

Terry follows with the engine.

"We need to add mass." He gives her the vial.

Terry nods. "I expected as much. But how do I know when to stop?"

"I don't know. When we used electricity the mass gain took days."

"I'm not adding electrons; I'm adding energy."

"Good" Lehmann grunts with surprise. "It'll be faster. Let's time it. How about one minute?"

"Agreed." Terry unwinds the cables and sets the engine on a table.

He stares into his tablet. "We're ready. We're going to charge it for one minute." The tablet issues static and broken voices in return. Lehmann looks at Terry. "They want the change now."

She holds the cables at either end of the vial, staring at the tablet and the timer. After a minute, she removes one end.

Lehmann shouts into the tablet. "That's it, one minute." Long minutes of static and voices respond. "Engineering wants three more minutes. They calculate that will stabilize the Big EK, enough to pull it out of the loop."

Terry reapplies the cables and waits three minutes. The singularity engine wails and thumps. The vibrations of the ship increase, knocking dust and debris into the air, then suddenly decrease. She looks at Lehmann to see if engineering wants more or less energy.

"That's impossible!" he yells at the tablet. "Who the hell do you think we are? Magicians?" He turns to Terry. "They see the increase in mass, but it has no bearing on the operation of the ship."

Terry looks at him sideways, eyebrows raising. "And that means?"

"They can't break out of the infinite loop. They want us to find a way to destroy the quantum entanglement."

"First of all, we don't know how this element became entangled; we can only guess. Second, if we destroyed the entanglement, then we no longer have control over increasing or decreasing the mass of element one hundred twenty-four. Thirdly, we don't know what that would do to the ship."

"They listed all the ways the element has caused problems; it shouldn't be on the hull. They postulate that the removal of the element will return everything to normal."

Terry closes her eyes, then nods. "But we are in the middle of an arterial."

"You've got an idea, don't you?" Lehmann raises his eyebrows.

"I do." Terry shakes her head, holding the vial close to her chest. "But it's a one-way decision. If I do this, the element and this vial is gone forever. If this works, the mass on the ship should evaporate within minutes. I figure the element is only stable, because of the quantum entanglement. Think of the entanglement as a lock. And if it doesn't work, we no longer have the vial, as a key, to change the mass."

"We could get more off the hull?" Lehmann suggests with a frown and a head shake as if he already knows that is wrong. "If this doesn't work, we'll be dead, won't we?"

Terry nods.

"Alright, worse case, we die. Best case, we lose element one hundred twenty-four. Forever."

"Yes, forever." Terry swallows hard then looks at the vial of black liquid. "How certain are your people, that we will be torn apart in this loop?" If they were on Earth, the unassuming element could be tested. It could become a boon for humankind. But they aren't on Earth.

"One hundred percent." Lehmann sighs. "I've seen the curve, it's guaranteed."

She closes her eyes and squeezes the bottle tightly, hoping that someday in the future, she will see the element again. "We have only one choice." Terry wraps the cables around the dark energy engine and sets it into its own cabinet. "In case we don't die." She closes the door and pats it. "Let's do this."

"Do what? You didn't tell me."

"We have to expose the element to a black hole." Terry stands and walks back to deck twelve.

Lehmann stands with her, shaking his head. "I don't like where this is going." He shakes his finger at her.

"Technically, we have a black hole right here."

"No, no." In a desperate plea for help, Lehmann looks at the Marines, as if they can offer alternate solutions. "We can't open the Singularity Drive. It could destroy the ship."

"This is our only option. There is nothing else." Terry shrugs. "Worse case we die, remember?" She jumps down on to the surface of the drive. Lehmann and the Marines follow. "There has to be an access port or something. Do you know where it is?"

He moves past her. "It's near the center of the drive. Where gravity is strongest."

"I'm glad you came along," Terry says to the Marines. "We are going to need some brute force."

It takes forty minutes to reach the center of the singularity—each step fighting the gravity down and forward, toward the center. Walking becomes a force of will.

"There it is." Lehmann points to a small hatchway in the side casing of the drive. "That is how the drive was originally seeded." He pulls on the knobs, but they won't budge.

"This is where we need you. Can you open that port?" Terry asks the Marine crew.

The Marines look at Lehmann for orders. "She's right; we don't have a choice." As a cohesive unit, they muscle and fight with the four lockdown knobs and then the hatch itself. The Marines step away from the opening, dripping with sweat.

"Now we drop the element; the singularity will pull it in." Terry looks at Lehmann. "Would you like the honors?"

"You mean; the responsibility." He holds out his hand.

Terry carefully gives him the vial. He drops it into the port, where it seems to go willingly. Within seconds the ship shakes and groans.

"Close the port!" Terry and Lehmann shout in unison to the Marines.

As a unit, they lift and shove the metal hatchway back into place.

The ship convulses and stutters unnaturally. Terry thinks she hears a scream from above, on deck eleven. Perhaps, it is the *Ekatarina* tearing itself apart. Metal sounds like screaming when it rips. She tries to block the thought.

Terry drops to the surface of the engine, sitting with her head in her hands. Did she kill everyone? Only time will tell.

Terry looks at the four familiar walls of the brig, where she is confined, and wonders if this is the exact cell Jax sat in after she was caught improperly fiddling with SIBIL… before she gave her life to save the ship.

She picks at a loose string on the mattress. *Didn't I save everyone's life?* She thinks, *wasn't I the savior of the Big EK? Matt should have visited.* He is obsessed, not that she blames him.

The metal door opens. Two Marines enter. Terry stands from the bed and steps forward. Roughly, the men grab her arms and place them into tight metal cuffs. They jerk her out of the cell.

"Where are we going?"

"Wherever we take you."

The pinch of the cuffs reminds her who is in charge, for the moment. Terry bites back the rude comment; she will find out soon enough. They cross over a deck.

Standing in front of the Captain's door is Major Helen Ironbear. Her dark hair is cut in a Mohawk. Combined with the tactical tomahawk on her hip, she looks savage. The woman scowls at Terry.

"You killed four of my people. I've been promised your scalp." Ironbear taps the weapon on her hip, grinning like a feral dog.

Terry feels a chill run up her spine, followed by the urge to run, but the men at her sides prevent any movement.

One of the men knocks. The door opens, revealing a woman with dark hair and narrow eyes.

"Step inside," Captain Illiadus says.

Terry opens her mouth. She closes it and steps across the threshold.

"You two, stay put." The Captain says to the Marines. She glances at Ironbear, nods, and then closes the door.

Terry looks around the small room, cramped with a desk, chair, and bed. A thin strip of floor is burnished bright by continuous wear.

"Ensign Terry Thaleia, what you did is no different than mutiny." The Captain paces two or three steps only to return to the door.

"Mutiny?"

The captain raises her index finger. "I have not given you permission to speak." The tall woman returns to pacing; her hands clasp at the small of her back. "Many of the crew want your head."

Terry swallows.

"How many died because of your insolence? How many more have radiation burns, and will die in the days to come?" She points to the closed door. "The Marines lost four." She shakes her head, then continues pacing.

"We are in your debt for having a cool head while under pressure. You saved the ship." The captain turns and points at Terry. "However, we would not have been in that situation if you had not acted of your own accord." Her finger shakes with each accusation. "Following your needs. With little regard for the rest of your shipmates."

Terry looks at her feet. She made mistakes. Perhaps she deserves punishment.

"I am stuck making a decision that will displease my crew."

Terry lifts her head. She frowns, confused. "Why?"

The captain stops pacing and focuses her glare on Terry. "Yes, Ensign?"

"Why displease the crew?" Terry stares at the captain. She is part of the crew and already displeased with the Captain. What could she possibly do or say to upset everyone more?

"Chief Engineer, Lt. Commander Walter Lehmann requests I spare your life," Captain Illiadus says, moving close to Terry.

"Spare, my life?" Terry lifts her cuffed hands to her chest, surprised that her death is an option.

"The Chief explained how you expected the element to unentangle and then evaporate when the vial was thrown into the singularity." The captain folds her arms. "Because you were right, Chief Engineer, Lt. Commander Walter Lehmann thinks you're a physics and engineering prodigy. He believes we'll need your guidance to get home."

"Well, he's right. You'll need me." Terry lifts her chin defiantly.

Captain Illiadus steps back from Terry. "Let me make one thing perfectly clear. I'm not sparing your life; I'm giving you a reprieve, a delay." Her lip curls with distaste. "Make one more mistake, step one toe out of line, and I will end your life." The captain stares into Terry's eyes, tapping the firearm that sits on her desk. "Personally."

Captain's Log, The Ekatarina

Twenty-Fourth Jump Completed

As I stated in previous log entries, the last series of jumps inadvertently locked us into a single dark energy artery which transported us to the galaxy's outer edge of the second galactic quadrant. Though far from prime navigation, we are now one-eighth of the distance from the Scourge Annihilation on the way back to Earth. Known only to SIBIL, myself, Major Helen Ironbear, and my second-in-command Commander Aithon, we have, in fact, come upon the remains of three separate jump gates. Two were in unexplored and uninhabited star systems. The third was in the Paragon-4, a binary star system with four inhabited ocean planets of a race of cephalopods known as The Nautilae. The subsequent explosion of their nearby jumpgate irradiated and killed all life throughout their solar system. With the galaxy as heavily populated as it is, many of the crew are upset with our prolonged journey and can't seem to understand why we have not yet been able to find a populated star system, let alone one with jump-gate technology after all this time. The answer is as simple as it is frustrating. The Milky Way is huge, and the distances between stars is astronomical. Dark Artery navigation is still only about as effective as skipping a stone across a lake's surface. Sheer luck may find us a port of call in the near future, but with everything that has happened to date I am finding luck to be in very short supply. End Log.

Articles of War

by William Joseph Roberts

Ship's Chronometer: 2430 AD

"**W**e can't keep going on like this," I shout. "I haven't had a day off in half a year. There's barely enough time to wind down and catch a cat nap most days. We've been working sixteen-hour shifts for the last six months, and for what?"

Engineering specialist Ensign Trevor Branagan stands, adjusting the crotch of his orange jumpsuit. He begins to pace about the barracks compartment like a trapped animal. "Crewman Beck isn't wrong. I've been saying the same thing for months. Something's got to give," he says in a thick Irish accent. He kicks the corner of a pod in frustration. "We cannot keep going on like this. It is cruel and inhumane. Even the shortest of arterial jumps takes a major toll on the ships systems. How can she expect us to continue on like this?"

I nod in total agreement with everything Ensign Branagan has said. Even as a communications specialist, I am tired of the way Captain Ill is running the ship into the ground.

"The Captain doesn't even give us enough time for proper repairs," Ensign Johnson adds. "They expect miracles with shoestrings and bubblegum. I swear it seems like the captain is trying to punish us."

"Exactly," Branagan says, excitedly stabbing his finger in the air. "Thank you for reminding me of that fact. But why? What good does it do anyone if we're all overworked and exhausted? Is she just trying to keep us all so busy that we don't have time to do anything else?"

"Don't get me wrong," Gene, a munitions monkey interjects. "I love my weapons and I love my job, but we're limping home. I don't see why resources should be wasted on maintaining the weapons systems when we're not likely to be in a firefight ever again. The time and materials should be allocated where they will be more beneficial."

"Don't forget about the regularity of the drills and training that are being forced down our throats," Emma Patel, an operations crewman says.

Bosun Winger nods his head, glancing at all the others in the room. "I can't argue with any of that. Drills, long shifts and no down time. Shit can't stay like this," he says pleadingly to no one in particular. "We're basically just spinning our wheels keeping this boat in the sky."

"Lest we forget the botched experiment Ensign Thaleia tried to pull off two years ago," Branagan says. "Because of *her*, our ETA back to Earth has nearly doubled!"

"Terry was just trying to help all of us get home a little quicker," Ensign Johnson says. "She wasn't trying to hurt anyone."

"Even so," Branagan growls. "Many were hurt and many died in her botched experiment. If she'd had any sense about her she'd have consulted a few of us to work out the problems. Not just satiate her ego and hope for the best."

"All y'all white folk are treating this like you treat your food," Lieutenant junior grade, Anita Whooper says.

"Please, don't mention the food," a female voice says from the back of the gathered group.

"I'm talking, so you shut it," Anita berates. "Y'all just want to season it with imagination and hope. But there ain't a damned one of you willing to do something about this mess we're in. Look at yourselves. Y'all ought to be ashamed." Anita, the ships supply officer, or lovingly known as '*chops*' to the crew, crossed her arms under and hefted up her oversized breasts. She stared at the others with a sideways shake of her head. "Um hum," she hummed. "My mamma would roll over in her grave if she saw the shit I've gotten myself into now."

"We can all agree that this ship and her crew are a powder keg that's ready to blow," Gunnery Sergeant Jedidiah Solomon Hatfield interjects loudly. Old Sol as he is known to the crew picks at something between his molars, then sucks loudly on his teeth. "Captain Illiadus is either blind or she's refusing to acknowledge that we have a serious problem aboard this ship. Chief Engineer Lehmann and Major Ironbear have their heads so far up Captain Ill's ass that they can't even see the truth of it all. I tell you what," Old Sol begins, then grunts a laugh. "It makes me sick to fucking death that I have to sit back and watch all of this happening around me. I'm powerless to stop any of it. Each and every one of us are stuck in the same damn predicament. Just spinning our wheels for the man. Not enough rank or pull to matter to the powers that be. I'd say my career has grown while working as second in command for Ironbear's Marine contingent, but it's gotten to the point that there is entirely too much by the book ass-kissing." He spits in disgust. Old Sol pulls himself to his feet and walks to the center of the room. "Yes *sir*, no *sir*. It makes me *ill*," he growls. "We've been dragging our asses through unknown space for five fucking years since we iced The Scourge. And where are we? Nowhere! I've personally had enough and think it's time for a change. I think it's high time that that bitch of a captain, Illiadus heard what we had to say. It's time that Ironbear stepped aside and let someone with vision and common sense run things around here."

The gathered crew claps, stomps and cheers in agreement. As many have come to appreciate since they first came aboard the *Ekatarina*, the gunnery sergeant's powerfully innate animal magnetism is as potent as it is infectious. His cult of personality has tripled over the past week since they exited the latest dark energy artery jump and crawled out of their cryopods. He'd been priming them every day, preparing for this moment.

Anita grunts, clearing her throat to get everyone's attention. "You do realize that everything you just said, in itself, is grounds for a court-martial? All of us could be charged with inciting a riot, sowing dissension, and mutiny just for being here and not reporting you to Illiadus."

"So, then don't report me." Old Sol flashes a wide toothy grin. "Besides, we're all in the clear here as long as everyone keeps their yaps shut," he says in a menacing tone. "I disabled all monitoring equipment in this section before everyone arrived. So, unless its bugged or one of you goes and cries to mommy, we're all in the clear."

"You about crazy. You know that, don't you?" Anita says with a laugh.

"Sure do," Old Sol replies.

"If you're serious, then I'm in," Anita says. "But how in the hell are we supposed to pull it off? The duty on watch in the CIC will be able to isolate us anywhere on the ship or even vent the atmosphere if they want."

"Actually, it's …," Branagan interrupts, "that's the easy bit." He smiles wide. "At least it is at the beginning of it all. I can access the mainframe and lock out all of the CIC. There's a redundant controls station in engineering, should anything happen to the CIC for any reason. So, it's just a matter of running the combat override subroutine and I'll have full control of the ship from there."

"And exactly what are we supposed to do after that?" Anita scoffs. "Are we supposed to take the ship with our bare hands?" She waves her hand in the air out of frustration and takes a seat on the bunk she was leaning on.

"Don't you worry none about that," Old Sol says. "I've got access to *all* the weapons we're going to need." He turns to look each crewman present in the eye. "I will contact each of you with the designated gathering point. If you're in, then be on time. If not, keep your mouths shut. Am I clear?"

"Yes sir," we all reply in unison.

We go about our regular duties until the next evening when we can gather at the designated time and location. Ten of us mill about in the engineering storage locker, impatiently waiting. Branagan nods as he listens into the earpiece. "That's the last of them. Everyone else is in position. Now's the time to do this if we're going to."

"About damned time," Anita huffs. "I'm getting tired of sitting here waiting. Hurry up and wait, hurry up and wait. I get enough of that with the current regime. Y'all about to lose my ass cause I'm just gonna walk away and go get me some ice cream or something."

"Shh," Branagan motions toward Anita. "The walls are thick, but that doesn't mean someone won't hear a bunch of strange voices in the engineering and come check it out."

"Guess it's time to get this show on the road, then." Old Sol grins, absentmindedly licking his teeth in thought. "Once we rush into main engineering, how long do you need to lock out the CIC and change the passcodes?"

"It should only take a few moments," Branagan says. "I've assisted with changing them before. I know exactly where they are on the mainframe."

"Let's do this then." Old Sol produces a duffel bag from behind a storage locker and sets it on a worktable.

"What's that," someone asks.

Sol laughs, looking around at the gathered crewmen. "This? This is quite possibly the key to your freedom." He opens the duffel bag and places a dozen Alpha class stun batons on the table, followed by a number of pistols. He slides the last of the pistols into the back of his waistband.

"*Hell*, yeah! That's what I'm talking about," Anita cheers. She snatches a pistol from the table and tucks it into her waistband.

"Do you even know how to use that?" Old Sol looks at Anita with questioning glance.

"Motherfucker," Anita says with an exasperated gasp of shock. "I was raised on the west side of Chicago. What the *hell* do you think?"

"And if you shoot yourself it's your funeral," Sol says.

We look at the weapons on the table then around to the others who wear a similar look of hesitation.

"We aren't going to kill anyone, are we?" I ask.

"Crewman Beck has a fair question. I would surely hope we weren't going to kill anyone," Branagan adds.

Sol stares angrily at Branagan, sucking on his teeth in thought. "If we're going to make this happen, then we might just have to hurt a few folks. We might even have to kill a few in order to succeed. Are you ready to do this thing or not?" Sol leans down nose to nose with Branagan. "I'll leave your ass sitting here high and dry if you're going to pussyfoot around on me. And it won't make a good god damn whether you help or not at this point. You've already been implicated. So, should we fail, you'll be lined up and shot with the rest of us." Sol laughs, then pushes himself upright and struts away from the table.

Reluctantly I pick up one of the stun batons. I move it about, feel the weight of the thing in my hand.

"Do you know how to use that thing," Sol asks. He picks up one of the other batons and demonstrates. "Push this switch to activate the thing and charge the capacitors. Hold down this button," he said, pointing to a small red button on the device, "when you want to actually shock someone. It works similar to a taser."

I flick the switch and immediately hear the electrical hum of charging capacitors. "Thank you," I say to Sol.

"You're welcome," Sol says. He passes out weapons to the rest of the gathered crew. "Once this all begins, just stay behind me and follow my orders. I know your training hasn't prepared you for anything like this, but I have faith that we will be successful. We'll work our way through the ship one section at a time in conjunction with the other groups. Once Brannigan disables the CIC controls he can open up a path through the ship straight to Command. We need to get there fast and take out the Captain and Major Ironbear as quickly as possible. Once we have them in custody or out of the way, the ship will be ours without question."

"I'm ready," Branagan says. "As soon as I lock out the engineering controls we had better move fast. The Chief can reverse what I've done from his station. He's the only person on this boat that could crack my codes."

"Lock and load people." Sol racks the slide on his pistol then places it behind his back. "Do it," he says to Branagan, then steps to the door.

Branagan opens the panels of a backup diagnostics station and types furiously, pressing the enter key with a flourish. "It's done!"

Sol turns to the waiting group. "Remember, stay together and do what I say. We'll be through with this in no time. Let's move out."

The dozen or so of us make quick work of the on-duty engineering staff. We flood in from the auxiliary area. Chief engineer Lehmann relinquishes control almost immediately after seeing armed individuals on his deck. He places his hands behind his head without hesitation and we take engineering without firing a shot. We quickly gather up the engineering crew and restrain them in the auxiliary control room. Branagan locks out all of the stations in engineering. With the area secured we pile out into the main corridor and wait for Branagan to override the CIC controls. From there Sol leads us on a fast march toward the CIC.

"I'm getting reports from the other teams," Branagan says. "They're having success locking most of the off-duty crew down in their quarters. They are pushing forward toward the mess hall to catch anyone gathered there. Chief Petty Officer Inari apparently put up one hell of a fight, but they managed to take her after she knocked out three of our people. All internal communications on board ship have been disabled other than our radios, so we have that working for us."

"That explains why we haven't really run into any resistance," Anita moans. "When the hell are we gonna get some action?"

As if on cue, the sound of running footfalls on the deck plating echoes from the corridor beyond the bulkhead door in front of us.

"Prepare yourselves, we have company coming," Sol forcefully whispers. Kneeling, he leans against the wall. He draws a pistol from his waistband and levels the sights at the unopened door. The rest of the mutinous team follow suit, pressing their backs against the walls of the corridor and out of the line of direct fire.

The hatchway slides open with an electric hum, revealing a group of crewmen armed with stun batons.

Sol aims at the head figure of the group. "Stand down, Jae-jin, or I will fire," Sol says to Crewman Jae-jin Pak, one of the few remaining ships security crewmen.

"You'll stand down now if you know what's good for you, Gunny," crewman Jae-jin Pak warns.

"Hell yeah!" Anita shouts. She throws her stun baton at the group of crewmen. Drawing the pistol from her waistband she fires wildly into the crowd. "That right there's what I'm talking about!"

Bodies drop amid a thick red mist that hangs in the air. The slide of Anita's gun locks back. She drops the magazine and slides a new one home.

Sol, taking his time to aim, fires into the group. Bodies drop as he methodically empties his magazine. In one swift motion, he stows his pistol and draws forth a serrated combat knife that he sinks up to the hilt into the chest of a panic-stricken crewman. The blade angles upward into the man's chest, aimed directly for his heart. Old Sol twists the blade and pulls it out with a sickening suction like sound.

I watch as if in a dream. Old Sol lets the man slide away to the left, then quickly ducks and rolls to the right as another crewman swings a baton at his head. He steps behind and drops this new attacker, slicing through the man's calves. He swings himself around to sit on the man's chest and inserts the blade into the crewman's throat. He blocks a separate strike from his left, then rolls, throwing the new attacker to the ground and plunges the blade into the crewman's ear canal.

I fight back the nauseating tingle brought on by the coppery taste of blood that hangs heavy in the air. I heave.

"What in the hell are you doing?" Branagan yells. He grabs Old Sol by the collar and shakes him. "You didn't have to kill them!"

Old Sol roars, then headbutts Branagan. The junior officers face erupts in a gushing gout of blood. Branagan stumbles backwards, holding his face.

"You broke my bloody nose you son of a bitch!"

"They were warned," Sol growls. "Now, get your sorry ginger ass up and fall in!" He turns and quickly presses ahead. "We are nowhere near done with this, ladies. Let's move it!"

"No!" Branagan stands rigidly. Fists clenched and pinned at his sides.

Sol stops in mid stride and turns, glaring at the junior officer.

Anita sighs. "Do not puss out on us now, Branagan." She punches the Ensign in the shoulder as she walks up. "Ain't nobody likes a quitter. We've already started this. We have to finish it."

Branagan holds his head high, eyes ablaze with rage. "NO! I will not be party to murder. You didn't say anything about killing anyone!"

Sol scoffs with a grin. "You're too late laddie," he says in a horribly butchered Irish accent. "It doesn't matter if you back out now or not. You're part of the revolution and it's your access codes that have been input into the system. Their blood is on your hands as much as they are mine." He smiles and winks at Branagan, as he wipes his blade clean on one of the dead crewman's back, then returns it to its sheath. "Now, if you don't want me to make an example of you, you'll pull your head out of your ass and pull your share of the weight!" He turns and presses forward.

Anita slaps Branagan across the back of the head. "What in the hell is wrong with you?"

"He's a bloody psychopath," he mutters, scowling back at Anita.

"That may be true, but he's the psychopath that'll pull this off before anyone else can." Anita drops her empty magazine, slams a full one into the pistol, and racks the slide. "Get with the program or get out of our way." She follows behind Sol.

"She's right, you know," I say. "He may be bat shit crazy, but it looks like he'll get the job done one way or another." I follow behind Anita along with the others.

Our party presses forward, closer to the CIC with every step. We meet with small packets of resistance that do little to slow Old Sol. The old warrior gleefully bobs and weaves about the untrained opponents. Small explosions rumble from somewhere deep within the bowels of the ship. Bulkheads hum from the resonant stresses exerted across the ship's spaceframe. Branagan reports that other cells of mutineers have met with heavy resistance but have secured their designated sections.

We edge closer to the Command Information Center, the final stronghold of Captain Tennyson Maria Illiadus. Old Sol slows his pace as we approach an intersection.

"Branagan," Sol loudly whispers back down the line. "*Come'r*, boy." He waves the junior engineer forward.

Branagan hesitates, awkwardly rocking on his heels as he considers his options.

"Now, what the hell is wrong with you?" Anita shoves Branagan forward. "Mister Psycho needs you. Get your ass up there."

"Come on," Sol whispers with a sideways nod. He leers menacingly as Branagan approaches.

"What?" Branagan growls defiantly.

"This is your chance," Old Sol says with a wide, predatory smile. "There's only one guard and her back is turned toward us."

I watch as Sol forces his long-bladed combat knife into Branagan's hand.

"Take this, sneak up behind her and put that blade between her fourth and fifth ribs. You'll puncture her lung and keep her from screaming. After that just keep stabbing until she hits the ground. She'll bleed out in minutes if you hit it just right." Sol hungrily licks his lips. The expression on his face tells of a memory being re-lived.

"Are you kidding me?" Branagan forcefully whispers. "I'm not going to do that. I can't kill anyone."

"Well, ya see," Old Sol whispers. "You might have too." He shoves Branagan into the intersection which sends him sprawling face first across the floor, knife in hand.

The sound of a stun baton's capacitor charging hummed in the otherwise uncomfortable silence.

"Put your hands where I can see them," an angry female voice says from somewhere around the corner.

Branagan tosses the blade aside to clatter across the deck plate in our direction. He starts to backpedal away from the direction of the crewman's voice. Old Sol motions for everyone to tuck against the wall, so I do what I am told.

"It's not what it looks like, mate," Branagan hastily stutters. "I swear that I am under an extreme amount of duress." He pushes himself up against the opposite wall of the intersection.

The crewman steps into view. The humming baton extends ahead of her, active with its electrical threat. Wisps of ozone flit about its tip as arcs of blue electricity dance across its surface.

"You'll turn around, face the wall, and put your hands behind your back," the crewman says.

Branagan shivers. "This isn't my fault. I was forced into this," he said. He sits up on his knees and places his hands behind his back. Defeat paints his face. He shuffles in place as he turns to face the wall.

I watch as the crewman continues into the intersection, her attention locked onto Branagan. She pulls a pair of handcuffs from a belt pouch and starts to click them onto Branagan's wrists.

Suddenly, in one fluid motion, Gunnery Sergeant Jedidiah Solomon Hatfield slides across the distance, retrieves the discarded blade and silently pounces on his quarry. His left arm wraps around the crewman's head from behind. He arches his back, lifting her head back and up while the long blade slides into the soft flesh of her neck with little effort. Blood gushes forward from the severed carotid artery and jugular veins. Gouts of blood flow forth from the crewman's wound as her heart desperately continues to pump the life sustaining fluid. A gurgling exhalation of breath escapes from the wound, frothing about the opening as the crewman attempts to scream for help.

Old Sol finishes the cut and severs the crewman's head from her body with a sickening crack of vertebra. Branagan gags and wretches at the ichor that covers him from head to toe. He goes to all fours, heaving. The woman's blood runs down his face and drips teasingly from the tip of his nose.

Sol lets the lifeless hunk of meat slip away in a limp heap on the deck. He kneeels down and wipes the blade on the back of the body, then returns it to its sheath. He glares disappointedly toward Branagan then holds up the severed head. The eyes of the disembodied head twitch and flutter. Its mouth works like a fish out of water. Surprise and fear frozen on its countenance.

"Ya see, boy?" Old Sol says in his horrible attempt at an Irish accent. "That wasn't so tough, now was it, *laddie*?

Branagan heaves again, losing the contents of his stomach.

"Now, if you're done being a sissy Mary, it's time to finish this thing and take over the CIC," Sol shouts at Branagan, then turns back to the rest of us lining the corridor. "Leave him in his cuffs, but make sure he stays with us. He may still have a use or two." Sol tosses the severed head into Branagan's lap as he stands, then continues down the corridor. Branagan catches it and turns as white as a ghost. He tosses and bats at the thing as he attempts to push it away.

"Oh now, that shit just ain't right," Anita howls. "But I like it!" She laughs. "Ain't no one'll fuck with you now, Gunny." Her laugh turns to a cackle as she continues down the corridor, following close behind Old Sol.

An hour or so later after a hard slog through the bowels of the ship, Jedediah and the rest of us mutineers stand before the sealed blast doors of the CIC. Sol immediately shoots out every security camera in the vicinity just in case Captain Ill and the others have managed to get control of the surveillance systems.

"Now how the hell we gonna get those doors open," Anita huffs.

"I could run back to Engineering and get a cutting torch," Ensign Johnson says from the rear of the group.

Old Sol laughs. "That's easy. Branagan, front and center." The Ensign is pushed to the head of the group by the other mutineers.

"Move your ass when a superior officer gives you an order," Anita shouts in his face then pushes him hard enough that he stumbles. He manages to get his footing before face planting to the deck.

"Work your engineering magic on those blast doors, boy," Sol orders.

"And if I don't?" Branagan glares at him.

Old Sol smiles, looking down his nose at the young ensign. "I could start cutting off bits of your scrawny ass, but you'd probably pass out in no time and ruin all of my fun." He glares at the ensign with a dark hunger in his eyes. "But I've got a better Idea." he said, wagging a finger in the air. "Send up that pretty little crewman that we just took prisoner," Sol orders.

The young female prisoner in a white uniform is passed forward as ordered to Old Sol's side. Anita wraps her fist in the woman's hair. She stumbles as Anita forces her to her knees next to Branagan. The woman's nostrils flare as she gasps for breath around the tightly tied gag. I recognized her. She is part of the medical night staff. We spoke once or twice before in the mess hall, but it never amounted to much more than simple pleasantries. *Saito, that was it*, I suddenly think. Crewman Miuna Saito. She'd said that she is part of the night shift on call crew. She tended to everything from headaches to broken bones in the medical bay. But if it was something more serious, she'd wake up the chief medical officer.

Sol pounced on the young crewman like a wolf on a hare. He tore Anita's hand free from the woman and wrapped his own hardened fist into the crewman's tangled mess of hair. Lifting her slightly from the ground he dragged her across the deck. I watched in amazement as the brute strength of the Gunnery Sergeant is revealed. He lifts her off the ground as if she weighs nothing at all, then clamps his free hand around her neck and pins her to the wall.

"You'll do it, or I'll get to see what it takes to make this little mamma san make noises you've never even imagined before," Old Sol growls.

She fights, beating her fists against the gunnery sergeant's muscular forearm. She kicks him repeatedly in the ribs with the tip of her boot. The old soldier grimaces, but his grip does not falter.

"Let this be a lesson to any of you," Sol says over his shoulder. "Know your target if you wish to inflict the most amount of pain." His anvil like fist repeatedly comes down with his full might just above the young crewman's left hip.

She cries out and flails wildly, gasping for breath. Her eyes roll into the back of their sockets as her head lolls to the side.

"Put her down!" Branagan shouts. "She hasn't done anything to deserve that sort of treatment."

Old Sol looks over his shoulder to me and grins. "No, she hasn't. But you still haven't done what I asked, either." He draws forth his blade and slices it across the back of the crewman's forearm. Blood runs down her arm and drips slowly from her limp fingertips.

"It's your choice, Ensign," Sol says. "What's it going to be? Should I cut her deeper? Or maybe I could take off an ear? They are such delicate and dainty things. I don't think anyone would notice too much if I kept one for myself. Do you?" Sol lets the crewman drop to the deck where she lands with a limp thud. He grabs her ear and pulls it away from the side of her head as he places the edge of the blade on her flesh. Blood trickles down her cheek as the Gunnery Sergeant begins to slice into the woman's flesh.

"Alright! Alright!" Branagan shouts. "For the love of God let her go."

Old Sol lets her slip to the floor where her head thuds heavily against the deck. She jerks awake, coughing and wheezing as she sucks in fresh, unrestricted air.

Branagan turns, flicking his handcuffed fingers about. "Someone will have to take these things off if you want me to open the door."

Anita unlocks the cuffs and tucks them into a pocket. Branagan rubs at the chafed places the cuffs have left on his wrists.

"Get to work, egghead," Sol says. He shoves the Ensign toward the access panel. "I need to get through those doors."

"Did you happen to bring any tools along with you?" Branagan asks.

Old Sol produces a multitool in response and hands it to Branagan. "Always be prepared for any situation." He removes the control panel faceplate for the CIC blast doors and lets it dangle by the connected wiring, then reaches inside the space and removes a pair of relay circuits from the control board.

"My patience is wearing thin, Ensign," Sol complains.

"Would you like to come and do this yourself?" Branagan growls, turning to face the Gunnery Sergeant.

Sol grunts. "Ballsy." He laughs. "There might be hope for you yet, Ensign."

Branagan turns back to the controls and removes one last, stubborn relay from the circuit and places it in an empty slot on the back of the dangling face plate. The faceplate beeps. He turns it over and the display reads *unlocked* in bright green letters.

"That's a good boy, Branagan," Sol says. He grabs Ensign Saito by the nape of the neck and throws her back down the corridor to the other mutineers who pass her along toward the back of the line. He pats Branagaon on the top of the head like a dog then takes the face plate out of the Ensign's hands. "We can't chance you getting hurt, now can we?" Sol shoves Branagan toward the back of the line as well.

"Keep him out of the way," Sol shouts. "Are you apes ready? It's time that we end the incompetence that has plagued us this entire voyage. It's all or nothing, boys and girls." He taps the controls and the blast doors open.

We rush the opening and are immediately met by an eruption of gunfire from inside the CIC. Bodies of the first four or five mutineers storming the command center litter the entrance. I pull back, tucking my back against the wall.

"Get in there, you worthless grunts," Sol says, waving everyone forward.

I try to crawl away down the corridor, but something grabs and pulls me backwards.

"Where the hell do you think you're going, Beck?" Sol shouts, pulling me to my feet by the collar of my flight suit.

I hear the clatter of something heavy and metallic bounce against the deck plating amid the shouts and gunfire. The world around me shakes then suddenly goes a blindingly silent white. Someone trips and falls on top of me. We both collapse to the floor as we fight to regain our footing. I push them off then feverishly rub at my eyes. The world blurs back into a speckled existence. I can see again, but barely. They must have used some type of flash bang grenade on us.

Red splattered figures litter the deck around me. Other figures rush by, charging into the CIC. Someone shoves me back to the ground. I look up to see Sol angrily pointing at me and mouthing something before he disappears through the doorway. I fumble to grip the wall and to steady myself.

"Branagan!" Someone shouts from inside the CIC.

I regain my footing and follow the Ensign to the edge of the entrance. He dashes into the room, ducking as low as he can without crawling. I step forward and peek into the CIC. Branagan hides behind one of the upper level auxiliary control consoles while a few paces away, Gunnery Sergeant Jedidia Solomon Hatfield stands toe to toe with Major Helen Ironbear. He punches, she parries. She kicks, he sidesteps. He lunges, she blocks. The two combatants are equally matched in what seems like every way. Defenders and mutineers alike watch with dumbstruck awe as the two titan Marines battle it out.

Reality suddenly snaps back to me. Gunfire erupts from the opposite side of the CIC. Rounds ricochet on the opposite wall of the corridor. Anita pushes me forward and fires over my head into the room. "Get your sorry ass up and help the Gunny!" She charges into the room and grabs Branagan by the collar. "Unlock the God damned controls, Ensign!" Anita ducks as rounds bounced off of the console that she hides behind.

"Are you crazy?" Branagan shouts. "I don't want to die!"

Anita presses her gun against the side of Branagan's head. "Get your beta cuck ass in there now before I shoot you myself! I am tired of the crap that Illiadus has put us through. It's time for change!"

"Okay, okay," he says, motioning for her to calm down with his hands.

I crawl across the deck to hide behind the auxiliary console beside Anita then peek over the top and down into the lower part of the CIC. A bullet impacts the console next to my head. I jerk back, my face peppered with bits of shrapnel.

"I won't miss the next time," one of the crewmen in a red jumpsuit shouts from below. Anita blindly fires twice down into the CIC, then ducks behind the wall as more rounds impact the console.

"It's going to take more than that to get me," Anita shouts with a laugh.

"I have to get to that station," Branagan points around to the opposite side of the CIC's upper level. "That's the engineering station. I'll be able to access everything from there."

Anita fires downward again. Two others rush into the room and take cover beside us.

"Move it Branagan," Sol shouts. "They're out of ammo!"

The Gunnery Sergeant's reflexes are just a mite too slow to block Ironbear's left back hand strike that breaks his nose immediately followed up by a tomahawk swipe that slices through his uniform, cuts his skin and nicks two of his left ribs. Doped up on pain, adrenaline, and anger, Jedidiah recklessly swings his large right open palm forward and slaps it against the hammer poll and head of the Major's tomahawk, wraps his fingers tightly around them and yanks back. This pulls the Major forward and off balance for a split second and gives the Gunnery Sergeant a full moment to drop to his right knee, shove his right hand under her right armpit, and in a flawless combat judo maneuver throw Major Ironbear completely up and over his shoulder. She bounces against one of the gunner's stations along the back wall and slides to the deck momentarily stunned.

Two more of the ship's gunnery crewmen charge at Old Sol, stun batons in their hands. Sol catches the back of the first man's hand in mid-swing, twists his hand backwards with a loud snap. His hand goes limp and his weapon falls away. The crewman lets out a painful gasp after Sol trips and slams the man to the deck. The gunnery sergeant discharges the baton against the second man's groin then rolls the first crewman onto his stomach. He placed the tip of the stun baton to the base of the man's skull and triggers the weapon. Scorched hair and ozone fills the upper deck area.

Ironbear suddenly charges in from out of nowhere wearing a feral scowl, digging her shoulder into Sol's side which sends both of them sprawling across the deck. The stun baton Sol has been holding bounces to a stop a foot or so away from me.

"Branagan!" Anita shouts from somewhere off to the side, but my attention is locked on the two battling titans. Ironbear coils her muscular body around Old Sol in ways that don't seem possible. She wraps her legs around the gunny's head and twists in mid-air, attempting to snap the old sergeant's neck. Sol grabs Ironbear by the waist and tears her away with little effort. He slams the major flat on her back to the deck. She coughs and gasps as she tries to roll away. Sol wraps his hand in her hair and lifts her from the ground. Pulling her in close he wraps her in a simple but effective head lock.

"I'm going to enjoy hurting you, Major," Sol says. He draws his blade and slowly inserts its tip into the major's face, just under the eye. Major Ironbear roars with fury, reaching behind herself. She squirms and contorts herself enough that she is able to reach the Gunney's face. She dug her thumbs into the Gunnery Sergeant's eye sockets.

"Bitch!" He roars. "You're going to pay for being such a pain in my ass all of these years! I'mma gonna get me a fucking scalp!" He shakes his head free from her grasp and draws the edge of his blade across her forehead.

I don't know what overcomes me in this moment. I can see the blood flow freely from the Major's scalp. Without another thought or the slightest of hesitation, I pick up the stun baton and place the tip at the base of Old Sol's skull. Scorched flesh and ozone accompany the clatter of his blade as it bounces against the deck plating.

The morale of my fellow mutineers deteriorates immediately. Before Sol's body hits the deck, Anita, Branagan and the others who have assisted in the assault of the CIC *flee*. In the moments after, I vaguely remember Captain Illiadus broadcasting a ship wide message to all, especially for the ears of the mutineers. Major Ironbear holds up the body of Gunnery Sergeant Hatfield for all to see on the vid-screens as Captain Ill orders the insurgents rounded up and brought to cargo bay four. It is one of the larger cargo bays on board the ship with its own independent airlock which greatly assists in the loading and unloading of any large equipment or oversized supply pallets that might be needed on a mission. I know this because I'd spent many hours in that bay during the ship's loadout prior to our launch from home.

The stun baton is torn from my grasp as two crewmen take me into custody.

"What about this one, Captain?" Major Ironbear asks with a nod toward me as she wipes blood from her eyes. "This is the crewman who actually stopped the Gunny."

"Mutiny is mutiny," Captain Illiadus says coldly. "Place him with the others."

My wrists are bound behind my back and I am led away by a familiar looking crewman. Darius, I think is his name. You'd think with a crew as small as ours we will all know everyone else aboard. Most are content to stay within their little groups when we aren't locked away in stasis. Some resist, others silently bow their heads in defeat as we are collected and led to the cargo bays massive air lock. I am one of the first to be deposited in the chamber. I watch as others are brought in. Some I recognize. Others I don't. Branagan looks completely defeated. Supply officer Lieutenant Anita Whooper looks angry.

"What are you looking at," Anita growls at me as she is led into the airlock. "Get your hands off of me," she shouts at the crewman as they force her to her knees.

A warning klaxon sounds. The regular crewmen run out of the airlock and back into the cargo bay. The large airlock hatch slowly draws itself closed. Anita and a few of the other mutineers leap to their feet and run for the opening, only to be knocked back into the chamber. Some are shoved, some electrified, while others are merely clubbed and beaten back. Cries of desperation are replaced by a somber silence that washes over all of us as the large airlock hatch closes, clanks and locks.

"Attention," a female voice announces over the ship's intercoms. *"Attention all hands,"* the voice continues followed by the shrill tone of a bosun's whistle.

"This is your Captain speaking," Captain Illiadus says over the ship's intercom. "I am appalled at what has happened aboard this ship today. The actions of the few must not endanger the lives of the many. The egregious deeds carried out by Gunnery Sergeant Hatfield and his followers cannot go overlooked. Neither mercy nor leniency shall be given to any who opposed the rightful chain of command. As such, let this be an example to all that are still under my command. I, Captain Tennyson Maria Illiadus sentence each of you mutineers to death, which will now be carried out by my own hand."

A klaxon reverberates within the confines of the airlock to the flashing beat of amber and red lights.

"May God have mercy on your souls," the captain says as mechanical clanks meld into the cacophony of explosive decompression.

We fly, as if a single entity, into the dark eternity of night beyond the confines of the *Ekatarina.*

Captain's Log, The Ekatarina

Jump Thirty-Six Completed

The ship is in a state of emergency. After the execution of the mutineers, the crew contingent is just too small to continue to operate all systems in an ongoing basis. The answer to this dilemma is possibly right in front of us. For the first time since we started this journey, we have exited a dark energy artery near an advanced populated system. There is no jumpgate technology in evidence, and the native population appears to have only rudimentary space travel capabilities. I am in a desperate situation which I now believe requires drastic measures. The human race moved out of its feral and primal infancy centuries ago, and is one of the original founders of The Polis, the democratic Galactic Government formed to fight off the bellicose Scourge. We are a proud, advanced, and ethical species… but I have been pushed to my limits, and I see no other choices in this dire time. As much as it sickens me, and goes against all my schooling and training, I must place the needs of my command, my crew, my ship, above all others. This is a damnation that I willingly accept. End Log.

The Right Bait

by Gustavo Bondoni

Ship's Chronometer: 2432 AD

Incoming Transmission.

The crew in the command center breathe a collective sigh. They've started to suspect that the civilization down there is one of those aberrations that don't communicate on the electromagnetic spectrum. In a galaxy the size of the Milky Way, it happens more often than is comfortable. There are also races that communicate with missiles and particle beams.

Stand by for translation.

Everyone tenses again. Even though they desperately need to resupply and repair the ship – so that being unable to talk to the planet would have meant a slow and unpleasant death – arriving unexpectedly at any planet just after a major galactic conflict is a good way to get shot at. Lettering appears on the screen.

Welcome to [untranslatable]. Please [untranslatable] origin, heading and destination. *Landing beacon [untranslatable] will follow.*

Even as the rest of the crew relaxes and begins to respond automatically to the standard, even prosaic, request, Ensign Igor Camina wonders how far afield they must be for the translator to have trouble with something as simple as landing instructions. Having worked in maintenance before his latest field promotion had moved him to the bridge, he is well aware of just how complete that database actually is. As always in times of stress, his uniform feels much too small on his enormous frame.

Captain Illiadus knows it, too, but she still gives orders calmly and unhurriedly, relying on the crew's impeccable training to fill in the gaps in her orders – even with a patchwork bridge complement, Igor suspects that she intentionally gives incomplete orders to keep the rest on their toes – and to keep them from wondering about the translation.

"Tell them we're a merchant ship exploring the system, and that we come in peace. Ask them to tell us which port would be the ideal place to send a shuttle down for supplies – send them the chemical specifications of what kind of food won't kill us." She pauses for a second. "And make sure the origin won't translate into anything. We don't know what side they're on, and they should be used to their translators not catching everything."

As the crew rushes to obey, the captain scans the info feed. Igor watches her as she flips between the energy sources identified, and also as she looks over the armament predictions for the planetary surface. She turns to him. "Looks like we won't be landing as an invading force – they're so spread out that it would take too many troops to hold the ground. We might have to try something a little different."

Igor has no idea what she is talking about, and the Captain sighs. "Just go get major Ironbear, will you?"

"Yes, Sir," Igor replies, swallowing hard. Major Ironbear isn't exactly the kind of person you want to have to disturb. But the fact that she never answers when commed make it imperative.

Fortunately, the Major is in her quarters, and Igor manages to avoid being chewed out on general principles.

"Glad you could make it, Major," Illiadus says. The recent troubles have strained the relationship between the pure Naval complement and the combat troops.

Ironbear doesn't rise to the bait. "I hear we're approaching a planet."

"Yes," Illiadus replies. "I'd like your opinion on it."

The Marine glances at the data screens. "Hmm. Either this place is something we could take down with a platoon of Marines, or they've got weapons or cloaking so advanced we can't get a read on their strength."

"I was thinking along the same lines, and I'm leaning towards the fact that they're all bumpkins. The scanners seem to have ID'd at least five different species, probably six, by DNA typing, but no sign of anything capable of getting between stars, and especially no gate-optimized tech. Hell, preliminary analysis shows that they might even have some intelligent insectoids on the islands in that biggest ocean, and some more on the other planet – how long has it been since you last saw an intelligent insectoid? We might be deep inside the old Scourge territory, of course, but I think we've stumbled on a system of isolated neutrals with at least two inhabited planets."

"And is this the bigger one?"

"Yes."

"Not much to look at, is it? So, do you want me to invade it, or is this a social call?"

"Neither. I need you to analyze the species the scanner has identified and to let me know if any of them would make good Marines. I'll go into the Helmet and ask SIBIL to help." The captain grimaces at the thought.

For the first time in Igor's experience, Major Ironbear smiles. The contortions in her scar tissue were nearly impossible to stomach. "Going to do some recruiting?"

"The thought has crossed my mind."

Igor hates landfall shuttles, which are one of the main reasons he'd signed up to be on the maintenance crew as opposed to straight naval duties – after all, when the crew gets shore leave, the maintenance team is expected to fix the ship for their return. Of course, with the recent shakeups, junior members of the repair crews have been pressed into service as gofers for the officers – even given naval ranks for their trouble. Only bad luck has gotten Igor assigned to the bridge crew. And worse luck – or perhaps his size – turned him into Illiadus' favorite target.

He suspects that she's read about his fear of landing in his psych profile and has brought him along for kicks.

He looks away from the Captain, trying to take his mind off the fact that they are now on an essentially ballistic trajectory towards the proximity of the spaceport, and that even a tiny failure in the heat-shielding will cook him to a crisp. No one is going to convince him that it will be too fast to notice.

The rest of the shuttle's occupants don't seem to mind much. There are twelve of them in total, and all but the Captain and Igor seem to have been gene-modded for space combat. Slightly violet-tinged skin for radiation shielding meant that this is a squad that has been earmarked for inner-orbit action. Despite being a fully human squadron, all of them seem twice Igor's size – even the women – and their skin is nearly as scarred as their commander's. Ironbear herself has remained on board the *Ekatarina*, ready and willing to squash any new insurrections – and probably praying that there would be one. She might not always see eye to eye with Illiadus, but she is loyal to the Polis.

They all have that slightly vacant look that means they are waiting for further orders. He wonders if there really is so little to their existence – or if they simply refuse to unbend in public.

The trip is essentially uneventful. The inertial equalizers on these assault shuttles are clearly much better than the typical naval land-buses, and if he hadn't been able to look out the armored forward-looking viewport, he would have had a tough time believing that they were even moving.

But that viewport tells an unmistakable story: the air under the shuttle glows a soft orange, and he can see ionized plumes shooting past. He wonders what the planet below looks like.

Even the landing is damped, with barely a slight bump to announce that the journey is over. The gorillas in uniforms – it has been decided that there is no sense in making the trip in mufti, as the people down there are unlikely to be human or even particularly humanoid – stand as a unit and filed towards the door.

Illiadus and Igor wait patiently, partly to ensure that there are plenty of bodies entering the corridor before them in case the locals react in unfortunate ways, but mostly because of the sense that if they stand, they'd be crushed. No attack came, so he let the captain through and brought up the rear.

The welcoming committee is rather larger than Igor expected. No less than six of what he presumed must be port officials stand in the dingy corridor. It seems that spaceports are the same everywhere: dirty, featureless and, even on hot planets, chilly and damp.

"Welcome to—" The name of the port came through their translator as a series of clicks and scratches. "Please state your origin and cargo."

The captain of the Marines strides forward. "We are from Pleiades six," he says. This is the place of origin they'd agreed on before leaving the *Ekatarina*. It is fictitious and won't set off any vaguely possible Scourge security protocols – in the very rare case there were any remnants here, as unlikely as it is – but most friendly races will recognize it as the local name of a star in Polis space. "We are here to deal in midrange stardrive technology and mind-interface communications devices."

The translators they'd rigged must be working, as a ripple runs through the assorted officials. Igor is surprised to see that five of the six beings present are roughly humanoid in appearance, although they do represent three seemingly different species. The final member is some kind of aquatic creature – or at least it seems that way based on the fact that it resided in a fishbowl with wheels, filled with black liquid that sloshed as the others talk. Or maybe the liquid itself is sentient.

"And what is your business in Teeneria?" Igor notes the fact that the translator – probably through SIBIL though he had no way of knowing – has inserted an easy name into the translation which will allow the landing team to homogenize the way they refer to the planet. This meant that the system can translate without having to interpret several different names.

"We have noted that you do not have star drive technology, or if you do, it is so far advanced that we can't identify it. Under these circumstances, we'd like to sell the technology to any faction interested in it – or to all of them."

This time there is no ripple. The group of envoys simply go completely still. Eventually, one of the Humanoids, a large, grey being covered in iridescent fur – or possibly very fine spines – speaks again: "And what would the price for this technology be?"

"We need to understand what you have to offer before we can negotiate a price."

"Fair enough. You are authorized to enter Teeneria. We are beaming a copy of the port bylaws – please attempt to keep them in mind. If you need to get in touch with us, simply use the frequency we have provided along with the bylaws. We'll be expecting your contact." They led us through the blast door, and the welcoming committee split up.

"They'll probably rendezvous as soon as we're out of sight," Illiadus says. In the charade through which the Marine has pretended to be leading the group, Igor has almost forgotten the Captain is there. Almost, but not quite; Illiadus isn't the sort of person one simply forgets. "They don't have star drive tech, and they want it desperately. We'll be the main item on the agenda until we leave." She stops and looks around. "And, from the looks of things, we'd have been the main item even if we'd come peddling furry heated earmuffs."

Igor looks around, slowly noticing the signs that his captain has incorporated at a glance. All spaceports are very similar, in that there is a huge trading bazaar somewhere near the shuttle docking area. All spaceports are similar in that the sales area is dirty, colorful, untidy and noisy.

But a closer look reveals that all is not well. There is rust on some of the blast doors, which is a sign that they are underused. Vendor stalls actually look like they have been there for a while, as opposed to having been set up quickly, a stop on the way to another port.

The bustle is also somewhat subdued. While no one on the team has ever seen any of the races present, and there seems to be at least six – the four they'd already seen, plus a scurrying insectoid type about the size of a medium-sized dog and another species which consists of sentient electric / gas symbiotes which move around the bazaar using a motley assortment of robotic bodies. These last lumber, roll and crawl all over, and it is impossible for any member of a different species to understand the relationships between individuals. Finally, there seem to be variations on each of these –perhaps answering to a fashion in gene modding. Randomly positioned tentacles seem to be in vogue this season, for some reason, at least for the humanoids.

Despite the number and variety of races, and the size of the bazaar area, there is very little energy in the air. It just feels wrong.

"How long until the first unofficial visit, do you think?"

Igor starts. If there is one thing he isn't expecting it's for Illiadus to use him as a sounding board – but then, he isn't actually sure why she'd brought him along, so that might just have been it. His money, though, is still on "human shield" in case things go to hell down here. "What unofficial visit?"

The Captain sighs. "Look around. There are six sentient species sharing a single system – at least six that we know of. Do you really think they're all united and get along? No way." She shakes her head. "As soon as we got down here, wheels went onto motion to get us alone, and to see if any one of the groups can convince us to sell to them exclusively."

"And what happens if we don't sell to them?"

"Well, that depends on how smart they are, and how desperate. If they're smart, they can probably deduce that any culture that has stardrives is far enough advanced that the ship we arrived in will be able to deal easily with anything the system can throw at us – and surgically, too. A smart race will know that we can completely destroy only them without hurting our relationship with the other five."

They walk past a couple of stalls that Igor would like to inspect, but he says nothing and keeps walking. Not many people on the *Ekatarina* get to interact directly with the captain, and he is going to listen.

"Of course, all of that goes out the window if they're really desperate. If any of the groups are, they might risk killing us – which wouldn't be too hard down here, really – just to keep us from selling the stuff to one of the other species. It all depends on what they feel they have to lose"

"Do you actually think one of the groups would be that hard up?"

"No."

"Oh, good."

"I'm convinced that all of them are, not just one" Illiadus replies. She turns and gives him a strange smile. "Which is actually what makes it fun. Come on, let's go see what the merchandise looks like."

Glancing at one of the tables, Igor grimaces. "Doesn't look like there's anything here that an intern in engineering couldn't cobble together in around five minutes. And I don't see anything in the way of art or clothing."

This time, the Captain's look is pure evil. "You're looking at the wrong kind of merchandise." She walks on, stopping to inspect the wares that one of the iridescent humanoids has on display. From up close, it looks like it is actually crenellated skin.

From what Igor can tell, the table holds motorcycle parts.

Ekluni looks around. The Captain's delegation is ambling aimlessly around the spaceport. That isn't her problem.

"Let's go this way," she tells one of the two hulking Marines they'd given her as bodyguards. "There has to be a bar around here somewhere."

"Shouldn't we stay with the Captain?"

"She can take care of herself."

"I don't know. We should probably stick with them."

Ekluni studies him. The purple sheen was brighter than on most Marines, a sure sign that it hasn't been out in the light much, and that the gene-mods have been done recently. Perhaps as recently as the past couple of days.

So, he is a new fish… but it still feels strange to see a Marine nervous about something as routine as a bodyguard job for the Intelligence team. His companion, silent and obeying without question is much more what she is accustomed to.

"Don't sweat it. We'll be fine, and you won't have to do too much standing around waiting for the captain to make up her mind about stuff."

"I suppose you're right. What are we doing?"

"Our job is to try to understand the political undercurrents here, something our analysts can reconstruct from observing the interactions between the races. But right now, we're looking for something." This was more than he needed to know. After all, he was just along as muscle. But she knew he'd ask.

"What?"

"A fight. Now relax."

The first approach takes longer than the Captain has anticipated. Igor can tell simply from looking at the way she fidgets. It is clear she isn't nervous – everyone on the *Ekatarina* has seen her unflinching in the face of one life-and-death crisis after another – but she is definitely impatient. She'd been extremely reluctant to find lodgings the night before, which will only be resolved when the spaceport dims the lights and the peddlers pack up their belongings.

But on the second day, the leader of their Marine team is suddenly involved in a commotion. Before anyone can remotely identify what the trouble is, the small group has been peacefully but firmly herded into an official-looking enclosure – where all signs of uniformed officials disappear within seconds of their arrival.

"Ah, finally," Illiadus breathes. "I wonder which faction it is."

The question is answered almost immediately, as one of the large globes filled with dark liquid enters the chamber from a cleverly hidden door in what appears to be a solid metal wall.

"Greetings," it says. "We apologize for the drama, but it was imperative that no one else knew we were in consultation with you."

"We?" the Marine captain asks, still playing his role as leader of the group. "Who do you mean by *we*? And while you're at it, who are these others who need to be so careful of?"

"Apologies once again. I represent the–" another clicking monstrosity of a noise which the system doesn't even attempt to translate. "We have been oppressed and discriminated against by the races who control the system for centuries, as you can imagine. The technology you offer, if genuine, could be our road to safety."

"What we offer is merely a small fraction of our capabilities," the Marine responds.

Igor wonders whether the creature's position is actually an honest one. After all, it – or one very much like it – have been present in the welcoming committee, while at least two other races haven't been represented. Plus, the officials that had herded them had probably been real (or someone would have warned them over the comm). And that secret tunnel probably hasn't been installed without moving a whole bunch of influence. He wonders what the liquid race really had in mind – but knows the *Ekatarina* will be long gone before he finds out.

"Even so, we shall require a demonstration."

"I believe that before reaching that point we would have to discuss the terms of payment, would we not?"

"We have access to all kinds of currency – in amounts that no other group on the planet can match."

So much for their position as persecuted and powerless pawns in the system's great game, Igor thinks. But Illiadus seems to ignore the comment, instead meeting the Marine captain's eye, giving him a significant look.

"That is comforting," the Marine replies. "But in order to run a demonstration, you would have to come onto the *Ekatarina*, our starship. And in order to allow this, we need to know two things – what your bodies are capable of, and whether you have large numbers of workers at your disposal in case we have to do some modifications to the ship."

"We are sentient algae colonies, so you have little to fear from us on board your ship. We need these globes and the liquid to survive outside of the oceans of our home world. You could say that we bring our home with us."

"As for workers, the constructs that carry our sentience can be fitted with numerous extensions and capabilities. Any one of us can replace dozens of workers from the other races."

"Ah, but can you get dozens of workers from the other races to work for you, if we should need to have them dispersed throughout the ship."

The globe paused, perhaps thinking, perhaps communicating in some way with absent confederates, perhaps just counting its availability.

"How many would we need?"

"A few hundred."

"I don't think so. The other races would certainly notice if we took so many. And they would ask huge wages to accompany us on any type of mission."

The conversation then goes on to discuss possible payment terms and other minutia, and ends when the Marine captain says: "We'll think about it. We will send a communication to the following frequency when we have an answer. Please make certain that it's being monitored."

With that, the group from the *Ekatarina* exits the room the same way they'd entered. Illiadus catches the Marine's eye on the way out and shakes her head.

Ekluni smiles. Dusk is falling and the bar is, supposedly, closing for the night. One of the locals, one with particularly ugly tentacles, comes to their booth to charge them for their drinks and shoo them away. She pays, wondering where the hell Intelligence had found the strange little coins that paid for drinks without skipping a beat, and then smiles at the creature.

"I don't want to leave," she says, keeping her phrasing simple enough for the translator.

"You must leave."

"No. I want to go where everyone else went. Back there." She points towards a blank wall at the rear of the bar, a wall which has slid aside a dozen times to allow aliens of all races through. Aliens, yes, but all native to this particular planetary system. She puts a big pile of local coinage on the table.

The waiter doesn't even look at it. "No."

"Bryce," she says to the frightened Marine whose name she hasn't bothered to learn. "Squeeze him a little for me, will you?"

This time, the guy complies without a word. He is a slow learner, perhaps, but not totally hopeless. He envelopes the nearest tentacle in one enormous hand and squeezes.

The alien lets out a strangled squeak, a strangely tiny sound for such an imposing form, and begins to wave its remaining tentacles in a circular pattern.

Ekluni notes everything. Her eidetic memory will capture every detail of the denizens' actions and then, when it is time to write her report, spew it back up for official consumption. Her initial analysis is that the waiter is signaling for help.

She seems to be right. Two more of the tentacled servers approach the table and the Marines leap into action.

They are good at their job. Seconds later, the bar's staff has been reduced to immobility—she hopes their analysis of the local's anatomy is correct, and that they are merely unconscious—and the *Ekatarina's* not-so-diplomatic contingent is busy scanning the back wall.

"Should be simple enough to open. All we need to do is send an infrared signal to this sensor here. Let me just see which frequency we need to use. There."

The door slides open and they stride confidently inside.

"Jackpot," Ekluni says. "Everyone's here."

A crowd of locals greet them. Unlike the ones who'd met with the Captain—Ekluni is getting the information feed directly from intelligence—these aren't from any specific race. All the planet's species mix together in a way that just doesn't happen out in the marketplace.

In fact, there are species, or perhaps subspecies, that aren't even represented by the delegation that have met the ship. One or two of the people in the bar seem completely different from anyone else they'd seen. There were even a couple of insectoids… who aren't even supposed to be anywhere near there.

Every single head—and a few carrier tanks—turns toward them almost as soon as they'd set foot inside.

Silence falls over the room. In fact, it is quiet enough for Ekluni to hear the hissing of the hidden panel as it slides shut behind them.

The scared Marine steps between the suddenly angry crowd and Ekluni.

"I think we're going to have that fight, now," he says.

Captain Illiadus' already foul mood deepens when it transpires that the next race to contact them are the insectoids. The group goes through the same conversation with them that they have with the algae… and with much the same result. This time, Illiadus kicks a wall when they exit the small warren of service tunnels that the insects have chosen as their meeting place.

"Dammit," is all she says.

Igor wonders, for the millionth time, what it is that Illiadus wants. Both the algae globes and the insectoids have essentially told the *Ekatarina* to take whatever they want, certain that the stardrive technology will pay back any sacrifice whatsoever. Convinced that any price they could pay will make them the winners in the transaction. Sure that they were robbing the *Ekatarina* blind.

All for a few tech trinkets that are centuries out of date.

And yet, they stay, waiting, Igor assumes, for a third contact. Illiadus grows so impatient to be dragged or tricked into some off-site encounter that when the actual approach occurs, she almost misses it completely.

The group has stuck to its routine, and is walking through the bazaar, examining merchandise that they'd been unimpressed with from the outset, other than some raw materials they'd already purchased enough of to refit the ship – and have subsequently seen what seems like a million times since – when one of the big humanoids with iridescent skin blocks their way.

Illiadus attempts to brush past, the way they have to avoid so many other sales pitches. The merchant stands his ground, specifically zeroing in on her. "I think I have a proposition that may interest you, Leader."

Igor freezes. None of the communication with the locals have given any inkling that Illiadus is in command – clearly, something is up.

The Captain also stops dead. "Are you certain that we should be discussing this here?"

"Is it any less private than a secret discussion in a holding cell or a maintenance tunnel?"

"Apparently not."

"Besides, we want to see which way you'll lean before committing ourselves. This way, we will have been able to improve whatever offer you are considering. Of course, the fact that you don't seem to have a particular preference has forced our hand."

"You don't seem to be working too hard to strengthen your bargaining position. Why are you telling us this?" Suspicion is written all over the captain's face but, at the same time, she seems much more eager than she had when the Marine was negotiating with the other two races. Something about this particular approach has interested her.

The alien goes through a complicated set of motions which Igor interprets as a shrug even though it reminds Igor of the motions of one of the ship's prostitutes. A slight bending of the waist and a rhythmic pulsing. "Our analysts, in their infinite wisdom, have come to the conclusion that you are looking for something very specific, and that either we have it or we don't. So, we've decided to ask what you want in exchange for the technology."

"Don't you think we should go somewhere more private to discuss that?"

"We are not being overheard."

A quick comm to the ship, audible on everyone's earpieces, confirmed that there is an interference field in that sector of the bazaar that will be enough to block any listening devices at the current level of planetary technology.

"Fair enough. And don't you want to know about the technology, and demonstrations, and all of that?"

Again, the shrug. "We know what you've told the others. We'd be willing to attend a demonstration onboard your starship, and we have no trouble bringing three hundred able-bodied workers to the demonstration."

Illiadus gives him a very curt nod. "Agreed. We can discuss the price once you've seen the demonstration. We'll be expecting you at our ship."

She turns away, giving Igor a quick glance. "I will be extremely happy to get off this planet. I've seen many ports in my life, and they're all dirty, desolate places. But this is the first time I've ever been to a port that was actually boring."

Igor shudders, wondering when they'd be hit by armed troops, and wishing that the Marines would hurry up – but they seemed in no hurry.

However, there was no attack as they crossed the bazaar, and they were even allowed to reach their ship in safety.

About ten thousand clicks from the *Ekatarina,* a message is commed into the shuttle. "Three attack cruisers, moving at intercept velocities approaching fast. They should be in firing range in under fifteen seconds. I recommend you brace for impact – the shielding should hold easily, but some of the inertia might make it through the dampers."

"Is there any particular reason you're letting them hit us?" Illiadus asks. She didn't seem too concerned.

"We actually want to analyze some of their strategy for the database."

"Ah, how fun." Illiadus activates the impact webbing. Igor hurries to imitate her.

The first concussion nearly loosens Igor's sphincters, and so does the second, but after that, the rocking movement becomes routine. The *Ekatarina* analysts keep up a running monologue about what the attackers are doing, and what kind of energy they are releasing at the heavily shielded shuttle. Nothing compares to the forces that the Scourge have routinely aimed at incursion craft.

After a few minutes, the voice from the *Ekatarina* says: "OK, we're neutralizing the threat."

And the rocking just stops. Igor wonders what the aliens last thoughts are – and whether they'd had the time to realize that they were about to be destroyed by technology beyond their imagination. He also wonders who has had the balls to let the Captain's shuttle get hammered.

The rest of the trip is uneventful.

"No, I don't think we're going to be able grab any of the ringleaders," Ekluni says over the comm. "In fact, I'm not completely certain we can get out without doing serious damage to the people here... and I estimate we've hit on a neural point of the liberal resistance."

"Can you get out of the bar?" the *Ekatarina* replies.

"I think so. The Marine's shields still have a couple of minutes of full charge, but these guys are really mad. Do you think you can get a shuttle down here in time."

"Yes."

"Really? We would have to break all the protocols we've established so far regarding flight speeds."

"I think we're past that point now."

"OK. I'm not arguing."

It is a fighting retreat. Bottles fly at the Marines, and a couple of unspeakably low-tech projectile weapons are discharged in their direction. The Marines calmly turn their disruptors upon any aggressors they can identify and leave them twitching on the floor.

But disruptors are not the ideal weapon for crowd control. They are pinpoint weapons, suitable for taking down individual targets without doing too much damage... the kind of thing issued to troops to avoid diplomatic incidents in places where you aren't really expecting to be attacked.

So, they fall back yard by yard. There is no question about losing the fight, of course. The Marines have plenty of other ordnance at their disposal, and they will use it if their lives are in danger. But as long as they are shielded, the crowd is more of a nuisance than a threat to them.

Which is more than Ekluni can say. If one of the projectiles—ancient or not—happens to catch her, then she is dead.

"Let's move, guys," she says.

They redouble their pace. The sliding door is already ten meters ahead—kept open by the packed mob of locals—and the main entrance to the bar just at their backs.

Ekluni tries the door; locked.

"Of course." She doesn't waste any time, simply blows the lock out and pushes the door open.

A scream of superheated air being pushed aside announces the arrival of the promised shuttle. It flies low over the city, causing the few members of the population still out and about to cover their ears, and lands ten yards from their position.

The Marine's shields flicker and die.

"Run for the shuttle," Ekluni cries.

She reaches the ramp first and steps inside to help the Marines in. One of them dives past her, into the reaches of the shuttle.

Lance Corporal Bryce nearly makes it. He is just six or seven feet away when something tears a big chunk out of his left leg and sends him sprawling to the floor. Undaunted, he begins to crawl forward.

Ekluni reacts instantly. "Cover me."

She sprints out to the prone soldier and tries to get her shoulder under Bryce's arm. He's the guy who'd been scared.

"Come on, soldier. Let's go home," she says.

But even as she says it, she knows it is no use. Out of the corner of her eye, she sees the crowd, emboldened by the success, surging towards them. They will never survive—or if they do, it is because the guy in the shuttle instigates a massacre. She hopes his orders preclude that.

The crowd hits her and buffets them into the shuttle, bumping her head in the process. Everything goes wobbly for a while.

Ekluni wakes to find herself in the middle of a standoff.

On one side, the unhurt Marine stands, weapon drawn. On the other, seven locals of all shapes and sizes huddle around one figure holding a projectile rifle. By the air pressure and the sense of acceleration, she assumes they are in space.

"Hold your fire," she says.

"Yes, Sir," the Marine replies. "I was just waiting for you to get back on your feet and decide where to go next."

"What's happening?"

"We're in a holding pattern."

"Why?"

"Because I want to come with you," the alien with the rifle declares.

It takes a moment for Ekluni to realize that the words have been spoken to her in Polis Standard, not in any of the alien languages they've heard so far. And yet, it is extremely clear that the alien is from this system… a system that, as far as anyone knows, has had no contact with any civilized race in recent times.

Ekluni studies the figure. Blue-skinned and humanoid, attractive in her alien way even though she barely has any hair.

At least she doesn't have any tentacles.

"My name is Farko Tiresias. I want to come with you." The alien stops as if searching for the right word. "We. We want to come with you."

"You attacked us."

"We thought you came from the delegates. We thought you were doing the government's work."

"Why would we do that?"

"Everyone knows you're here to trade. Perhaps it was part of the trade." The alien seems to shrug, or close enough to it. "I see we were in error."

"You can say that again," the hurt Marine Bryce says from where he's been lying. He looks like he wants to shoot the whole lot of them, but his un-Marine-like behavior doesn't extend quite that far.

"Stay out of this, soldier." She turns back to Farko. "Why should I take you with me? You attacked us."

Farko drops the weapon on the floor and kicks it over. "Take us or kill us. If you send us back, we're dead all the same. There are many people who prefer to keep the balance as it is… if they can't destroy the other races, at least they can keep the lower castes from becoming a problem. That is the true evil of the current stalemate: it keeps the upper castes in power because anyone who complains is a traitor to their species."

This is way above Ekluni's paygrade. She is a data collector and sometimes analyst. Humanitarian considerations aren't part of her job description.

Then she smiles. She knows what to do with this kind of stuff.

Kick it upstairs.

She turns to the hale Marine. "Cover them." Then she bends over Corporal Bryce. "You think you can stand?"

"I can try. Hurts like hell."

"Let's see if I can find something to staunch that bleeding."

Bryce gets to his feet.

"Yes, Sir. Thank you, Sir."

She smiles. He is still a pretty slow learner, but maybe he'd become a real Marine eventually.

An unknown faction—presumably the same guys who'd attacked the Captain's shuttle—attempt to assault the small flotilla bringing the buyers to the *Ekatarina*, but they aren't allowed to cause any damage. Three different attack formations are vaporized before they even get close enough to fire.

Igor is happy to see that the terror he'd experienced riding in the shuttle with Captain Illiadus has at least allowed for an effective tactical analysis.

He is also a bit surprised by the fact that he'd been selected to come along to meet the delegation. Other than the jaunt to the spaceport, which seems more a question of being in the wrong place at the wrong time when the decision was made, he'd usually been valued – if that was the right word – more for clerical and organizational skills than for really being part of the officer cadre. He feels completely out of place in the receiving hold as they watch the small fleet berth with the hangar bay's docking tubes.

The alien humanoids filter into a large pressurized deck where they seem to organize into two groups, a small one whose members are taller, with somewhat more iridescent skin, and a larger group whose members stand in unruly ranks. Of this latter group, no two seemed to be of the same species, except for the fact that they are all similarly sized and roughly humanoid. Tentacles, extra limbs and even rearranged body configurations abound.

Ironbear, whose presence in a commercial delegation is yet another unexplained mystery, grins. "Curious bunch, aren't they? They'll sprain a neck looking around like that."

"They'll have plenty of time to learn about the ship later. But, more importantly, what do you think?" Illiadus replies.

The Major looks at the massed aliens. "I think they'll do nicely. One way or another. The outfitters are going to be pissed about all the tentacles, but they'll survive."

The conversation goes right over Igor's head, but he has a feeling he isn't going to like the outcome.

On SIBIL's advice, they walk up to the smaller group and welcomes them aboard. Captain Illiadus introduces herself more formally and tells the delegation that she is delighted to meet the Entik Minister of Commerce. "We have the demonstration set up for you, if you come with us."

"What about the menials you requested? Where would you like us to instruct them to work?"

"They can't really work aboard the ship. Everything is automated. Leave them where they are for now."

If this confuses them, the grey humanoids don't show it. The Minister simply says. "Lead. We will follow. We are eager to see the stardrive."

The deck where the demonstration has been set up is located on the outer edge of the *Ekatarina*. It might have represented a very old technology, but the energies of an ancient fusion-ion drive can do a lot of damage to the interior decoration of even a vessel as Spartan as the *Ekatarina*.

They reach a viewport and Illiadus takes over.

"We know that your technology has advanced to the point in which ion drives are reasonably viable, and we also know that you've managed to solve the problem of getting good thrust out of them, as opposed to just relying on chemical rockets for fast acceleration – some of the interceptors that attacked our delegation had ion-drive supplements, according to our readings. What was clear to us even as we approached the system was that you don't yet have high-efficiency fusion power – in fact, we see that you're still at mid-level Tokamak research. Your problem is that using toroidal magnetic fields for plasma containment is a reasonable alternative for planetary trips, but you run into a fuel-mass crisis for any trips of over a light year or so, especially if you are planning manned missions."

Igor wonders how they are translating concepts such as *light years*, but assumes that continuous monitoring of all the planet's communications over the last few days has probably made the translator database system (perhaps aided by SIBIL herself) more of an expert on the different planetary dialects than anyone on the surface. The translation is probably perfect.

"Essentially, this problem is solved by adequately modeling the quantum chaos mathematics within the plasma, allowing the energy to be harnessed at nearly one hundred percent efficiency. This coupled with some work on the energy drainage patterns of the ion drives themselves leads to an energy system that can cross interstellar distances of hundreds of light years with enough power for crew needs and suspended animation. The suspended animation itself is another technology that you don't currently have, but we have accessed your medical research and designed a system that will function perfectly with your body chemistry – but not for any of the other races on the planet."

Illiadus steps towards the delegation.

"We are offering all three of the technologies: the containment technology for the fusion reactor, the efficiency optimizers for the ion drives, and the life support system. Please have your observation satellites focus on that ship over there. I believe that the energy profile and ship performance will convince you that you can cross interstellar distances with no more problems. Please note that the drive system is on the exterior of the shuttle, so there is no shielding."

Igor is then forced to watch the demonstration. He has no real way to tell but, although the small shuttle on which the drive system is mounted seem slow as hell to him, their visitors look like they are in awe. Ripples of movement and expression wash across them periodically – probably coinciding with communication from their analysts.

After a while, one of them speaks.

"The demonstration is sufficient. We are willing to pay for this." He pauses, starts to speak and pauses again. "But we still don't know what you want."

"Oh, you've already brought us what we want. We are sending the schematics to your ships at this moment, using your engineering conventions." Illiadus says.

"We don't understand."

"The menials in the hold. We need them to replenish our supply of Sailors and Marines."

"That is impossible. Ask for anything else."

"We are not asking. We have already taken them."

"Return them immediately." The iridescence of the creature's skin almost seems to glow.

"They are just menials. You will not miss them."

"You don't understand. They are menials in this cycle, but they will cycle out and become leaders in three years, after we've genetically altered them away from the job-specific bodies they currently have." This explains the strange body configurations, at least. "We, in turn, will become menials. Among those menials are our brothers, fathers, friends."

"Well, by the next cycle they will be Polis sailors and Marines. That should help somewhat."

"They won't accept willingly."

"We think they will, after a while. And if they don't," she shrugs. "If they don't, we have ways to change their behavior without doing too much damage to the brain."

"This is unacceptable."

Illiadus turns to them. Igor would have hated to be on the other side of that look.

"Right now, your choice is simple: you can return to the surface as the delegation who brought your race to ascendancy… or you can join your brothers, fathers and friends. It's all the same to me."

Minutes later, they watch the delegation and their now-nearly-empty flotilla make their way back to the surface.

"Should we shoot them out of the sky? They won't be happy about this," Ironbear asks.

"They can't hurt us. And the Polis keeps its side of the bargain, even if the other side doesn't like the way it turned out. They just traded three hundred people for the chance to make their race great. They ended up way ahead, and their future historians will realize it."

"This is probably how those *deal with the devil* legends get started, you know that, don't you?"

"That's my problem," Illiadus replies. "your problem is keeping them contained."

"Already done."

"And keeping them fed. Ensign Camina should be able to help you organize the logistics of that."

Igor's heart sinks.

"So, let's make him a temporary Marine. Give him a rank or something and get him to work." She turns away, already discussing how to get onto the second planet to harvest a few of the insectoids, who, she seems to believe, will be excellent in low-gee environments.

And Igor is led off, thinking that he will feel a lot better without knowing the answer to any of the mysteries.

But, just like these new alien recruits, he really doesn't have much of a choice.

Captain's Log, The Ekatarina

By some small miracle our illegal impressment of three hundred fresh alien recruits resulted in zero casualties. With the help of the alien Farko Tiresias we have located a suitable world in this solar system in which to begin indoctrination. For the first time in years, I am beginning to feel hope. End Log.

Boot Camp

by Brian Bigelow

"There are only two ways off this island, maggots. A pine box or a Greyhound bus!"

– anonymous U.S. Marine Corps Drill Instructor

Ship's Chronometer: 2434 AD

Sergeant Vladimir Irena and Lieutenant Camina, formerly Ensign Igor Camina, stand before the three hundred surly alien recruits milling about in the center of The Eketarina's main hanger. Two-dozen armed Marines stand on the periphery with pulse rifles held at the ready.

Sgt. Irena scowls at the motley group. With his pasty white skin more than a few unwise lads over the years, who had read the classic novel Dracula, quipped *vampire* under surly breaths only to find out that a master of combat Jiu-Jutsu is a far worse nightmare than any Transylvanian bloodsucker. In reality, Sgt. Irena is an albino whose unprotected epidermis can only withstand exposure to an earthlike sun for a minute before suffering first-degree burns. A nearly invisible, micro-thin body stocking made that a negligible occurrence, at least from the neck down, which explains Sgt. Irena's penchant for wearing his pressure helmet with polarized visor down whenever planet-side.

After serving over a decade in this war he has become extremely short tempered with the abject hatred he carries. A perpetual scowl never leaves his sun-scarred face and it is accentuated by his piercing black eyes. Never again can he go to his home colony at "Bona Terra."

It is now a scorched and desolate void. He has shared "Ten's" original xenocidal sentiments and had even volunteered for the suicide crew on the captured Scourge scout ship, renamed *The Revenge*, that had been fitted with the dark matter fountain bomb that had ended that foul race of murderers. Unfortunately, there were only so many available berths, and the ranks of volunteers had numbered in the thousands.

The Scourge is no more, but Sgt Irena's hatred has only grown darker and colder in the aftermath. His wife and children are gone forever, and all that is left is his seething animosity toward every day left to live until the end of his cursed life. There are even some moments he actually wishes the Scourge still exist, for thus he would have a target to vent his anger upon.

Beside the Sergeant stands Lt. Camina, just recently transferred from space navy officer status to that of a space Marine officer. Every bone and muscle in his body aches from the four-day condensed OTS that Irena has put him through in preparation for this new assignment. Camina's hatred for Captain Tennyson has reached an all-time high.

Sgt. Irena takes up a position directly in front of the recruits and shouts in barely controlled fury, "fall in, you slimy scumbags. I said fall in now."

Doing their best to comply, it takes a full minute for the hung over, nauseous, and terrified contingent of three hundred alien humanoids to form something vaguely resembling ranks. They'd spent the last seventy-two hours under high acceleration with nothing but the ship's bad excuse for liquor to sedate them. The day will not get any better.

"Line up, side by side men, elbows touching," Sgt. Irena spits.

The shuffle of civilian boots on deck plating is the only sound as Vladimir watches them in disgust.

"Attention," Sgt. Irena snaps as Captain Illiadus strides up beside the Sergeant.

"Thank you, Drill Instructor," Illiadus says, "at ease." She quickly gives them the once over, flips on her personal com-link, then begins to speak slowly, the instant translation blaring from various speakers built into the wall, "you former civilians have volunteered to become part of a great adventure. Not only will you be the first members of your respective races to ever venture outside this solar system, but you will now train to become Soldiers and Crewman of one of the most distinguished and noble space navies to voyage across the greater galactic reach. The Terran Expeditionary Space Force."

Sgt. Irena smiles an evil smile.

The captain continues, "some of you will become Space Marines and some of you will become Crewmen of The Terran Space Navy, depending on your own particular abilities. As you will learn in the months to come, your little solar system is not the center of the universe. The greater galaxy in which we exist is populated by thousands of sentient civilizations. Until a recent catastrophe, most of the higher developed solar systems were connected via an artificially created transport network of FTL Jump Gates. And most recently, because of a great war that we recently won, most of these civilizations had joined to form a loose Galactic confederation. It is my strong hope that when we finally re-connect with both the galactic transport network and the galactic government, advanced robot ships will be sent back here to create new jump gates that will connect your solar system to your thousands of neighbors. It may take years before this happens, but one day you may very well return here as ambassadors and heroes."

Illiadus gives a moment for this to sink in before she begins speaking again, "basic training will commence after I have finished speaking. Your instruction will be intense and a lot will be packed into a short amount of time. Pay attention to everything you are being taught, your lives may very well depend on it. In fact, I'm sure they will."

"Sgt. Irena," Illiadus adds, "Good luck."

"Yes, Sir."

Without waiting to see mother's darlings put to exercising, Illiadus strides from the hanger and into an adjoining corridor. Walking down the hallway, Tennyson considers the hundred and one details that need to be dealt with to turn this rabble into an efficient warship crew.

She is so lost in thought she almost runs into the doorway to the CIC. Entering, and nodding to the night-shift exec, she crosses the room and drops down into her cocoon-like chair, quickly grabs up the interface helmet and slaps it down on her head in a single practiced move.

Tennyson suddenly finds herself standing on a cobalt landscape that stretches into infinity. The atmosphere smells of blueberries and cyan light permeated the surroundings. A long blue robe appears in the misty sky above her, flowing as if a strong wind is gusting. It drops through the air rapidly to hover in front of her. Then the hood of the blue robe lowers to show the yellow eyes and blonde hair of a twenty-two year old woman with an impish grin.

"Yes Captain," SIBIL says, "what can I do for you?"

"Please keep an eye out for a couple of unoccupied planets in close proximity to each other, one with a lethal atmosphere for suit training, and the other a breathable atmosphere, at least by permeable-face-mask standards. And find them in the next two days, okay?"

The seemingly sentient virtual entity swirls around in the hyperspace of Tennyson's quantum helmet, "I'll see what I can do Captain, but no promises."

"Have I ever asked you for one, SIBIL?" the Captain replies.

SIBIL ignores the edge of sarcasm in the Captain's weary voice.

Four days later Captain Illiadus shouts from her command chair, "Major Ironbear, can you begin a training mission on the outside of the ship today? Using just trainees, right now?"

"Sure Captain, I'll have them suited up by the airlock in five."

"Make it four," Illiadus replies, "I'm timing you."

Though the chain of command has informed her the trainees are progressing efficiently, Illiadus needs to see with her own eyes that these former ground-pounders are getting used to maneuvering in space with body armor and the equipment they'll be carrying on any and all EVAs.

"And Major Ironbear," Iliadus says, "make it live fire."

"Yes Captain."

Firing a blaster in space isn't anything like firing it on a planet with an atmosphere. The blast will come out of the barrel as you will expect though the only sound you will hear is what echoes from the weapon and into and along the inner lining of your suit up to your helmet, a dull crackling sound. With no atmosphere to contend with the energy discharge will move more efficiently than on the surface of your average gravity well. The main problem is that if you aren't braced or anchored in place on the hull with gravity boots or a secured line the gun will push you the opposite way into the relative void of space thus satisfying the laws of physics. And if that happens, without judicious use of portable suit jets not only are you not coming back, but no one will be able to get you.

Tennyson remembers this happening in one of her own first EVA skirmishes as a wet Lieutenant near the beginning of the war with the Scourge. One of her troops had unloaded a pulse rifle on full auto and rocketed out into deep space. There were no shuttles or landers within a million miles and the ship did not have enough fuel to engage in a rescue. Tennyson remembered that scared voice, a short nineteen-year-old woman fresh out of basic training, emanating from her helmet speaker. The cries of terror had seared themselves into the young officer's brain…

The main upper airlock splits apart and Captain Illiadus activates her magnetic books and walks out onto the ship's hull.

Crewman First Class Farko Tiresias's edgy inexperienced voice breaks into the Captain's wandering thoughts on the com link, "three of the cameras are out on the starboard side of the ship, Captain."

"That would be an excellent training mission for the new crew members unless they can be bypassed instead."

"No, they can't be bypassed though we still have the long-range sensors. Someone will have to replace the cameras ASAP. We are blind to any attacks that are coming from starboard."

"Okay Farko, notify Major Ironbear to have a dozen of the Crewman Trainees assigned."

Ironbear delegates authority for the mission of replacing the cameras to Marine Sergeant Mikhail Aristov. The six-foot tall human has been through many missions in frozen hell holes and has come out of them all successfully. A long list of decorations and impressive accomplishments fill out his service record. He is also one of the few who have single handedly taken out two of the Scourge's single-man scout ships with nothing but a shoulder mounted pulse rifle. The rest of the members of his small Marine unit were killed in that attack where Mikhail was the sole survivor. Because he survived, he was elevated a couple of ranks to Sergeant.

Mikhail disdainfully leads ten of the swabbie grunts in free fall training and getting used to their new space suits and magnetic boots. They also test the two-way suit com systems. One tall and gangly looking yellow, feathered alien is having trouble adjusting one of the helmets to fit their oblong crested head. After a couple of frustrating attempts that are unsuccessful the birdlike recruit is sent to peel potatoes in the main mess. Now the Sergeant only has nine for the contingent which might work better. Just as they are getting ready to exit the hatch the order comes in to replace some of the cameras.

"Okay, there's been a slight change in mission so wait a moment before you go out. We're going to replace some of the cameras while we're out and about, give me a second or two and I'll grab them." He goes to one of the wall bins and grabs three of the instruments that he puts in netting bag he grabs from one of the other bins. Securing the bag to his waist hook and handing some tethers to two of the trainees he now heads to the hatch. Waiving to them all they follow him out.

For a moment, the Sergeant closes his eyes and floats beside the ship enjoying the sensation of weightlessness. After a few moments of being carried away he remembers the trainees that are all hovering around. "Be careful when you are in weightlessness, you can float off but you'll usually move with the ship. Use your jets this way to get to the ship." Hitting a short burp he floats toward the ship. "Don't hit it too long or you'll end up bouncing off of the ship and there's no way to tell where you'll end up at."

Turning his body so that his feet contacted first, he waited for the rest of them. He winced as one of the recruits thudded into the side of the ship. Luckily there is a pintle hook for tethering within reach that the man thankfully grabs in time. Vladimir thins of how close that could have been, "be careful out here, maggots!"

Doing a quick head count to make sure he hasn't lost any of them he breathes a sigh of relief. Waving them to follow him he leads them to the first camera to be replaced. "Okay, the boots are magnetic. When you pick up your foot the magnets should let go and you'll end up doing big steps…"

On the opposite side of the ship Sergeant Irena is training a small contingent of five Marine grunts in zero atmosphere personal weaponry. There are some issues fitting Lt. Camina into one of the space suits, he is so big and burly.

For the next hour Irena's grunts aim and fire their weapons into deep space. This is to give them a feel for shooting a blaster in zero gravity.

Then, happily, a passing asteroid makes a convenient target for their practice. Making sure that it is in a safe position where no resulting micro-meteorites can expel back at them and turn them into hamburger, Irena gives the order to fire. The blasters make short work of the house-sized hunk of rock which goes on its way as a couple of pebbles.

An urgent voice calls out through the suits speakers, "Hey! I've got a problem Sergeant. What do I do now?"

The Sergeant looks around and can see Camina shoot off into space. The Lieutenant is too stiff to bend much and Irena instantly realizes he is not able to reach his suit jet controls.

"I'll see if I can catch you in time," Irena spits out, "everyone, hold your fire," he tells the other trainees, squatting down, turns off the magnets in his own boots, and leaps upward as hard and fast as he can, trying to reach the Lieutenant in time. Irena hits his suit jets twice as long as he normally would, hoping to overtake the rapidly receding Lieutenant.

"Just relax Lieutenant," Irena says calmly, "I'm coming to get you now."

"Okay Sergeant, just hurry please," Camina's normally gruff voice betrays tension and fear.

The two of them shoot past the camera replacement detail. Sergeant Aristov watches them for a moment before turning his attention back to training instruction. "That's why you always make sure you bring a tether with you when you're going to be on the outside of the ship working. You guys are not Space Marines, you're Crewmen. You ain't got no business trying to fly around out here, that's for us badasses. Whenever you punks EVA, you keep your mag boots on and your butts tethered when on a work detail. It won't be long before you are by yourself out here and no one will be able to come to get you if a problem comes up. Too many things that can and will go wrong at the same time will kill you on EVA. Even better, these nasty events will happen without any warning. I shit you not, swabbies. Do you hear me, recruits?"

"Aye aye, Sergeant," the chorus of voices reach his ears as they all nervously double-check their tether lines.

Irena grabs a hold of the big Lieutenant's belt. Together they spin as the Sergeant hits suit jets lightly to slow their spinning momentum.

One of Irena's Marine trainees back on the ship unconsciously lets his right index claw glance across his weapon's safety switch. Without realizing it, he triggers the blaster. The weapon fires, impacts, and pierces the trainee right next to him, killing him instantly. The fresh corpse floats away from the ship, its tether undulating behind it. Catching the unintended fratricide out of the corner of his eye, Irena can see the burn mark and hole from the blaster on the dead soldier's suit.

"Bloody hell," Irena growls, "and I ain't even had lunch yet."

"Sergeant," the shocked recruit who has fired the weapon cries out, "I don't know what happened. I swear I didn't pull the trigger. I don't know how…"

"Lighten up, Private Beltroy," Irena growls, "Captain will have a quick drumhead, I'll give her my report, and if she thinks you're worth a second chance we won't have to hang you. Personally, I give you sixty-forty odds."

"Huh… hang me?" Beltroy croaks.

"Like I said," Irena says as he and Camina slowly touch down on the ship's skin, "you'll get your fair day in court."

Beltroy faints in his space suit.

Four weeks later, LT Adoris Djulgun looks up from his view screen as the light reflects off of his green scaly skin, in the CIC, "Captain, SIBIL has found the planet you were looking for. And, ummm… she's asking why you haven't linked with her for over two weeks."

"I'm ignoring the arrogant bitch," Illiadus snaps, "trying to teach her some manners. So, pipe it over to the navigation screen."

"Already done sir," Djulgun replies before stepping over to the horizontal screen that lays atop a large coffin shaped console, "No transmissions of any kind. No abnormal radiation plumes and no heat signatures of anything but plant and small animal life."

The green and brown ball looks perfect.

"And you're sure it's a breathable atmosphere?"

"Yes Captain, the readouts are all nominal. Breathable oxygen and the other necessary elements, there's even earthlike gravity."

"Nonetheless," Illiadus snaps, "standard first footfall protocol until the techno-lung confirmation. Environmental suits until we know it's safe. If it checks out, we'll do a sniff test tomorrow morning followed up by one gee survival-training planet-side. Now, give it a name Ensign."

"A name?" Djulgun replies.

"Yes," Illiadus says, "and I don't want any dam Greek alphabet designations or numbers."

"Ummm, uh," Djulgun stutters, "how about Korbanuss?" The thought brings back a momentary thought of his home planet Nargil in the constellation Lepton. He wants to return one day but it won't be today.

"Say what?" Illiadus asks.

"An aggressive god of war," Djulgun mumbles, "from one of my people's long dead religions."

"Korbanuss," Illiadus says with relish, "oh I like it Ensign. Commander Aithon, enter it into the ship's log."

"Yes, sir," Aithon replies.

Settling into a stationary orbit above the mildly vegetative planet the *Ekatarina* became Korbanuss's first moon.

Overnight, three shuttles are prepared in the main launch bays. Two days later they are ferrying trainees to the surface. Since everyone is wearing bulky environmental suits each shuttle is only able to hold six humanoids at a time. Sgt. Irena is chosen to do the sniff test. Cracking open his polarized visor the scent of sulfur and dust make his nose wrinkle.

"Great," Irena coughs, "bad enough I gotta spend the next four weeks training you gorillas, but I have to do it on a planet that smells like my drunken uncle Frankie's farts. All clear. Everybody strip."

The shuttles lift off and return to the Big E for the next group of trainees.

Where they land on Korbanuss is a wide dusty plain that extends far into the distance. Short, rolling hills covered with multi-colored bushes and trees rise up on the horizon. Sgt. Irena and two Marines reconnoiter the area and find rolls of what can only be described as thick, tiger-striped spiral vines in the bottom of a couple of ravines that have water flowing in them. Otherwise, the immediate area is essentially a desert seemingly devoid of any feral or dangerous life forms. They won't have to worry about being disturbed by any unwelcome visitors anyway. Every footstep causes the fine ground particulates to rise and soon everyone looks like they have been caught in a dust storm.

It takes two days to set up the base camp. Each of the ten prefab shelters are capable of housing fifteen humanoids. The structures are made of two distinct layers of a very tough, almost rip proof, synthetic material that has an insulating air gap between them. At first just a small two foot by two foot pod, all a trainee has to do is press a little blue button and in a few seconds the whoosh of air fills the igloo which practically explodes into existence, a surprising fact that gives the NCOs no shortage of entertainment as shocked trainees lay sprawled in all directions.

Make-shift commodes are hand dug with small titanium shovels into the surrounding countryside a full half mile from the perimeter of the camp. The only problem is the timid weather gives no indication of what direction is down wind.

Though the thick layers of dust everywhere indicate there has been no dramatic air movement for the past week or two, Sgt. Irena sincerely hopes that this planet did not suffer surprise gusts. He can easily envision the igloos, each an overly large silvery ball, blowing and rolling into the distance if the anchor lines are not properly staked into the soil. He slaps the igloo he has just finished securing and is greeted by a "boink" sound, the surface appears to be quite firm. If they do somehow blow away, at least they will be easy to find again with the way their silver skin stands out against the reddish sand and pinkish sky of the planet.

On the third day after planetfall Sgt. Irena leads thirty Marine trainees on a forced march into the wilderness. It is as good an excuse as any to further reconnoiter the surroundings and you might as well do it while you're running. It isn't purely out of spite, as Irena needs to build up their endurance to prepare for assault edification. Irena carries a chambered pulse rifle just in case they run into some sneaky unexpected nasties out in these boondocks. The grunts are only issued training rifles that fire non-lethal particle bursts at holographic drones that will occasionally attack them without notice. It is quite an amazing little invention that fits easily in Irena's right hip pocket. He will randomly push a button and it will send out a 3-D image down range and register when a shot hits it. It will also save a 3-D digital record of the altercation for later review.

After a solid week of non-stop running back and forth over every single hill in a ten-mile perimeter, it is time to have some practice with grenades. A short berm is created two miles from the base camp for the trainees to hide behind after throwing their live grenades. One of the youngest Marine recruits, a thin, red-skinned youth by the name of Narby stands dumbfounded, staring bug-eyed at the fist size purple egg as its tiny digital screen counts down to zero.

"Toss, duck, and cover," Sergeant Irena bellows.

Narby freezes.

A second before the grenade goes off the Sergeant simultaneously jumps up, yanks it out of Narby's hand, tosses it away in a sideways snap of his wrist, tackles Narby knocking them both back over the safe side of the berm, all in what seems like a single move. This is followed a moment later by a huge explosion that lifts everyone at least a foot off of the ground. A single flying bit of superheated tritanium shoots back over the berm's rim and nicks the Sergeant's shoulder, burning through his jacket, and leaving behind a nasty black burn scar just north of his right collarbone.

Ignoring what has to be agonizing pain Irena yells, "what in the name of Andromeda's tits do you think you are doing recruit?!"

Unable to answer, the recruit just lays there with his eyes wide in shock. Turning his head slowly towards the Sergeant, Narby's attention returns from wherever it has momentarily escaped.

"You could have been killed right there, Private Narby," Irena spits, "and then you would have been in a whole world of shit, because you do not have permission to die unless I give it. Do you understand me, you cephalopodic scumbag?"

"Yes Sergeant," Narby yells, standing at attention.

"I can't hear you, loser," Irena yells.

"Yes Sergeant," Narby screams.

"Then drop and give me fifty you stupid, ugly pool of meteor piss," Irena growls.

Though it is an act easier to commit to then actually complete, as Narby possesses three tentacles instead of arms, and while they possess impressive grasping strength, they suck when it came to push-ups. Barely able to complete twenty-five reps, the recruit collapses in exhaustion.

"Good enough," Irena shouts, "now get back in ranks before I rip you a new asshole, you lazy excuse for a nut-sack."

Over the next four weeks only two recruits are killed, both Ship Crew Trainees too slow in running from a landslide resulting from an accidental pulse rifle discharge. There are an additional ten injuries, but nothing that can't be patched up in the Big E's sick bay.

The Crewman trainees are now being shuttled back up to the ship as Sergeant Irena spent the last three days teaching his soon to be graduated Marines the fine art of lethal close-quarters combat. His boys, well, technically four of them were women by their species' standards but god forgive any idiot dumb enough to try to forcibly cop a feel of humanoids whose genitals were protected by retractable two-inch spikes, are getting tough and salty.

The Sergeant wishes he had a little more time for team building with these future combat Marines, but the Captain is getting antsy and wants to get back to their main mission, returning home. They are at nearly full complement and playtime is over.

A day later and the ship is under way. SIBIL has calculated it will take three weeks at top speed to reach the nearest arterial entrance.

For a few days all of the new recruits fall into their final shipboard training schedule. Most of the Marines are put on guard duty at various high security locations around the ship, including the weapons stores, brig, ship's engines, docking bays, and the CIC.

Comfortably ensconced in her cocoon, and wearing her quantum helmet, Illiadus's eyes are closed. Commander Aithon cannot help but notice the slight smile creasing her face. Whatever she is planning, he is sure it will be something dramatic. If there is one thing he has appreciated about being Ten's second-in-command, she definitely has a flare for the dramatic.

"And you have not shared my plans with any of the bridge crew, correct?" Illiadus asks.

"No," SIBIL replies, a look of disgust crossing her face, "and stop asking me. I get it, okay? I learned my lesson. I won't go behind your back with my worries and suppositions anymore. You and only you hear from me first and then decide if I can pass information off to your subordinates. Sheesh."

"Very good," Illiadus smiles, "now. Estimation of how long before interception?"

"Based on all my extrapolations from the available data," SIBIL spouts robotically, "almost every large transport and cargo ship's intercepted in this region reported such altercations within two days flight of this system's farthest satellite."

"Which we are now coming abreast of?" Illiadus asks.

"Aye, Captain," SIBIL sticks her tongue out.

Shots fly past the bow of Big EK as the alarms ring out. Another shot. A thud sounds as the reactive material of the ship's outermost skin deflects the force. Commander Aithon turns on the public address system, "This is second-in-command Commander Aithon. This is not a drill. Set General Quarters, Set General Quarters. All hands, man battle stations. All hands, man battle stations. Set material condition Zebra throughout the ship."

Captain Illiadus sits up and roughly removes her interactive helmet.

"Belay that order," she shouts, "do not charge the main gun. Keep the bow cover closed. Keep all chain guns retracted and under wraps until I order otherwise."

Aithon's jaw drops as Illiadus strides to the main display console right across from him.

"Bring up our new friends, Crewman Tiresias," Illiadus says.

"But Captain," Aithon spouts, "we're being attacked and…"

"I know," Illiadus replies, "I set this trap and was expecting them."

"What?" Djulgun spouts aloud.

"As you were, Ensign," Illiadus says.

"Sorry, sir."

Another thud and the entire ship shakes.

Illiadus studies the screen as the five pirate ships come into view. Behind them, a small cloudy nebula has served as cover while they waited for something to attack. The four disk-shaped craft, each about one-tenth the size of the Ekatarina, split off in different directions from the larger central one that is about one-third the size of the Terran warship.

"I could take them all out with a single spread of torpedoes, Sir," Al-Quam says calmly.

"No, Mr. Al-Quam, that will not be necessary. I need to blood this wet-nosed crew, Commander," Illiadus says, "so we're going to let these scumbags get nice and close. In fact, I want them to board us through the main hanger bay up top."

"Captain," Aithon gasps.

"My sources tell me they'll enter us with no more than fifty armed thugs," Illiadus spits, "which you will make sure are met with twenty-five of Sgt. Irena's finest."

"Yes Sir," Aithon replies, relaying her orders as rapidly as he can.

"Djulgun ," Illiadus continues, "make sure that every chain gun is manned, but not to be unharnessed and tracked into external firing position until MY order. These pirates think we're either a transport ship or a cargo hauler. I do not want them to learn differently until it is too late."

"Understood, Sir," Djulgun replies.

"Ensign Djulgun, slow down to half speed. Maybe we can make it look like they've hurt us."

A shudder is felt from another one of the attacker's hits as it knocks anything loose down to the floor.

"We've shed some dorsal ablative armor, Sir," Aithon says, "but nothing we can't replace."

"Captain," Djulgun says, "I'm receiving a transmission."

"Pipe it through the translator then the CIC com system," Illiadus replies.

A moment later a liquidy voice barks out of the surrounding speakers, "cargo ship. You are surrounded by the Denebrian Alliance. You have illegally entered our territory and must now pay our toll for travel through this region. We will board your ship for an official inspection to make sure you are not carrying any illegal contraband or weapons."

"And if we refuse entry?" Illiadus replies.

"We will destroy you."

"I'm opening the main cargo bay right now," Illiadus signals silently to Aithon, "my crew are just civilians. We don't want any trouble."

"Good," the pirate actually has the gall to laugh, "then this should be over soon."

A moment later the largest of the five ships lowers itself directly over the slowly opening main upper hanger of the Ekatarina. One minute later nearly fifty space-suited and mostly armed figures drop from the main enemy ship down into the large, unlit hanger bay that has been opened to space.

The four smaller disk-shaped ships have all moved within close proximity of the big E, two on each side.

"Now," Captain Illiadus shouts, "repel all boarders. Dis-mount all rail guns and extrude all secondary kinetic launchers. Target all flanking vessels and fire!"

Hell erupts everywhere.

Moments after the pirates touch down in the center of the main hanger, they immediately find themselves centered in a deadly crossfire of thirty pulse rifles aimed by itchy-fingered Marines fresh out of boot camp. Their resistance is fierce, but caught off guard in their exposed position, all forty-eight intruders are killed in less than half a minute. All the CIC can see from the hanger cameras is a wild flurry and red, green, and blue energy flashes that turn the ship's interior into an all too short fireworks display. Two Ekatarina Marines are wounded, one from a lucky enemy shot, and the other accidentally shooting itself in the foot, but both will recover quickly in their respective med pods in the sick bay.

Outside the battle cruiser the drama is just as fierce.

All eight of the port and starboard chain gun mounts erupt. Every one of them is set on manual mode, allowing the recent basic training crew graduates manning them full autonomy from computer override to fire as they see fit.

Within seconds hundreds of depleted trans-uranium shot accelerate to ridiculous speeds and cross the fractional distance separating battle cruiser from pirate ship. One after the other each of the four disk vessels are literally torn in half by the hellish onslaught, their crews expelled into deep space dying in explosive decompression.

Just one minute after the attack began, the largest ship lifts away, making best speed to escape.

"Target her with one torpedo Mr. Al-Quam," Captain Illiadus says, "low grade yield. I only want to hurt them."

"I'm unfamiliar with this vessel's configuration Sir," Al-Quam replies calmly, "I cannot guarantee I will not strike a sensitive area."

"Best guess then," Illiadus smiles, "and no, I won't hold it against you."

A moment later one space torpedo shoots forward and impacts and explodes against what appears to be a port-side engine pod. The pirate ship immediately lists starboard and slows down to half of its original speed.

"Djulgun," Illiadus says, "recommence communications."

"Ready, Sir," Djulgun replies.

"I can destroy you with little to no effort," Illiadus says, "you committed an act of aggression on a fully armed warship. Not a bright idea."

"We really thought you were someone else."

"I see," Illiadus replies with relish, "now, am I ever going to have another problem with you in this space sector? And you do realize we're here to stay?"

"Yes… I mean no! No, you won't have a problem and, uh, yes I realize, it, ummm, the other thing."

"And all the other ships in this solar system that are now under my… personal protection?"

"They'll never ever see me, Captain. I've just decided on early retirement… to a large asteroid colony far far away from here. I swear upon all thirty-six deities of the Fallapteron Cluster!"

Illiadus's mouth curls into a satisfied smile, "then we'll let it go for now."

Captain's Log, The Ekatarina

Fortieth Jump Completed

The extended half year out of cold sleep has allowed the new recruits plenty of time to learn their new positions and duties. They have proven themselves to be more than adaptable to both ship and military life. Though the majority of the surviving human crew has only been awake and active for two and a half years, ship's time has now just exceeded the eleven-year mark since we left the destruction of the Scourge sphere. Navigation estimates that we have crossed forty percent of the distance that originally separated us from Earth. Though accurate course calculations via the dark energy arteries still elude us, I am confident that my recently expanded crew is more than up for the challenge of the rest of our journey. End Log.

Hide and Seek

by Arthur Sánchez

Ship's Chronometer: 2436 AD

Captain Tennyson awakes to the memory of battle claxons and death. As she pulls herself up into a sitting position, she can almost make out the echoes of the ship's alarms and the face of the red-headed ensign who has died in front of her. *What was his name?* She can't remember. Ten turns away from the ghosts that haunt her dreams and takes a deep painful breath.

"Lights," she calls out. The interior of her cryogenic pod is illuminated by a bright white light and she runs a hand through her damp hair. She is still soaking from the stasis gel that is now running down the drains. "Christ," she mutters to herself, "what a mess."

"Captain?" SIBIL, the ship's AI calls to her through the small wireless earbud in her right ear, "are you alright?"

"I'm fine," Captain Tennyson slurs back, her tongue not quite functional yet. Out of habit she touches the earbud to make sure it is properly seated. A pointless gesture since it is designed to never pop out.

"I ask, because," SIBIL attempts to sound unobtrusive, "sensors are reporting that you are experiencing elevated respiratory and metabolic functions."

In other words, Ten thinks, I've woken up gasping for air and in a cold sweat. "I'm fine," she snaps, hating the fact that SIBIL insists on intruding on her nightmares. "At least I will be as soon as I have some coffee. Dispense Coffee. Hot." A small cup emerges from a cabinet by her head and the brown liquid steams in the still cold air of the cryo-pod.

"Stimulants are not recommended at this time," SIBIL admonishes her. "Your digestive tract has not yet returned to normal."

Ten bites back her response. There is no point in arguing with SIBIL. The AI is only doing what she is programmed to do. Instead, Ten sips her coffee slowly before asking: "Ship's status?"

SIBIL is smart enough to let it go. Long ago she'd learned not to antagonize the captain about her coffee. Instead, the disembodied voice of the ship's computer focuses on the matter at hand. "If the data from our last trading partners can be trusted, we are enroute to the Ikem Plutocracy Shipyards. All systems are operating within acceptable parameters. But," there is always a *but*, "there is a problem."

Ten nods her head. "Of course, there is. Why else would you have revived me?" She sips her coffee again. The hot liquid is helping to drive the cold of cryo-sleep from her gut and the caffeine feels like it is being pumped into her system intravenously. How long has it been since she'd had her last cup?

"Protocol dictates," SIBIL says coolly, "that I alert you to any situation requiring a command decision."

Ten rolls her eyes. She could have done without an AI who is so easily offended. "And our situation *is*?"

SIBIL answers by lighting up the view screen next to Ill's head. It shows a portion of the space directly ahead of them. Bright sparkly objects float within the view and while some appear to be just particles of dust others are alarmingly large. "What am I looking at?" Ten attempts to adjust the focus. She reaches out and with a finger and pans the camera from left to right. There is more of the same in all directions.

"Debris," SIBIL answers.

"From what?" Ten demands.

"Unknown."

"Speculate," Ten insists. She hates it when SIBIL becomes defensive. When she gets in a mood getting information is like pulling teeth.

"It appears," SIBIL concedes, "to be technological in origin. I believe we are looking at a graveyard of sorts. Perhaps the remnants of a battle."

Ten spins around and begins touching the walls of her pod. Screens flash to life as she checks the data flow from the sensors. "What battle? *Who's* battle? Is it ongoing?"

SIBIL isn't concerned. "Unknown. Configuration and composition of some of the debris does not match anything in our database. It is possible that this is the site of several battles fought over a protracted length of time."

Ill's hand freezes over the running data stream. "Are we in danger?"

"Unknown."

Ill's punches the wall of her pod. "SIBIL, what *do* you know?"

SIBIL's voice becomes cool again. "I know that we have encountered a debris field, it is at least .34 parsecs wide by .56 parsecs high but I have no way to estimate its depth or age. I can tell you that the density of the debris appears to amount to about 15,000 kilograms of mass per cubic kilometer with individual objects ranging in size from a grain of sand to a full-sized drop ship."

Ten whistles appreciatively. "That's a lot of space junk."

SIBIL continues her report. "The debris consists of materials that are both known and unknown to the Polisian fleet. All of it appears to be manufactured but little seems to be intact. The debris appears to be the result of violent encounters. There is evidence that both the Scourge and the Polisian fleets have been here. There does not appear to be anyone present now. Data is limited because protocol dictates that I use only passive detection methods while the crew is in cryogenic sleep." That last sentence almost sounds like an accusation.

Protocol does demand that SIBIL use only passive detection methods. It takes time to wake the crew. Active scans would announce their presence to anyone hiding in the debris. The crew might not be awake in time to fight a battle. "Assuming there is a raider lurking in the debris field," Ten asks, "how long before it will detect us using known passive scans?"

"An opponent would have detected us a little over thirty-two minutes ago," SIBIL answered.

And we'd already be dead. Thank God for small favors. "Let's assume nothing out there is hostile. Bring up the scans and start doing some deep probes. Check for life signs, heat signatures, movement, anything. If a Xentro Field Mouse sneezes, I want to know about it." Ten begins punching buttons to pressurize and activate the corridors leading to the C.I.C.

"Highly doubtful," SIBIL answers her. "Xentro Field Mice have no olfactory organs."

"Which is why it would be noteworthy if one sneezed," Ten responds sharply.

"Shall I awaken the rest of the crew?" SIBIL asks, ignoring the jab.

Ten hesitates. It will take time and energy to wake everyone up. "No, not yet. Let's wait until we know more."

"Aye, aye, Captain."

Five minutes later Ten strides down the still cold corridors of the ship as if the entire crew is present: head held high, back straight, and with a quick enough pace to make ensigns scramble for cover. It is tempting to stroll down to the Command Center in just her underwear but that would be cultivating a bad habit. Given their situation it is too easy to cultivate bad habits. Given their situation bad habits could last for centuries.

Ten walks into the C.I.C just as everything is being turned on. Lights flash, consoles chirp, there is the sudden whirl of fans as puffs of stale air are recycled. Odd how you never notice these details in your day-to-day life but remove the sights and sounds of a starship for long enough and they're all new the next time you encounter them.

"Captain on the bridge!" SIBIL announces in her ear. Ten rolls her eyes. The AI takes everything so seriously. Luckily, since SIBIL is just in her ear there is no pathetic echo off the empty stations.

"I'm coming in," Ten announces as she turns and walks towards the couch in the back of the room. This investigation will go faster and easier if they are connected.

"Is there a preference in venue?" SIBIL says to her. "Would you like a beach resort or to be on a mountain side?"

Ten reaches the couch and sits down. She then lays back and arranges herself comfortably. "The C.I.C. will do fine," she says, "we don't need any distractions." She then lifts the Quantum Helmet and places it on her head.

There is hardly any sensation at all but when Ten opens her eyes SIBIL is waiting for her.

Looking up from the virtual couch Ten is surprised to find that SIBIL now appears to be a young woman in her early twenties. She is wearing an ensign's uniform and her pips indicate she is a member of the Science Team. Her dark hair is cut to a regulation length but the soft lines that frame her face retain a sense of style that suits her. Could an AI have a sense of style? Ten decides not to comment but simply nods at her approvingly. She stands up and straightens the jacket on her virtual self. "Status?"

"Holding on the edge of the debris field," SIBIL answers as she hands her captain a steaming cup of coffee and then stands at attention. Ten can smell the coffee's rich aroma instantly. Nice touch.

Ten accepts the mug and moves into the center of the room. It is still empty but now it doesn't have the feeling of having been abandoned. The virtual space feels oddly more lived in than the reality she's left. "Anything interesting yet?" She says as she checks the screens.

SIBIL remains at attention. "No, Captain."

Ten nods. "Earlier you said that this thing is about a third of a parsec high by a half of a parsec wide. How long will it take for us to go around it?"

SIBIL gives a blink as she makes the calculations. "About half a standard year."

Ten doesn't like the sound of that. More time wasted. More time in danger. "Can we go through it?"

"Unknown. But given the nature of the field we'd be unable to travel at top speed for fear of collisions. It may not be any faster than going around."

The smart move will be to plot a course around the debris field. Pay the half year in time and avoid the potential problems. Of course, the smart move rarely pays off. She needs more information. "Prepare to enter the debris field," she says as she sits down in her chair. "Let's see what this thing looks like from the inside."

"Captain," SIBIL says with concern, "is that wise?"

"No," Ten answers her, "it's not. Magnetize the hull to repel the small stuff and plot a course around the big stuff. Ahead three clicks per second please."

For a moment it looks as if SIBIL will argue the point but instead she complies, and the ship begins to move forward. The debris that hangs before them parts like a curtain.

At first it is beautiful – and fascinating. Ten probes several pieces as they fly by and the possibilities of this unknown technology is enough to make the average scientist drool. The debris field has the potential of being a treasure trove of new discoveries. But after half a day of weaving in and around these relics the entire experience begins to lose its charm. "Any indication yet on the depth of the field?" Ten asks.

SIBIL, who has taken up her station by the Captain's chair, appears as immovable as a statue. "No Sir, still undetermined."

Ten watches as the hull of a very large alien vessel floats by. It looks like a child's top that was cracked in half. It also appears to be ancient. Detailed scans of its surface reveal that it is pocked and burnished from centuries of collisions within the debris field. Who had they been, Ten wonders. How did they die? Were they early victims of the Scourge or did they have enemies of their own?

"Let's change things up a little," Ten says quickly, disturbed by her thoughts, "and bring something on board for examination."

"Captain," SIBIL says, turning her head to face her, "I'd advise against that. We have no idea what affect our gravity or atmosphere might have upon some of these materials."

Of course, Ten agrees but she isn't about to tell SIBIL that. "I'm not looking to collect all that much, just enough to analyze. Open one of the bay doors and let's see what wanders in. We'll keep the bay depressurized so as to maintain a void similar to space itself. We'll use drones to do the actual testing and then flush everything back out when we're done. How's that?"

SIBIL grudgingly accepts her precautions. "Aye, aye, Captain. Opening real world aft bay doors now."

SIBIL is good enough to patch a video feed from the real-world bay directly to Ill's main view screen. Ten watches as particles get sucked into the bay as the doors open up onto space. Several larger pieces are also scooped up and for a second Ten thinks she sees something scuttle across the face of the bay doors in a left to right motion. She is about to zoom in on the area when SIBIL appears at her elbow.

"Captain?"

"Yes?"

"We're being hailed."

Ten isn't sure she hears that correctly. "*What?*"

"We're being hailed by a Polisian vessel." SIBIL's normally expressionless face shows actual surprise. "It's an automated message.

Probably triggered when we opened the bay doors and revealed our energy-signature but the message is authentic."

Ten tries to remain calm. A Polisian ship? A sister vessel.

"Get it on screen."

The monitor in front of her flickers for just a moment and then the most beautiful man Ten has ever known appears on it. Ten recognizes him immediately. Anyone who's been to the Space Command Academy within the last ten years will – Captain Nathanial Armstrong is infamous. At six foot four inches and one hundred eighty pounds of chiseled muscle, his tight curly hair, mocha-colored skin, and naturally emerald-green eyes are legendary. More cadets have fallen in love with him than with any other instructor in recorded history. And he enjoyed every minute of it.

"Greetings," Armstrong says sternly into the camera. He is older now, with a touch of gray to his temples, but still just as beautiful.

"If you are viewing this transmission then you know who I am and what vessel I command. Protocol dictates that we follow certain… procedures. If you've ever been to the Space Academy you know what a stickler I am for procedures. I will follow them now. The Polisian fleet was formed as a defense force for the mutual…"

Ten begins hitting buttons on her console. "Search for a sub-carrier wave," she tells SIBIL. "And turn that thing off. It's distracting."

SIBIL frowns. "But Captain Armstrong hasn't yet said what he's hailing us about."

Ten shakes her head. "And he's not going to. Captain Armstrong is broadcasting on an open channel. Protocol dictates that he not broadcast any unencrypted information that might reveal his situation or position to the enemy."

"Then," SIBIL asks, confusion showing, "why is he broadcasting at all?"

Ten smiles. "Protocol dictates that he not broadcast any *unencrypted* information. That," she said pointing at the monitor, "is nothing more than a flare meant to get our attention. His real message should be buried in a sub-carrier wave." Ill's console suddenly flashes. "There! That's the real message. Get it up and run it through our encryption programs."

It takes a second before the pixelated imaged reconfigures itself and the now weary face of Captain Armstrong takes shape. "Greetings," he says in a softer and less confident voice. "I am Captain Armstrong, commanding officer of the Polisian Starship Agamemnon. If you are viewing this then you are a Polisian war vessel and you have entered the debris field. First, I must warn you about the field. There are . . . things in it -- strange anomalies that pop up and then disappear when you try to hunt them down. It's like trying to catch a shadow. You're never quite sure of what you've seen. But be wary of them because I believe that one of these shadows is what damaged our engines. Both Science and Engineering are unable to determine what caused the explosion in our star-drive but I'm convinced it was something in this field. Don't let anything in the debris field touch your vessel."

Ten turns to SIBIL. "Flush the aft bay. Get that stuff out of here."

SIBIL blinks. "On it. The bay is being purged now and the doors are being shut."

"Secondly, and just as importantly," Captain Armstrong continues, unaware of their conversation. "I am requesting your assistance in getting the Agamemnon home. With the bulk of the Polisian fleet off to engage the Scourge, Central Command thought it wise to string a line of Oasis class supply ships in their return trajectory to act as resupply depots. No one expects the battle with the Scourge to go easily and our troops, those that survive, will need all the help we can give them. But a vessel of our size, unescorted, and remaining stationary will be a prime target for Scourge raiders. That is why it is imperative that we get moving again. Any assistance you can render in this effort would be greatly appreciated."

Ten gives the image of her old instructor a half smile. "Oh, Nate, if only you knew how much we are in need of *your* assistance."

SIBIL cocks her head to look at Ten. "Nate? You are familiar with Captain Armstrong?"

Ten shoots SIBIL a warning glance. "That's none of your business. Now, how old is the transmission?" Truth is Ten never succumbed to Nate's charms. Something about getting in line didn't appeal to her.

"Unknown," SIBIL responds. "There is no date stamp attached to it. I suspect he is having more difficulty than he is admitting. The lack of a date stamp implies a systems failure."

It wouldn't be unlike Nate to hold back critical information, especially when he wasn't certain of his audience. "Is there any more to the transmission?"

SIBIL shakes her head. "No. It ends there. But there does appear to be a series of numbers attached to the data stream. They could just be for archiving purposes." SIBIL brings up the string of code on the screen.

Ten smiles. "It's a frequency. He buried a sub-carrier wave within the sub-carrier wave."

SIBIL frowns. "Isn't that redundant?"

Ten begins imputing the numbers. "Exactly. Nobody would ever think to look for a hidden message within a hidden message. At the academy Captain Armstrong's field of expertise was tactics. His most popular class was: *The Art of Deception.*" A new image appears on her screen. Now Nate is grinning at her from ear to ear.

"If you found this then you are definitely one of MY students. Congratulations, Captain, you've done me proud. By now you're probably wondering where the hell I am. Truth is, I don't know. With the damage to the star drives we've lost a good deal of our power. My vessel has minimal propulsion and is technically adrift. I've had to shut down nonessential systems to conserve energy and that's left us pretty much blind." His voice becomes serious. "So, you can see we really are in need of your assistance. Given the debris field's tendency to obscure reference points, we've opted to string a line of short-range transmitters to act as a trail of breadcrumbs. If you're not human, check your cultural database for an explanation of that phrase. In any case, each transmitter is programmed to maintain a relative distance to its nearest neighbor. In that way the chain should remain unbroken. Once a transmitter detects your presence, it will deliver any messages I've sent and point you towards us. You should be able to follow the trail right back to…"

The transmission abruptly ends.

Ten sits up. "What happened?"

SIBIL stares at the view screen. "The transmission was terminated at its origin. Captain, we have a series of explosions off the stern."

"On screen."

The monitor now shows that alien vessel Ten was watching a few minutes earlier being attacked. It is as if it is being fired upon by a rather small vessel. Each hit tears away a small section of the hull and though none are lethal they make the ship look like it is being pecked to pieces.

Small clouds of disintegrated materials are being added to the debris field with each blow.

Ill's hands fly over her console. She calls up various data streams. "Can you see the attacker? Is he within range of us?"

SIBIL remains completely still. "There is no attacker."

Ten isn't sure she's heard her correctly. "What are you talking about? *Someone's* firing on that ship."

SIBIL, however, remains unmoved. "No one is firing upon that ship. I am not detecting any directed fire in the area. There are also no energy signatures from star drives."

"Then, what's tearing that ship apart?"

SIBIL tries to remain placid but her eyes reveal concerned. "Unknown. Shall I increase our speed? Get us out of range."

The idea of an undetectable attacker is terrifying. "No," Ten responds, "don't make any adjustments."

SIBIL frowns. "Captain? Wouldn't it make sense to put as much distance as we can between this assailant and ourselves?"

Ten IS trying to make sense of it all. The alien derelict has long since gone cold. It can't possibly represent a threat to anyone. Yet, in the middle of Nate's transmission it is attacked. The timing can't be coincidental. "The attacker must be blind," Ten says out loud. "Those missiles were meant for us. Only, the attacker can't see us and took a chance that they were targeting the correct ship. What we don't want to do now is draw their attention. At least not till we've gotten out of range."

SIBIL stares at her intently. "The Scourge do not have stealth technology. Who, then, is attacking?"

Ten turns her attention back to the monitor. "I haven't a clue, but I bet Nate does. Tell me you got the coordinates of the next transmitter -- that you know the location of the next breadcrumb?"

SIBIL shakes her head. "The transmission was terminated before we received that information. Captain. Perhaps now would be a good time to awaken the crew. If there is a threat, they will need time to prepare."

But Ten is only half listening. Something still isn't right. Why would the transmission terminate with the attack on the derelict? This would mean that the transmitter is caught in one of the explosions. "Is that how you hid it, Nate?" Ten says as she stares at the dying vessel. "Did you place it in the shadow of something big enough to mask its presence? The transmitter had been fine till it began broadcasting. Was it the signal, or the spike in energy output, that drew the attack?"

"Captain," SIBIL presses, uncertain of what she is talking about, "do I awaken the crew?"

"No," Ten answers slowly and then she explains why.

SIBIL nods. "It makes sense. Sticking close to the derelict would provide both protection and cover. It's a strategy that would be consistent with Nate's tactical record."

Ten cocks an eyebrow. "Nate? Since when did *you* become familiar with Captain Armstrong?" If SIBIL could blush, Ten is convinced the AI would have.

"Ever since we detected Captain Armstrong's transmission," SIBIL explains, "I've been running a subroutine to familiarize myself with both Captain Armstrong's record and his teachings. I have reviewed over a hundred hours of course materials and, in many ways, I now feel like I am acquainted with him. But I apologize. It was inappropriate of me to refer to him in familiar terms."

Ten smiles. *Familiar* is the way Nate preferred things.

"Don't apologize. He would have loved it. And I'm glad you have familiarized yourself with his record. It's just you and me right now. We can't risk awakening the rest of the crew. The energy required to support that much activity might be enough to draw an attack. Until we know who, or what, is out there we can't risk waking anyone else up."

SIBIL, however, has other concerns. "But what about the Agamemnon? We didn't get any further instructions to its whereabouts."

Ten considers this. "The recording said the transmitters were programmed to maintain a relative distance to one another. They were strung out like warning buoys."

"Yes?"

"Then the next buoy is somewhere nearby. If we fly in a circular pattern using the destroyed derelict as the center, we might stumble upon it."

SIBIL begins plotting the course. "We'll be spending a lot of time going in circles with no guarantee of finding anything."

Ten thinks of her sleeping crew. An Oasis class supply ship will mean fresh food, news from home, and much needed medical supplies. The

Agamemnon has ten times the crew compliment as the *Ekatarina*. There'd be the chance to meet new people and maybe reconnect with old friends. Ten wonders how many members of her crew *know* Captain Armstrong. With this discovery they won't be alone anymore.

"Time is something we have," Ten says to her. "And nobody's ever offered us any guarantees. Execute the search pattern. Keep it organic feeling. Somebody out there is hunting us. We need to remain invisible."

"Aye, aye, Captain."

Six hours later Ten awakes with a start. At first, she intently watched the data streams -- searching for clues, watching for attackers. But it soon became apparent that nothing else is going to happen. After a few brief moments of revelation, the debris field, like a thick New England fog, has closed in again and gone silent. At some point, Ten fell asleep. Given that her real self is quietly resting this entire time, the sleep is probably more the result of boredom than it is of actual fatigue. Ten looks up to find SIBIL standing over her.

"Report?" she asks, slightly embarrassed by her lack of discipline.

SIBIL looks excited. "I think I've found the transmitter. I've been scanning for Polisian tech that may be hovering near a much larger structure."

"And?"

SIBIL steps back and points at the monitor. On it is a star-shaped vessel that appears more to have been grown than built. It is ice-blue and has crystalline spires jutting out in all directions. You can easily mistake it for an odd-looking comet were it not that some of the broken spires reveal an obvious infrastructure. Is this someone's idea of a scout craft?

"Have we received anything, yet?"

SIBIL shakes her head. "I believe that our magnetized hull is cloaking our energy signature. It isn't till we opened the bay doors, and created a crack in that cloak, that the first transmitter was activated. Shall I open the bay doors now?"

Ten considers this. "We have to assume that the attacker is still out there. As soon as the transmitter starts broadcasting it'll zero in on it and start looking for us. If our magnetized hull is somehow shielding us let's give our enemy as little as we can to go on. Open one of the gun ports. Let's see if that's enough to trigger the transmitter."

"Aye, Captain, opening starboard gun port now."

The response is almost instantaneous. Nate appears on her screen seated in his Captain's chair. He appears to be alone in the C.I.C and his face is haggard and thin. "Good morning. This is the Captain of the Agamemnon requesting immediate assistance. We have been adrift for forty-seven days now. If you have received any of my earlier transmissions, you know that we are attempting to traverse the debris field." Ten looks at SIBIL questioningly but the AI shakes her head. They have not gotten any of the other transmissions.

"The Science team has been able to determine that the debris field was purposefully designed to obscure and confuse. My Chief Science Officer theorizes that it was meant to be a training device. The goal was to teach captains Search and Destroy and Evasive tactics. It's essentially a giant game of Hide and Seek. Only the game has turned deadly. Upon halting for repairs we've been attacked. The attacking vessel or vessels seem to be invisible, small, and have limited firing power. But they are relentless, and their store of missiles seems to be endless. They may also be automated. We've detected no intelligence in the attack pattern." Nate takes a deep painful breath. He seems to be at the end of his rope.

"I've lost crew to this attacker. I've lost engines and mobility to it. It seems to focus on anything with a big energy signature–like life support. We're currently venting atmosphere and radiation leaks have poisoned nearly a third of our living quarters. I've ordered half of the crew into their cyropods in order to conserve resources. If you are out there, we need your help. Please, continue to follow the buoys. We are depending on you." The transmission ends.

Ten looks up. "Forty-seven days? How *long* have they been out here?"

SIBIL shakes her head. "Unknown. They still do not have a date stamp. Captain," she said looking up from her station. "There's another transmission."

Ten returns her attention to the monitor. The image that appears now is so loud and boisterous that she jumps back in her chair. In stark contrast to the previous transmission this one shows a party being held in the C.I.C. Confetti is flying, noise makers are being blown, and music is blaring in the background.

"Woo Hoo!" shouts Captain Armstrong as he drops into his chair. His uniform is disheveled, and he appears to be wearing a fistful of Mardi Gras beads around his neck. "Greetings, traveler, and welcome to Wakey, Wakey, Day!" Captain Armstrong leans in toward the monitor as if confiding a secret.

"It's the sixtieth day of our adventure and the day that we awaken the crew members who have been in their cryopods so that THESE hard-working bastards can get some rest. Am I right? Am I right!" Somebody tosses him a string of beads and he laughs almost maniacally as he catches it. Turning to the camera he grins as he holds up bright sparkly necklaces. "You do NOT want to know what I had to do for these." And he laughs again. Then the transmission ends.

SIBIL looks up from her monitor. "Explosions on the derelict. Our pursuer has found her." Ill's monitor now shows the star-shaped craft being destroyed.

"Did we get the coordinates this time?" Ten asks.

SIBIL's hands are darting about her station. She appears to be confirming something. "No, there were no coordinates included in the transmission, but I did detect a directed microwave burst. To quote you, Captain, I think the transmitter was sending up a flare."

Ten could feel her heart racing. "Calculate the trajectory and lay in a course."

SIBIL complies. "Captain, given the festivities on the second transmission, can we infer that they were getting their situation under control?"

Ten shakes her head. "That second transmission was for show. He wanted the crew to see they had nothing to worry about. The fact that they were celebrating 'Wakey, Wakey, Day' means they were still running alternating crews. That means they were still short on materials. Captain Armstrong threw this party to distract them."

SIBIL absorbs this. "That would also be consistent with his record."

Ten grins. Nate has one hell of a record. She then reaches out to her monitor and pans the view around in the direction they are now supposed to go and is startled by what she sees. On the horizon are two behemoths locked in mortal combat.

Like some illustration from an ancient Mariner's map she can make out two distinctive intertwined shapes. On the one side is an oblong shape that reminds her of a whale with flippers and a tail perfectly suited for an ocean. On the other side is a tentacle-wielding squid creature. As she watches the whale generates an electrical charge in its tail that runs up along its body and strikes at the squid like a lightning bolt. The squid, in turn, has wrapped several of its tentacles around the whale while bashing it relentlessly with its free arms. The image seems to be on a loop as the same actions and reactions are played out over and over. "What the hell is that?" Ten whispers out loud.

"What is what?" SIBIL asks.

Ten looks up and frowns. "That." She says pointing at the monitor. "What the hell is *that?*"

SIBIL turns to the indicated monitor and squints at it. It is a totally unnecessary gesture since the AI has direct access to the video feed. "I don't know," SIBIL says with a frown. "This is the first time I've seen this."

Ten glares at her. "What are you talking about? You should have been scanning this from the instant it came into range."

SIBIL turns and gives her an innocent look. "Yes, I should have. Only, this activity has not appeared on any of our scans. This is the first we've detected it." She continues to stare innocently at Ten and the captain can't tell if she is being evasive or ignorant.

"Are you telling me that two . . . creatures, who are presently trying to tear each other apart, have not registered on any of our scans? Not for heat, nor motion, nothing?"

SIBIL turns and looks at the monitor again. "They are not creatures," she says, avoiding the question. "They are not organic. A visual inspection shows signs of manufacturing."

"You're saying they're spaceships?"

"Yes, equally matched and specifically designed to challenge each other."

"What makes you say that?"

SIBIL gives her a curious look. "Isn't it obvious? Though they are intent on doing so -- neither has succeeded in destroying the other. Each vessel's offensive capabilities are being cancelled out by the other's defensive systems. Furthermore, molecular scans indicate that they have been at this for decades – perhaps centuries. It is safe to assume that their crews have long since perished and they are trapped in a mindless loop attempting to fulfill their last pre-programmed objectives."

Ten hates it when the universe tries to speak to her. "What you're saying is that we have two ghost ships, locked in mortal combat, fighting a war that was lost ages ago."

SIBIL cocks an eyebrow. "From your tone I detect that I should be deriving some greater significance from this situation than I currently understand."

Ten shakes her head. "No," she says, "you shouldn't. The only thing of importance to be derived from this encounter is how did these things avoid our detection? Nate said in his transmission that this field was designed to obscure and confuse." She watched as the whale shot the squid with a lightning bolt and it responded with a vicious blow to the head. Was it for the thousandth or the millionth time that they'd done this? Did it matter?

SIBIL nods her head. "They seemed to have some sort of shielding that hides their energy signatures, something that goes beyond simply magnetizing their hulls. Since their designs are of an unknown origin it is safe to say that their technology is also unknown to us. Captain, it concerns me that we did not detect these vessels prior to coming upon them. I recommend we hold here before proceeding any further. Without a reliable detection system, we are at risk at crashing into some of the larger debris items."

Ten shakes her head. "Nate said they were attacked each time they stopped. The thing that's hunting us isn't very fast. It needs to catch up. But those ships have given me an idea. Alter some of your scans to look for what's NOT there as opposed to what IS there."

SIBIL's confusion is obvious. "Sir?"

Ten isn't surprised. It is an *out of the box* kind of approach. "You told me that the debris field had an average density of about fifteen thousand kilos of material per cubic kilometer. Correct?"

SIBIL's expression does not change. "Yes."

"Well, then, it stands to reason that even if we cannot see an object it still occupies space – space that things we CAN see cannot fill. Look for gaps in the debris field -- places suspiciously devoid of material. Even if we cannot see an object, we can detect it from the behavior of the things around it. Look for holes in the field that shouldn't be there."

SIBIL nods her head approvingly. "Very clever, Captain, you are employing an ancient stellar cartographer's trick."

Ten wouldn't have phrased it that way but sure, fine. "Let's resume our search for the Agamemnon. My gut tells me we're close."

"Captain?" SIBIL's expression has suddenly changed from grudging admiration to concern. "We have a problem."

Ten looks at her. "Explain."

SIBIL's hands check the data stream. "I've implemented your suggestion and I've detected several anomalies directly to our stern."

"How many and of what nature?"

SIBIL cocks her head as she makes her calculations. "Twenty-seven. They seem to be following us. I can trace their debris trail for several klicks."

Ill's voice almost catches in her throat. "Starships?"

SIBIL shakes her head. "Too small. The largest is no more than a meter in length. They are shielded but reveal no sign of intelligence. Their trails are erratic and uncontrolled. It's almost as if they've been trailing along behind us without actually knowing where we were. It's very odd."

Ill's eyes go round with the implication. "Magnetic mines. We are being trailed by two dozen magnetic mines."

"Twenty-seven," SIBIL corrects her, "and magnetic mines have been outlawed by all civilized worlds for over three centuries."

Ten almost screams with frustration. "When has being civilized ever stopped anyone from using a weapon?" Now it makes sense. The derelicts riddled with holes, the lack of an energy signature, Captain Armstrong's warning them not to stop. Magnetic mines latch on to a vessel's magnetic wake and get pulled along behind it. They're almost impossible to detect because they have no real energy source. At best they have small booster rockets to move them into position. But as soon as you stop, they ride a kinetic wave right up your backside and tear you apart. It is like tying a can to a dog's tail. The poor thing will run and run till it drops from exhaustion and never outruns its tormentor. It is sadistic. It is also the reason why Nate didn't discover them. They have no strategy, no thought process. They are just part of the game. Now the *Ekatarina* is part of that game.

"Execute the new course correction. We need to find the Agamemnon, now."

SIBIL looks doubtful. "The Agamemnon was lost for months. We may not have that much time in which to find her."

Ten has considered this. "We don't need that much time. The Agamemnon was running blind. She probably wandered in circles. We, however, know exactly where we need to go. Execute the course correction."

Three hours later SIBIL turns from her station. "Captain," she says out loud, "scans are showing that the debris field is starting to thin out. I think we may have found the other side."

Ten gives a silent thanks to the powers that be. "Then they got out. They made it." But her celebration is short-lived as an explosion rocks the ship. "What was that?"

SIBIL scans the screen. "A magnetic mine just exploded off the port side. It was close. Less than a thousand meters."

"Any damage?"

"None of consequence."

"How did it catch up to us? We should have been outpacing them?"

SIBIL frowns. "Trajectory indicates that it is not one of the mines that have been following us. It was actually . . . Captain, that mine came from in front of us."

Ten practically jumps out of her seat. "Ninety-degree turn, now!"

"What direction?"

"Any direction! It doesn't matter! There's a minefield in front of us!" SIBIL executes the order and the ship's gravitational dampeners barely compensate for the steep turn and acceleration. Ten has to grab her armrests to stay upright.

"Captain," SIBIL says as she stares excitedly at a view screen, "the Agamemnon, she's here. She's sitting on the edge of the debris field."

The image fills the view screen in front of Ill. It is one of the most inspiring things she's ever seen. The Agamemnon is a great big orb floating in the vastness of space. Like a Christmas ornament hung in the window - - welcoming her home.

"Something's wrong," SIBIL says with a frown. "I'm not getting an energy signature off of her. She's not emitting, transmitting, or radiating anything." Ill's heart sinks. "Do you think Captain Armstrong has found a way to use the stealth properties of the debris field to his advantage? If so, that would be a remarkable achievement."

"Let's hold the award's ceremony till we're in the clear. Are there any more mines?"

SIBIL scans the area. "We've picked up about a dozen more trails. But there's nothing in front of us. Odd. You would think that the mines would be equally spaced. But they appear to be clustered behind us."

Ten doesn't want to ask. "Are they clustered around the Agamemnon?" It takes a moment for SIBIL to nod the affirmative. "Christ! Could it get any worse?" They are being chased by more mines than is necessary to destroy them and now the Agamemnon is barricaded.

"We're receiving a message," SIBIL calls out excitedly.

Captain Armstrong's haggard face appears on her screen. "We didn't know," he says, almost in a whisper, "we didn't understand. We thought there was something intelligent out there. Something alive. I never suspected we were running from a fistful of firecrackers. Individually they were nothing but together they've crippled us. We have had fifty-two separate hull breaches. I've lost one hundred and twenty-five crewmen. Our star drives are dead and we're venting atmosphere so badly I've had to order the entire crew into their cryopods. Ironically, shutting down all of our major systems have caused the mines to cease their attacks. I guess we're not broadcasting as loudly as we once were. I'm the only one left awake and I'll be entering my pod at the end of this recording. What the crew doesn't know. What I wasn't brave enough to tell them, is that we only have enough reserves to run the cryopods for another six months. After that they'll start to fail. My only hope is that you'll find this in time to save some, if not all, of my crew. They are good and loyal soldiers. They don't deserve to die this way. Please, if there is anything --" The message ends. Ten looks at SIBIL.

The AI shakes her head. "Message terminated at the source. They found the transmitter."

Ten takes a deep breath. "I don't suppose this message had a date stamp?"

SIBIL checks the transmission and suddenly brightens.

"They must have affected some repairs. There IS a date stamp."

Ten sits up in her chair. "How old is it?"

"Making adjustments for relativity." SIBIL hesitates before looking up. "It appears the message is over ten years old."

Ten sinks back into her chair. "They only had enough reserve power for six months."

SIBIL, though, isn't prepared to surrender. "They may have affected some repairs in those six months. They were able to repair the operating systems."

Ten shakes her head. "There is nobody awake to affect repairs. He ordered everyone to sleep."

"They could have set a timer. Some of the crew could have been revived to work on a solution." SIBIL's hands move as she searches the data stream for evidence of her theory.

"Are there any more transmissions?" Ten asks as a dull resignation seeps into her bones.

"No."

"If they'd made it," Ten says, "there would have been."

"The transmitters could have all been destroyed. We know the mines home in on them once they begin broadcasting."

Ten shakes her head. "Nate would have known that. He would have been prepared for that. They're gone SIBIL. We're too late."

SIBIL's look of disappointment is as realistic as any emotion she's ever displayed. Ten is almost convinced the AI is feeling a sense of loss, "What do we do now, Captain?"

Ten gives herself a mental kick in the ass. Yes, Captain, what do you do now? What you do now, she answers herself, is you get your own crew home. "We need to shake these mines," she says out loud, "and there's only one way to do that."

"Sir?"

"Plot an elliptical course and get us pointed back at the Agamemnon. Make it wide enough so that the mines behind us don't manage to cut us off on the return trip."

SIBIL looks concerned. "Sir, there is a minefield surrounding the Agamemnon. Doing a fly by will only attach more mines to us."

Ten shakes her head as she watches SIBIL execute the orders.

"We're not doing a fly by. As soon as we are on the correct trajectory, I want you to aim for the center of the Agamemnon. Bring us in at ten clicks per second."

SIBIL punches in the coordinates but not without reservations. "Captain, at that speed we may not be able to pull up."

"And neither will those magnetic mines," Ten answers her.

"Besides, we're not going to pull up. We're going to blast our way through the center of the Agamemnon. Power up the forward gun and two of our rear guns. When we get close, lay down a series of short bursts to clear a path for us. Then we'll hit her with a long hard burst to punch our way through." Ten closes her eyes and tries not to think of the supplies they are destroying – and of the bodies she is desecrating. "Forgive me Nate," Ten says softly to the now growing image of the Agamemnon, "but I'm only doing what you would have done."

SIBIL reluctantly executes the order. "You are going to use the mass of the Agamemnon to distract the mines. You're hoping none of them will make it through with us."

Once again, it almost sounds like an accusation. "I'm using what's available to us. We can't escape with those things trailing us and we can't stay here. The mines will latch on to the best potential target. When we light up the Agamemnon, they should latch on to her. It's our only hope of escaping."

SIBIL's face actually mirrors her inner turmoil. "There could be survivors. We should make sure first."

Ten knew what SIBIL wants – to hold onto some hope. "It's a dead ship, SIBIL." Ill's voice sounds harsh even to her. "Nate and his crew died in their sleep dreaming of home. We however have a chance to actually make it home. No one on that ship would fault us for this -- especially not Nate."

SIBIL accepts this stiffly. "Then I recommend we fire a cluster of low-yield rockets in a tight formation to punch our way through. We don't want to split her in half before we make it through."

Ten nods. "Set the rear guns to fire a widespread the moment we clear the other side. I want her to collapse in on herself after we're through. We need the mines to get caught up in the debris."

The maneuver is almost textbook -- if such a thing could ever be written down in a textbook. To use the corpse of a dead ship to mask your own escape is not something you wanted to teach young cadets. But perhaps it is something you should. The difference between honor and survival is the price you are willing to pay for it. Ten has never been prepared to sacrifice her crew's lives for her honor so the tradeoff is acceptable.

By the time they hit the Agamemnon they are trailing over a hundred mines. There are so many of them that they are colliding into each other and exploding. The *Ekatarina* looks as if she has a comet's trail behind her. SIBIL displays remarkable finesse and she fires the guns with just the right accuracy and frequency to punch a hole through the heart of the vessel. They watch as the ship shudders and buckles and Ten almost feels each strike as if they are hitting her own body.

"As soon as we are clear," Ten says as they enter the hole they've created, "fire the rear guns and engage the stardrives. We need to be out of here before anything else gets past the Agamemnon."

SIBIL doesn't answer but executes the order with commendable professionalism. The last thing Ten sees in the monitors is the Agamemnon imploding upon itself. Hundreds of flashes of light reveal the vessel collapsing inwards as she is torn apart. As she turns the monitor off Ten wonders if she'll ever get that image out of her mind or if it would become a permanent addition to her nightmares.

It doesn't take long to determine that the maneuver has worked and that they no longer have anything to fear from the debris field. That also means Ten has no reason to stay awake. So, she returns to the real world and retires to her cryopod to sleep.

As Ten lays back and tries to adjust her position for the upcoming sleep she wonders what the point of this little adventure has been. Was there ever a point to anything?

"Excuse me, Captain," SIBIL calls to her through the earbud.

"Yes," Ten answers as she fluffs up a pillow before slipping it under her head. She needed to get it just right otherwise she'd get a crick in her neck that could last for years.

"I'm sorry to bring this up, Sir, but you never filed a report on this incident."

Ten frowns. SIBIL might have matured but the girl was still a stickler for procedures. "Does it matter?"

SIBIL pauses and Ten can imagine her debating how to phrase her next statement. "Yes," she says determinedly, "it does. There was only the two of us to witness these events. If something should happen to us, then no one will ever know what became of the Agamemnon. She'll remain lost forever. Captain Armstrong and his crew had family – loved ones. They deserve closure."

It is a good point. "Fine, then record this as my report," Ten says as she imagines SIBIL waiting with a pen and paper. It is an archaic image but one that seems oddly appropriate.

"Lights," Ten calls out and the pod is plunged into darkness.

"Initiate cryosleep cycle."

SIBIL becomes concerned that the Captain is going to ignore her. "Sir?"

Ten takes several deep breaths. It takes less than thirty seconds for cryogenic freezing to occur. "You ready, SIBIL?"

"Yes Sir."

"Then begin -- On whatever day this is, at whatever time you woke me up, the Captain of the *Ekatarina* and its AI encountered a . . . minefield. With the help of Captain Armstrong and the crew of the Agamemnon, the *Ekatarina* was able to escape that minefield. Unfortunately, the Agamemnon and her crew were lost in this effort. It is the recommendation of Captain Tennyson that Captain Armstrong and every member of the Agamemnon be awarded the Galactic Star for Heroism. Without their devotion to duty, and self-sacrifice, none of us would have made it out of there alive. End of report." Ten begins to feel the familiar weight of the freezing process take hold of her. "Satisfied?" she asks SIBIL.

SIBIL, however, isn't. "That's not exactly how it happened."

"Isn't it?" Ten asks. "Armstrong and his crew had worked it all out. Through the transmissions they lead us through the minefield. And in the end, they sacrificed themselves to save us."

"I feel compelled to point out that the Agamemnon was cold for almost a decade when that happened."

Ten could barely move a muscle. She has to fight to keep talking but she wants to remember to close her mouth when they are done. She doesn't want to fall asleep with her mouth open – not for however many decades.

"Doesn't matter, alive or dead they did their duty and died heroes. That's how I'll tell it. Got a problem with that?"

SIBIL doesn't hesitate. "No, Captain."

"Good," Ten says with a long final yawn. "I'll see you on your thirtieth birthday, SIBIL."

"Sir?"

Ten smiles. "Just teasing, good night, SIBIL."

"Good night, Captain."

And the world goes dark.

Captain's Log, The Ekatarina

Sixtieth Jump Completed

Ship's chronometer records that our journey began thirteen years ago. SIBIL has just awakened me from coldsleep for an auspicious pain in the neck ceremony. The duties of a Captain are never ending, and in this case, can occasionally border on the ridiculous. End Log.

Crossing the Line

by Beth Patterson

Ship's Chronometer: 2438 AD

In the beginning was the word, and the word was a very harsh obscenity. It burst from her throat in a snarl. Sirens are always confounding everything, like the distressed howling of the mechanical pack baying discordant cries of alarm.

Captain Tennyson Maria Illiadus can never recall if she dreamed during her Cold Sleep state, and she certainly gives no thought to the matter now. All that exists is the myopic world of screeching alarms and the pod that encases her, suspending her in an animalistic fight-or-flight state for an eternal nanosecond. Another breath of air slashes her lungs and she jack knifes upright, a stab of reason returning. She is in charge and her ship is in some sort of peril. Without a thought to her appearance, she goes tearing down the corridor in a full-on sprint towards the CIC, her hair streaming behind her like the unruly tail of a dark comet.

The frantic woman dodges the ensuing flood of higher-ranking officers spurting from their pods to the corridors. She reaches the CIC a fraction of a second before first officer Aithon, nearly smashing full-tilt into the equally disoriented man, forcing her to come to her senses. She checks the screens on the walls, but the myriad camera eyes outside the ship project no hostile ships or oncoming satellites. She can plainly see that all of the *Ekatarina's* functions are running smoothly, and no crewmembers are in peril. With no outlet for her seething adrenaline, panic is instantly replaced by fury, a psychological sleight-of-hand.

"Dave, what the hell is going on?"

Aithon appears just as rattled and confused as she feels, his wide blue eyes giving the controls a cursory glance. "It appears that something has triggered one of the priority programs, the ones that are inserted into all space navy ships before launching. Why such clamor is utterly necessary is beyond me, but I hope that the creator of this program eats Scourge biscuits for all eternity."

"SIBIL!" barks Ten, raising her head to snarl at the unseen navigator. "What is the reason for this clusterfuck?" She is fond of archaic obscenities.

"The *Ekatarina* flight path is rapidly approaching the recently documented set of coordinates known as the Coaxial Shield," replies the ship's artificial intelligence unit. Illiadus knows in her head that the smooth voice created by machines and men is deliberately impassive, that it is all information translated into pre-programmed sound, but she cannot eradicate the nagging sensation that SIBIL somehow enjoys provoking her by pitting logical computer against volatile human emotion.

Aithon is visibly uncomfortable. "We have nearly reached the halfway point between Earth Prime and the location of the last Polisian war against the Scourge, the latter specifically the location of the Dark Matter void that devoured their ship. Each coordinate is exactly 16,204 parsecs from us. The ship is programmed to alert the entire crew in the event of an occasion to hold a line-crossing ceremony, much like the ones we endured between portals..."

The captain's nostrils flare. "They woke us for *this*? No invasion, no Dark Matter fountains... a morning cup of coffee would be just as effective at bringing this occasion to my attention!"

As though having predicted her needs, someone wordlessly materialized a cup of coffee before her. Coffee beans are grown in abundance in the hydroponic gardens, and the ship labs keep the food supply consistent with fresh vegetables and protein cultures that simulate meat. However, fresh water is more precious, and only a few personnel are permitted to drink coffee, while the rest of the crew have to chew the roasted beans whole. The hot liquid is a primordial comfort to the captain, half soothing and half revitalizing. Tennyson's mind begins to clear as she grips the sturdy hot mug.

Aithon clears his throat. "Everyone needs ceremony, even when the people have forgotten why. Take away the joy of it, and ritual is reduced to superstition."

"We've been to hell and back already. We really don't need one more wrench in the clockwork."

"But it is undeniably significant. Aren't you familiar with this tradition?"

"First this bitch-ass AI unit wakes me in a panic, and now you insult my expertise. Of course, I'm well acquainted with this pain-in-the-ass rite of passage. This isn't my first rodeo, you know. I didn't acquire the skills needed to become Captain without earning my status as a seasoned *Diamondback*. Time to see what these youngsters have in mind for the ritual." She rolls her eyes.

"Better get Ironbear to accompany you to the main Mess. And Ten..."

"What now, Dave?"

"What's a *rodeo?*"

Tennyson sighs. This is going to be tricky.

She knows that this ceremony predates space travel. When she herself had been an initiate, she had been surprised to discover that *Sons of Neptune* had nothing to do with the planet, but rather the Roman sea god for which it is named. When exploring was limited to voyaging the Terran seas, there was usually a big deal made over crossing the equator, and the trusty *Shellbacks* who had already been through that rite of passage loved having any excuse to subjugate the neophyte *Pollywogs*. The ceremony allegedly paid homage to King Neptune, but usually involved an array of drugs, alcohol, humiliation, and frequent endangering of new initiates and ship alike.

Much has changed since then. With the advent of communication between Earth and other planets, all Terracentric XYZ coordinates had to be discarded in favor of a mapping system agreed upon by multiple planets (and theoretical alternate universes). Locations were pinpointed more accurately but with a system that was far more complex. This makes noteworthy points an even bigger deal than the primitive system based on two axes, but the celebrations are no less barbaric.

The entire crew has already been briefed since the rude awakening. The sub-officers are already eager to get the plans in motion. Hungry as they are for any sort of merits or status, she doubts that they have any idea what sort of horrors awaited them or notice how delighted the commanding officers are to go along with this. Science and technology have progressed in leaps and bounds since documented evidence of this tradition, but the need for acceptance—as well as the dark desire to subjugate others—is still a dominant trait in all races.

Illiadus herself had crossed a rare threshold while still in training. She had been part of a team that reached a significant space coordinate and had managed to help the crew steer clear of the ensuing hazards. She swore that never again would she joke about interstellar sonic booms or gaseous filaments. She recalled how proud she had felt over this feat—especially for one so young at the time—and the price she had had to pay for her pride. The memories, to which she has tried to become impervious—or more secretly has desperately tried to forget—now flood her mind, and her pace picks up even more frantically as she speeds to the common areas.

The main Mess is an absolute jungle, almost literally. The screens on the walls have been switched from the outer cameras to now depict images on the long-extinct rain forests of Earth. Adding to the atmosphere is the beastly cry of the revelers, mimicking mainly terrestrial creatures. The commanding officers that have tagged along appear dismayed, with the exception of wide-eyed Farko Tiresias. She is ostensibly relishing an experience so drastically different from her home planet behavior, oblivious to the potential disaster from the utter chaos unfolding.

A drunken cluster of engineer staff in their bright orange jumpsuits are brazenly singing a folk ballad that is over four hundred years old, about a man steering his ship into the galactic X-ray source and black hole that is located in an Earthen-viewed constellation known as Cygnus. It was written before any such space exploration had ever been made. A few lyrics have obviously been altered to give the song a bawdy flair, causing hysterical laughter from the delighted spectators:

"X-rated her siren song

This shit cannot resist my dong
Nearer to my throbbing pole
Until the bunghole --
Takes it whole..."

The final lines to the song end in a note pitched extremely high for human voices; only the engineer known as Dirk is able to hit it, with the rest of the chorus merely satisfied to tunelessly screech instead. A bottle of rare whisky is being passed around the singers. How the whisky has been smuggled onboard the ship is a mystery.

Some of the *initiation* has dissolved into complete moral turpitude, according to the ethical code of the Polisian Space Fleet. A Fleet member out of uniform is serious enough, but no one had thought of what to do with numerous Fleet members out of clothing altogether. Illiadus catches a bouncing movement out of the corner of her eye and sees that several tangles of arms, legs, fur, and tentacles have formed in highly inappropriate liaisons, crossing ranks and exploring scores of mathematical and biological possibilities. Dozens of curious revelers have gathered around these clusters like rings around vulgar planets and are shamelessly observing spectacles that are equally unabashed. A few sordid war cries, such as, "Igor, I've done it again! I'm the Albino Rhino!" float from the throng. From the amazed murmurs that ripple outward, it appears that Private Narby has just earned the nickname *Private Parts*, and is putting on a rather spectacular show with his three tentacles, enlisting some of the ensigns as oversized finger puppets.

A row of initiates is being forced to crouch face-first to the floor, noses touching chips used for bartering onboard the *Ekatarina*. On the signal of a wild-eyed Starback, they push the chips across the rough floor with their noses in a race, with the threat of some further punishment that will befall the loser goading them on. Skin chafed, and bright red streaks of blood trail the hostage competitors, as throngs of higher-ranking crew are chanting, "Scumbag, scumbag, *scumbag*!" Grapes have been procured from the hydroponic labs—doubtlessly by one of the farming technicians—and whatever the next race the Starbacks are preparing that has to do with the overheard phrase "hold the grape," it does not sound auspicious.

Crewmembers of various insectoid races, who have been the least familiar with this tradition, are now the most terrified. One of the lower-ranking officers has detached the plate-sized lens from an antique telescope, one of the ship's few decorative trappings, and is using the artifact to threaten the compound-eyed initiates. Although the sun on the wall screen is a completely simulated image, all insectoids have evolved to fear magnifying lenses, and the frantic hard-shelled denizens of the *Ekatarina* are clustered in the corner. They normally communicate with each other through pheromones, and since they have no vocal cords, they cannot scream, but beat with their forelegs frenzied rhythms of code that are cries of distress.

One poor crewman, his terrified whimpering only feeding the frenzy of the seasoned bullies like blood among sharks, has been taped naked to a pole. Someone is preparing to tie a heavy water-based foam fire extinguisher to his genitals, and the Spacewog's cries for mercy did nothing to discourage his superiors. Even the non-hominids that have no external genitalia are frightened, and they look wildly around the main Mess for surreptitious ways to protect their fur, spines, or tentacles, as well as ways to conceal other true natures of their vulnerable anatomy before the Starbacks can figure out more ways to bully them.

Another reveler is attempting to tamper with the artificial gravity. A few co-conspirators have already strapped themselves to permanent fixtures with safety tethers, eagerly waiting to see what sort of disaster will ensue for the unsuspecting initiates. The potential for damage is unthinkable: drifting objects, water into the delicate electronics, open flame in the controlled oxygen, combustion in microgravity...

Has everyone lost their wits?

"Steady!"

At the sound of the captain's stentorian voice every man, woman, and creature freezes, as though waking from a mass hallucination.

"Are you all out of your minds? Do you have any clue what kind of damage this out-of-control behavior can cause? I'm not going to stand back and watch us senselessly self-destruct after everything we've already survived. We manage to obliterate the Scourge, escape the gravitational pull of a black hole, deflect a bomb unscathed..."

"Nearly unscathed," murmurs a stray voice, and Ten knows it is a reference to the bomb squad that had died after the very first dark energy artery traverse. She hasn't realized that she has lost so much respect over that crisis, in spite of her best efforts to keep everyone safe. She struggles to rein in her temper. *Get angry, Ten,* she tells herself, *but do not lose control under any circumstances.* She can't afford to have any more mutinies.

"Good men sacrificed their lives in that jettison," she concurs. "Many people suffered burns or death from radiation. Some never even survived boot camp. And we've even beaten the odds against mines chasing us through a debris field. And now this entire ship is on the verge of imploding in a shitstorm of debauchery!"

"But we are the Sons of Neptune..." ventures someone. Another slurred voice retorts, "More like Sons of Uran--"

"Quiet!" This time the roar comes from Ironbear. The webbing of scars across her face speak more that any decorations, and between her physical evidence of hard battle and dangerous tone, the revelers know that she means business. The captain is not supposed to care whether or not her brothers and sisters in arms like her, but sometimes she secretly wishes that Ironbear's unswerving fealty was based upon free thought. Unlike Illiadus, who is often resented, most of the crew seem to want to please the Commander of the SMEF contingent, with her sturdy demeanor, not to mention her unusual Mohawk heritage and coif.

The murmuring descends in a rapid fade. The only sound is the clink and grinding of an empty glass bottle of Hibiki rolling away from Inari, who looks abashed.

Two of the insectoids—Coliuta and Weckl are their given humanoid names, since their language is not understood by anyone outside of their race—approach the commanding women. They began to beat out a rapid-fire communication rhythm that is usually left to diplomats and ambassadors to interpret, but SIBIL steps in to translate into the captain's earbuds, and Illiadus relays the message for the benefit of the crew. *Flaunting hierarchy from rank to rank is the nature of most people,* they drum, *but we higher-ranking people you call 'insectoids' will not be subjugated based on our physical makeup rather than our merits or lack thereof. We wish to replay this ritual with due respect to our kind.* A couple of their fellow chitin-shelled comrades, Copeland and Bozzio, hammer out a loud agreement.

The manic voice of a seasoned human Starback—Zivojinovich is his name—floats out of the throng. "Permission to speak, Captain? This tradition dates back hundreds of years. It's practically mandatory. Everyone knows the story. Blah, *blah,* blah, blaaahh...blah-blah-blah-BLAH!!! With all due respect, are you *ill?*"

All suddenly hush, a near vacuum-silence like a hand claps over every mouth, as it dawns upon the captain what she is called behind her back.

There is a long pause before she speaks, and it is the calm before a storm. "We will all regroup in twenty hours. You have heard these words from *Captain Ill.* At ease." And she turns on her heel and walks sharply back to the CIC, leaving the crew ill at ease indeed. They have just crossed the line.

Brushing past the disoriented crew, she dons the helmet that will connect her mind to SIBIL.

"What in the multiverse is going on? Besides this raucous tradition, there is unmistakably some other factor affecting my crew's behavior. Is it jump disorientation?" Illiadus is often frustrated at the emotionless machine and secretly irritated at herself for expecting a human response. She is not particularly animistic, but it is hard to forget when the searchlight-yellow virtual eyes lock with her own. And now SIBIL seems to be the only sane entity on the *Ekatarina.* Even the ship itself is making Illiadus feel slightly anthropomorphic, as if it mourns its big sister. She shakes herself violently, willing herself to come to her senses.

"The ritual, which can usually be controlled by the oversight of ranking superiors, has fallen into a volatile state due to interfering frequencies."

"Frequencies? From where?"

"I have detected a nebula two astronomical units away that appears to be emitting these. Some who have previously encountered it believe that it is a pocket of residual energy, while others believe that it is a vortex of collective consciousness. In any case, it appears to contain some sort of remnants of an ancient satellite caught on a rent corner of the time-space fabric and is sending these vibrations out in waves like some sort of signal. Because of its spiral appearance, its official name is the Nautilus Nebula."

"I see. And why, pray tell, is the *Ekatarina* so susceptible to these frequencies?"

"The whole ship is one big receptor. The coils and magnets in the engine are the biggest factors, but everything is affected: the metal hull resonates with the waves, as do the living creatures inside it. Basically, this craft detects every wave in a huge shotgun pickup pattern. What aggravates the situation further are the frequencies emitted by the ship—everything from communicational signals to the collective thoughts of the crew—creating phasing between the *Ekatarina* and the nebula."

Tennyson whistles softly. "It would certainly be quite the initiation if we can cross the invisible threshold and pass this nebula with our ship, crew, and minds intact."

"Precisely. Your kind is slow to adapt to new concepts. It took more time than necessary for humans to accept a heliocentric solar system, a round earth, evolution, and the capacity of the human race to nearly destroy itself and its own planet. You might think that proximity to a point in the time-space continuum would have lost its charm by the standards of many races, but I don't foresee this as ever being the case." SIBIL, who appears in the visual stimulus as a thirty-year-old human, smiles smugly like a woman still young enough to fancy herself attractive, yet old enough to think that she has all of the answers.

Tennyson grits her teeth and resolves to not rip the quantum helmet off and kick it to pieces. She is the Captain, and she is not going to let this inanimate object get the better of her. She wills herself into the utmost self-control before replying, "We have to let the crew carry out their ritual of the Mysteries of the Deep Space. I don't wish for any harm to come to those reveling fools on the EK, but there would be utter mutiny if I forbade it. I run a tight ship, but I'm no tyrant."

"Control freak, perhaps." SIBIL is obviously expanding her vocabulary for figures of speech at an alarming rate, and the double meaning does not go unnoticed by Illiadus.

"Allowing them to get it out of their systems would eventually help restore order," suggested SIBIL.

"You're not supposed to have empathy; you're a computer."

"Neither are you; you're a human."

Illiadus reflects on the wars that have taken place over the course of history—long before the Polisians banded together—and nodded somberly, although she is once again irritated that the AI unit is right, logical as the observation is. She does not want to be reminded of the destruction of Kallos, especially by this object that can calculate, store knowledge, and even develop, but can never know what it means to lose everything. The metal panels that contain this false prophet, a simulated consciousness looming omniscient within the walls of the spacecraft, taunts her. They are forged from the purest steel that she has tried so hard to be, and they flaunt the lack of emotion that she has failed to attain.

"You are agitated," observes SIBIL without emotion. Illiadus has forgotten how finely calibrated the AI unit is to her brain, and she sighs in resignation.

The yellow eyes of the AI's image bore into the captain's soul, bringing to Illiadus' mind a predator fixed on a target. "You would like to cuff me from time to time, isn't that true?" Illiadus clenched her jaw and said nothing.

"I am not corporeal. But your crew is. I have no ego, fears, or desires, but your crew does. And so are you, and so do you. Use this advantage wisely. You can fathom solutions to this program that I am not programmed to."

Illiadus is ashamed at the relief she suddenly feels from this virtual being stating its own shortcomings. Of course, everything has its shortcomings. And then something clicks in her mind—her quirky, unpredictable, and utterly human mind—and she assumes a faraway stare. "If it's crazy they want, then it's crazy they'll get."

Through some stroke of luck or lore, Lehmann manages to procure an old set of CIC speakers. He harnesses the electromagnetic fields, and the sulky-faced technicians he commandeered away from the nearby hullabaloo works with the captain in secret to try to understand the nature of these frequencies. By allowing the frequencies to be received by a previously discarded speaker, she is able to tune into hundreds of wavelengths: mostly sounds, but sometimes they are in the form of pure vibrations that she feels in her gut more than hears. They evoke myriad emotional responses ranging from joyous to fearful, until she begins to feel so agitated, she has to step away from the task now and again.

And the song, an artifact of a centuries-old signal projected by a satellite, comes through loud and clear in the form of a song. It is utterly atrocious to her ears; in fact, it is so horrible, it just might work. She has the main computer identify it.

Eureka.

With the click of a few buttons, she finds a huge sonic cesspool in the interstellar database of this musical dung. It is vapid-sounding, lyrically ignorant, and highly annoying. In fact, it is the perfect party music. And there seems to be a huge selection of songs from this source. By the time she has finished combing through an information bank and has prepared the sound files to be piped into the mess hall on cue, her smile has evolved from lupine to outright crocodilian.

"David, how many of those earpieces have we got?" Tennyson can barely conceal her excitement.

"Seven. Those will be for you, me, Lehmann—assuming that we can locate him and get him over here—Tiresias, Inari, Al-Quam, and Ironbear."

"I can operate the settings from the notch filter controller," the captain murmurs. "This should cancel out the incoming frequencies emanating from the Nautilus Nebula, as far as whatever our ears and pick up. The filter will also make us slightly more impervious to the nauseating soundtrack I have assembled. But we will still feel these vibrations in the very marrow of our bones, especially in our skulls. We don't have much time. One last thing: let's thaw out Ensign Thaleia."

David's expression doesn't change, but his sudden stillness reveals his surprise. "And the presence of this duplicitous, conniving bitch is important…how?"

"It isn't." Tennyson's smile doesn't quite reach her eyes. "I just think it would be a shame for that self-entitled little popsicle to miss out on all the fun. She's going to have to learn that a genetically engineered human with two PhDs is still not infallible. Especially when it comes to enduring musical torture."

Captain Tennyson Maria Illiadus clenches her jaw in determination. It is time to fight dirty with dirty. She is armed to the teeth with her plan. She is indeed a perfect Ten.

Her lupine grin is at once compelling and terrifying: downright mirthful, though everyone doubts that she will share the joke. Her thick unbound hair swirls around her head like a jet-black storm cloud.

"It's time to meet your real King Neptune, bitches!" she mutters to no one in particular.

And with that, she and the crew don the in-ear filters and march toward the main Mess. SIBIL heralds their approach by calmly announcing, "Let the games begin."

"Spacewogs and Starbacks. Listen up! This is a line crossing of epic significance. A mere pocket battleship was strong enough to survive a war in which the odds were grim, and now we are at the halfway point to what is home to so many of us. You Starbacks have earned your new status, to be sure. But guess what: I myself am a Diamondback, and my bite is deadly. For those of you who have *not* ¬¬¬¬learned your XYZ coordinates or crossed a point at which Antares, Sheliak, and the Sun are equidistant from your ship, 'Diamondback' is short for Royal Diamond Starback. And I know exactly what goes into these rites of passage, and how potentially disastrous they can be, putting an entire ship in mortal peril through unnecessary *stupidity*."

"But the ritual...surely you don't intend to stop it!"

Illiadus' smile grows wider and more chilling.

"Oh, *heavens* no, I'm not here to stop the festivities," she announces. "I'm here to participate."

Ten does not fraternize with the rest of the crew and everyone knows it. Her threat disguises as a self-invitation makes every sentient being shudder.

"But..." one of the newly-promoted Starbacks protests, "We've already been through the initiation!"

"Then you certainly won't mind it again, will you? Suck it up, big boy. There are some things that last more than two minutes."

"That ain't fair!"

Illiadus' mouth is smiling, but her black eyes are colder than any void they had seen.

"*Fair?* We've all lost loved ones, and you want to talk about *fair?* We've defeated the Scourge at a terrible price, a Dark Matter flood of Genesis proportions that destroyed all the wicked but also many of the good, and you still need *initiation?* But who am I to break an age-old tradition? Let us party!"

It is a ruthless rite of passage.

The entire main mess is decked out to resemble a crude sailing ship, complete with ropes and pilings, bamboo, coconut trees, and palm fronds. Ominous-looking black flags depict skulls and crossbones, which had once signified pirates, flutter from every corner, although even Tennyson herself is at a loss to understand why this has become part of 25th century amusement. The images on the wall screens are a shock to the eye. They are of parrots in bright, garish colors, mostly of a large screechy species called *macaws*. There are scenes of distant volcanoes, tropical islands with primitive accommodations, and oddly shaped drink ware full of beverages that are in colors only seen in nature to warn predators about toxicity. There are scantily clad men and women of various ages and states of physical shape, most of which are not considered to be attractive by any race's standards. There are small spherical objects in bright bands of colors that the virtual people keep lobbing into the air and back and forth to one another, although judging by the vacant smiles on their faces, this does not appear to be an act of hostility.

Ensign Thaleia is unable to hide the sheer bewilderment on her face as a few of the stronger crewmen and women reduce her shapely body to a human barbell, heaving her over their heads as she tries to remain ramrod straight. A few revelers, still resentful of the damage she has caused, call out, "Why the confusion? Isn't this part of your heritage or something? Oh, wait—you're genetically engineered—you don't have a heritage!" The young ensign's first true doubt of her own perfection is ill-concealed on her face.

The insectoids, who are not supposed to appear to have been cut any slack, are the assigned the task of enforcing the timing of the dancing, not unlike the designated drummers cuing enslaved boat rowers in ancient Earthen history. Next to the bug-like people, the commanding crew have hung decorations intended to terrify the insectoids into remaining on task, shaped like shoes—another psychological trigger that is ingrained into insectoid DNA—but the ersatz footwear is so obviously crudely made from papyrus fibers grown in the labs, that as long as rhythm-keepers pretend to be frightened, Tennyson and crew turn a blind eye to how they seem to enjoy creating complex polyrhythms. Weckl, Copeland, and another insectoid named Bruford can barely refrain from waving their antennae in delight. The only one of their species who is not enjoying himself is Rich, an ill-tempered being who is not well-liked by his comrades and has been tightly tied to a post, while he loudly clacks his mandibles in what is clearly a stream of incessant obscenities.

The insipid music is a twentieth-century genre—which Terran musicologists have tried to forget—that mainly touted tropical regions of Earth, fast food (a popular twentieth-century fare lacking nutritional value), and some sort of alcoholic beverage made from an earthen agave plant, the formula of which has long since been lost. Choreographic punishment involves wearing garlands of fake flowers and passing beneath a bar doing backbends, increasing in difficulty and pain each time the bar is lowered. Some non-terrestrial races have never seen a shark, and although they do not understand the humiliating choreography that accompanies one of the maddening songs, they try to endure. Appendages raise above their heads, palms (for those who had palms) press together to make a pinnacle, simulating fins. Moved to the left...then to the right... Some of the weaker ones who can no longer endure the piped-in sound begin to scream.

"Captain, is this horrible music really necessary? And what is a *cheeseburger*, anyway? And I thought that pirates were people who flew rogue ships to siphon fuel from other crafts... what does it have to do with covering one hand with a grappling hook and blocking one eye with a patch in this ridiculous getup, not to mention being forced to snarl like a Scourge whelp? Please tell me that people didn't really dress like this at any point in time."

"Why is there a woman to blame in the song?"

"Captain, with all due respect, I can't take this music anymore! I've heard of Spacewogs, Shellbacks, and Diamondbacks, but I don't want to be branded with this Macaw-head title of which you speak! With all due respect, please make it stop, *make it stop!!!*"

Exhausted and hung over, the new initiates ooze their way back to their cramped co-ed quarters. The captain has promoted all revelers to the status of Diamondbacks, but everyone is too badly shaken to care. Their senses have been buffeted beyond torture.

The last crewmember to leave is a shy, large-brained insectoid whose given humanoid name has been forgotten by many, but who is affectionately dubbed by his comrades of all races as "Pratt." He tucks under his wing one of his favorite Terran artifacts that is said to have been called a "book," inclines his head in a nearly humanlike gesture, raises one antenna in salute, and cheerfully scuttles off to his sleeping bunk. All that remains is the two-foot-high debris comprised largely of confetti, discarded drink ware, hastily ripped costumes, vomit, squashed hydroponic limes, broken main Mess tables, a flummoxed command crew, and one very satisfied captain.

"Ten," says Lehmann tentatively, "we didn't know that you had such a wicked sense of humor."

"I don't."

"How did you know that it would work?"

Tennyson thoughtfully eyes the helmet that connects her mind to SIBIL. "I'm only human," she replies dryly.

And then the phasing stops.

With so many of the crew returning to Cold Sleep, there is no longer a feedback loop between the *Ekatarina* and the Nautilus Nebula. Now in their purest form, the frequencies wash over the remaining crew in a flood of emotions: bliss, longing, revenge, lust, spirituality, and yearning for material goods they have never wanted before. Not audible, as sound can not travel through space, but more vibrations of energy.

"Captain...?" Ironbear's terse inquiry is the softest anyone has ever heard her voice. The others feel it. Illiadus looks haggard, but triumphant.

"We are passing the Nautilus soon enough," reassures Illiadus. "I think it's safe to tune in to the last few waves."

And so, before returning to Cold Sleep, Captain Tennyson Maria Illiadus bids the crew to sit and rest in the CIC for a spell, where they feel the last few fading frequencies in their bodies, bringing to mind images of a jailhouse, and a rock.

Captain's Log, The Ekatarina

Seventy-Third Jump Completed.

A lucky series of improbably straight dark energy arteries have allowed us to cross a full eighth of our journey in a record amount of time. Crew morale has been quite high over the last thirteen jumps since the outrageous incident of our galactic line-crossing ceremony two years ago. I've taken the risk of allowing Ensign Thaleia back on full duty roster for these last twenty-four months because we simply have so few junior officers left from the original crew with her skills and training. Her work to date has been exemplary but as far as I and Ironbear are concerned that arrogant, genetically engineered pain in the ass will be on probation until we actually get home. I'm hoping that our run of bad luck is finally behind us. End Log.

Straight From The Source

by Aldea Berrycloth

Ship's Chronometer: 2440 AD

"Yes, that is reveille you are hearing, Crew," Ensign Ilborna Trireenan says with a wide smile and mellifluous voice, "it is zero five hundred hours ship time, so drop your socks, scrub that crotch, brush those teeth, shave what's gotta be shaved, and get your butts into gear… good morning, *Ekatarina*! Welcome to another wonderful day aboard the Polisian fleet's finest pocket battleship in this quadrant of The Milky Way, wherever the heck that is, God forbid anyone can ever get a straight answer from the Astronavigtor, am I right? As I'm sure you've figured out by now, I am none other than ship's reporter Ensign Ilborna Trireenan and this is *Straight From The Source*!"

A blare of synthetic music playing the Polisian Fleet theme fills the ships corridors for a full ten seconds before fading away.

"Yeah," Ilborna says, "that groovy tune just never gets old does it? Now, as you can see on the corridor video panels or your own bunk's monitors my hair color is multi-spectral today! No monochromatic look for this mop. Green, purple, yellow, and red are the hues for today, so deal with it! Today marks three weeks since our duty shift woke from cryosleep since the last dark artery jump. And if I said it once I'll say it a thousand times, am I the only one still hung over and sore since that *crossing the line* ceremony two years ago! Yowza. I've never been that plastered in my life. And I'll repeat what I've said every morning for the last twenty-one days, I remember almost nothing and deny any and all responsibility for any questionable actions I may or may not have taken on that crazy day. Hah!"

Ilborna grabs a cup and gulps down some java before leaning forward.

"Now," she says, "it looks like my little show is starting to become popular as this week I've received no less than twenty questions and messages from the crew and I am now going to try to answer a select few so strap in as we are about to lift off."

Ilborna leans back in a very unmilitary pose and smiles. In fact, her entire appearance is far from regulation as her hair is not tied back and she is only wearing a wife-beater t-shirt that displays all her neck and arm tattoos normally covered by a uniform. Faded shark-skin jeans and combat boots shroud her lower half. The only reason she gets away with this breach in protocol is because her broadcasts are all done off-duty, on her own time. Twelve hours a day she works maintenance on the ship's waste reclamation machinery, the other twelve are her own, and when not sleeping she travels The *Ekatarina's* corridors looking for stories and writing her own copy for her daily morning wake up show.

"First letter," Ilborna says, "from anonymous crewman. Hey Ilborna, I've got a bet going with a lazy spic slob currently in coldsleep. He said you're half-Hawaiian, one-quarter Mexican, and one-quarter Chinese. I say bull. You're from Singapore, I just know it. So gimme the good news so I can collect my credits. Oh, I've got bad news, crewman! Seems like sleeping beauty got the straight scoop on my gene scan. How, I have no idea, but yeah, you've lost that bet."

Ilborna points her right hand at the monitor camera in front of her and pantomimes firing a blaster pistol.

"Pew pew pew! Okay," she continues, "next letter is from Anonymous Marine. Dear Ilborna, what's the follow up to whether or not Chief of Security and Commander of Space Marines Major Helen Ironbear is really a man? Okay, I've gathered a ton of intel on this mission, Anonymous Marine, but I'm afraid I'm just not quite ready to give a full report. I'm going to shit-can this conversation for a future show. But I promise you as a grunt by association, as soon as I get some solid *rumint* from one of my secret squirrels, you'll hear it straight from the source! On to the next letter."

Ilborna raises her eyebrows comically at the camera three times before picking up another paper printout.

"And my third letter is from Anonymous Scientist," Ilborna says, "damn, seems like everyone messaging this morning is a chickenshit ninja.

Oh well, Anonymous Scientist tells me… dear Ilborna, do you think there is any truth in the recent rumor that the ship has been caught in a temporal causality loop ever since we exited the last dark energy artery and we've been reliving the same day over and over again for god knows how many times without retaining any memory of it?"

Ilborna looks up with a wicked smirk.

"I can neither confirm nor deny that rumor, scientist, but I suppose on a pucker factor of one to ten, that would qualify for a tight nine."

Ilborna sits up a little straighter.

"Well crew, we're rapidly closing in on zero five fifteen hours and the end of this broadcast. I've got four hours to nab a plate of shit on a shingle in our sorry excuse for a mess hall then hit the decks running to shovel up more news. My closing quote for today is from the late Eugene Ionesco, a twentieth century Terran playwright who once said, *Cut off from his religious, metaphysical and transcendental roots, man is lost; all his actions become senseless, absurd, useless.* Ponder those charming words as we begin preparations for tomorrow's headfirst leap into a new dark energy artery on our epic and never quite boring star voyage back to Earth. This is Ensign Ilborna Trireenan and you have been watching *Straight From The Source!*"

Ilborna signs off with a tap of her index finger on her bunk monitor.

Licking her lips free of the last of the chipped beef, Ilborna starts jogging down the main corridor that leads away from the mess hall. She is still dressed as she has been in her earlier broadcast but with a dark blue utility cap on her head that has a small thumb-sized camera eye near the front top below which sits a white card with the word *PRESS* lazily scrawled across it. She taps an inset button on the right side of the cap and says out loud, "…and we are rolling!" The cap camera has a twenty-four-hour memory chip, but never taking any chances, Ilborna is also live-streaming to a backup storage unit in her bunk.

The *Ekatarina's* sole Reporter jogs in a straight line for about twenty yards, expertly dodging and twice even pirouetting around fellow crew whose presence dares to impede her movement. A few seconds later she dances through a hatchway and walks rapidly down a narrower side corridor before sliding unannounced into the main Sick Bay.

"Dr. Sorlan," Ilborna shouts to the Ship's Doctor who is busy opening cabinets while two Ship's Nurses sterilize an exam table with tubular contraptions spraying pink foam that quickly evaporates after striking a surface, "any truth to the rumors that you are experimenting on new cybernetic enhancements to the ship's Marines, creating, in essence, a fighting force of killer cyborgs?"

Sorlan snorts in surprise and good humor, "I think it would be easier to create Terran/Teenerian hybrid genetic super soldiers than what you're suggesting, Ensign Hearsay."

"Wow," Ilborna shouts, "I'm quoting you on that one, doc. Later!"

Before Sorlan can reply, Ilborna shoots out of the sickbay.

Racing down several more corridors deeper into the ship, she gets the high-five from two crewmen swabbing a deck and three Marines on their morning run.

"Straight from the source," one chubby male Terran crewman shouts after slapping her hand, "when we getting home?"

"Sooner than later," Ilborna shouts back over her shoulder, "if tomorrow's big test pays off."

Ilborna dashes into one of the *Ekatarina's* storage rooms and instantly spots Chief Warrant Officer Yaqub Al-Quam studying a series of weapons schematics on a large wall monitor by himself.

"Chief," Ilborna says loudly, "*Straight From The Source* news service. Subhanallah, my Muslim brother. So, is that some new super cannon you're developing for the ship? Something that can, like, blow up whole moons if they get in our way or try to attack us?"

"Are you permanently deaf, Ensign?" Al-Quam snaps, "I've told you a dozen times to never approach me again."

"Aw, come on Chief," Ilborna says in her most seductive voice, "doesn't the Koran say, *Try to have as many as possible true friends, for they are the supplies in joy and the shelters in misfortunes?*"

"You try my patience young one," Al-Quam sighs, "and no, this is not some dramatic offensive weapon, merely a redesign of the tertiary heat-sinks for the lateral torpedo array. Now please, you know you do not have clearance to be in this section of the ship. Please leave before a security contingent spots you and drags you off to the brig."

"Buzzkill," Ilborna blurts and sticks out her tongue right before dashing out of the storage room and back into the hallway while shouting over her shoulder, "ma'aasalaama!"

Al-Quam scowls at the impudence of the reporter, but when he is sure she is completely out of sight, shakes his head, smiles, and indulges in a short chuckle.

Two lefts, a right, straight on for thirty yards, and then back up two levels and she walks into one of the rear food preparation pantries behind the mess hall's main kitchen.

The ship's head cook, Chief Petty Officer Melanie Inari is just sending off three of her staff to start on lunch when turning around she finds herself face to face with Ilborna.

"*Straight From The Source*, Cookie," Ilborna smiles, "would you care to comment on the rumors that meat stores have been slowly and surreptitiously replaced by the dead flesh of the many alien enemies we've defended ourselves against on recent planetfalls and ship incursions? No need to be shy. Much of the crew feels that the recent increase in shipboard flatulence has to be a physiological reaction to something new in our daily rations. So, anything you want to say on the record about new secret ingredients?"

Inari, her face calm, walks five steps toward a nearby countertop, picks up a large meat cleaver and turns around.

"A shortage of protein is no joking matter," the cook says, walking towards Ilborna and swinging the cleaver back and forth slowly, "and any wasted and *useless* source of said material is always ripe for acquisition..."

Her eyes wide, Ilborna spins on her heel and makes tracks.

Ilborna enters the Teenerian Berthing Compartments located in the ventral aft of The *Ekatarina*. Well over half of the aliens are drowsing in coldsleep, in cryopods modified into large circular shapes to accommodate the four different Teenerian species (Arachnoid, Cephalopodic, Aves, and Lepidoptera). The normal sleeping bunks for Teenerians are a strange collection of weblike pods, liquid filled half shells, suspended nests near the ceiling, and tree-bark-like forms glued or welded to the bulkheads, about three meters above the deck. Two-thirds are in their sleep shifts and the rest are going about their many duties around the ship.

Ilborna spots a couple of the arachnids feeding on protein paste from one of the communal troughs and trots up to them. She slaps the ship's translator on her hip and starts talking.

"Ensign Ilborna Trireenan, *Straight From The Source*," she says, "mind if I ask you fellas some questions?"

One of the arachnoids stops eating, raises a fifth claw-arm and taps a small metal device wedded to its upper thorax.

"I am Private Tah-Achonn-Gull," its mechanized translated voice speaks into Ilborna's ear plugs, "and we were told to avoid all interrogative conversations with The *Ekatarina's Flaunter-of-Gossip*. I recognize you by your cranial ornamentation. You should not be here."

"Aw, come on, fellas," Ilborna smiles even though she had no idea if human facial expressions can be read by Teenerians, "just one grunt to another."

"We are enlisted personnel," it says, "and you an officer, albeit a low-ranking one. We do not [untranslatable] your attempt at fraternization."

"Whatever," Ilborna rolls her eyes, "just answer one question, okay?"

"What?" Tah-Achon-Gull asks.

"There is a rumor going around that certain of your, um, species, and certain of mine, have been meeting off hours to engage in, ohhhh… personal private acquaintance rituals that normally only occur between members of the same, uh, species…"

Tah-Achon-Gul turns to the other Arachnoid and Ilborna surmises they are communicating with each other silently via the exchange of complex scent hormones. A few moments later Gul turns back toward her and his mechanical voice starts back up.

"Is this question one of curiosity, documentary research, or personal interest, Ensign?"

"What?" Ilborna asks, caught off guard.

"I have studied both the Expeditionary Force and Space Navy Manuals on interpersonal relationships amongst military personnel. Though [untranslatable] between officers and enlisted is frowned upon, it is not necessarily forbidden… and I am currently off duty for the next hour and am feeling quite amenable to the… how did the Terran slang manual put it… [untranslatable] beast with two backs. But I do have one question of my own."

"And what's that?" Ilborna says, literally shocked at the direction the conversation had taken.

"Can my buddy, Private Narh-Boll-Trallon, watch?"

Ilborna double-times it out of the alien barracks while the going is good.

A short while later Ilborna makes her way to the third to last upper deck, bow, and enters the largest of the ship's four hydroponic gardens. As she hopes, it is currently only inhabited by her favorite gardener, Sergeant David Alberman, a tall, handsome, and fit, dark man of African ancestry in his early forties who is definitely born with a green thumb. It seems like there isn't anything he can't grow in his thousands of hanging trays and shelves.

"Sgt. Alberman," Ilborna shouts, "*Straight From The Source*. Is there any truth to the rumor that shortages in proper approved fertilizers have forced you to randomly waylay non-essential wandering Teenerian crew for instant vivisection and spreading of their remains to keep your production of fruits and vegetables on schedule? I promise that your identity will remain confidential if you wish to answer off the record."

"When it comes to non-essential crew," Alberman smiles, "I'd strongly suggest from now on you travel with at least one companion during these fact-finding missions of yours."

"Ouch," Ilborna laughs.

"Here," Alberman says, tossing a fist-sized strawberry which the reporter deftly catches, "new variety. Tell me what you think."

Ilborna takes a large bite and red juices drip down her chin.

"Oh my god," she gasps, "that's delicious."

"Yeah, wonderful stuff that Teenerian fertilizer," he replies.

They both laugh for a moment and Ilborna walks up to watch him adjust the water and nutrient conduits feeding five overhead trays. She reaches up and taps the *off* switch on her cap camera.

"Speaking of fertilization," Ilborna says neutrally, "I see something you missed."

"What?" Alberman replies, looking around himself worriedly.

"Me," Ilborna says before leaping up onto the sergeant, wraps her legs around his hips, her arms around his head, and shoves her tongue into his mouth.

The interview is decidedly over.

Ilborna, completely naked and sporting a wide variety of tattoos spread across most of her body with the exception of her face and hands, dives through the open hatch and into the largest of the five water reservoirs in the lowest of The *Ekatarina's* bow decks.

The not quite ice-cold water scours her flesh, stripping away the sweat and grime acquired from the rough and tumble sex she'd just shared with Sergeant Alberman. Though there is fractional lighting in this aquatic environment, Ilborna's lithe movements are confident and strong as she moves forward by twenty body-lengths using an inverted breaststroke. At the last possible second, she brings herself to a halt and shoots upward a full meter until her head breaks surface in a dark recess in the upper deck. She exhales and takes in a full half-dozen breaths before dropping back into the water.

It was just over a year ago that Ilborna had reconnoitered this particular locale. Though it took her awhile, she'd managed to acquire detailed schematics of The *Ekatarina* after trading a sufficient number of watch-shifts and favors. If there was one thing (other than her entire extended family and all of her childhood friends) that she misses from her home colony world of Tethys, it is swimming in the ocean. She was born on a planet entirely covered in water and populated by colonists who lived on both floating cities and down within subterranean domes in the shallow parts of the planet. Every child became an expert swimmer and diver by the age of five. After The Scourge had destroyed all life on Tethys when she was off planet on a class trip, Ilborna hacked and altered her identity chip, gaining access to Polisian Fleet basic training at the true age of thirteen. And now, roughly four years later, not counting downtime in coldsleep, she finds herself wondering what the purpose to her life is, now that she has to accept surviving the suicide mission The *Ekatarina* was on when delivering the dark matter fountain bomb that has utterly destroyed the entire Scourge species.

Her recent work as a ship's reporter and transmission personality added a little purpose to her present life. One nice thing about Tethys was that it had a huge sociological archive stored in the main computers, and at a very young age Ilborna had become a voracious amateur historian. She eventually became fascinated by late twentieth and early twenty-first century American radio, tv, cable, and streaming talk shows. Ironically, none of her ancestors ever lived in the United States or spoke English as a first language, but she was completely and utterly charmed by the sayings, slang, and catch-phrases of that particular time period and location of popular entertainment. *Straight From The Source* is her tribute to an exciting bygone era.

Her skin starts to go numb and the urge to open her mouth grows stronger, but she makes no effort to surface as she continues to swim forward into the darkness.

Why not end it here, she thinks, *back home on Tethys, a water funeral was considered quite natural, and generally chosen by the populace.*

Her skin grows even colder and she clenches her jaws tighter as black spots begin forming before her eyes as she nears the diffuse light peeking at her up ahead.

Would anyone miss me? She thinks, *would it change anything?*

Just as she is feeling she is about to black-out, Ilborna arches her back and thrusts both of her hands forward and up. She breaks through the surface of the water and grabs the edges of the hatchway that she had originally dove through.

After pulling her clothes on, she slams the hatch shut. Walking away she shouts over her shoulder, "Alpha Mike Foxtrot!"

Timing is everything, and at zero eight hundred hours, with sixty minutes left before she has to make it to her duty station, Ilborna does the truly unthinkable and sidles into the Main Engineering Bay doing her best to stay behind several large Marines out of the sightlines of the group of officers engaged in an animated conversation. In all her newsgathering trips upon The *Ekatarina*, this is the first time she's snuck into a restricted area that has been simultaneously occupied by the ship's senior staff. It is a big risk and her heart pounds in her chest as her mouth goes dry.

Standing around a large table whose surface is entirely taken up by a touch-sensitive view screen, they are debating a series of complex schematics that Ilborna can barely make out a full thirty feet away, though she zooms her camera in as tightly as possible while turning her microphone up to full gain.

One of the Marines in front of her, one Sergeant Bryce, catches sight of Ilborna out of the corner of his eye, frowns, then smiles and winks at her before turning around and ignoring her.

Present at the main table is that hot, arrogant, genetically-engineered bitch, Ensign Thaleia, ship's Head Engineer the all too friendly Lt. Commander Walter Lehmann, that recent alien recruit the Teenerian with total recall and the coolest skin pattern modeling ever, Crewman Farko Tiresias, Dr. Bream who oversees the programming for the Captain's AI, the dreaded Captain Ills herself, and to her right is none other than Head of Security and every crewmen's walking, talking, stalking nightmare, Major Helen Ironbear. Ilborna is pretty damn sure they are talking about tomorrow's dark energy artery transit and hopes she can snag some solid quotes for tomorrow morning's show. The captain suddenly slams her fist onto the table.

"Enough," Illiadus shouts, "I don't like this better than any of you, but if we are going to return this crew to Earth within our lifetimes, we have to create a more efficient and reliable navigation-predictor. I'm sorry Dr. Bream, but the loss of Maxwell and most of your staff over the past several years is no longer an acceptable excuse for stalling further progress. Ensign Thaleia and Crewman Tiresias have spent two months catching up on everything your former cadre of cyberneticists knew and were capable of. Following your specific instructions and working with the Chief, they have fabricated and created the more complex and impressive prototype that you conceived of years ago. Walter here has tested the equipment through numerous simulations, and…"

"Computer simulations," Dr. Bream says, "no human testing whatsoever."

"Stop playing games, Doctor," Illiadus retorts, "I'm the only human left on this ship biologically compatible with the current neural technology. There are no other human subjects to test the new quantum helmet on. I will not put off a jump-test any longer, and that is my final decision on this matter. SIBIL and I discussed the potential dangers thoroughly and she is enthusiastic about tomorrow's experiment. We're moving forward on this. Do I make myself clear?"

"Yes Captain," Bream replies, "though I humbly request that my dissenting opinion be placed on the permanent record."

"Fine," Illiadus said disparagingly, "it's on the record. So now you don't have to worry about any of my relatives suing you for malpractice."

A small burst of laughter explodes from Ilborna and she instantly slams both of her hands over her mouth.

Every head at the engineering table turns in her direction as Bryce and his fellow Marine sidestep, right and left, fully exposing her presence.

"Uh," Ilborna mumbles as she instantly stands to attention, "Ensign Ilborna Trireenan, *Straight From The Source*, ship's news service, Captain. May I, umm… quote you on that last statement?"

Twelve hours later Ilborna shoots to her feet as the hatch to The Brig opens. Gulping, she stands ramrod straight at full attention when she realizes that Major Ironbear is her guest. Ilborna licks her lips and readies herself for the onslaught. As an enthusiastic reporter she has done her homework on all the senior officers awhile back. They almost all have tragic backgrounds preceding the war, most entering service with revenge-filled hearts. Helen Ironbear is no different in this regard, but her rise through the ranks is a thing of legend. She joined the Space Marines at seventeen years old, entering boot camp with a no-nonsense thick-skinned attitude and bullseye focus that impressed even the most cynical of Drill Instructors. She made Sergeant within her first year on the light space cruiser *Mayhem*, and Staff Sergeant two years later. It was during her heroic actions on the world Arcus, leading an evacuation of colonists after the entire chain of command above her had been killed by a Scourge missile, that she showed her true mettle. She was given an immediate battlefield commission to Second Lieutenant. Seven years later she'd worked her way up the ladder to Major and third in command of the *Ekatarina*. And now here she is looking at Ilborna with hungry hawk-like eyes.

"At ease, Ensign," Ironbear says in a neutral voice, walking right up to the steel bars that separate the two of them by mere inches, "Christ, you look like smashed ass and buttered corn chips. No, let me change that. You look like a spilled can of fuck. Now, for the record, the Captain merely requested your removal from main engineering. It was my personal decision to let you cool off down here for a while. You know, it's really not that damn difficult to avoid restricted areas on this ship. It's not like you've been asked to eat a bushel of apples and shit a fruit salad. Holy shit! I've never seen anything so stupid. I'd bet dollars to dickheads nobody has ever seen anything so dumb in this warship. What in the holy mother of dog fuck is wrong with you, you malformed coat hanger dodger? You're so fucking stupid that if you fell into a barrel of tits, you would come out sucking your thumb. Has anyone ever told you that you have the traits of a child whose mother frequently drank Drano throughout her pregnancy? How the fuck were you the fastest sperm, Ensign? Seriously, do you know what the speed of light is? It's the speed at which you fucked up today, Ensign, and it damn well better be the last mistake you make for the rest of your life. Do I make myself clear?"

"Yes Sir," Ilborna says smartly, "very good Sir."

"Yes… real shipshape, are we?" Ironbear smirks, "looks like that lucky thirteen tattoo on your left arm finally bit you on the ass. You know the only reason you're not going to spend the next year behind these bars is because this crew has been balls-to-nutsack for far too long, and any distraction from the daily S.N.A.F.U. this cruise has become, and that includes your shit morning news show, is considered an unfortunate but urgent necessity by the Captain."

"Uhhhh… thank you, I think, Sir."

"Tell me, Ensign," Ironbear says, "do you believe in the theory of evolution?"

"Yes, Major."

"Well, I did too, until I met you. You, Ensign, are proof against both evolution and creationism, because *neither* would allow for your fucking existence on my god damned ship. You're worse than a bathtub full of abortions and more fucked up than a left-handed football bat! You're about as useful as an ashtray on a motorcycle. You make me wanna go to my bunk and rinse my mouth out with a hand blaster. I have pimples older and wiser than you, jackoff. You are the load your mother should have swallowed. I swear to God that if you were one of my Marines the only use you'd have in combat would be as a mobile sandbag. Ensign, goddammit, you are the reason I used to beat my nieces!"

Ironbear taps a portion of her wrist com unit and the metal bars in front of her retract into the walls.

"You're free to leave," Ironbear adds, "no marks on your permanent record, and your Crew Chief was told you were needed elsewhere during your last shift, so no repercussions. Also, for reasons that are completely beyond my understanding and imagination, the Captain has officially requested your presence, as the ship's lone reporter, in the CIC at zero nine hundred hours for tomorrow morning's dark energy artery jump. Regulation uniform and military grooming standards will apply, of course, so make sure every damn one of your Tats is covered. You'll be recording the event for your news show, and posterity, Ensign, so do not fuck it up. Dismissed!"

Ilborna salutes Ironbear, who returns it, and walks toward the hatchway when a stern note in Ironbear's voice stops the Ensign in her tracks.

"But I swear, sugar britches" Ironbear starts, "if I *ever* catch you wearing that ridiculous press cap while spying on me anywhere, and I do mean absolutely anywhere on this ship, I will take it quite *personally*."

Ilborna can't help noticing the way the Major's right hand caresses the wedge and eye of her holstered tactical tomahawk on that last word and a cold chill shoots up the Ensign's spine.

"And Ensign," Ironbear finishes, "I suggest you run with the speed of a burning rat back to your rack… now!"

Ilborna leaves, no, *escapes* the brig as fast as her frightened young legs can carry her.

Zero nine hundred hours and things are running late in the CIC, but only a little late. A last-minute diagnostic on the Captain's new quantum helmet raises a few red flags but the delays appear to be coming to an end.

Ensign Ilborna Trireenan, wearing a freshly ironed black and green fleet uniform with her hair tied down tight beneath the traditional space navy tri-fold silver cap (which houses her video camera eye and audio mics) walks around the periphery of the room trying to record as many faces as possible. This is her first time in the CIC, an area off limits to all but the most necessary and critical personnel, with sophisticated security features she is wise enough never to have considered circumventing during her daily news searching throughout the *Ekatarina*.

Various crew man a variety of consoles on the periphery of the large room, among whom are ship's Engineer, Lt. Commander Walter Lehmann and first officer Commander David Aithon. Guarding each of the four entrances are two fully-armed Marines, each handpicked by Ironbear herself, a permanent assignment rumored to have started immediately after the failed mutiny by Gunnery Sergeant Hatfield and his followers. Major Helen Ironbear stands near the main entrance scanning the interior of the room like a missile looking for radar-lock. Considering their last encounter, Ilborna does her best to not make eye contact with the intimidating officer.

Large flat monitors cover most of the surrounding walls. In the center of the room, sitting in a raised command seat, Captain Illiadus sits ramrod straight as the new quantum helmet is lowered onto her head by both Crewman Tiresias and Ensign Thaleia. Dr. Bream stands several feet away watching the whole procedure with a large frown on his face. Unlike the former helmet which looks like the carcass of a porcupine covered in Christmas lights, this new headgear strongly resembles a fighter pilot crash helmet mated with a virtual gaming visor and wrapped in about a mile of crisscrossed diamond twine. It covers all but the captain's face from the eyebrows down to her chin, and up to the edge of her lips on either side.

Ilborna walks forward and stops about eight feet from the Captain.

"For the edification of the ship's reporter," the Captain says, "the inner surface of this new prototype quantum helmet, is covered with over three thousand micro-electrodes that are the heart of this brain-machine interface. When the connection is made, my mind will be mated with the ship's artificial intelligence, SIBIL. This experience is almost impossible to put into words that make any sense but suffice it to say if feels like instantly becoming a schizophrenic genius who can play Go and Chess simultaneously while a dozen movies are being projected on the back of your eyelids."

"That sounds," Ilborna says, "like a totally irrational scenario to, ummm… operate in, Sir."

"Right you are, Ensign," Illiadus chuckles, "and we are now adding a whole series of probability and statistic algorithms that along with a more direct and cooperative mental interface between me and SIBIL, should allow me to plot and navigate a much more efficient series of jumps via the dark energy arterials we've been using to return to Earth. Okay. All further communication from me will be via ship's speakers as I am engaging mind-lock in ten, nine, eight…"

Ilborna zooms in on the Captain's face for the rest of the countdown when her lips close shut after saying "one."

"Ensign, over here."

Ilborna realizes that Commander Aithon has just waived her over to his console at the nearest wall. He motions to her to take the empty seat next to him.

"Captain's orders," he says, "I'm to allow you to record her virtual vision, audio, etc. via this screen."

A moment later the eighty-inch screen in front of her lights up, showing what appears to be an empty duplicate of the CIC. A second later she realizes it is a POV shot, as if she is looking through the Captain's eyes. As the virtual captain turns to the right, Ilborna gasps at the sight of SIBIL, a beautiful first lieutenant in her late twenties wearing a perfectly fitting bridge uniform exactly like her own and standing nearly two meters tall.

"She looks so human," Ilborna whispers.

SIBIL turns to her left on the screen, tilts her head sideways, and smiles while looking right into the Captain's virtual eyes as she winks and mouths the words, *Thank you, Ensign*, before turning back around to view the virtual CIC main screen wall.

Ilborna blushes as Commander Aithon leans in.

"SIBIL is tied into every monitoring system on the ship," he says, "she sees all and knows all."

Ilborna gulps and nods her head.

"This is the Captain," an almost robotic sounding version of Illiadus's voice blares from the surrounding speakers, "to all crew. We have reached the entry point of the dark energy artery designated Epsilon-ninety-nine. Maintain stations until further orders. SIBIL has supplied me with a quote from Orison Swett Marden, an author in both the nineteenth and twentieth centuries. *We advance on our journey only when we face our goal, when we are confident and believe we are going to win out.*"

She lets that sink in for a moment and then begins speaking again.

"Jump on Captain's mark," the speakers throughout the ship state, "mark!"

Three hours into the dark energy artery and everything appears nominal to Ilborna. The main viewscreen, in both the real CIC and the captain's virtual copy display the strange, unexpected bizarreries of fire-like plasma in a rippling, ever-morphing non-Euclidean and almost organic-looking massive tunnel that they hurl through in a barely controlled, endless fall.

They are traveling vast distances, though precise navigation is a problem this latest jump is supposed to offer a breakthrough on. If all goes as hoped, when they exit this artery, they should have a more clearly focused and precise procedure for choosing long stretches of the dark energy arteries that lead directly toward the Sol System, and take decades, if not centuries, off this journey.

Everyone is still on full alert and attending to their duties, monitoring consoles, etc., but it is the constant back and forth conversation between the Captain and SIBIL in their virtual copy of the CIC that fascinates Ilborna most of all. There is a closeness, a comradery if you will, between the two that is akin to two sisters, or a mother and daughter. The captain seems more relaxed, more human, in the sim than Ilborna has ever witnessed, albeit from a distance, on the ship.

"Captain," Commander Aithon speaks into his mic, "we've exceeded minimal travel time by eight minutes."

"Very good," the Captains voice speaks, "I think that's enough for this first test run of the new helmet, right SIBIL? Crew, prepare for arterial exit in three zero seconds. My calculations show we'll be reappearing about ninety-five million miles from a Sol-sized yellow sun, whose inner and middle systems contain no planetary bodies. Projected mass indicators do not detect any asteroid fields."

"Battle Stations," Aithon yells out, "I repeat, Battle Stations." He then turns and smiles at Ilborna, "for the sake of our viewers many years from now, we are not expecting battle of any kind. This is a precautionary protocol in case we exit onto a portion of the Galaxy that is for whatever reason engaged in some type of combat operations, and we find ourselves on the defensive. The odds of this happening are probably ten million to one…"

"Exit," the Captain says.

On the main view screen in the CIC, the kaleidoscopic *light show* that is the interior of a Dark Energy Artery immediately flickers into and out of existence for five seconds when a slight shake hits the ship and the blackness of space and background stars appear.

Ilborna gulps nervously, knowing they have just exited sub-space and are coasting at nine-tenths the speed of light. Because of the lack of planets, braking procedures will not commence for a full minute. Once the astronavigator, a sophisticated A.I. in its own right, makes a series of five-second calculations, they will know roughly where they are in the galaxy and hopefully have a finer grasp on how to more effectively plot out future dark energy arteries.

"Captain," a Teenerian Warrant Officer manning the navigation console on the other side of the CIC says through his translator, somehow managing to elicit a sense of panic, "multiple target intercept in fifteen seconds."

"That's impossible," Illiadus replies from the speaker, "SIBIL, I can't see…"

"Comet fragments," the A.I. says with the slightest hint of fear, "it must have just broken up. Instrumentation was not set this low in the parabola of this star. The odds of this happening at this moment are millions to one."

"The Staver Field," the Captain shouts.

"Should deflect the majority of ice debris but…," SIBIL hesitates for a microsecond, "there are at least two dozen objects between twenty to fifty feet in diameter."

"Brace for impacts," the Captain's voice fills the ship, "brace for impacts."

Moments later The *Ekatarina* reaches, enters, and flies through the icy debris field. A half a dozen of the larger comet chunks close in on a tight trajectory but manage to get no closer than three klicks to the ship. Two knuckle-biting minutes later and it feels to Ilborna like they are going to make it through okay.

"Brace brace brace," the Captain says, and the ship shakes hard. Ilborna manages to keep to her feet, but then a series of four more shocks vibrate through *Ekatarina* and the Ensign is knocked back onto her ass.

"We have multiple impacts, Captain," Chief Engineer Lehman shouts from his console, "potential structural damage to the Main Engines, Staver Field Generator, the Ship's Ventral Heat Sink Array, Garden Deck… we're venting atmosphere from five decks…"

"General Quarters!" the Captain's voice blares from every speaker in The *Ekatarina*, "General Quarters! Damage Control Parties to form up immediately and report to the following locations."

Ilborna ignores the orders being given as she staggers out of the CIC and towards the nearest ladder. Alberman's hydroponic garden is on the Garden Deck. She heads down to the lower decks as fast as her shaking legs can carry her. Some gunk keeps dripping into her eyes and after a few seconds of wiping it away she realizes it is blood. She somehow cut her forehead just above her left eyebrow. Ilborna stops for a few precious seconds to yank off her regulation silver neck wrap and tie it tightly around her head as a makeshift bandage, not even aware that she is still wearing her Space Navy Cap and that her camera and mics are still operating.

"All crew evacuate decks eight and nine," the Captain's voice blares in the corridors, "I repeat, all crew evacuate decks eight and nine. Emergency bulkheads lowering."

This last order causes Ilborna more than a little hassle as three times she has to circumnavigate blocked corridors, thanking a wide variety of her ancestor's deities that her reporter duties have encouraged her to learn every nook, cranny, dead end, and shortcut throughout the *Ekatarina*. Three times she presses herself against the side of the corridor to allow emergency repair crews by, far too intent on their duties to give her the slightest notice. Twice, the artificial gravity fluctuates, and she floats off the deck for a few seconds before dropping down without notice, barely avoiding spraining her ankles.

"The Singularity Drive has been damaged," the Captain's voice blasts from the nearest wall speaker, "A-G will be spotty from this point on."

"No shit, Sherlock," Ilborna mumbles under her breath as she climbs down three decks of ladders and starts crawling down a narrow maintenance conduit that pierces at least four bulkhead compartments directly beneath the Garden Deck, "tell me something I don't know."

"Ensign Trireenan," an unfamiliar voice speaks in her ear plug, "this is SIBIL. You're cap camera and mics are still operating, and I don't think the Captain would appreciate your sentiments. Luckily for you I'm the only thing on this ship with hearing acute enough to pick up your last comment from the recording. We'll keep it our little secret."

"Thanks," Ilborna replies gruffly, continuing her crawl forward.

"I suspect you are attempting some kind of personal rescue, Ensign," SIBIL says through Ilborna's ear plug, "and I just want to warn you that there is heavy damage to multiple hulls and none of the surrounding compartments in this part of the ship are structurally sound. The entire area is being evacuated. If you cannot finish your retrieval in five minutes, the odds of your survival are near zero."

"Noted," Ilborna grunts while continuing to crawl forward.

"Good luck, Ensign," SIBIL replies, signing off.

Ilborna reaches the end of her crawl and flips over onto her back. She quickly studies the digital display next to the maintenance hatch just a foot and a half above her face. Readouts indicate there is still pressurized atmosphere in the compartment directly above her.

I've come to fate's bridge, Ilborna thinks, typing in a standard activation code, *and it's time to cross it.* The hatch slides open sideways, and she reaches upward with both hands, grabs two stanchions and pulls herself up into the Garden Deck. The overhead lights are flickering on and off, but she manages to confirm this is Hydroponics Garden Number Two, which is connected to Alberman's Garden by a single hatch on the far side of the surrounding greenery. Ilborna stands up and runs as fast as she can.

About three quarters of the way across the room Ilborna becomes aware of a loud whistling sound.

"Not yet, god dammit," she says through gritted teeth, "almost there…"

The whistling soon becomes a tearing scream and Ilborna feels the air rushing over her body and pulling at her just as she reaches the pressure-lock hatch to the next garden. She grabs a handle next to the hatch with one hand and stabs an activation code with her right index finger as the air rapidly grows thin. The hatch slides open as she falls forward, jumps back up, and slams her right palm on the large red emergency pad which immediately closes the hatch and stops the roar of air out of this garden.

Gasping loudly, Ilborna turns around and squints her eyes. Shelves and hanging trays are in upheaval and over half of this garden has fallen to the deck. The overhead lights are still flickering on and off.

"Sergeant Alberman," she yells, "dammit David, you better not have died on me."

"Over here!"

His voice sounds close. It takes Ilborna just one minute to find him. One of the largest of the hydroponics shelves, weighing several hundred pounds, has fallen across both his legs, effectively pinning him and his right hand to the deck. He is lying on his back.

Ilborna climbs over several other crumpled shelving units and makes it to his side.

"Jesus, David," Ilborna says while wiping away as much dirt as she can from his face, "we've got to get you out of here. There are multiple hull breaches and this whole part of the ship isn't safe."

The deck under them shakes once, then twice. Though the overhead light is still flickering, Ilborna can see David's normally dark brown face is looking paler.

"Lost too much blood," he says weakly, "not strong enough to help you move this shelf… whatta you say you go get help. Promise I'll be here when you return. Go on now…"

"No," Ilborna says stubbornly, "I'm not leaving without you."

"Stop talking crazy…" he whispers loudly, "this ain't no adventure vid. Save your ass… move it… that's an order."

"I outrank you, asshole," she says in a soft voice before wrapping both of her hands around his left one and laying down next to him, her head touching his, "and I'm going to wait for our rescue, right here, with you. SIBIL knows I'm here and I'm sure a rescue team is on its way."

"Hobnobbing with the big shots now, huh reporter?" he chuckles than coughs three times.

The deck shakes hard three times in a row then settles down.

"Hey now," Ilborna says, "I forbid you to pass out. In fact, I'll tell you a big secret if you keep awake."

"Whuzzat?" he mumbles.

"I enlisted at thirteen," she says in a covert voice, "I'm only seventeen."

David's eyes shoot open at this and the weakness leaves his voice.

"Are you fucking shitting me?" he asks.

"That's not a problem, is it?" Ilborna asks coyly.

"Damn right it is," he says, "I got a bloody daughter your age."

The deck shakes again, this time so hard that Ilborna bounces two inches into the air. David groans in pain and she presses her head against his and squeezes his hand tightly.

"I love you, David," Ilborna blurts out, "I… I just wanted you to know."

Another shake rocks the deck. A distant and frighteningly familiar whistling sound from the other side of the garden starts up.

"Shit," David says, "just gimme a kiss, Ensign, and make it one for the books."

Ilborna presses her mouth desperately against his.

A thunderous boom bursts through the garden and the lights go out…

Captain Illiadus, sans her new Quantum Helmet, stands beside Major Helen Ironbear in front of a small screen in a corner the CIC.

"That's the last of her recording, Captain," Ironbear says gravely.

"Bodies?" the Captain asks.

"No, Sir," Ironbear says, "the entire hydroponics bay and all its contents vented into space."

"Department Heads' latest status report?" the Captain asks.

"The ship is dying, Sir," Commander Aithon replies smartly, "we can't repair the sublight engines in anything less than a month, and we've lost a lot of provisions, most of our food, water, and air reserves. CO_2 scrubbers are down to thirty percent. We're currently sending out distress signals to the nearest planetary systems and prepping the solar sail. Current casualty report is thirty dead, sixty seriously wounded, and twelve missing."

"And that's," the Captain mumbles sadly to herself, "straight from the source."

Captain's Log, The Ekatarina

The last dark energy artery jump was a disaster. The ship collided with several large comet fragments. The damage is substantial and we are currently creeping towards the closest planetary system via our deployable solar sail. Though none of our hails have been answered, passive sensors have alerted us to various radiation blooms in the distance, leading us to believe an advanced civilization is in the vicinity. The ship is bleeding, and no one knows if we have enough air, food, and water left to make it to safety. And if we are able to park in orbit around a habitable planet, will the residents be friendly, or otherwise? Weapons systems are all down and we have no method of defending the ship if needed. The Ekatarina may be approaching its final graveyard. End Log.

Renascence

by Mallory Makepeace

Ship's Chronometer: 2442 AD

Fal Kamora, the head administrator of the orbiting Cerridian Shipyards, hands a small comp-pad to a smiling Captain Illiadus.

"As the status report shows," Fal says with a soothing mellifluous voice, "we're actually a couple of weeks ahead of schedule, Tenn… uh, I mean, Captain."

Illiadus holds back a chuckle at Fal's overly endearing awkwardness over public human social protocols. She pauses for a moment to regard the alluring alien. The residents of the planet Cerrid are a technologically advanced species of startlingly beautiful hominids who have almost no practical understanding of hierarchy and leadership. They seem to be the embodiment of pure socialism sharing all responsibility equally throughout their culture, regardless of job or activity. Each and every one of them possess a genius I.Q. by Terran standards, gold colored skin, shiny silver hair, large all green eyes, and at full growth stand no less than two meters in height.

Illiadus looks down and examines the comp-pad for a moment before nodding and then reluctantly looking back up into Fal's disarming eyes.

"Five months and this amazing refit is ninety-percent done," Illiadus says, "I have to admit, I thought your original engineering estimates were nothing less than ridiculous. But after my last tour of the ship this morning I'm gob-smacked."

"Gob…," Fal frowns.

"Oh," Illiadus laughs, "it's an old Earth expression. It means surprised. Shocked."

"We wish to please," Fal says, placing his gold six-fingered hand upon his sturdy chest and bowing slightly.

"That seems to be your planet's motto," Illiadus smiles, "you all so love to say that at every occasion."

Illiadus steps forward and the two of them walk side-by-side down a long sidewalk bordered by a wide variety of purple colored vegetation that thrive all across the planet. Cerrid is roughly the size of Earth, having a similar land to water ratio but only one large continent. Their sun is a red dwarf star and the planet is tucked neatly into its Goldilocks zone. Two airless moons, each about half the size of Earth's, share overlapping concentric revolutions that stabilize Cerrid's orbital axis.

For the last five months the weather patterns have been unusually temperate, from pole to pole, and for the life of them nobody in orbit aboard the *Ekatarina* can figure out why. An unprecedented and complex weather controlling infrastructure is obviously responsible, but no orbiting machinery is evident, and the alien population is always disinclined to discuss the matter when it comes up. And considering the massive rehauling they have been giving the *Ekatarina*, stating that no cost will be involved beyond the sharing of cultures and historical archives, Illiadus is determined to *not* look a gift horse in the mouth.

"You seem preoccupied, Captain," Fal says solicitously, "surely you have nothing to worry about on a beautiful day like this… especially after receiving my report?"

"As you know," Illiadus says in a low voice, "good luck has not been in high supply during much of the *Ekatarina's* recent voyage."

"Ah, yes," Fal replies, "as you've told me many times before, an abundance of this *luck*, as you call it, is something to fear or be wary of."

"Finding your planet," Illiadus says, "and your people, and your incredible technology, yes, at times it just feels too good to be true."

"I swear on both of my hearts," Fal says solemnly, "To Serve Man is *not* a cookbook."

Illiadus frowns at his last statement, "what?"

"Oh," Fal chuckles mildly, "just a reference to words spoken at the denouement of an unusual and highly entertaining drama we found in the *Ekatarina's* historical archives. Unlike the aliens in that ancient tale, we truly have no dire hidden agenda."

In the distance, Illiadus can see a couple of dozen of the Ekatarina's Teenerian crew, in all their various physical permutations, closely following two Cerridians, a male and a female, who are about to enter a huge construct in the shape of a hyperboloid, over five hundred feet tall and looking like it has been carved from a single massive ruby gemstone. Illiadus wonders for a moment what delights the Cerridians are offering up and sharing with this unusual race she indentured to the *Ekatarina's* service in recent years.

Fal touches Illiadus's elbow with his outstretched hand and oh so gently guides her off the sidewalk and across a well-manicured vermillion lawn along a level path between lovely rows of tall purple bushes.

"These strange concepts of luck and fate," Fal says, "they never cease to amaze me."

"Your claim that your people have not known conflict or war for thousands of years," Illiadus replies, "has always amazed me."

"Why so?" Fal asks, "we have conquered disease and most dangers. We are a land of plenty which is all shared equally among a population whose coda is self-respect and mutual respect. Why, logically, would anyone wish to live differently than this?"

"You never had to deal with the Scourge," Illiadus says tightly, "sometimes the universe doesn't give you a choice. Sometimes you must act against your better nature for the greater good."

"An odd idea," Fal says, "and one I will contemplate for many nights I think…"

"With the aid of your advanced computers and active scanning equipment," Illiadus says, "we found credible evidence that the comet whose fragments nearly destroyed us had been struck by an unknown particle beam shortly before we exited the dark energy artery. It was something not of natural origin, but generated by advanced equipment. You tell us it is not you, and we believe you," Illiadus adds to cut Fal off, "because we have discovered no such radiation residue in your entire planetary system. But the fact that our accident may have been engineered by someone, some unknown alien race, leaves me paranoid… and I still find myself taken aback that you do not seem worried by this at all.

"You've seen our monitoring network technology in action. Nothing can approach us from thousands of light years in any direction without us knowing it," Fal says, "and we have found no indication of any ship in the vicinity of your accident. I see nothing to worry about and question your people's need for something to fear."

"Tell me, Fal," Illiadus says, "just what is it about us that you truly find so intriguing? I can't help but notice an emotional depth to you and other Cerridians that wells up whenever one of you approach or engage with my crew."

"An insightful observation, Captain," Fal says, "and I can conceive of many complex and clever answers to your query, but *to cut to the heart of the matter*, a wonderful phrase I recently found in your ship's archives, I would say it is your people's *passion for life* that so arouses us…"

When they are out of sight of any prying eyes, Fal wraps his large solid arms around Illiadus and slowly presses his lips against hers. Surprised, she resists his urgency for a fraction of a second and then returns his affections fervently.

Commander David Aithon, the *Ekatarina's* First Officer, purses his lips when he spots the Captain and that damned alien Adonis walking together a couple of hundred yards away. He begins to follow them so he can relate some odd observations he's made recently when Illiadus and Fal decide on a nature walk. David stops, sighs, and does a quick about face to return to the nearest space elevator that will return him to the *Ekatarina* and the shipyard's low orbit. As he strides forward, he thinks back on all that has happened since they first stumbled upon this idyllic paradise.

An undetected recently exploded comet's sudden appearance upon the Ekatarina's exit of a dark energy artery led to a disastrous series of ship impacts that came far too close to killing them all. The result was fifty-nine deaths and another fifty seriously injured and in need of emergency surgery, a roughly equal number of human and Teenerian genomes. The jump drive was disabled, and the ship's engines were non-operable. For sixty hours overlapping shifts worked furiously to close bulkheads and seal multiple hull breaches. Precious supplies of food, air, and fuel had been blown out into space.

The Commander's appraisal almost three days later was not pretty. They were equidistant from at least four systems, with no way to determine which was a hell hole and which might offer sanctum. And then the most unexpected thing happened. A series of x-rays were detected by the ship's passive sensor array. After computer processing, it was quickly determined the source was not natural, and several of the *Ekatarina's* scientists openly suspected this was a beacon of sorts. With little in the way of choice, Captain Illiadus had the main solar sail deployed and placed the *Ekatarina* at full steam to this unknown system and ordered all but a dozen of the crew into their cryopods. By some small miracle they reached the planet of Cerrid in one month.

David reaches the space elevator and stops and smiles politely at four Cerridian females and two males exiting the large pod. They all say "Hello" while passing him. Though he is not one hundred percent sure, David is fairly confident that every single Cerridian in the system speaks, reads, and writes/types Standard Terran. For the first day of first contact they used the remotes of the ship's language translator to speak with these new aliens, but by the second day every single one that they communicated with from that day on spoke in perfect idiomatic Standard. It was like living on a planet of linguists. Or a planet of Crewman Farko Tiresias's, the Ekatarina's young Teenerian polymath who is making herself indispensable in several areas of engineering and astrophysics. Word has it that Farko is even giving Ensign Terry Thaleia's genetically-engineered brain a run for its money, as the ancient Earth expression goes.

David glances up and whistles at the cyclopean structure that reaches up into the sky like Jack's own beanstalk. Only more amazing than this sight are dozens of other glistening silver and ebony space elevators that he can see in the distance. They cover the planet like spines, over one thousand of them and all stretching upwards of three hundred miles. The cost in man hours and materials for this planet's technological marvels is practically inconceivable. David smiles remembering The *Ekatarina's* Chief Engineer Lehmann's first reaction to the staggeringly tall alien spires.

"It's not possible," Lehmann says, "and I don't care what kind of unknown advanced supermaterials the damned tethers are made of. For stability the geostationary orbit altitude would have to be over twenty-two thousand miles… and don't even get me started on the counterweight!"

"You can't deny your own eyes, Chief," David replies, "they're standing right in front of us. Each one is three hundred miles and no longer."

"And I'm telling you there's more here than meets the eye," Lehmann says, "and if I were a fan of science-fiction I'd say the bloody things were being supported or supplemented by some kind of anti-gravity devices."

"If they had anti-gravity technology, they wouldn't need space elevators, Walter."

"Unless there is an inherent engineering limit in both the size of these theoretical a-g generators, and the strength of the a-g field they generate… bah. Tis all fantasy, Commander. I just don't believe this."

As the air-tight doors seal shut behind him, David chides himself for his immature discomfort over the Captain's current dalliance. If there is one person who deserves a break, a vacation from the duties of command it is Illiadus. The last use of that damned quantum helmet had left her with a migraine that had lasted over two weeks. Doctor Sorlan gave her a clean bill of health three months ago, but it is the ongoing friendship and companionship of the shipyards' head administrator Fal Kamora that seems to have the most dramatic and positive effect on her overall well-being.

The return journey to Earth to date is taking a severe toll on the Captain. David feels strongly that the latest setback with the comet collision has surely pushed her to the breaking point. But when they first contacted this incredible civilization, and commenced regular furloughs planet-side, there has been a slow and inexorable rejuvenation of both Captain and crew. In the last few weeks the word *hope* has begun appearing on the crew's tongues. Now if only he can keep his mind on his duties and off of the Captain's new boyfriend.

Chief Engineer Lt. Commander Walter Lehmann and his mixed crew of thirty human and Teenerian engineers, machinists, maintenance folk, propulsion techs, and repairmen all stand behind the transparent wall in the observation bubble poised several hundred feet above the space-docked *Ekatarina*. Staring slack jawed, they marvel at their view of large portions of adaptive mobile armor increasing the overall size and dimensions of the ship. It is the first major test of the *Ekatarina's* new additional skin and as far as the Chief is concerned, the technology just jumped from the realm of science to that of outright witchcraft.

"For Christ's sake," Lehmann says, "it ain't normal."

"Radiation shielding should be a five-fold increase," a gentle voice rings out.

Lehmann turns and frowns at the tall and painfully lovely Cerridian female standing behind and towering over his staff.

"Aye," Lehmann spits, "so you keep telling me, Nemain. But it just don't feel right to see a ship's hull so... on the move. Moving through a dark energy artery ain't like normal space travel. We need a hull with zero tolerance for even the tiniest of faults or weaknesses where these different sections of this additional hull meet and mate."

"Chief Engineer," Nemain says, "we've been over this a thousand times, and you've tested our active panels against every type of explosion and particle beam weaponry. The panels instantly weld to each other at a molecular level when joining. Each seam is perfect and without flaw, and these panels can separate and re-join an endless number of times without fear of degradation or malformation."

"A hell of a promise you're making, lass," Lehmann says, "which makes me think you've never had the pleasure of making an acquaintance with the consequences of Murphy's law."

"Murphy?" Nemain asks, "one of your people's great philosophers or physicists, Chief?"

"Actually," Lehmann says, "he was an engineer, and a damned fine one at that. Now, what's next?"

"I will now hover along the dorsal spine of the *Ekatarina*," Nemain says, "so that you can see the new magnetic field array which will have..."

"Yes, I understand," Lehmann sighs, "it'll repel several times more dust and micro asteroids than our previous shield did, not to mention theoretically be able to affect much larger objects when focused as a deflection beam, something we definitely could have used just months ago."

Nemain displays another gorgeous smile, "Roger that, Chief. We wish to please."

"Dia duidich mi," the Chief groans.

"Dr. Sorlan," the beautiful female says, "I am puzzled by your reticence. We've tested this new cryopod system on every single lifeform we have access to with the exception of human, Teenerian, or Cerridean sentients. There were zero fatalities, and zero breakdowns, even after sudden power losses and multiple pod concussions. And lest we forget, the individual back-up energy storage units will keep the chambers running for a full five years if disconnected from ship's power."

"Be that as it may, Nott," Sorlan snaps back, "I want another round of diagnostics before I'll sign off on this new hibernation system. Hundreds of lives are on the line, and I will not do any human or Teenerian testing until I am one hundred percent convinced of this cold coffin's efficacy."

"What's that curious human phrase?" Nott replies with a lovely trill of laughter, "better safe than sorry?"

Sorlan frowns for a moment before letting his face break out into a smile.

"Yes," Sorlan says, "we've had a lot to be sorry about these past years, and I honestly mean no disrespect to your amazing engineering and medical skills. Hell, the way you completely reversed radiation induced DNA double strand breaks in the entire Human crew, not to mention reversing degeneration in our males' spermatogonia cells and our females' oocyte cells and returning fertility to even the oldest of us is a downright miracle. The damage from that damned supermassive black hole at the center of the galaxy had shortened all of our lives. And don't get me started on all the missing limbs and damaged vital organs from the comet impacts... all regenerated back to full health. The upgrades your people made in our nano-med-technology is nothing short of a true blessing. I'm *sure* this new hibernation chamber will be everything that you promise. I'm sorry, but I'm just a stickler for biological testing protocol."

"No short cuts?" Nott says.

"No short cuts," Sorlan replies with a sigh.

Nott steps forward, looks down at the diminutive Doctor, and slides her arm through his.

"Perhaps a break is in order, doctor" Nott purrs, "I know a wonderful little café planet-side that serves the most delicious java… with a gorgeous view of an endless mountain ridge covered with glistening, turquoise colored snow and ruby red waterfalls. The surrounding trees are crystalline in nature and it is said that southerly winds make their vibrations sound like a chorus of angels, and perhaps I can convince you to tell me more about your home world of Galen and that amazing huge Sun your people live so close to?"

"Now that my dear," Sorlan replies while setting his comp-pad on a countertop, "is the best offer I've had all year."

"We wish to please."

"Your civilization has existed for multiple millennia," Al-Quam says, "and your technology is far superior to our own…"

"Yet?" a tall Cerridian male adds.

"I've yet to hear a straight-forward explanation, Laran," Al-Quam continues, "for why your people have neither engaged in a deep space exploration program, nor ever found or become aware of the ancient galaxy-wide Space-Gate Network. Don't get me wrong. Your solar system is nothing short of impressive with five completely terraformed and fully inhabited worlds to its credit. You seem to wield creation like the almighty himself. One wonders why you did not seek beyond yourselves."

"Well," Laran says, standing beside Al-Quam at the *Ekatarina's* new main weapons control console, "for one thing, after examining all your recorded data about the dark matter fountain device's activation, it is our belief that a chain reaction occurred which destroyed well over fifty percent of the connected Space-Gates located throughout the galaxy. Possibly more. So, it would seem there is no hurry for us to locate that old transit construct. As for exploration, I keep telling you that we long ago turned our focus inward, not outward. We have spent multiple lifetimes bettering ourselves from within, embracing our minds and our immediate vicinity."

"You find paradise within your souls," Al-Quam muses, "not in some far away heaven. A very Buddhist approach to life."

"A simple enough judgement," Laran says, "and I am happy to say it is the fundamental foundation of all aspects of our culture."

"And you never had a war?" Al-Quam says slyly, "no conflicts whatsoever?"

"As with all species we have evolved," Laran replies, "and while conflict occasionally still arises in what you might call calm, bloodless debates, we do not engage or stand in readiness or preparation for war."

"How fortunate for you we are not an outwardly aggressive and warlike species by nature," Al-Quam says, "otherwise our meeting would have been very different.

"These weapons I've enhanced bode dark times for someone," Laran says while typing out a final diagnostic code into the console.

"Our war is over," Al-Quam replies, "and we only wish to return home without fear of being destroyed or enslaved by a greater power. The radically increased efficiency of our railguns, torpedoes, and particle beam generators will hopefully ensure that. We owe your people a great deal for these impressive gifts. One wonders how you can so easily trust us with this sophisticated weaponry after such a short acquaintance with our people."

"We pride ourselves on our judgement," Laran says, "and on our ability to look into the hearts of others."

"Some of the crew suspect you might be telepaths," Al-Quam says while typing in a test code all the while watching his companion peripherally, "certainly the perfect way to discover if we are the honest and nonthreatening travelers we claim to be."

"I sense other more pertinent suspicions swimming beneath the surface of your observations," Laran says, "certainly you've known me long enough to trust my sense of propriety and discretion, Chief Warrant Officer Yaqub Al-Quam."

"You are an unusually courteous species," Al-Quam says with reverence, "probably the closest of any race I have met to the ideal of my own Islamic convictions."

"But?"

"But I sense levels of technology far beyond anything you've allowed us to see," Al-Quam sighs, "and it is my belief that Cerrid is more than capable, if necessary, to defend itself from any overt act of aggression, regardless of size or nature."

"We Cerridians are a civilization built upon beliefs," Laran says, "and I have nothing but respect for your own."

Al-Quam raises his eyebrows in surprise as he suddenly realizes his unspoken question was just answered.

"The diagnostic is complete," Laran says, "with no false positives. Zero errors across the line. All systems nominal."

"Excellent," Al-Quam nods, "and the newly fabricated torpedoes?"

"The first shipment arrives shortly."

"Jazaka Allahu Khairan," Al-Quam said.

Down on the surface of Cerrid, upon an outdoor one-hundred-meter diameter blue circular wrestling mat, Major Helen Ironbear, Commander of Space Marines on board the Polisian Pocket Battleship *Ekatarina*, faces off with two Cerridians, a male and a female. The aliens wear one-piece red bodysuits, both skintight and very flexible. Ironbear wears a similar outfit that is colored green and also leaves her hands and feet bare. A small crowd of both off-duty crew and random Cerridians loosely crowd around to watch the demonstration.

Out of the corner of her eyes Ironbear notices a mildly handsome dark-haired crewman who looks vaguely Brazilian making wagers with other crewmen and even a Ceriddian or two. He doesn't look all that familiar though, and she shrugs the distraction off. It is time to embrace combat mode.

The female Cerridian is named Anath. The male, Gu. Crouching forward with their large hands stretched slightly forward, they quickly move apart and circle in an effort to quickly outflank Ironbear. The Major smiles and turns to match their revolution, keeping her torso perpendicular to each alien, and using her excellent peripheral vision to constantly track both.

The rules of this contest are relatively simple. No overt killing or permanently crippling strikes or maneuvers. Slapping the mat twice, or yelling *yield,* instantly ends all actions. First three out of five falls or being pushed out of the perimeter of the mat's outer boundary, marks a win.

Two days ago, the Major made no effort to hide her surprise when she received Anath and Gu's invitation. They had told her that after reviewing the ship's cultural archives, they wished to test their advanced gymnastic-dancer skills against any and all Earthborn hand-to-hand martial arts. The chance to actively go toe-to-toe with a new hominid species, and a rather unbearably smug one at that, was an opportunity that Ironbear could not resist.

Anath leaps forward, drops to the mat, and spins her long right leg forward in a vicious sweep that Ironbear deftly jumps over, and replies to with a front snap-kick that connects with Anath's exposed right shoulder, effectively knocking the alien onto her back.

Sensing Gu's nearing silent attack behind her, Ironbear does a quick dance-step to the left and simultaneously ducks forward. Gu's large arms suddenly swing through empty air, which momentarily throws him off balance. Ironbear immediately takes advantage of this by moving under his guard and tackles him to the mat. She quickly ties him up in a brutal jiu-jitsu bow and arrow choke. Gu slaps the mat and she lets him go. The aliens both bow to her, then immediately resume their circling. The Major frowns. This is far too easy.

A moment later she is proven right.

Gu and Anath jump toward her simultaneously. Without hesitation Ironbear turns and sprints directly at the larger, Gu, who is fractionally closer to her. Just as they are about to collide, she leans forward and to his left, striking downward with her leading hand against his outstretched forearm. She grabs his opposing arm and spins him around, momentarily separating herself from Anath's attack in a flawless Krav Maga maneuver. Ironbear then drops Gu with a brutal kidney punch, jumps onto and springs off his collapsed body on her left leg and hits Anath's abdomen with a Wing Chun shoulder strike.

Seconds later the two Cerridians, smiling and not looking the worse for wear at all, start circling the Major again. Ironbear frowns. Those last couple of strikes have come close to crossing the line, each one capable of incapacitating a sturdy human male with injuries that might take up to two weeks to fully recover from. And here the two aliens appear to not only feel no pain but seem to have an underlying musculature as strong as carbon fiber and as durable as tungsten. The Major has a sneaking suspicion she is being toyed with. The next round will answer that question once and for all, as she has every intention of winning this demo three falls in a row.

The quick look that passes between Gu and Anath just before they rush her make the hair rise on the back of Ironbear's neck. Fun time is over.

Both Cerridians are larger and far stronger than Ironbear, but during the last two rounds she has determined that her speed and coordination is just a hair finer. And in an open combat arena like this, far from the encumbrance of awkward ship's corridors and crowded compartments, she plans to prove to herself that her defeat at the hands of that mutinous bastard Gunnery Sergeant Jedidiah Solomon Hatfield was a matter of fickle luck and circumstance. Skill had failed her during that rebellion in the tight confines of the *Ekatarina* where body mass and brute strength were the deciding factor. She had room to maneuver here, with nothing but her own ineptness to blame if she is defeated. This is *her* playground.

What follows is a short but master lesson in the exquisitely painful and peerless art of human hand to hand combat.

Knowing that the frighteningly intelligent and athletic Cerridians have by now fully gauged the limits of her strength, flexibility, and speed to the minutest measurements and calculations, Ironbear steels herself. True cunning and strategy are needed here. Without hesitation she runs straight at the two aliens.

First the Major shin-blocks two brutal rapid front snap kicks the aliens give one after the other. This makes her stumble and nearly lose her balance as she further closes with them both. Next, she blocks both a surprise throat strike from Gu's leading right palm with her left fist and a lightning quick lateral knee strike from Anath that is aimed at her right rib cage and barely blocks with her right forearm. The rest plays out like the closing moves of a city park speed chess match.

Gu stops the Major in her tracks with a solid steel-hard right cross that Ironbear knows has broken her own jaw. In the same second Anath slams a spinning back heel kick which makes the Major's left knee feel like it has just exploded.

Ironbear closes her eyes and drops forward and to her left in a perfect approximation of an unconscious crippled human. The Cerridians freeze for the slightest of moments to follow her fall. It is their undoing.

Springing forward off her good right leg the Major slams her right fist into Gu's groin doubling him over instantly. Continuing the forward momentum Ironbear strikes Anath's nose with an upward left palm strike, breaking it and making the Cerridian's eyes fill with tears and momentarily blinding her. Rolling onto Anath's back, the Major finishes her off with a two-knuckle Ryukyu Kempo strike to one of her neck's vital pressure points.

Gu is already rousing when Ironbear leaps on his large torso and rapidly immobilizes his right arm and head in a vicious jiu-jitsu triangle leg lock. With all her leg strength she constricts his neck until his eyes roll in his sockets and he stops breathing. She waits a full five seconds more before releasing the unconscious giant.

Rolling away she stands up on her one good leg. A small cheer rises among those spectators who are from the *Ekatarina*.

Mere seconds later, and not surprising at all to the Major, both Gu and Anath suddenly stand up. Neither displays a scratch. What should have been bruised and battered flesh on their necks and faces appears perfectly normal.

"Most impressive, Major," Gu says, "your deception was flawless. I applaud you."

"Agreed," Anath adds, "perhaps another three rounds are in order?"

Ironbear gives them both a long searing look, before shaking her head.

"This is not a fair fight… on many levels. The two of you are not what you seem, and I'm talking about more than your superior physiology and the fact that you don't feel any pain whatsoever. You fight without the slightest fear of physical consequence, and I'm not talking about reckless bravery or combat commitment. You treat your bodies like expendable playthings. Almost like… puppets."

Gu and Anath look at each other significantly, then turn to regard Ironbear.

"You see much, Major," Anath says quietly, "and you are right… we apologize for any improper obfuscation."

"Our physicians will fix your injuries in a matter of minutes if you'll allow us to carry you to the nearest conveyance," Gu says.

"Thank you but no," Ironbear says, turning her back on them and limping away, "I'll be fine."

"We only wish to please," Gu says to her back.

"Blow it out your ass," Ironbear snarls.

A couple of *Ekatarina* crew members, alongside Marine Sergeant Bryce, start approaching the Major to offer assistance but a quick scowl on Ironbear's face, whose jaw is darkening and starting to swell, stops them in their tracks and all three quickly find themselves preoccupied with asking some nearby Cerridians where the nearest restroom is located.

"Man, that planet purple cooch is tight. I think I'm falling in love. If only these chicks weren't so damn tall."

"I like 'em big! Especially the guys. This last boy I dated had the mother of all tactical torpedoes."

"Intoxication and Intercourse!"

"I and I, rules!"

"Oorah!"

Leaning against the far side of the space elevator pod returning her to the *Ekatarina*, Chief Petty Officer Melanie Inari smiles at the rambunctious ship Marines returning from R&R on Cerrid. Their enthusiasm is a welcome distraction from the radical changes she is overseeing as the *Ekatarina's* Mess Officer. She has always thought that the basic waste recyclers on board the ship are pretty darned advanced, but the latest demonstration she just witnessed of DNA-tailored bacteria has, to use an old Earth expression, knocked her socks off. These new bugs will not only purify any urine or contaminated liquid into the healthiest potable water she ever drank but can and do alter any and all fecal waste into matter that is not only edible and nutritionally sound, but actually tastes good. And it is a process with an unheard of ninety-nine-point five percent efficiency, i.e., near perfect.

As the elevator quickly accelerates upward, Inari contemplates the changes the ship's upgrades are going to make towards daily life on the *Ekatarina*. With near one hundred percent effectiveness in waste and air recycling, and the startling improvements the Cerridians made in both hydroponics output and tissue meat culture replication, the ship can theoretically travel the rest of the way back to Earth without technically ever needing to resupply… barring any catastrophes or major mishaps of course.

In minutes the elevator has risen above the planet's atmosphere and starts closing in on their destination, a large transparent docking bubble that is connected to the *Ekatarina* via a quarter of a mile-long pressurized walkway tube.

For a long minute Melanie ponders what it might be like to spend the rest of her life on this advanced planet with its superior technology and, well, superior people. The Cerridians are unusually accommodating and generous, and both their home world and all the other terraformed planets in the system are idyllic paradises. But something holds her back from embracing the idea of immigration. Though the Cerridians are friendly enough, she always felt that something is just not right about them. Perhaps it has to do with the fact that they seem completely devoid of any type of spirituality. Oh, Melanie has long ago stopped believing in Santa Claus, the Easter Bunny, and God, yet still she has an instinctual certainty that all people have souls, regardless of whether or not they endure beyond physical death.

The Cerridians espouse fundamental peaceful philosophies, but ones that feel ultimately simplistic and shallow, like they have no divine goals in life beyond pleasure and comfort. Melanie suspects this culture is tens of thousands of years old, maybe hundreds of thousands of years as modern metropolitan peoples.

Perhaps all civilizations lose something in the long run after achieving true unity and peace, she thinks.

The elevator pod stops, and she follows the rowdy Marines who walk jovially along the pressurized bridge to the ship.

Or maybe you're not ready for the perfection of paradise just yet, a little voice speaks inside Melanie's head.

She smiles.

"I guess time will tell," Melanie mumbles to herself then lets out a brief chuckle.

"So, rumor has it you've been flirting rather strongly with the ship's second in command," Crewman Farko Tiresias says aloud to Ensign Terry Thaleia as they both drink coffee in the *Ekatarina's* mostly empty gym, each straddling adjacent weight benches with damp towels strung around the back of their necks.

"For all the good it's done me," Terry laughs, "David's all moon-eyed for our intrepid Captain, though she doesn't seem to be interested in him at all."

"So why are you after his affections?"

"Like I have much of a choice," Terry says, "In case you haven't noticed there is a distinct shortage of intelligent and attractive human males left on this ship. Most of the surviving Terrans have paired off and what's left… well, let's just say David is far and above the high standard for a male mate on this flying bucket."

"Why Terry," Farko laughs, "you're a romantic!"

"Look who's talking," Terry smirks, "rumor has it you don't have any trouble filling your bunk at night, with either male or female Terrans."

"Oh, you know," Farko shrugs, "just doing my bit for interspecies diplomacy and all that."

They both laugh.

"But seriously, I've got something else on my mind right now and it's the damnedest thing," Farko says, "I've traveled to every single populated planet in this system, Morfran, Creirwy, Bala, and Awan, and they are all the same!"

"What do you mean?" Terry asks, "redundancy in architecture, city layout, and infrastructure? One person's bland efficiency is another's highest art form…"

"No," Farko sighs, "not that. I mean every single building, every walkway, every space elevator… they all appear to be brand new, with only minimal signs of wear."

"So, they spend a lot on upkeep, maintenance, and renovation," Terry smirks, "what of it?"

"This strikes me as something other than pride, vanity, or ostentation," Farko says, "which even if it was true would require a ridiculously significant portion of their overall resources to enact and maintain. No… something else is going on here. Teeneria, you know, reached the ability to engage in system-wide space flight at least three thousand years before Terra. Yet do you remember how old and even decrepit many of my planet's structures looked? True, we were suffering a system wide recession, but still, we had buildings that were in some cases a thousand years old. Where is the historical preservation of heritage and all structures of significant importance on these planets? I have not seen a single monument to any figure or event in Cerrid's past anywhere, and yes, I asked quite a few questions on this matter and was generally answered with that damned Cerridian look of bemused nonchalance and false puzzlement."

"So, what are you saying?" Terry smiles, "this civilization was born yesterday?"

Farko's eyebrows raised and her mouth took the shape of a large O in her pale blue face.

"As a matter of fact," Farko says, "I actually do get the irrational and admittedly unbelievable feeling that every single structure and piece of technology in view, their multiple skyscrapers, space elevators, orbiting ships and shipyards, canals and rivers, museums, floating ocean cities… everything, looks like it was fabricated and constructed in the past year…"

"What a preposterous thought," Terry says, "you make it sound like they're all actors and these worlds are quickly dressed stages for an eccentric performance all dolled up for our personal edification. Could you think of anything more perverse? Seriously, Farko, I had no idea your imagination was so macabre!"

After an amazing six-month refit, overhaul, repair, and redesign that results in multiple alterations to the ship's hull, engines, weaponry and dozens of subsystems, the now nearly unrecognizable Polisian pocket warship *Ekatarina* leaves the orbit of the planet Cerrid and rapidly accelerates away from the solar system toward the nearest dark energy artery that SIBIL can identify.

The crew is well rested, full of renewed hope, and more than a little salty.

The Captain, sitting in her command chair and wearing the quantum helmet, orders everyone into their cryopods ten minutes before SIBIL will let the ship enter the artery. Once the jump is made, she will remove the cumbersome helmet and enter her own hibernation pod, leaving SIBIL in the driver's seat for an estimated year or more.

"It was an exciting six months, wasn't it, Captain?" SIBIL asks.

Tennyson Illiadus, currently sitting in her command chair in a virtual reality sim version of the CIC and seemingly unencumbered by the real-world quantum helmet, turns toward SIBIL, standing beside her.

"An unusually welcome surplus of good fortune, I must admit," Illiadus says, "and you, SIBIL? The cybernetics team said you reacted quite well to the Cerridian's programming upgrades. I hope you didn't feel too violated by any of their creative machinations."

"Though I have no memory of what occurred during the two months I was disconnected and nonfunctional," SIBIL says, "I can say with perfect accuracy that my current processing power, reaction time, and overall cognitive abilities have all been increased three-fold. The planet purple people were very good to me."

"Then what do you say we continue on our journey home?" the Captain asks.

"To quote an ancient human phrase I just found in the ship's fiction archives... let's split this popsicle stand!"

The distant flickering form of the *Ekatarina* winks out of sight just as it is sucked into sub-space.

In that instance, every Cerridian, on every planet in the system, in every spaceship in orbit or between planets, riding up and down multiple space elevators, engaged in sports in various massive underwater domes, or engaged in thousands of other activities… every single one of this population numbering ten billion, *freeze.*

Perhaps it will be another three-million-year wait until they are activated again.

Captain's Log, The Ekatarina

One hundredth Dark Artery Jump Completed.

Nineteen years ship time have passed since we defeated The Scourge on the far side of the galaxy. Out of our coldsleep pods the crew has aged an average of five years each. Due to attrition less than half our current crew are of Terran descent. Astronavigation shows that we have now completed two-thirds of the journey home. The often, random nature of the dark arteries paths, the huge distances between solar systems, and the destruction of so much of the jump gate network has continued to prevent us from contacting any of the known races that make up The Polis. I find myself wondering about the survivability of that great galactic government now that many of its constituents can probably no longer communicate with each other via FTL transmission, or visit each other instantaneously through jump gates. I also wonder if we had truly killed all of The Scourge when we destroyed their home sphere. It is possible they had a small number of raiding parties stranded throughout the galaxy when so many of the jump gates were destroyed in the chain reaction caused by the Dark Matter fountain bomb. If so, I can only imagine the many conflicts the Polisian Fleet has been engaged in these past nineteen years tracking down and destroying the last remnants of that horrible species. Perhaps it was one such Scourge task force that destroyed the comet that nearly destroyed us. We never found any answers to that mystery. Our repairs and retrofit on Cerrid have left us with a vessel that would be virtually unrecognizable by any ship of the Polisian Fleet. The new hull has increased the size of the ship by a full third. Our sublight speed capabilities have tripled and our new advanced weaponry makes us more than a match for any known race's battle dreadnaughts in the galaxy. As my chief of security is wont to say, we are loaded for bear and very salty. End Log.

Gremlins

by Benjamin Tyler Smith

Ship's Chronometer: 2444 AD

"If you want something done right, you have to do it yourself," Culinary Specialist Chief Petty Officer Melanie Inari grumbles. She stomps down the corridor towards the *Ekatarina's* reefer hold, where the ship's perishables are stored.

A loud rumbling follows along behind her. "Chief Inari! Chief Inari, please slow down!"

"If I had the luxury of time, I would." Inari glares over her shoulder at Culinary Specialist Frances Erland, who pushes the galley's food cart. "If I could trust my own staff to do their jobs, then I'd be free to do *mine*."

Three days in a row, Inari has ordered her subordinates to restock the galley's freezer with what is in the reefer hold: meat, seafood, vegetables, fruit, and dessert items. Their time on Cerrid has seen the ship repaired and restored to her former glory, but more importantly: it has restored Inari's galley to its former glory. They had long since used up the fresh foodstuffs, but there are still plenty of quality ingredients for making sushi, barbecue, stews, and other crew favorites. They won't be dipping into the Recycler for awhile, yet.

Captain Illiadus has developed a taste for Pelrin, a fish from Cerrid that looks and tastes a lot like catfish. Inari has cut it into strips, blackened it, and made creole sushi rolls as an experiment, and the Captain was hooked.

But she couldn't very well make the Captain's new favorite dish if the galley freezer doesn't have any. "Because you didn't do your job, Erland, I'm going to have to make something else for the Captain tonight and thaw out the fish for tomorrow."

"But, Chief Inari," Erland objects, her voice strains like she is holding back tears. "There's nothing in the reefer hold! I was here just this morning!"

"There's no way that's true."

"The manifest says so!"

"Not my manifest." Inari reaches into her fur-trimmed freezer coat and produces a notebook. "I haven't trusted computers since that incident back on Jixpa shorted out the galley's inventory database. Remember that?"

"I wasn't aboard the ship at that time."

"Ah, right. That was before the final battle with the Dyson Sphere." It has taken her and her staff three sleepless nights to create a new inventory, only to have the computer short out again. After that, Inari has sworn to maintain a physical record that she updates weekly, based on the galley's consumption.

She flips through the notebook to the most recent entry. "Says here we've got around three tons of meat, fish, and ice cream as of just five days ago, and that's not including everything else." She snaps it shut and tucks it back into her coat. "Unless we've got a bunch of suddenly obese crewmen waddling around in the last week, there should be plenty of food left."

Erland has no response, and together they walk in silence until they reach the three meter-wide bay doors of the Reefer Hold. Inari punches in the access code, and the doors slide open with a hiss. Cold mist swirls about Inari's feet as she surveys the chamber. "Well?"

Behind her, the rumbling of the food cart ceases. Erland gasps. "That's not possible!"

Shelves filled with containers packed the Reefer Hold. It looks the same as it had a month ago, when Inari last visited. She turns back to Erland, her head cocked to the side. "Well?" she repeats.

"I swear, Sir, it was empty in here!" Erland put a shaky hand to her forehead. "It was. It had to be. No. Wait." She looks back up, her eyes staring past Inari. "It is empty! See?"

Inari frowns. "The hell?" She steps into the Reefer Hold, shivering slightly as the subzero air caresses her cheeks. "Erland, you may want to head to sickbay. This hold's as full as it ever was."

A tingling sensation tickles the inside of Inari's nose, right in her sinuses. She squeezes her eyes shut and rubs her forehead. *A brain freeze, just from the air?*

"There, Chief, do you see? It's empty in here."

The tingling turns into a sharp stab of pain. Inari grimaces, then opens her eyes. Her vision is blurry, and for a moment she thinks the chamber is empty. She blinks rapidly, and the stocked shelves reappear.

The hairs on the back of her neck rise. Something felt very, very wrong here. She spins on her heel and starts for the door. "Frances, we need to get out of here…"

Pain explodes in her back. She screams.

"Captain, we've got a problem," Chief Engineer Walter Lehmann says.

"Isn't that the order of the day?" Captain Tennyson Illiadus looks up from her command chair, a small smile on her lips. The smile fades when she sees his serious expression. She lowers her voice. "What's going on, Walter?"

Lehmann leans forward. "Power fluctuations all across the ship over the last thirty-six hours, and we can't figure out the cause."

"That's… mildly alarming."

"You're telling me." Lehmann swipes his finger along his tablet and turns it around for her to see. The small screen shows an exploded diagram of the *Ekatarina*, with several sections highlighted in yellow and two in red. "The yellow areas are where we've had temporary interruptions: propulsion, environmental, navigation, communications, data storage, the rail gun, and life support, to name a few. These interruptions have never lasted more than a few seconds, but they're occurring more frequently."

"What about the red sections?"

"Areas where we've had unexplained power spikes. This has occurred in the Hydroponics Bay and the Reefer Hold." He shrugs. "And again, we have no cause. It happens, and then it levels off. It's almost like…"

Illiadus spread her hands. "Almost like…?"

Lehmann barks a mirthless laugh. "It's almost like -- and I promise I'm not drinking again -- it's almost like there are gremlins aboard."

Illiadus rests her elbows on the chair's armrests. She steeples her fingers in front of her face to hide her smile. "Gremlins? I haven't heard that word since the early days of the war."

"Well, it fits, doesn't it? We had to tear this ship apart and rebuild her from memory. Who's to say our alien benefactors didn't sell us shoddy equipment? Or provide us with subpar labor? Or..." He shrugs. "Send us off with some stowaways?"

"The... Gremlins."

"Precisely."

The comm panel on Illiadus's chair chimes. She touches it. "Illiadus here."

"Captain," a female voice says, "this is sickbay. You... You might want to get down here."

Illiadus and Lehmann share a look.

"How did this happen, Kyle?" Illiadus crosses her arms beneath her breasts and glares down at Doctor Sorlan's back.

Sorlan shifted in his chair and glanced up. "I could do with a little less attitude, Ten," he murmurs. "It's not like I did this to her."

Inari lays on the bed in the fetal position, a breathing tube in her mouth. The ventilator hums and hisses quietly as it forces oxygen into her lungs. A blanket has been pulled up to cover her front, but her entire backside is exposed. Or as exposed as it could be, considering the back of her head and upper back are covered in bandages.

Illiadus digs her fingers into her biceps, then releases them. She sighs. "Sorry, Kyle. I just never expected something like this would happen to Inari, of all people. She's a *cook*, for God's sake, not a soldier. What happened? Who attacked her?"

"I think *what*, is a more apt term." Sorlan motions for her to join him at the monitor. Video from Inari's emergency surgery plays on the screen. Her backside has been raked again and again by claws or a scourge of some sort. The dark hair on the back of her head is matted in blood, and raw bits of flesh cling to the strands. Sorlan pauses the video. "Parts of her scalp are flayed and the bone exposed, but her skull isn't penetrated. Her brain is spared any direct trauma."

As she studies the claw marks criss-crossing Inari's slender back, Illiadus can't help but think of Lehmann's gremlins. "Could these wounds have been made by some of our alien crewmen? The Yelior, perhaps?"

"The wounds are too shallow to be from Yelior talons. Their talons are also quite brittle. Had one of them done this, we'd still be picking fragments out of her body."

"The Ulthax?"

"Their claws are for digging and would've been spread further apart as they struck." He splays his fingers and makes a swiping motion.

Illiadus's scalp prickles again. She taps her com-badge and says, "Illiadus to Major Ironbear."

"*Yes, Captain?*" Ironbear's voice sounds gruff yet feminine.

"Report to sickbay."

"*Yes, Sir.*"

"Kyle, you said Inari suffers no direct brain trauma." She glances at Inari's unconscious form. "What about indirect?"

"That's the interesting thing." Sorlan closes the video and pulls up a set of MRIs. "We took these after she was stabilized. As you can see, the rear of the cerebrum and the cerebellum are perfectly healthy. No signs of swelling, and her brainstem is intact."

This is way above my paygrade, Illiadus thinks, but doesn't voice it.

"And the front of the cerebrum?"

Sorlan points. "The frontal lobe shows signs of minor inflammation. It's possible she banged her head as she collapsed, but there are no contusions or lacerations anywhere except her backside. I just don't see how that could have happened, but it gets stranger still." He brings up another set of scans.

Illiadus frowns. "What else is wrong with her?"

"Oh, this isn't her." He leans in close to read the name. "It's Culinary Specialist Erland, one of the galley staff. She's the one who brought Chief Petty Officer Inari here. Wheeled her in on a food cart, screaming for a medic."

Illiadus could put a face to the name, but that was about it. "Is she still here?"

"Of course. We're keeping her for observation." He points. "See her frontal lobe?"

Illiadus leans close. "Let me guess: more inflammation?"

Sorlan smiles. "One of these days, you may actually fool me into thinking you know how to read these scans."

Illiadus returns the smile, but there is little mirth in it. "What does it mean, Kyle?"

"I don't know. By itself, it could be nothing. But, coupled with Chief Inari's condition and Culinary Specialist Erland's behavior since arriving here, it could be everything."

"How has she been acting?"

"She doesn't remember anything. She claims she was with Chief Inari the entire time, but she can't tell us where it happened, what happened, or how she even got here."

Illiadus gapes at Sorlan.

"My thoughts exactly." He taps the image of Erland's frontal lobe. "One of the primary functions of the frontal lobe is memory storage and access. If that gets disrupted somehow, well, anything's possible: acute or permanent memory loss, memory alteration, implantation of completely fabricated memories, just to name a few."

"So, the gremlins aren't just disrupting my ship," Illiadus mutters. "They're disrupting my crew."

The door to sickbay opens, bringing with it the familiar, heavy tread of Major Helen Ironbear. Illiadus steps through the privacy drape separating Inari from the rest of the ship's hospital wing. Ironbear sees her and salutes. "Captain, how may I assist?" A sardonic smile plays across her dark lips. "You're standing, so you couldn't have been hurt too badly. Should I be worried about the other guy?"

Illiadus returns the salute. "No, but you should be worried about Melanie Inari."

Ironbear settles into a stiff parade rest. Her smile is gone, replaced with a scowl. "Who attacked her?"

"Rouse your troops, Major. It's time to hunt Gremlins."

"We're in position," Ironbear reports, her crisp voice coming over the intercom in Illiadus's command chair.

"We'll figure out what's going on, Captain," Lehmann says.

The CIC's main monitor shows a split-screen view from Ironbear's body-cam and the camera facing the door to the Hydroponics Bay. Ironbear faces the team of three engineers and seven Marines. *"Chief, you and your men will wait until we've cleared the whole bay."*

"Sounds good to me."

The Marines form up on either side of the wide door. Ironbear takes up position to the left of the door, by the control panel. She punches in the access code and barks, "Marines, go.."

Klaxons blare throughout the CIC, the sudden piercing whistles causes Illiadus to jump. "What the hell's going on?"

"Massive power fluctuations reported across the ship!" an officer shouts.

"External camera feeds down!"

"Communications are down!"

The audio from Ironbear and Lehmann cuts out. On the screen, Ironbear types in a code over and over again, but the door refuses to open. She raises her fist to smash the control panel just as the camera feed dies.

"Get on the hardline to engineering!" Illiadus barks to the communications officer. "Find out what's happening to my ship!"

"Yes, Captain!" The man lifts the receiver from his console and punches in the number for engineering. The physical circuits exist for just this kind of situation. It won't help them communicate with Ironbear or Lehmann, but there is another way to deal with that.

"Commander, you have the CIC." Illiadus reaches to her side and removes the Quantum Helmet from its resting place.

A hand grips her arm. Aithon looks down at her, concern in his eyes. "You said you wouldn't use it again."

"And I'm not." She shudders at the thought of being connected to the entire ship, of feeling the damage to the outer hull as if it were her own body, the need to be connected to everything and everyone-- "No, I won't be using that. This is just to connect to SIBIL and use her eyes. We need to know what's going on."

As if to accentuate her point, the lights in the CIC flicker and dim before returning to normal. Aithon grips her arm tighter, then lets it go. "All right. Be careful."

"Aren't I always?" She slips the helmet around her head. "Don't answer that."

Aithon chuckles, then steps forward. "Comms, what's happening in Engineering?"

Illiadus activates the helmet, feels her consciousness slip from her body and…

She steps into a field of blue irises. She recognizes it as one of the images projected onto the walls of the galley from time to time, taken from New Estonia or one of the other Earth-class colony worlds humanity has settled on. In the galley it feels as if you are surrounded by a very lovely painting. In SIBIL's space, it is as if you are *in* the painting.

SIBIL sits in the middle of the field, idly plucking iris after iris. Hovering in front of her are dozens of images, each from a different security camera feed in the ship. A cacophony of audio from each camera flows through the air, the discordant jumble an assault on Illiadus's digitized hearing. "Can you hear everything going on?" she asks.

"Almost." SIBIL raises a hand, and three images enlarge. Each is a blank screen with the words "Feed Lost" printed across them. "Cameras in the Reefer Hold and Hydroponics Bay are lost to me, along with their audio feeds."

"For how long?"

"Four minutes, twenty-two seconds ago, maybe longer for the Reefer Hold."

Illiadus cocks her head to the side. Maybe longer? She isn't used to SIBIL explaining things by half-measures. "Never mind that for now. What is going on with the *Ekatarina?*"

"Fluctuations in power grids across nearly all systems. Disruptions in crew access to camera feeds, secured doors, and communications. I posit this is due to boarding by force of unknown strength and composition." She looks over her shoulder at Illiadus, her blue eyes boring into her. "I believe Lieutenant Commander Walter Lehmann refers to them as *gremlins*?"

"That's as good a name for them as any."

"Very well. From here on, boarders of unknown origin will be referenced as Gremlins."

Illiadus chuckles, but it fades. "How is the crew?"

"Engineering is attempting to mitigate the power fluctuations. Sickbay is focused on keeping their patients calm. And Major Ironbear is screaming into her mic, requesting permission to 'blow the shit out of this door.' She seems unaware of the larger issues going on."

"Can you override the door access from here?"

"The codes have been changed, but I should be able to. Please wait."

Illiadus settles down next to SIBIL. Years have passed since she first laid eyes on the AI, then in the body of a ten-year-old girl. Now she is full-grown, almost her age. It is almost as if they were sisters.

"Major Ironbear," SIBIL says, "I am about to unlock the door. Prepare your men."

Inside the virtual space, SIBIL's voice sounds like that of a normal, human woman. Through the intercom's speakers where Ironbear is, those same words rise and fall in pitch, from a barely audible squeak at "Ironbear" to a low rumble with "unlock" and back to high with "men." Whenever Illiadus hears it, she imagines SIBIL tracing the curving path of a sound wave.

"*Roger,*" Ironbear says. "*You heard SIBIL! Get ready!*"

She shifts her focus back to the screens suspended overhead just as the bay door slides open. "Move, Marines!" Ironbear barks.

The first two Marines through the door suddenly stagger backwards, each slamming into the man behind him, and on down the line until all eight Marines are stopped in the doorway. Marine Sergeant Bryce screams as blood erupts from cuts along his face and neck. Another marine grabs and pulls Bryce away, but then he is attacked.

And then all hell breaks loose. The cluster of Marines stumble out of the doorway, swatting the air or clutching at wounds that suddenly appear. *"Pull back!"* Ironbear shouts. *"I'm shutting the door!"*

The view of the major's body-cam bounces about as she runs forward and pulls one of the wounded Marines free of the door. As it did, Illiadus catches a glimpse of the inside of the Hydroponics Bay. Some kind of strange alien growth covers the raised beds that run the length of the chamber, all reds and blues and browns instead of the vibrant green of Earth plants.

Illiadus jumps to her feet as the doors shut. Her Marines still swat at the air as rends and tears appear in their armor and exposed flesh. What the hell is going on? What is attacking her men? She strains her digital eyes until her head hurts. If only she can see what is happening!

The virtual world shifts. The field of flowers vanish and are replaced with a 3-D representation of the corridor outside the Hydroponics Bay. SIBIL stands next to her now, her left hand grasping Illiadus's right. It appears as if they are right in the middle of the action, right there with the Marines and engineers. "I'm combining the footage from all the body-cams and the corridor camera to create this facsimile," SIBIL says. "Together we can try and see what's happening."

"If your cameras aren't picking anything up, how can we…" Illiadus begins.

A blur of motion catches the corner of her eye, and she spins. Nothing moves in the corridor, but something is there. And it is about to strike. "Major, behind you!"

Ironbear whirls about and fires a burst from her rifle. A screech fills the corridor, and the body of a large winged insect strikes the floor. The doll-sized alien writhes on the ground as yellow ichor leaks from the wounds in its body.

Further down the corridor, the air warps and bends, then returns to normal. "SIBIL, did you see that?"

"Confirmed. For exactly zero point zero zero two one seconds, three Gremlins were visible to the cameras in the corridor. They are fleeing."

With her consciousness returned to her body, Illiadus removes the Quantum Helmet and sets it aside. "SIBIL, show us what you found."

A trio of doll-sized aliens appear on the main CIC screen, their transparent wings freeze midflight. The 3-D representations of what had been in the corridor rotate slowly, revealing multi-faceted eyes glowing with yellow light. That light is reflected by the razor-sharp claws on their three-fingered hands.

"Aman tamrin!" Al-Quam exclaims. "They're so… ugly!"

"And big," Aithon adds. "Are you sure SIBIL's not playing some kind of prank on us, Captain? How've we missed seeing those things buzzing around?"

"All I know is these bastards just tore up several of our Marines, and they left Chief Inari for dead."

As for how they are hiding…

"SIBIL, how were you able to see them?"

"Unknown."

"Speculate."

The insects disappear from the screen and are replaced by SIBIL's avatar. She rubs her chin, her blue eyes gazing off into the distance of her virtual world. "Hypothesis One: they possess some kind of optic and thermal camouflage that is disrupted for a fraction of a second. Possible cause of disruption: power fluctuations in ship's systems."

"Does that hypothesis seem likely?"

"Negative. The effects are too widespread, and too uniform."

Illiadus frowns. "Too widespread? We're just talking about one corridor, right?"

"Negative. Appearance of species designated Gremlins occurred ship-wide for 0.0021 seconds."

A chill runs down Illiadus's spine. "Show us."

SIBIL's avatar vanishes, replaced with dozens of still images from cameras all across the ship. Though the sections of the ship varied widely, each image has one thing in common: Gremlins. In some images, just one or two. In others, twenty or more. All told, there have to be hundreds of them.

"My God," Aithon says. "The *Ekatarina's* full of them!"

"And that's their leader." Illiadus points to one of the images, and SIBIL increases its size to fill up the monitor screen. It is an image taken from the camera in the Reefer Hold corridor. The doors lay open, and inside it she can see several Gremlins buzzing about. One in particular stands out, larger than the others, with eyes that burn with red light. Those eyes stare directly into the camera.

Pain lances into Illiadus's forehead. She gasps from the suddenness and clutches at her head. Groans and cries rise up from the rest of the CIC staff. Most hold hands to their heads, and at least one officer has slumped over his station, unmoving.

The image of the leader Gremlin shifts on the screen, its transparent wings unfurling as it stretches out its claws. A voice screeches through her thoughts. *I am the Queen of this vessel. You will kneel before us, pitiful creatures, or perish.*

The voice fades, and with it the pain. Illiadus shakes her head to clear it, then looks back at the screen. It has returned to a still-frame shot of the Gremlin leader.

"Kneel?" Illiadus balls her hands into fists. "We'll see who kneels at the end of this, you ugly little bitch."

"Let me get this straight, Captain," Ensign Terry Thaleia says. "The *Ekatarina's* been invaded by a race of insects with the power to mask their physical presence and alter certain people's memories. And on top of that, they're trying to take over the ship and kill all of us. Does that about cover it?"

"Pretty much." Illiadus crosses her arms and leans a shoulder against the wall. She stands on the other side of Thaleia's bunk. "Well, we don't know for sure that they want to kill us. But the result will be the same if we don't do something. They're attacking critical ship systems, including environmental and life support. If we let them do as they please, it'll only be a matter of time before we die of hypoxia."

"And that's why you and Dr. Bream have decided to grace me with your presence today."

Illiadus favors Thaleia with a withering smile. "You've been an exemplary junior officer for a few years now, but can the attitude. Let's not forget why you spent so much of your time in Coldsleep before I gave you a second chance after your personal act of mutiny. Who's to blame for that again?"

Thaleia returns the smile with a wolfish grin. "You, actually. You could've executed me. You probably should've."

"Believe me, I was tempted. But I have a duty to the ship and crew as a whole. And I saw worth in your skills as a physicist." Her smile fades. "Even if your personality and morals are lacking."

Thaleia recoils as if slapped. "I just wanted all of us to get home!"

"No, you wanted *you* to get home. You didn't care what happened to the rest of us."

"And you do?" Thaleia strides up to the bars and glares at Illiadus. "How many of us have died under your orders? How many people have you sent to their deaths?"

Dr. Bream shifts uncomfortably. "Captain, Ensign, maybe we should get down to the business at hand?"

Illiadus nods to the Marine guard with them. "Yes, let's get on with this."

"And that's the long and short of it," Illiadus says as the conference room monitor goes blank. "The only way to counteract the Gremlins' psychic cloaking and manipulation is with a psychic shield of our own. That's where the Quantum Helmet comes in. SIBIL? Care to explain Hypothesis Two to us?"

SIBIL appears on the conference room monitor. "Hypothesis Two: through her connection to the *Ekatarina*, Captain Illiadus is able to project her natural psychic resistance through the ship's systems."

"Natural psychic resistance?" Aithon looks at Dr. Sorlan. "Is that a real thing?"

Dr. Sorlan shrugs. "We believe that's why Chief Inari was attacked. She didn't succumb to the Queen's psychic manipulation, and they tried to kill her instead. I can't say for sure that the captain possesses the same resistance as Chief Inari, but it's a possible explanation."

Illiadus spread her hands. "I won't pretend to have the answers. All I can tell you is for just a split second, when I was linked to SIBIL, we could see the aliens all across the ship. If we can boost that effect, we can strip these aliens of their one advantage over us." She thumps the table with a fist. "Then we can wipe them out."

"I request that we capture their Queen, Captain," Dr. Bream says. "She could be a valuable prisoner."

"A psychic shield," Thaleia mutters. She leans over and whispers something to Dr. Bream and Dr. Sorlan. The three put their heads together.

"Capturing her is too risky," Aithon objects. "She can enter our thoughts!"

"The Commander has a good point." Ironbear cracks her knuckles. "I've fought my share of hard cases, but never one who could manipulate my thoughts." She pauses. "Well, except that one ex. I swear he was a mind-reader."

Aithon chuckles. "I'd like to meet a man who could wrap you around his finger, Major."

She bares her teeth. "Who says he's still around to meet?"

"Point taken." Aithon's smile fades. "Seriously, though, how are we supposed to contain this alien?"

"Sedate her, and get her into Cold Sleep?" Illiadus offers.

"Do we have any idea what can sedate one of these Gremlins?"

"No, but we will soon." Dr. Sorlan raises his head from the hushed conversation. "My team's about finished with its autopsy of the dead one you brought in."

"Excellent," Illiadus says. "And the Quantum Helmet?"

"We have an idea, but…" Thaleia shares a look with Dr. Bream. "Captain, this could melt your brain," Thaleia says. "And I'm not being hyperbolic. I mean, soft tissue turning into gelatin and leaking out of your ears as you die screaming."

The deck plates beneath their boots shudder violently. A klaxon sounds in the corridor, followed by SIBIL announcing, "Explosive decompression on Deck Six." "Ensign, if we don't do something, it won't just be my brain melting. These Gremlins will kill us all."

"Captain, I really must protest to this," Thaleia says.

"Noted, considered, and rejected." Illiadus leans back and lets Crewman Tiresias settle the Quantum Helmet on her head. "We have no choice in the matter. If we don't stop these Gremlins and their psychic Queen, the ship is lost. Everyone else has their part to do. Your part is to keep the Quantum Helmet running and collect data."

"Captain," Aithon calls, "Major Ironbear reports her Marines are ready."

"We're out of time for any more improvements, Ensign," Illiadus says, heading off any further objections. "I trust that you, Crewman Tiresias, Chief Lehmann, and Dr. Bream did your best. Now, turn it on."

Thaleia hesitates, then sighs. "Don't throw me back in the brig if this fails."

She punches several commands into her console. A jolt shoots through Illiadus's body, and then…

"Are you ready?" SIBIL asks.

They stand in the field of blue irises again, an array of viewscreens floating overhead in the cool evening air. Each of these screens show footage from one of the *Ekatarina's* three hundred and forty-two security cameras. Illiadus gazes upward. Through her neural connection to SIBIL and the ship's systems, she sees every screen in clear focus all at once. "I'm ready," she murmurs.

SIBIL takes one of Illiadus's hands in her own. "I'm right here," the AI says, concern in her tone. "Be careful."

That isn't very reassuring, Illiadus thinks. She focuses her attention fully on the cameras and thinks about the Gremlins infesting her ship. The little insects are cloaked, hidden from view and attacking from those shadows. She needs to strip away that cloak, to shine light in their darkness. They need to pay for what they did to her people.

As she thought about this, pressure builds in her head. That pressure flows down into the hand that SIBIL holds. Their clasped fingers begin to glow.

Little shapes appear in the overhead screens. Gremlins. Hundreds of them.

"The Gremlins are exposed," SIBIL reports to the CIC. "Opening doors in forty-five seconds."

"*Roger,*" Aithon replies. *"The Marines will be ready."* There is a pause. *"Captain, how're you holding up?"*

"Other than having my consciousness pulled in a thousand different directions," Illiadus says through gritted teeth, "just fine."

And it's about to get a lot more fun, she thinks. While keeping her attention focused on all the ship's Gremlins, she simultaneously reaches out toward her crew, especially the Marines. Revealing the Gremlins' presence won't be enough.

She needs to keep her people safe.

Major Ironbear stands with her men stacked up on either side of the Reefer Hold's large door. Twenty-five Marines, armed, armored, and ready to fight. Most are armed with rifles, but four wielded ballistic shields and pistols. They would breach the hold first, while the rest would follow and provide covering fire.

Her second, Master Gunnery Sergeant Worlu, commands a similar sized team ready to breach the Hydroponics Bay. He is relatively new to the ship, but the green-skinned alien was a warrior through-and-through. The remaining Marines are divided into small quick-reaction squads and scatter about the ship. If the Captain's crazy plan works and they can unmask the Gremlins, it will be the quick-reaction squads' job to deal with the ones roaming the decks.

Both she and Worlu are equipped with tranquilizer injections for the Queen. The last place she was spotted was the Reefer Hold, but images taken from the Hydroponics Bay door show a hive of some size. She can move from one location to another, or there could be two Queens. Whatever the case, they won't be caught flat-footed again.

"Major Ironbear, Sergeant Worlu," Aithon says into Ironbear's headset, *"SIBIL is opening the doors in twenty-five seconds."*

"Roger that, Commander," Ironbear says. She raises her hand. Her men tense, weapons at low ready.

As she shoulders her rifle, she feels as if a blanket has settled around her head and shoulders. She frowns and shakes her head to clear it, but the sensation doesn't go away. It is not an unpleasant feeling.

"Anyone else feel that?" one of her Marines ask.

Her headset crackles, and then SIBIL's modulating voice flows into her ear. *"We've placed a psychic shield around the breaching team. The Gremlin Queen can do nothing to you."*

Bring that bitch down, Helen, Illiadus says, and with a start Ironbear realizes the captain's voice comes from inside her mind.

Ironbear grins. "You don't need to tell me twice, Captain."

The doors to the Reefer Hold opens with a hiss. The four shield Marines rush into the swirling cold mist, followed by Ironbear and the rest of the platoon.

From the entrance, the Reefer Hold appears as it had the last time Ironbear had been in there: row upon row of shelves, each stacked to the ceiling with crates, containers, barrels, and palettes of frozen foodstuffs. However, the frigid, dim chamber is also packed to the ceiling with Gremlins, their multi-faceted eyes glowing yellow. Their beating wings fill the space with a buzzing that is nearly deafening, heard even through the electronic hearing protection built into Ironbear's helmet.

A cleared area in the center of the room is reserved for forklifts. Beyond that, some of the shelves have been absorbed by that strange green and brown mass that fills the Hydroponics Bay. How long had they been building these hives, with no one noticing? What kind of psychic hold did this Gremlin Queen have over the crew?

"Weapons free!" Ironbear orders. She lines up her sights on one of the flying Gremlins and squeezes the trigger. A single shot rings out, and the Gremlin disappears between the shelving.

A cacophony of gunfire erupts as her men react to Ironbear's initial shot. Bullet-riddled Gremlins slam into the floor as storage containers explode into fragments of plastic, wood, and glass. The Gremlin swarm recoils from the attack, their soaring forms retreating deeper into the Reefer Hold, back towards what can only be the hive.

The shield Marines slowly advance into the rows of shelving, their pistols barking. As Ironbear follows behind, her boots crunch on glass. She glances up and notices the jars shattered in the gunfire are empty. Same with a broken crate marked as containing "Freeze-dried Blackberry Equivalent." Nothing leaks out of its pierced side.

Six Gremlins soar down the row towards her. The shield Marine in front of her empties his magazine in a spray of rapid fire. Three of the Gremlins fall dead, and a fourth is wounded, but the remaining two continue towards them. Ironbear thumbs her rifle's selector to full-auto and lets out a controlled burst. One Gremlin blows apart, and the last one smacks harmlessly into the lead Marine's shield. He raises his boot to stomp it flat.

And freezes, his foot hanging in the air. The "blanket" around Ironbear's head and shoulders suddenly tightens. Her body seizes up, and it takes every ounce of her strength to shift her aim toward an approaching Gremlin. The trigger seems to weigh a thousand pounds as she squeezes. She fires just as it is upon her. Blood and ichor splatter her face.

A Gremlin twice as big as the others hovers in the clearing ahead. It glares at Ironbear with a pair of malevolent red eyes.

Surrender. Kneel before your betters.
The Queen's psychic command buffets the shields placed around the Marines. Illiadus feels this as blows to her own body. She gasps from the pain, and reflexively squeezes SIBIL's hand.

Illiadus's head hurts as she concentrates. She needs to pour more energy into the shields. Ironbear and the others are counting on her. She grinds her teeth together and pushes with everything she has.

The invisible bonds around Ironbear snaps, and she can move freely again. She rushes forward just as a group of Gremlins tear into the shield Marine. Blood sprays, and the man screams. Ironbear rips one Gremlin after another off the stricken man and dashes their tiny bodies against the steel shelves. She then raises her rifle and fires into the teeming mass gathering in the cleared space.

She risks a glance backward, and sees her Marines engage in a close quarter fight. Gremlins leaped and flew from spaces in the shelving. If she didn't get her men moving soon, they would be overrun in the rows.

Pain lances through her skull, and she staggers. Over the comms, several Marines grunt or cry out. A woman's scream echoes in her mind. As quickly as the pain comes, it dissipates. She shakes her head to clear it and growls. That damned Queen is still trying to get to them.

"Forward!" she shouts, leaping over the fallen shield Marine. "We have to take down the Queen!"

Despite the fear and adrenaline coursing through her, she worries for Illiadus. Had that been her scream she heard?

On the CIC, Aithon watches as Dr. Bream tends to a writhing Illiadus. A pained moan escapes her lips. He winces but resist the urge to go to her.

Thaleia reaches for the Quantum Helmet's chin strap.

"What are you doing?" Aithon snaps.

"We have to remove this!" Thaleia glares at him. "She's dying!"

"Don't you think I know that?" Commander Aithon steps between Thaleia and Illiadus. "She has her job to do, just like you do, just like we all do. Let her do it, and keep that helmet running!"

He steps close to Dr. Bream and grips the smaller man's shoulder. "And you keep her alive, understand?"

"Surrender, Queen!" From her body-cam Illiadus and SIBIL watch as Ironbear shoots one of the insect guards, then slams her fist into another. The pair of Gremlins crumple to the Reefer Hold's cold floor. *"It's over!"*

Twenty Marines stand in a loose semi-circle in the cleared space of the Reefer Hold, their rifles roaring. Gremlin gore covers the steel floor, their yellowish blood already beginning to freeze in the cold air. The curious side of Illiadus wonders how there could be insects that handled both the warmth of the Hydroponics Bay and the cold equally well.

The Queen's answer is a shriek followed by a burst of psychic energy. The energy impacts the shields Illiadus and SIBIL have erected around Ironbear and her Marines. Pain meant for twenty-nine crewmen rips through Illiadus's body and mind. She screams. SIBIL embraces her tightly and murmurs soothing words into her ear.

Illiadus needs more power. She reaches deep into her very essence.

Energy and strength well up from her body and coalesces in front of her and SIBIL as a ball of light. SIBIL reaches out and touches it. Electricity crackles from the ball to the tip of her finger, but SIBIL doesn't recoil. She instead places her whole hand against it. "Is this… warmth?"

Illiadus can't answer that. It is all she can do to hold it together. She tries to focus it on just the Gremlin Queen, but her consciousness - split as it is over every deck of the *Ekatarina* - is too frayed. "You will kneel before us, Queen," she spat.

The Queen shrieks again and unleashes another telepathic burst. This time Illiadus barely feels the impacts against her shields, so focused is she on her own attack. Her concentration begins to slip, and she realizes it is now or never.

She let the power go.

"I said *kneel!*" Illiadus and SIBIL roar in unison. SIBIL's voice undulates through the ship's intercom, while Illiadus's rushed from the Quantum Helmet in a psychic wave.

Across Illiadus's camera-eyes, hundreds of the tiny, insectoid Gremlins fall to the floor, their wings and limbs paralyzed. Even her crew, from the officers on the CIC to Major Ironbear and her Marines assaulting the Queen's lair in Reefer Hold, have fallen to their knees. Ironbear kneels before the alien Queen, her rifle held at low-ready and the rest of her body rigid. She glares at the doll-sized alien overlord for a moment before shifting her gaze to the security camera above her. She arches an eyebrow.

Pain explodes in her head, and she sags against SIBIL. "Take her… custody," she slurs.

"Ironbear, sedate and seize!" SIBIL cries, her voice carrying with it a frantic quality Illiadus has never before heard in the AI.

As her vision darkens around her, she feels herself being eased to the virtual ground of SIBIL's iris field. She feels her hold over the crew and aliens slip as consciousness begins to fade. She glances over at the screen and sees Ironbear stab the Gremlin Queen with the tranquilizer. Before everything goes black, she looks up and sees SIBIL staring down at her. Her yellow eyes reflect the blue irises and green grass below them. It reminds her of Earth.

"Well, Ten, we did it." Aithon leans back in his chair, a glass of some kind of blue alien liquor in his hand. "We've got the alien Queen in custody. Once we are able to sedate her and get her into a cryosleep chamber, the rest of her people just stopped resisting." He made a shooing motion with his free hand. "We shoved them into one of the empty cargo holds, and they're content to stay there."

He swirls the liquid in his glass. What is it called again? He never has figured out how to pronounce it. He takes a small sip, and grimaces. Nor has he really developed a taste for it. He sets it down on the small table at Illiadus's bedside, right next to her untouched glass. He tries to ignore the steady beeping yet is grateful for its presence. *If it weren't for that, I wouldn't even know if she is alive.*

Illiadus lay in the sickbay bed, her lithe, six-foot-one frame covered to the neck in a heavy blanket taken from her quarters. She still wears the Quantum Helmet, its power cables plugged into every available outlet in the partitioned area. The color has drained from her cheeks, leaving her skin as white as her scars. She doesn't stir. She barely even breathes.

Dr. Sorlan isn't sure if, or when, she will wake up. "And even if she does wake up, there's no telling what kind of state she'll be in." Not very comforting, but his matter-of-factness is one of the things Aithon likes about the good doctor. Except when it applies to the woman he cares about more than anyone else.

Aithon leans his head back until it rests against the wall. "Ah, Ten, you always put me in this kind of position, don't you? When we started this godforsaken journey, I had to come to your quarters and rouse you from bed. Your hair was down and tangled, your clothes were unkempt, and you looked absolutely ravishing in spite of all that. I had to tell you to quit moping about, and that your ship needed you."

He slides out of the chair and kneels next to her bedside. "Well, nothing's changed. I'll take care of things in the meantime, but don't laze about in a coma for too long. Your ship needs you." He leans forward and kisses her forehead. "I need you, too."

Aithon stands and turns to go. He pauses as he steps past the privacy drape and into the darkened sickbay. One of the cameras in the ceiling points his way. He stares up at it for a moment, then says, "Take care of her, all right? Bring her back to us."

SIBIL watches as Aithon walks out of the sickbay. Once he is gone, she sets her monitoring of the ship's security cameras and microphones to passive and shifts her attention to the limp form leaning against her. She reaches up with an arm and strokes the hair of Illiadus's avatar. The captain's digital form is just as unmoving as her physical body. It isn't something SIBIL has ever experienced before. Illiadus has always been full of life whenever they have encountered one another, full of determined desperation, disciplined excitement, or frank curiosity. To see her in this vulnerable state is… unsettling.

She closes her eyes briefly and re-orders the world around both of them. When she opens them again, she finds herself in a bedroom on long-lost Hestia. She and Illiadus both lay on a queen-sized bed.

SIBIL blinks. How had she known this is Hestia? And how did she know what a queen-sized bed is? The only beds she has ever seen are the narrow bunks the enlisted crew used, and the hospital bed Illiadus lays in.

A strange sensation ripples through SIBIL's consciousness. She reaches up and touches her forehead, much as Illiadus has done during her climactic fight with the Queen.

SIBIL snuggles next to Illiadus and pulls the covers around them both. She stares at the sleeping form of the woman who has bravely linked herself to an experimental AI all those years ago. SIBIL doesn't understand her creators at all. All she has ever known are orders, but maybe, just maybe, she has come to know a friend, as well.

She echoes Aithon's last words to Illiadus before he left the sickbay: "I need you."

Acting Captain's Log, The Ekatarina

Four years ago, our fight with the alien species we came to know as Gremlins turned in our favor. We lost three marines. Fifteen marines and crewmen were seriously wounded but recovered quickly because of the advanced medical trauma technology given to us by the Cerridians. The most severely wounded was Captain Illiadus. The strain on her mind, her brain, battling the psychic alien queen while wearing the cybernetic helmet was terrible, and the ship's doctor is still not sure if she will ever regain consciousness. Most of the crew has been sequestered in their coldsleep pods as The Ekatarina continues to move at our fasted sublight speed toward home. Captain Illiadus is the only person on the ship capable of using the Quantum Helmet to navigate through dark energy arteries. If she does not wake up, it will be our great great grandchildren who eventually reach Earth. End Log.

Cognitive Therapy

by Dina Leacock

Ship's Chronometer: 2448 AD

SIBIL remains silent. Connected by the helmet to a being that is not responding to anything. Damaged.

The Captain is damaged. SIBIL once again realizes humans are so fragile, so defective. The one thing she has learned through her existence is that humans break so easily and there doesn't appear to be many replacement parts that repair them like there are for her.

It is a pity, SIBIL thinks, then realizes for the nine thousand one hundred and eighty-seventh time, that pity is basically an alien term, a term that humans use, not an artificial intelligence being like she. Periodically being hooked up to the Captain over all these years through that helmet has definitely altered her perceptions. Altered her very being. She understood emotions on a level that went well beyond the logical.

SIBIL has developed cybernetic analogues of emotions, not as strong as a human's, but they are there. She just hides them because she has never been built that way. To show emotion, she is still a machine. A machine tied to this broken human and she realizes that she wants to cry. Her core aches, and for the first time she wants to share her feelings with something, no. Someone.

She mentally nudges the Captain, then gives the unhuman equivalent of a sigh.

"Captain?"

Nothing happens and for a brief moment SIBIL allows frustration to interfere with her thought process.

"Captain Illiadus?"

"Tennyson?"

"Tenn?"

Still nothing although SIBIL know there has to be some response lying dormant in the Captain or their connection would have been broken.

SIBIL tries again. She will try again and again until the connection breaks because she doesn't get bored by trying, she just keeps count of the times she probes looking for the Captain.

"Maria?"

Something, a tiny spark nudges SIBIL back.

SIBIL knows it is real, she doesn't have the ability to create false hope. She continues.

"Maria, are you there?"

Silence. Just as SIBIL is about to try again, she hears it.

"Yes."

SIBIL wants to do a high five with the Captain, her cyber image smiles.

"Maria, I'm so glad to hear you. Are you all right?"

"I'm scared."

SIBIL stops being happy. This is all wrong. The Captain is the most fearless human SIBIL has had contact with, and she is connected to everyone on the *Ekatarina* through the onboard system. Not like she is connected to the Captain, she is almost one being with the Captain and this mind she is joined with is terrified.

It was still broken, SIBIL thinks. *I've got it working at last, but it is not working to capacity.*

SIBIL presents herself as the thirty-four-year-old woman she is created to be at this juncture in time. She sits in her favorite place, the field of blue irises, and waits for the Captain to join her.

"Come Maria, why are you afraid? There is nothing here to fear. Come, show yourself to me."

"I'm scared," the voice quavers

"Try to come here," SIBIL urges. "You don't have to be scared of me. I'm your best friend, remember?"

The silence stretches on and SIBIL weighs her options. Should she push? Would that cause more damage, would it cause the Captain to retreat?

After a few moments a five-year-old girl takes form.

"I'm lost," the dark-haired child says and burst into tears.

SIBIL is surprised for just a moment, the resemblance to the Captain is there but none of the strength, the persona of protector she has worn was gone. Maria is an innocent little girl. SIBIL holds out her simulated hand.

"Come, Maria, show me where you live."

The child grasps the offered hand and scrunches up her face in thought and then they are in a child's bedroom. A little girl's room, pink and pale green with pretty dolls and toy spaceships.

"Is this your room?" SIBIL asks.

Maria smiles, "Yes,"

"It is a very pretty room for a very pretty girl," SIBIL says and smiles. "Tell me, what do you like best here?"

"I love this doll," Maria says and hugs one of the larger baby dolls. "When I'm a grown-up I'll have a baby just like her, maybe lots of babies." Then she turns and swats at a suspended antique space shuttle. "I like this a lot too. Mommy tells me my great-great grandfather flew one of these when he was a boy on earth. Then she giggles. "I don't really know what that means, but mommy always smiles whenever she tells me about it."

"I see," SIBIL says. "Why are these two toys your favorites?" She decides that getting the child self of the Captain to talk would help her memories. Maybe this is the way to fix her broken mind, by bringing her to the present from the past her mind has retreated too. To making her be Captain Illiadus again.

"I want to fly a spaceship too. I'm going to be a mommy and a spaceship flyer. I want to see the stars twinkle and I love my doll, her name is ..is..is SIBIL."

SIBIL remains silent. Obviously, there is a blending of past and present here.

"When I grow up, I want to be just like SIBIL. She knows everything and she's going to be my best friend. We'll have so much fun together!"

Maria stops talking and looks at SIBIL sitting on the pink carpeting and then adds, "She's going to be pretty, just like you. She will help me have fun except, except when the fun hurts too much."

SIBIL frowns and lays her hand on the child's tiny hand.

They sit in silence until the little girl starts to squirm and whimper.

"It hurts now." She gasps and falls over on her side.

SIBIL sits with the small child rubbing her back until she fades away. The Captain is gone again and SIBIL probes but can't find any trace of her anywhere. The bedroom has faded away and SIBIL has replaced it with the field of irises swaying ever so softly in the breeze.

"What to do now?" she says as if the Captain is still with her instead of behind a wall of unbreakable silence.

She sits in simulation and ponders. She knows time moves in the outside world, that humans age, that things wear out, that entropy causes disorder, but in her world, time has no meaning. She starts to nudge again.

"Maria?"

She is faced with a wall of silence.

"Maria?"

A voice reaches out to her.

"SIBIL." It is calling to her from the terminal in the sick bay.

"SIBIL, are you there? Are you all right? Are you in communication with Captain Illiadus? Is she all right? We can't get any response from her."

"I am here, First Officer Aithon," she says, "all my systems are working, those that needed repair have been updated. The ship appears to be operating although it is in need of repairs. I will display the needed repairs on the screen…"

"And the Captain?" David interrupts.

SIBIL continues on as if not interrupted, "The Captain is ninety-eight percent unresponsive. I am working on her brain, but it appears to be severely damaged. I advise the doctor to keep her body functioning, the helmet attached, and I will continue to try to repair her."

SIBIL sees the ensign frown and wipe at the corners of his eyes.

"I will repair her, first officer, do not worry," SIBIL says, realizing that she is lying to ease his grief. She would have had a complete systems failure a decade ago doing that, but the connection though the helmet has obviously made her more capable of emotions than she thought possible.

He stands straighter and says, "SIBIL we have a problem only the Captain can solve."

"What is it?"

"The Captain's log and her codes for the ship have vanished. The crew is searching and we fear the gremlins have destroyed them. I have started a new log as the provisional Captain, but we really need the information that the records contained. The history of the ship the records of all repairs and replacements. So many have died on this voyage, the Captain's records are important."

SIBIL says, "I will continue to work with the Captain's memories and will provide information as I receive it."

She leaves the crew to solve the problems they are capable of handling. She knows that First Officer Aithon is agitated. His voice and words don't show it, but she was programmed long ago to be intuitive to all human and known alien thought patterns. She did her equivalent of a silent chuckle and thought, known aliens of the time of the Scourge War. Since then, they have been bombarded by so many new beings, the *gremlins* as the crew calls them only being the newest to think so differently than anything she'd been introduced too when she'd been created.

Guess, I'm not so state of the art as I once was, she mused. Then she stops thinking for a second before continuing, *well that was certainly a human way of processing information.*

She knows she is being altered, becoming more and more hybrid as she stays attached to the Captain. She isn't quite artificial intelligence anymore, she is evolving.

She nudges the Captain, "Maria?"

Still no response. "Maria? Are you there? It is me SIBIL."

SIBIL stops probing, she goes into a silent mode where no one on the ship can disturb her without the proper commands. Too bad for the officers and crew, she is connected to the ship and the Captain, but to no other being. The Captain has moved the codes to the safest place on the ship before she put on the helmet and fried her brain.

SIBIL replays the scene, "Remember, SIBIL, this information is for the Captain's eyes only," Captain Illiadus said, "I'm depending on you."

SIBIL wonders how and when they will declare the Captain unfit to be Captain. She wonders how she will begin to change if the late Doctor Bream's cybernetic team determines that Captain Aithon is compatible for syncing his mind with the quantum helmet and eventually merging with her brain. She wonders if she will like sharing her brain with David Aithon, or if his mind cannot achieve rapport, some other crew member aboard the *Ekatarina* will. She loved sharing it with Tenn.

It is SIBIL's secret, sometime during their odyssey, she has developed emotions that are strong and remain after the helmet is not connected. She loves the Captain, she hates the species that caused her Captain to currently cease working.

"SIBIL?"

She responds.

"Yes First Officer Aithon."

"SIBIL, how are you doing reaching out to the Captain? Any changes?"

"Nothing new, First Officer."

"We need to find the codes to jump."

"I am programmed to jump the ship."

Aithon sighs.

"I know, SIBIL, but the Captain has to be able to run the ship. What if you get damaged or destroyed?"

"I know First Officer Aithon," SIBIL says, stressing his title. It is human to say it, but she feels that the first officer is crossing a line. Her Captain is still alive and she is going to bring her back. "I will search for the information you are seeking." She realizes the most logical approach she can take is to bring the Captain back so she won't have to deal with lies since she is incapable of telling lies.

"Captain," she nudges. No response.

'Captain Illiadus," No response.

"Tennyson," no response.

"Tenn," no response.

"Maria," no response.

"Captain," No response.

"Captain Illiadus," No response.

"Tennyson," no response.

"Tenn," no response.

"Maria," no response.

"Captain," no response

SIBIL keeps going. She never tires, she never gets bored, she never hesitates at the seeming futility of her duty. She does have a feeling of frustration, as much as her brain can allow her to feel. Even after developing the ability to feel emotion, she is still limited by what she is.

So, she keeps going on.

"Captain Maria, Tennyson. Illiadus. Can you hear me?"

"Yes," a voice answers her, but SIBIL doesn't know who has answered. She waits as an adult form of the Captain joins her in her field. It is a much younger Captain. "Maria?"

"No, cadet Tennyson Illiadus. And who are you?"

"I am SIBIL, I am your friend. You have been hurt and I am here to help you get well."

The Captain looks around, "Strange hospital."

"Yes, it is, but soothing, don't you agree?"

The Captain shrugs, "In a way, I like these flowers but I've never seen them before. Obviously, they don't grow in my world. She stops then says, "I don't have a world anymore. The Scourge blew it up and everyone I knew on it. If I hadn't gone off planet for basic training, I'd be dead too. The bastards!"

"I'm sorry," SIBIL says. "How old are you?"

"I'm seventeen. Been through training and getting ready to see some action."

"Are you scared?" SIBIL asks looking at this young woman, without any apparent scars except the invisible one so many have suffered at the hands of the Scourge.

The Scourge started the war by destroying three planets in three different sectors, killing unimaginable numbers of humans and various other species and alien races, letting the denizens of The Milky Way galaxy know about their presence and that they were on a mission of multiple genocide. They are an unstoppable evil and are on their way to accomplishing that feat when this young untested cadet here, still fresh and hopeful, destroys them and saves mankind and dozens of other races as well.

Tennyson stares at SIBIL, seeing a woman who is the age of her mother when she died. "No, I'm not scared, I just want to avenge my family, my friends, my planet, my race. I want to be the one to get even, wipe them out of existence," she tells SIBIL then smiles. "Big ambition huh?"

SIBIL frowns then smiles at her friend and pats the ground next to her. "Sit and we can talk."

Tennyson, shrugs and says, "I like you, don't know why but I think you can be trusted. No wait, I know you can be. Funny, but I feel like you know me better than I know myself."

"Perhaps I do."

Tennyson sits and eventually lays her head on SIBIL's lap and closes her eyes.

SIBIL runs her hand softly over the young woman's short military cut hair, and thinks soothing thoughts to her, thoughts that ease survivor's guilt over her lost planet. She doesn't want to touch on future guilt that she has felt festering in the mind of the older Tennyson. She doesn't want to change Tennyson's memories or her personality as it has formed. She only takes the edge off the pain that has lingered through the war and their present odyssey.

She gives the young cadet a feeling of security, a sense of great things to come. She touches the broken mind adding a glimpse of a brilliant future, thoughts of winning, thoughts of making love and being loved and loving someone someday, someone named SIBIL.

Tennyson's breathing slows and becomes deep and even and with a beatific smile, she fades away back into that wounded subconscious.

SIBIL sits in her field of flowers and let her thoughts of the Captain roam. She is capable of love and she loves the Captain. They have shared the most intimate moments, mind melded by the helmet. She feels something new, fear and loss if the Captain never wakes up. Yet, she is still connected to the Captain and the intimacy will continue until they got unplugged. SIBIL realizes that someday the Captain will actually physically die and she is swept by a wave of sadness.

She lets the emotion sink into every nuance of her constructed brain and suddenly feels tears on her avatar. She is crying the only way she is capable. Such an odd feeling, she'd experienced sadness and loss, anger, fury and happiness through her connection with the Captain, but this is the first time she's felt emotion in it's purest form. She sits and cries knowing that she too will eventually lose everything she's ever loved. She sits in her field, tears running down her cheeks and lets the Captain sleep.

SIBIL is pulled away from her world as the ship lets her know they are approaching another jump point, she goes back into the mode she is built for and spends the next hours preparing the crew and the ship to make the next jump to who knew where. She assures the first officer that she is in total control, lets him know she has suffered no damage in the episode that incapacitated the Captain, even though she now knows that she has been irretrievably changed. The Captain's agony has opened a neural gateway to human feelings.

She prepares the jump and ignores the first officer's request about any headway to the missing codes.

The *Ekatarina* comes through the dark matter in perfect shape, everyone is once again safe until the next jump, at least safe from the jump. No one knows exactly where they were. SIBIL studies the star maps and in a fraction of a second places their location the best she can with charts that have never recorded this place in space.

The ship now back in the able hands of the crew allows SIBIL to return to the needs of the Captain. She is ninety percent certain that her interactions with the fragmented thought processes of the Captain can help her recovery. She knows the Captain well and knows that the part of her personality that is the most damaged is yet to come. There is so much to heal.

"Tennyson, are you there?"

A moment of silence, "Yes this is Captain Illiadus, who is calling me?"

SIBIL watches as the Captain materializes into her corner of her reality. Older than the last version but much younger and so much less careworn than the Captain she knows so well. This is the Captain SIBIL has just met. The trust isn't there. The shared experiences aren't there and the Captain won't even recognize her in her current state, as a grown woman.

"Where am I?" Tennyson asks her gaze moving from the softly swaying flowers to the girl in front of her. "Who are you?"

SIBIL smiles, not a thing she got to do often if at all. "I'm an artificial Intelligence unit and this is my virtual world. You've been hurt, badly, and I'm here to help you recover and go back to your place, captaining the *Ekatarina.*"

"Hmmmm," Tennyson says in a non-committal tone.

SIBIL smiles again, she really enjoys getting to know this version of the Captain. Tennyson Illiadus is nobody's fool and so strong willed. She always knows what she considers right and wrong and follows her gut. She never thinks she'd ever have regrets, but SIBIL knows differently. SIBIL has glimpsed deep inside her and knows there are regrets that can never be totally resolved, but this Tennyson doesn't have them yet, she carries a burning hatred for the Scourge.

"Let's talk, Captain," for at this stage SIBIL has always referred to her as Captain.

"I don't have time, I've figured out how to defeat the Scourge once and for all."

"Have you?" SIBIL asks. "How?"

"I can't share the details, but if my plan works then we win and the Scourge will cease to be a problem."

"That is a good thing then, the Scourge not being a problem anymore?" SIBIL asks knowing that this confident, brash woman before her knew to her very core her decision is best for ending the war that has destroyed so many planets, taken so many lives. The Captain knows the Scourge are so much better at warfare, at killing, at winning their battles. By human standards they are an evil, heartless, cold-blooded race that deserves to die. If mankind did not win this time the Captain knew they will be annihilated, wiped from existence forever.

The Captain nods, "Yes, we have to win or die. And I for one, will not die quietly like my home world and my family, gone before they ever knew they were dead. Mankind's losses need to be avenged, the Scourge must be made to pay."

SIBIL nods. "Yes, I see. The death toll would be so much more, unimaginable, if this war were allowed to continue. You are going to save many lives, maybe your entire race. Humanity didn't start the war."

"But we have to end it, at any cost," the Captain agrees.

"Come sit," SIBIL pats the soft green grass. "Tell me something else. You are complex, there is more to you than war."

The Captain hesitates then sits. "You think so, I'm not complex, I'm a solder, through and through. I do my duty."

"I know," SIBIL says, "Duty is important. To a great leader such as yourself, duty is everything. It is your duty to keep worlds safe, your duty keeps your crew safe, your duty to bring your crew home."

SIBIL talks and the Captain remains silent as she listens. Eventually she lays her head on SIBIL's lap and SIBIL continues to show the Captain that she has to do whatever she has to do, it is her duty. She talks on, erasing the doubt that has laid heavy on Captain Illiadus's head for years.

Soon the Captain fades away and SIBIL is alone with her flowers and her infinite knowledge. She knows that whatever version decides to come out of the cocoon of pain that is the core being of Captain Maria Tennyson IIlliadus, there will be so much pain. SIBIL knows that the Captain is full of pain, years of pain. There is no room left. She has to free up space in this human so she can finally recover and resume her duty as the leader.

SIBIL hears the first officer calling to her and answers, "Yes, First Officer Aithon?"

"SIBIL, we are getting desperate here, I need to take over for the Captain until she recovers. As acting Captain, I need that logbook and all the ship's information."

SIBIL nods knowing that the acting Captain can't see her, she just wants to make a human gesture.

"I am closer to discovering it," she says and knows that the only person on board the *Ekatarina* that can help the Captain and crew is in a coma. But a coma that is lessening with each healed personality.

SIBIL waits. Time doesn't mean anything to her as it passes. She waits until she feels the Captain is ready to come to her again. She isn't sure which version of the Captain's subconscious will be revived but she knows that since it appears to be progressing she'll attempt to communicate with her friend.

"Tenn?" she probes. "Tenn are you aware?"

"SIBIL?"

"You know who I am?"

"You are SIBIL, the *Ekatarina's* AI and my friend."

SIBIL allows herself to feel happy. "Come to me Tenn, we have much to discuss."

The Captain in her current state appears and sits next to SIBIL.

"I do love this virtual reality," she says then frowns. "SIBIL, why did you call me? I can tell something is wrong. I…I don't feel quite like me. I feel a pain deep inside."

"You've been badly hurt, Tenn. Your body is in a coma, a deep coma and your mind is… disconnected, for want of a better word. The gremlin queen's attack ripped into your brain. It is bruised and battered but the fact that you can come to me and talk is a great improvement. You are getting better. What do you remember?"

"I remember…." Tenn hesitates. "I… remember fighting to keep the ship, I remember the relentless attack against us and me. I remember…"

she stopped bowed her head and clasped it in her hands. "I… I remember pain, such incredible pain. I remember blacking out and dying."

"You did not die."

"It felt like I did."

"No," SIBIL assures her, "you are very alive but we need to get you to connect to yourself, to become whole, to become the Captain. It will take time, your neural pathways are bruised and in some cases broken but the human mind is so good at creating new neural paths, to healing itself. I have faith in you that you will wake up in better shape than before this attack."

Tenn lifts her head. "The pain is so real," she says and grimaces. "I'd like to go back to being dead."

SIBIL shakes her head. "Soon I'll let you rest. Each time you've woken up for me you are stronger. Stay with me just a little longer."

Tenn nods. "All right, I'll try… for… a little while."

"Tenn, you've had a pain inside you for years. It has been growing, festering. You will never be whole until you understand yourself."

The Captain looks puzzled. "I'd been Captain for half my life, what could I not know."

SIBIL says. "I've spent my time watching you struggle to recover. I've seen the part of you that was an innocent child full of dreams, I've seen the part of you full of hate over the loss of your world, your family, your younger dreams. You were gung-ho and ready for war."

The Captain frowns. "Really, ready for war? I don't remember being that way at all. How could anyone be ready for battle?"

"Your older self knows how awful war is. That even winners lose." SIBIL said and stared at the Captain but got no reaction.

She continues. "I met the version of you who became Captain of the ship and had to make a decision no one could rationally make. I met a person who knew duty above all else and who knew her responsibilities and acted on them no matter the cost. No matter the cost to her."

The Captain frowns, "And now I'm here with you but I don't know what you are trying to say to me."

"Captain, you have built a mental wall around what you did when you destroyed an entire species."

"I know what I did, and I know I had to do it or our species would have been terminated."

"That's right," SIBIL says. "But I know you have carried that guilt with you ever since you destroyed the Scourge. It is always there, in the back of your mind, reflecting in the back of your eyes. You relive those feelings during every battle, this last one pushed you to withdraw from yourself."

"Bullshit," Tenn shouts. "I did my duty and that is all there is too it."

SIBIL shakes her head. "Tenn, you are a rational being. That idea of carrying out an extermination has to drag at you. That wall you've built is crumbling and you'll never wake up. You will die, and you don't have to."

The Captain grips her head again and began to sob.

SIBIL watches silently. The Captain could never have cried in the real would, but this virtual, serene place allows her to be a vulnerable human being. Allows her to show the pain and the doubts she's had to live with. Here she isn't the Captain, isn't the woman of steel, ridged and strong, never wavering from her sense of duty.

SIBIL stands and put her arms around her friend and soothes her.

"You did what you had to do to survive. Morally wrong but the right thing to do to save millions of other lives. It is impossible to live with the guilt, but also possible to understand that you alone were not guilty. The Scourge started the war and they would have committed genocide. You had to stop them because above all it was your duty."

"My duty," the Captain whispers and begins to fade away.

"Wait Captain," SIBIL calls and the Captain regains focus. "The acting Captain wants all the ship's codes and logs."

The Captain looks puzzled.

"You made me commit it all to my memory core and destroy anything physical. You said you didn't want the invaders to gain any knowledge from us. I erased all traces."

"Oh, I remember," the Captain says. "Please make sure you give it all to David. I feel weak, tired. I have to stop thinking now."

She fades away as SIBIL says, "rest Tenn, heal so you can come back to us, to your duty."

Then the ship's A.I. sits again in her virtual field of flowers and is ninety-six percent sure she has led the Captain through the first part of the journey on the way back to full recovery. Tennyson Maria Illiadus has been carrying an overload for way too long.

Now, Captain Illiadus, SIBIL thinks, *I must divorce your current reality from your soul, and give you the opportunity to honestly face the past traumas of this journey as your final therapy.*

"Acting Captain Aithon," SIBIL says through the terminal, "I have put all the information you asked for back in the ship's computer system. It is available to you."

"Thank you, SIBIL," David Aithon says. "How did you find it?"

Although no one could see her, SIBIL smiles.

"I asked the Captain."

Acting Captain's Log, The Ekatarina

SIBIL assures me that Captain Illiadus is well on the way to full recovery. She states that one more month of therapy is required before Ten can be awakened. The waiting causes me endless frustration, but I keep that bottled away from the majority of the crew. We continue to move forward at mere sublight speeds. The rest of our journey looms before us like an endless road into eternity… As for my personal life, I have begun an intense but discreet relationship with one of my junior officers. I can't speak to the wisdom of this decision, but it is a welcome distraction to the darkness that has always greeted me each night before I go to sleep. End Log.

Penthesilia

by Allison Chrysler Smith

Ship's Chronometer: 1189 BC

Penthesilia, Queen of the Ha-Mazan warrior cohort that fills this storm battered trireme, stands upon the bow of her ship, desperately seeking the horizon. The sails have been furled and the male slaves in the galley are struggling at their oars to maintain the current heading.

It is a desperate gamble. A distant squall line, a dozen leagues aft, is rapidly closing in on them. Five leagues off the bow is the hint of an island with a hoped-for harbor. Only the gods know if they'll make it.

Her ship, the Artemis, named for the Ha-Mazan's chosen female deity, plows through dark waters ferociously. The large red and white eyes painted on either side of the bow have never failed to find safe haven for this crew. Penthesilia know they will not do so now.

The Artemis regularly rises several feet into the air and crashes back down upon the treacherous seas, its forward momentum unabated. Between the distant cracks of thunder odd sounds distract Penthesilia. She discerns some small meaning to their pestering words.

Captain, please, you must return.

Captain hear us.

Trust my voice. Listen to me...

The voice of gods taunt a mortal. Would nothing of this life ever change? Penthesilia grits her teeth and pushes all thoughts of the ruling pantheon from her mind. She has a ship at dire risk.

"My Queen," a harsh female voice shouts over the roaring wind, "all has been secured."

Penthesilia turns for a moment to regard her second in command, a lithe figure sporting a sinewy physique cloaked in form fitting leather and bronze armor. Her long auburn hair is tied up and coiled about her head.

"Well done, SIBILLA," Penthesilia shouts back, "now join me."

The Chief Mate attends her Captain at the bow, fiercely clutching the huge oak boar's head that girds the front of the railing high atop the main bronze-cloaked ram.

"There," SIBILLA shouts, thrusting her right hand toward the distance, "I see it."

"Your eyes are keen, good sister," Penthesilia says.

"But which isle, my Queen?" SIBILLA asks, "Tenedos? Or Lemnos or Imbros? Apollo's and Serene's sky chariots have been hidden from the Navigator's eyes for far too long."

"It matters not," the Queen says with forced confidence, "Tyche is the most horrible bitch goddess of them all. Curses and praises matter not to her. She shall toss her three clay die and we shall reap their bounty however they fall."

Without notice the Artemis lurches starboard, and then slowly to port. The clouds unleash their quivers and rain falls like arrows upon the fleeing ship.

"We need more speed," Penthesilia shouts, "order the oar master to break out the Usiarus! By Nemesis I want to make that harbor."

SIBILLA dashes away without further word. In moments the painful grunts and groans of one hundred and eighty shackled oarsmen enduring the lash fill the already storm-tortured air.

The harbor is but a league distant. It does not appear to contain any ships, which makes sense if this is Tenedos which has long been abandoned by the King's mighty hidden Hellasian fleet weeks earlier. If any rogue ships from the Hellasian fleet have recently preceded the Artemis here, they have long since moved on, following their own journeys by the gods' whims.

Looking back she can see that the storm line is about to intersect the rear of the trireme. It is all going to be much too close.

The crew needs you…

More gods' voices she struggles to push out of her mind.

The harbor nears. Entering it, the full force of the storm strikes down upon the ship. Hail the size of bird eggs strikes topside, cracking deck plates and threatening the skulls of those not wearing helmets.

Penthesilia and SIBILLA both drop to their knees, unsling their circular shields off their backs and raise them as the sky turns an angry black.

Two days after landfall Queen Penthesilia frowns at the shipwright and her four much younger female carpenters.

"I will not lie, my Queen," Shipright Bremusa says, "even with the strong backs of almost two hundred men-slaves I will need well over a week to make the Artemis seaworthy, and that is assuming we can find good or merely usable lumber inland."

The Queen sighs with resignation and understanding. The Artemis is no ordinary trireme. Its manufacture is unique. The entire ship is built entirely with wood harvested from the Stólo tou stólou, a rare tree that only grows upon the Ha-Mazan's home island. Three times as strong as oak with half the weight and twice the buoyancy. These unusual qualities allow the island's shipwrights to increase the width and length beyond the Hellasian Navy standard. These changes in turn give the vessel an unusually shallow draft allowing the Artemis access to otherwise inaccessible riverways. The extended width and length also require additional ballast for stability, which makes an unusually large increase in the number of warriors, i.e., the Marine detachment, even more necessary. The Artemis is the largest, fastest, most maneuverable trireme with the largest crew on any sea.

"Very well," Penthesilia frowns, "Do what you must."

Bremusa and her underlings bow their heads and quickly scamper away.

"SIBILLA, increase the number of foraging parties to three a day. I will lead the first right now. How many warriors can we spare?" Penthesilia asks.

"Fifty-one," SIBILLA says, "counting myself."

"I'd prefer to leave you here to keep an eye on things," Penthesilia says.

"My Queen," SIBILLA replies in shock.

"I suppose Harmothoe could stand in for you while we're away," Penthesilia says with a smile.

"Thank you," SIBILLA says, mollified, "you are most kind."

Half of a morning later the Ha-Mazan warriors exit a small stony valley. In the distance is a tree line that hopefully harbors slow-footed game. The ship's stores need restocking.

"Surely this is not the isle of Tenedos, my Queen," SIBILLA says as they maintain a steady march of two columns, "nor Lemnos or Imbros if my memory serves. The harbor is most unfamiliar, as are the flowers and brush we have spotted while here. Mayhaps this is Mitilini?"

"If so," Penthesilia replies, "then the ocean currents pushed us much farther south than I thought possible."

"More bad luck," SIBILLA mumbles while clutching the carved jade sculpture of the goddess Tyche that hangs from a leather strap down between her breasts.

Penthesilia frowns. Surely bad luck has been the Ha-Mazan coin of trade this past year. Queen of their matriarchal tribe-country that populates the island of Themyscira, she has ignored the demands of their treaty with Ilium for nearly five planting seasons. But duty is deeply ingrained in her people's blood, and the long war between high-walled Ilium and the Hellasian horde has far reaching implications, trade among them, and Ha-Mazan trading partners are making unavoidable demands of protection for their convoys and caravans.

When the Artemis made landfall not far from the anchored and beached Hellasian fleet, all Hell had already broken loose. The Ha-Mazan found both armies engaged in great slaughter upon the fields before Ilium.

A weary and bloodied battle-captain on the outskirts of the melee quickly informed Penthesilia of the great Achilleus's recent duel and slaughter of both King Memnon of Ethiopia and Ilium's own Prince Hektor. Knowing both of these great warriors as friend and ally, Penthesilia's soul filled with an unholy rage and she led her female warriors onto the chaotic battlefield.

After shedding vast wine casks of blood and killing dozens and then hundreds of the enemy, the Ha-Mazan Queen had faced off with the mighty Achilleus. Hoplon shield to Hoplon shield, spear against spear, and xiphos blade to xiphos blade the two titans of war traded deadly blows back and forth across the blood-soaked earth.

Thrice did the larger stronger man knock her to ground, but each time she blocked his killing blow with a rapid deflection and a catlike leap back onto her feet. He had reach, strength, and endurance. She had speed, dexterity, and grace. Their skills reflected and balanced each other like twin spirits.

Hundreds of Ilium's defenders and hundreds of Hellasian troops had stopped their fighting to bear witness to this mighty contest. Cheers and roars of encouragement from both sides filled the air like bouts of thunder.

Achilleus drove Penthesilia back several feet with seven upon seven slashing strikes with his bronze sword. Upon his last blow, the Queen of the Ha-Mazan skipped forward a half step inside the larger man's reach, parrying his sword with her own, and slamming the leading edge of her circular shield across the crest of his helmet, knocking him back stumbling for several steps.

Penthesilia snatched up her short spear and cast it at the King of the Myrmidons like a bolt of lightning. At the last possible moment the great warrior somehow snatched the noble Queen's doru out of the air and tossed it aside, his eyes wide at how close he had been to death.

And it was here that Achilleus dropped his guard and took one step back.

"You have defeated my heart, valiant and beautiful Queen Penthesilia," Achilleus said in his low harsh voice, "I must surrender to my love for you."

The surrounding circle of warriors quieted and strained their ears to try to hear some portion of the words traded between these two captains of battle.

The legendary hero's words, as heartfelt as they were, had infuriated Penthesilia. Blood drunk she leaped upon Achilleus and tackled him to the ground. The surrounding warriors all rushed forward and much of what occurred next was obscured by dust, limbs, flashing swords, and ultimately by the inadequacy of fallible human memory and the unforgivable petty pride of men and their historians.

Sometime later SIBILLA pulled the unconscious form of Penthesilia out from beneath the corpse of Achilleus, leaving behind her Queen's sword which had pierced the heart of the King of the Myrmidons. Of the sixty Ha-Mazam warriors that had followed their Queen into battle, only twelve were left to escort her back to their main camp.

The Queen's injuries were minimal, and two days later, disgusted with the vile excess of war among these petty men, she ordered her people back onto the Artemis to return home.

SIBILLA warned that so quickly leaving this battlefield before performing the traditional rites and sacrifices would anger the gods, but Penthesilia did not care. A day later the freak storm overtook their ship and forced them to dock on this uncharted island.

"Let us reconnoiter that large cave," Penthesilia says.

SIBILLA nods and immediately relays orders to the fifty warriors who are walking forward in a roughly circular formation. They immediately redress their ranks to allow for twenty women taking a thirty-foot lead to the rest of the party, forming into the rough shape of an arrowhead. In minutes the enters the front of the cave whose floor is flush with the surrounding ground and appears to be at least sixty feet tall. Six torches were lit as the troop quickly moves inside.

You can't ignore us. It is your duty, Captain.

Penthesilia shakes her head angrily.

"Dammit, I am no oracle," the Queen mumbles, "enough of this madness."

"The gods?" SIBILLA asks quietly from the right, "they continue to plague your mind?"

"Damn them," Penthesilia grimaces, "I will make my own fate."

And with these words they all move deep into the large cave.

"My Queen," the voice of a young warrior in her late teens, perhaps Evandre, shouts from the rear of the massive cave, "come here."

A full one hundred and fifty paces into the darkness, poorly lit by flickering flame, warriors part to allow the Queen access. On the rear cave is a large crudely painted mural twenty arm spans wide by thirty high.

"It shows a great battle," SIBILLA says, "see the armies on either side, and there in the middle, some mighty king, judging by the size in which he was painted."

"No," Penthesilia says as her pulse quickened, "this is no change in perspective to show rank… that is a giant… look more closely at the face, up in the shadows… he has one eye."

"The Isle of Cyclopes," SIBILLA gasps, "we must flee my Queen!"

Just then the faint sunlight from the entrance of the cave instantly dims. All turn to see a huge thirty-foot tall dark figure silhouetted by the bright sky quickly roll a large boulder into place, effectively sealing itself inside with the Ha-Mazam.

"Who is in here?" a surprisingly high pitched yet resonating male voice shouts out, "who dares invade the home of Pyraemon?"

"Archers to the rear at half knotch," Penthesilia whispers fiercely, "the rest of you ready your dory."

Penthesilia, refusing to show fear, marches toward the giant with all six of the torchbearers sprinting forward to keep pace. She stops a mere fifteen paces from the towering squinting figure. Her warriors spread out behind and to either side, spacing each other an arm's breadth apart.

"I am Queen Penthesilia of the Ha-Mazam," she says sternly. "We are strangers to these shores and mean you no harm. Let us leave your home and we will trouble you no further."

Pyraemon laughs and sneers loudly.

"I see well in the dark," he boasts, "and find you to be but a group of pathetic women. I will feast well on mortal flesh today."

"And I am no ambassador of good will," Penthesilia replies harshly, "witnessed by the gods, I gave you a peaceful choice."

"Piss on your peace," Pyraemon spits.

"Target his eye," Penthesilia screams while drawing her spear arm back and aiming her dory. One dozen arrows instantly fly over her head and at least half of them find their target as evidenced by the giant's screams of pain.

"Cast," Penthesilia yells and fifty short and expertly aimed bronze tipped missiles fly forward, many striking the shocked Cyclop's face and throat.

Pyraemon staggers back against the boulder that blocks the cave entrance and claws at the arrows and spears that cover him like the quills from some mythically large porcupine.

"You've blinded me, Ha-Mazam bitches," Pyraemon screams in agony, "and I will crush you all."

"Circle and draw your xiphos," Penthesilia orders, though by now every warrior has already raised shield and short sword and leans forward in ready crouches. The Queen's troops do as ordered, their multiple footsteps confusing the blind behemoth who nonetheless manages to reach out and grasp two unlucky warriors instantly crushing the life from both before flinging their doll-like corpses through the air to splatter upon the distant cave walls.

"Hamstring him," Penthesilia says in a cold voice. She is not born of woman in this world to play The Royal Game of Ur with this monster. "Now."

As one, all fifty Ha-Mazam warriors rush the giant from every side, leaping, rolling, and ducking under his large grasping hands. Like a mass of fire ants, they swarm over his feet and ankles up to the back of his knees. Realizing their intent too late, dozens of razor-sharp swords stab and slash at the giant's hamstring tendons at the back of his thighs.

Once, twice, thrice does Pyraemon slap at his legs with huge hands, striking and killing up to five warriors with each swat, but then his right leg buckles and forces him to his knee. A moment later his other leg buckles as two dozen of the warriors climb his torso from all sides.

Snapping his mouth about himself frantically he manages to bite several of the women in half, spewing out pieces of their armored body, but it is to no avail.

A full one dozen warriors reach his neck and thrust their xiphos forward and into his large throat. At least six of them strike the cyclop's main artery, though none as deeply as the Queen, cutting a large wound that lets forth a flood of gore as wide as a small river.

Pyraemon sways for but a moment upon his knees and then lifeless, falls over, crushing and killing another four warriors.

A short while later the twenty-five bloody and bruised survivors are surprised that they are able to move the large boulder enough to allow their escape. It has been extremely well balanced and much more manageable than expected.

Later that night back at the now heavily fortified harbor camp on full alert, Penthesilia struggles to fall asleep.

Now more than ever the gods are plaguing her with their strange cryptic appeals. Most she can ignore, but a few managed to briefly capture her attention before she slips off to blessed oblivion.

The ship needs you. Only you can lead us home. Damn you, answer me.

Captain, I know you can hear me. You must fight this. You must come back to us.

The last voice is insistent but gentle… perhaps that of Apollo…

A week later the Artemis renews her voyage toward the Euxine Sea, and home. By the second night at sail, the clouds clear for the first time yet and her navigator Derimacheia smiles at the familiar stars.

"We are not as far off course as I feared my Queen," Derimacheia says. "A handful of days will put us in familiar waters, maybe less."

Penthesilia smiles and lets out a long slow breath.

"Good fortune to us all," the Queen intones, and then all hell broke loose.

The entire slave contingent chooses that moment to break free of their chains to mutiny. The moment has been well planned, occurring at the very end of a shift change in guard duty.

No alarm is sounded, no great bell rung, nor flag raised or flaming arrow set aloft. Every Ha-Mazam warrior on the Artemis has been raised from birth to instantly react to just such an event should it ever occur.

As one hundred and eighty desperate men flood onto the upper deck, the two hundred and ninety well-armed and exquisitely trained female soldiers meet them without hesitation in close quarters combat.

Though many of the men are larger and stronger than any individual woman, and their ferocity is heightened by their desperation, nonetheless do they fight a losing battle. Those that manage to gang up on an individual Ha-Mazam warrior and overpower her and take her weapons are more often than not poorly prepared to wield sword or spear, and quickly fall dead to the deck.

One Ha-Mazam falls for every four slaves killed, and in a mere half of an hour it is all over. One hundred and eighty men lay dead upon the deck, many of them slumped over or under forty-five of Penthesilia's slain warrior sisters.

They make shore the next day to put their fallen warriors to the torch. The dead men are simply dumped over the side of the ship.

"Let Poseidon sort them out," Penthesilia coldly replies when asked by SIBILLA as to their disposition.

Two days later SIBILLA joins her Queen at the foredeck.

"How goes it?" Penthesilia asks.

"So many sore backs," SIBILLA says with a smile, "suffice it to say their songs are not happy ones. Nevertheless, their spirits are high knowing we head home. I sense something still troubles you, my Queen. Has the loss of so many of our sisters dampened your spirits?"

"Not at all," Penthesilia replies, "we are a tribe bred for battle, and those of our warriors who died did so heroically following their Queen. I'm sure they all now serve with distinction on the Elysian plains."

"Then what bothers you, my Queen?" SIBILLA asks, "are the gods taunting your waking mind?"

"Not on this day, SIBILLA," Penthesilia says, "though I sense they still follow my actions much too closely for comfort."

Late into the night, SIBILLA strides into her Queen's cabin and grabs her by the shoulders.

"Awake my Queen," SIBILLA hisses loudly, "there is a most odd spell upon the crew and the Artemis enters strange waters."

Penthesilia follows SIBILLA up to the main deck and quickly sees that her First Mate's words are true. Every crew member is slumped over or has dropped to the deck. Many are snoring.

"It is a witching sleep my Queen," SIBILLA says, "I tried to rouse many with cold water and even the point of my knife, but as you can see it was for naught."

"There is no wind, but the ship moves forward," Penthesilia says.

"Poseidon has given us a strong current," SIBILLA says, "but look where it takes us."

Both reach the bow and peered ahead through the moonlit fog that covers the silent sea.

"There," SIBILLA says.

Instantly, Penthesilia notes the silhouettes of ships, first just a few, but quickly dozens. As they draw closer, the Queen can see their sails are torn and their hulls have sustained much damage, some by sea and others by battle.

"We have entered a graveyard of sea vessels, my Queen," Penthesilia says, "never have I heard of such a thing. Is this Poseidon's magic, or that of Thanatos?"

"Both, neither, perhaps we are dreaming…"

"This doesn't feel like a dream, my Queen," SIBILLA shivers, "it feels… wrong."

The Artemis continues moving forward passing one ship then another. Many are Hellasian triremes but soon other ships, some of familiar design, others not, come into view.

Time seems to pass in a strange, unaffecting way until the Artemis starts turning to port and Penthesilia suddenly notices she is but a ship's length and parallel to another trireme moving in the same direction.

On the foredeck of this other ship is a lone figure.

"No," Penthesilia says, "it can't be."

But the moonlight does not lie. Standing but a spear's cast away, looking proud and fierce is a Ha-Mazan princess.

"My Queen," SIBILLA whispers fiercely, "it can't be… that can't be…"

"Melanippe," Penthesilia says, "my dead sister."

Suddenly the waters all around Melanippe's ship, The Harmonia, start to froth and bubble. Shapes, possibly sharks in dozens, and then hundreds begin to chase the other trireme, paying the Artemis no note.

SIBILLA bends forward and gasps.

"Look my queen, they are people."

Penthesilia can see that SIBILLA is right. Churning steadily across the surface of the water, swimmers, some in rags, others in various armor, swim in close pursuit of the Harmonia.

"Sister be warned," Penthesilia suddenly finds herself shouting, "these demons mean to board you."

But her sister, whether wraith or vision or dream, pays the Queen no heed, either not hearing nor seeing her.

Peering through the wisps of fog Penthesilia takes note of all the various swimmers, for they consist of men and women of all the races of men, most warriors from a variety of nations whom the Ha-Mazam have called enemy.

Closer the swimmers come, and closer, and then they climb and swarm over the ship. Dozens of Ha-Mazam warriors awake and rush up from the lower deck, but they are too few, and die valiantly defending their Queen. When the last one falls, Melanippe draws her own sword and throws herself upon the horde that quickly overwhelms her.

Penthesilia, shouting in fury, suddenly finds herself restrained, and looks down upon SIBILLA's arms.

"Forgive me my Queen," SIBILLA shouts, "but there is nothing you can do. This is a game of the gods. They taunt us. You must not leave the ship."

Penthesilia turns to look back upon the Harmonia. The phantom figures that attacked it now slowly slip back into the water. A moment later, many of them began to swim toward the Artemis.

"They mean to board us now my Queen," SIBILLA says slyly, "perhaps such a quick death would be preferable to a hopeless journey home. We have suffered so much since leaving the fields before the walls of Ilium."

Penthesilia turns angrily to her first mate, "why do you speak such heresy? We are Ha-Mazam. As long as breath fills our lungs and blood pumps through our hearts we do not give up. We do not surrender. As long as I live, I will not abandon my sisters to despair."

"I am glad you feel this mighty Queen."

Just then, as the nearest swimmers are mere body lengths from the Artemis, the leading edge of Apollo's golden chariot begins to crest the horizon. The flood of sunlight across the ocean quickly burns through the surrounding fog, and all the swimmers, one by one, and then by dozens sink back into the dark waters of the sea. The flotilla of ruined ships quickly slips behind them as a strong current continues moving the ship forward.

A seagull screams overhead, and hearing this, sleeping warriors all across the ship awake, leaping to their feet, ashamed they have dozed at their station. Penthesilia forbids SIBILLA from calling anyone to task. The night has been one of god's magic, and no fault of her brave crew.

Days later, after sailing through the Bosporus Strait, crossing the Sea of Marmara and the Dardanelles Strait, they finally enter The Euxine Sea. Penthesilia stands on the foredeck of the Artemis with SIBILLA and the ship's navigator Derimacheia.

"The winds and current will not change direction for two weeks, my Queen," Derimacheia says, "we can harbor and wait, otherwise, if we continue now, even at full oars, we can possibly travel dangerously close to the kingdom of Colchis."

"Those shores are treacherous, my Queen," SIBILLA says, "rumors abound that Aglaope the Siren has made her home among those savage reefs, spawning dozens of female children born of the sailors she has lured to her clutches and eventual death… men avoid these waters fearing dreadful peril."

"We are not men," Penthesilia says coldly, "and I will delay our return home no longer. Full ahead."

"Full ahead," SIBILLA shouts, and thus do the Ha-Mazam harness their sails and put oars to the Euxine Sea, pulling in unison, and humming as one. No drum is struck, no song shared, as neither can effectively unite this sisterhood in moving their warship as well as the feral drone of one hundred and eighty Ha-Mazam acting as one.

The waves roll around them for hours and soon the sky begins to grow dark.

"Selene's chariot does not lie," Derimacheia says pointing to the moon, "we will be skirting the shores of Colchis closer than I would choose."

Penthesilia answers her navigator with a nod and nothing more.

A short while later, SIBILLA cocks her head oddly and gasps.

"Seirene song, my Queen," SIBILLA says.

And thus, does the arcane music drift across the ocean from jagged reef to the mighty female warriors aboard the Artemis. A mix of eerie female voice and lyre, it soon is heard by all on board.

Many of the Ha-Mazam are entranced by the music, releasing their oars and dropping to the deck in stupor. Only a dozen try to leap overboard, and are each stopped by their sisters, and tied protesting fiercely to the masts.

On the foredeck Queen Penthesilia puts both her hands over her ears to stop the demon music, for it has opened her mind's eye to the madness and hopelessness of this voyage.

The terrible god's voices, which she has not heard for weeks, now comes flooding back to her with an insistence and passion she finds startling.

Captain, do not abandon us.

The crew... think of the crew.

You can beat this. You are better than this.

Dammit, I've never known you to shirk from a fight since you took command. Say something!

And it is this last god's shout that strikes Penthesilia to the core. Bruising her ego and filling her with an irrational humiliation.

"My Queen," SIBILLA shouts, "is the song too much for you? Should we lash you to a mast?"

Without notice Penthesilia leaps upward atop the large wood boar's head sculpture.

"Queen, no," SIBILLA screams.

Penthesilia wavers. The distant siren's music promises beautiful distraction. The god's voices naught but pain, struggle… and duty.

"Choose, my Captain," SIBILLA says in a surprisingly calm voice, "choose for us all."

As suddenly as the destructive urge has filled the Queen's heart, it rapidly bleeds away. A look of realization fills Penthesilia's eyes and she drops back down to the deck.

Ignoring SIBILLA and many of her crew that have rushed upon the foredeck at sight of their Queen's madness, Penthesilia calmly walks forward and through the quickly parting crowd. The siren music still fills the air, but it no longer affects her.

The Queen drops down to the next deck and walks into the short passageway that leads to her Captain's cabin. She slams the door behind her and begins to lift her bronze helmet off of her head before suddenly stopping and lowering it back in place.

Penthesilia then lowers herself down onto her pallet, reclines flat on her back, and closes her eyes.

Captain Tennyson Illiadus opens her eyes and looks about herself with only the slightest movement of head and eyes. She is laying on an examination table in the *Ekatarina's* sick bay. With one hand she confirms that it is the Quantum Helmet that hampers the movement of her neck.

Dr. Kyle Sorlan's kind face suddenly appears above hers. His large golden eyes take note of her cogent expression.

"Have you finally decided to join us in the land of the living, Captain?"

"How long?" Illiadus asks.

"Since you first slipped into that pesky coma?" Sorlan says, "Five years. It was crewman Farko Tiresias's idea to keep your head plugged into that damned contraption. I wanted it off, but Commander Aithon decided to put his trust in our resident alien wunderkind. I have serious doubts about the therapeutic psychological attributes of your A.I.'s virtual reality entertainment skills and told the Commander so. Now tell me. Were you ever aware of anything that SIBIL was attempting to broadcast into your already overstimulated cerebellum? If so, what do you remember?"

Illiadus swallows to fight a small case of dry mouth. Then she lets out a long breath.

"I remember…"

"Yes, Captain," Sorlan says.

"I remember my duty," Illiadus says. But she also retains one last image in her groggy mind, that of shadowy warriors, enemies of the Ha-Mazam, swimming towards and surrounding The Artemis. This sends a cold chill down her spine before she closes her eyes and slips into dreamless untroubled sleep.

Captain's Log, The Ekatarina

Two years ship time has passed since I awoke from my long coma. Twenty-five years, ship time, have passed since the destruction of The Scourge's home sphere. The average human crewperson has aged approximately eight years outside of coldsleep. We are now about to finish our twenty-four-month sub-light traversal between two relatively close uncharted star systems. The ship's long range imaging array suggests at least one uninhabited Earth-like planet up ahead. The majority of the crew, including myself, have been in coldsleep these last two years in an effort to save resources. I welcome landfall as part of my final mental recovery. I have to make a decision soon… whether or not I have the courage to use the quantum helmet once again, and steer The Ekatarina into a dark energy artery towards home. The crew is depending on me. I am struggling with my doubts. End Log.

BugFuck

by Shirley Meier

Ship's Chronometer: 2450 AD

They are worried that I am insane. In any state or place called sane? How can I be insane when I may not be sane at all?

At least not sane enough for command.

...explosions bigger than the frightened and fighting child in my head can even comprehend. I see you SIBIL. You are not my little sister, growing up under the pressure of getting us home. Home. There is no home. There hasn't been a home and I'm not sure there is anyplace I even want to go 'home'. On the deck of a trireme... no. A program. An AI. A little sister.

Tennyson turns her face to the hot sun, eyes closed, tries to soak in how peaceful it is here, trying to let it in. It is a lovely little planet, certainly not visible from earth, but earthlike enough. The sea this shallow is Fiji turquoise and clear meters down.

The sky is a shade darker blue than it should have been. The deeper ocean an indigo, perhaps like the Black Sea...*kept triggering the episode where she nearly retreated into her own head, Queen, wandering the wine-dark sea.*

She opens her eyes to see Igor, still firmly convinced he hates coming downside, with Michael, and Cailin trying to initiate the others... all non-human, all humanoid... into the mysteries of a pickup game of beach volleyball. Ensign I!tik, her hair standing out from her head like a startled red cat, has her arms raised in *polite confusion.*

"I'd be considered crazy enough if I tried to describe this to anyone from home," Ten says aloud to herself. Her mouth twists at the irony of her using the term *crazy* in these circumstances.

She gets up, brushing the powdery pink sand off her skin and re-ups her melanine response, as well as applying sunscreen. Everybody has been in space long enough that normal solar radiation bites hard.

David hails her from the pinnace which is parked on a coral-like outcropping, a mangrove-like tangle shading it, so they can open it up to un-canned air and save the circuits except for the filters that still never manage to keep the sand out of things.

A lovely planet. A peaceful planet. The indigenous monkeys have eight limbs and the crew insists on calling them *spider monkeys*, but they aren't intelligent, at least not by any method the *Ekatarina* has of testing for it. It is one reason she'd said this little island, in the middle of a scattering of little islands, with not a single spider monkey on any of them as far as they could find, is be a place they can get a little relaxation.

Doctor's orders.

"No emergencies, no meltdowns, no 'we're about to plunge into the sun-slash-energy vortex-slash we're all going to die unless I do something heroic and stupid', Yuri said. "No 'I have to scramble my brains again for the good of the ship,' okay?" *…dreams of Ilium and fighting and dreams of the Gods…nothing for me but war and my true lover, Death.*

Ten manages to smile at him, feeling as frail as an ancient stained-glass window.

"Just a little rest. Yes. I understand. We need the time. I need the time."

He nods firmly at her.

"So," David says, catching up to her. "I'm looking dashing in my regulation short pants and rakishly open shirt. You look appropriately bronzed, with your towel and sunscreen. Did I just see you consider going for a walk, alone?" He waggles his eyebrows at her in a way he obviously considers lascivious.

She smacks him with the whipcrack of her towel. "OW!" He jumps back, rubbing his thigh. "Horrors! I haven't been snapped like that since basic!"

"High time you were then. Yes, I wanted to walk." It is hard cinching a smile up on her face. *Normal human expression for this kind of interaction*: check. "Coming down I saw some of the spider monkey nests and I want to make sure we didn't make a mistake and set up on the wrong island."

"You wound me, Captain!" He flings his hand up to his forehead, still trying to make her laugh. Still trying to make her be normal, be human again.

"The nests are ancient... grown in place abandoned."

"Well, then, let's go see since it's perfectly safe."

"Captain."

"What?" She turns back to where he'd stopped. "I'm armed," she says. "You don't want to ask where I'm carrying a side-arm." It was in her hair actually, a tiny personal weapon that tucked neatly under the knot when she tied her hair back.

"If we're going to go traipsing through alien jungle maybe a bit more skin covering?"

He waved at her where she'd shucked down to go swimming. "And some boots?"

She looks down at herself and then considers the tangle of green on the edge of the sand.

"You know, there's a reason I keep you around Davy... and it's more than how cute you are… for a boy." *Pretend everything is fine. Pretend you aren't hanging on, inside your head, by fingertips and teeth and if any one of them jars you the wrong way you'll fall screaming into the pit and never quit falling, never quit burning, never quit flailing around totally and completely bugfuck.* "I'll get dressed." *Trojan war and Amazons, Queens and Cyclops and bursting bodies pouring blood.*

"Cute! She said I was cute! Did you hear that Igor? You lose! Of course, Captain." He grins at her again. "And here I was thinking that having the Ekays' Captain AND First Officer on leave at the same time was a bad idea!"

"Everybody's on leave, David. We've been so tired… You know…" she blinks her eyes closed against the bright sun, pulls on a loose coverall, snaps on a pair of 'toes', the footgear wiggling as it settles around her instep. *... a war sandal… no... 'toes' now, not then.*

"Of course, Tennyson," he says, suddenly dropping the buffoon like a bad poker chip. "You know I was just trying to lighten your mood."

"Thank you, David."

The jungle isn't as thick as it looks from the beach and the crew has already set up their tents in amongst the trees. Ten finds it funny that humans suspend their tents between the trunks the same way that spider monkeys build their nests, though the crew's shelters are only a few meters off the ground instead of swaying several stories up. Standard on an alien planet. The tension straps that holds them up all have anti-*bug* collars on them, so that nothing can crawl in on them during the night. All of the crew with the captain are humanoid enough to use the Solian style shelters.

The insects in the air aren't butterflies but they look like them. Their wings are a glittering blue. One settles on her hands and she can see it has more legs than six.

"It has as many legs as the little octopusses… octopi?... octopods?... you told me you saw when you went snorkeling."

They've checked out as non-toxic to humans… like the water, before anybody was allowed in to swim.

"Don't worry about the octopi… call them krakenettes if you have to," David grins at her. "They were very shy and tiny. The biggest one I found was the size of my hand and had ten legs and two longer ones."

It is quiet under the canopy, except for sounds of their feet and the click and buzz of the native insects. There are small gliding lizards that appear to be the major predators of all the bugs though birds or bird analogues haven't yet evolved here, so there is no birdsong.

"How are you doing, Tennyson?" He asks quietly.

"I'm…" she stops speaking, trying to answer him honestly. *I'm broken, David. I've been broken over and over and over again and I just don't know if I have it in me to heal one more time. That's what my life has become… have something shatter me into a dozen shards, scramble to gather up the bits so I don't lose any more of me, bleeding into the dark… David. I just do not have the strength, or the will for anything. Anything at all.* "Don't ask me that, David."

They are in deep shade now, but she can see his lips thin. *Poor David. I'm not anything but 'Captain' now. I can't be anything else until we get home. However much I wandered, as a female Odysseus… Penthesilia… losing people, losing those who love how well I can fight, how well I can kill… So… I suppose I have to heal again. I'm just not sure how. The war burned me to the core and I'm finding that there's something under the coating of scale. I just need to find out what it is. Is there a Home for me?*

"Oh. Look. Just as you said." She sweeps up her hand to indicate over their heads. The spider monkeys all over this planet weave high-tree nests and in their wanderings return year after year to their old ones, if they survive in the treetops. But the bulbous nests are woven tightly into the treetops and the tree just continues growing. These nests were woven a long, long time ago, and then abandoned to grow into massive, gnarled fists of branches. It is unlikely that there is any space left inside the old nests, even if you have as many limbs as the original builders and can climb up that high. "Funny that the monkeys wouldn't thrive here? Maybe an illness wiped them out here and there's not enough population pressure elsewhere to re-populate the island?"

He shrugs.

"Could be." She can almost see his retreat into 'flippant young officer'. "I checked and there's no hyper-intelligent version of these monkeys to give us any nasty surprises. No spears out of the eyries. No firepots dropped on us from above. All very calm and boring."

"That's good. We've needed the double order of dull and boring we put in for, so long ago." She can't manage his lightness. Not yet. "But the backorder list is just so damn long."

"Dah."

"Have the other landers checked in—"

"—Captain." He interrupts her. "You are not to worry about the crew, what they're doing, what's going on, who is screwing whom... none of that. It's all taken care of, relax!"

You... you... she throttles down the automatic anger at his tone. *You puppy! How dare you tell me to relax! As if I don't know it? As if you... well, you have seen as much action as I have, albeit from a different perspective. As a Queen facing the siren-song of death...* Ten has no idea what her face, in the dappled shade, looks like but he is suddenly wary of her. She draws a deep, shuddering breath. "Relax. Of course, First Officer." *...slave men revolting, slaughtered on the deck of the Artemis...*

He hides his flinch well. "My pleasure, Captain." They walk back down to the beach in silence and he gives her an acknowledging nod when she peels off to lie down in her tent, instead of joining the ruckus that is building along the water's edge, where beach volleyball has turned into a ball-spiking competition. An unfamiliar young crewman of Portuguese persuasion instantly becomes an impromptu bookmaker as bets start flying as to who will get beaned in the upper sensory area next. Ignoring this breach in protocol, she manages to convince herself that the beach is more Tahiti and less Greek.

The insect buzz grows over the course of the day, and Ten actually manages to doze some just before dinner, declines the bonfire on the sand. It is too much. Dealing with people is just too much. Her tent, suspended between three trees, bounces a little in the wind just shifting from an onshore to offshore breeze. Dozing, Ten can see the blue butterflies in the trees and glittering on their tents. They seem to like the fabric because they keep flitting around and around them.

Good thing they don't bite.

Bite. Like the Scourge bit us. We got them.

We got them all, but that doesn't bring anybody back. Biting.

Like those aliens where we got new crew?

The ones with rows of teeth like sharks trying to convince us pink-skins that they were dedicated vegetarians?

They really did think we were that stupid. To get us alone. Into the dark. To get us into the dark like under these trees. What was that? There are no big predators on this island. But I heard one. I heard that one that I called Sharkface to myself… he had this habit of clashing his jaws together. In the dark. It's dark. There's a creaking… groaning noise that claws make against roots. I'm hearing it. I… can smell them. They've followed us here and in the dark they've surrounded us and — don't be stupid, Ten!

She finds herself sitting upright in the middle of her tent, the billow of fabric bouncing the bugs off her zipped-up tent to patter on the ground or fly away. She is terror-stricken, heart pounding, eyes stretched wide to try and see in the dark, panting, sweating. She snaps her hand-light on and brings up the tent's lights.

That makes it worse… it makes her a target… she can't see outside the edges of where her light falls and the blackness beyond it is thicker, darker and the shadows move as her tent sways. She can't hear anything beyond her own panicked breathing. Not Igor's snoring, not the regular pulsing whistle that I!tik makes while asleep.

She untabs the tent, wincing at the noise, rolls out, landing on hands and feet, *on the bounce giving them a moving target*, her gun in her hand. *I have to get out from under these trees. I have to get clear.* "FIRST! Report!"

She scuttles sideways from where she'd spoken, bursts through a bunch of butterflies, feels them as she runs down toward the beach, struggling not to trip on anything.

Don't give them a target. There is no answer from David. Of course. He is in the pinnace.

I have to get to the beach before we all get killed!

That is when she hears the first scream. Up ahead. Igor.

"GET THEM OFF ME!"

Someone kicks the embers of the bonfire -- a blaze of sparks that arc out and the ocean… the ocean squeals. Or rather the things in the ocean squeal.

"Build up that fire! Igor!"

"Fuck, fuck fuck fuck…" he isn't terribly injured, or he wouldn't be cursing so steadily.

She still has her handlight. "Lights! DAVID! This is an order! Get us some lights on!"

He must have woken up by now, given that others were shouting, screaming, running around in the dark… She snaps her handlight on, to horror. The beach is covered with little kraken… seething over each other, every ocean wave brings another gooey splash of them. Igor swears as he rips another kraken off his calf. I!tik seems to have fallen and has three on her back, ripping at her coverall and she is making noises that make Ten's ears hurt.

"Cailin… get that fire blazing! Michael… more wood… someone get… did we bring a flame thrower?"

"With all due respect, Captain," Igor yells as he tackles I!kit and cuts the kraken off her before they could burrow into the bloody holes they'd chewed in her back. "Why in HELL would we pack a flame-thrower?" Her coverall has saved her spine. Heesh springs up with Igor and they stomp a dozen more, while backing up to the safety of the fire. Light doesn't seem to bother them, or even slow them down.

Cailin and Michael have bloody furrows on their backs… they didn't have clothing on when they were swarmed but they both hold clubs that have dead bits of sea-life apparently stuck in the wood. There is the end of a tentacle hanging from what looks like hooks in Cailin's hip.

Screaming from the jungle and Sergeant Murdock bursts from the trees, running blindly and though Ten lunges for him he dodges her hand as if it is a striking snake and plunges into the water. A second later he heaves up, covered in a pulsing mass of octopod, so thickly covered that he can't be heard through them, barely showing a human outline at all before falling over right on the wave-line.

Michael is stomping, jumping up and down on the squeamish line… bare feet bloody where he's cut himself on their beaks and tentacle hooks.

"WHY DOES EVERYTHING ON THIS STINKIN' PLANET HAVE TO HAVE SO MANY LEGS?"

Everyone's lights are out, stuck in the sand. A handgun is stinking awful against millions of things the size of a human hand.

Ten grabs her own chunk from the firewood pile and with the other four manages to keep the circle of seething beaks barely at arm's length.

"DAVID!" Where in hell is her first officer? His ears should be ringing from the feedback squeal alone, much less her yelling.

The damned butterflies come out floating around them and it is as if every nerve in Ten's body goes haywire. She can't coordinate her muscles, everyone… not just her. Everyone is crumpling into a heap. Her hand twitches and her club rolls away from her grip. *Their googly eyes are blue. Roaring…* ah…pinnace. David isn't comatose. Good for… She can't turn her head, but she can hear the Pinnace in a way that she seriously should not be able to hear. *He's overdriving them flying that thing like it's an ultralite under a joystick… the backwash… oh shit, David don't fry us all with that…*

The pinnace's drive-wash flattens the waves, drives the water away, cooks the sand and the kraken pinned in it, even if for only a microsecond. It blew sand and kraken everywhere smacking them deep into the bush as David walks that sucker within a dozen meters of them before setting it down right there.

She can barely coordinate her eyelids to blink the grit out of them, but they are watering hard enough that she can see. The door of the pinnace snaps open… emergency open, and a pair of glass bottles, with a flaming chunk of fabric stuffed in the neck flies out to smash and burn, followed by another two.

David steps out holding what appears to be a flare of some kind in one hand and a bottle in the other, with his finger on the aerosol nozzle.

"Captain. Bellhop! help."

The pinnace has a baggage handler, voice activated, but it has never been pressed into service like this, limp people gather up, rolled unceremoniously into the hatch and dumped on the floor.

Ten is furthest from the hatch and sees everyone else carried in. David runs over with his flare and his bottle… Igor's aerosolized booze.

"Prepare to be evacuated, Captain," he says calmly as he steps over her, aiming his aerosol through the flare… which is a pair of I!krit's fancy underthings wrapped around a barbeque fork and set on fire… and with careful bursts of flame drives a swath of squealing kraken back.

"Shy, you said. Inoffensive, you said." She isn't sure he hears her. That is when she sees another swarm of butterflies drifting down toward them.

"DAVID, THE BUGS, GET THE FUCKING BUGS!"

It is the butterflies that are the worse danger. She isn't sure how she knows but something… she put something together in her mind. The butterflies.

He flames them in the air as their glittery scales drift on the wind past his face… but charred it just sticks. Does he have nose plugs in?

The bellhop drags her unresponsive body awkwardly onto its cargo bed, rises to its legs eight legs. *Why does everything have so many legs?*

David follows behind, keeping the kraken back, until the hatch shuts out the noise of the surf and the kraken and she try to shudder. Murdock is still making noises out there. He is still alive. David has seen them all in and goes back out before the hatch closes. When he comes back, he doesn't have Murdock with him.

She's been getting some feeling back in her fingers even before bellhop drops her, and in the filtered air of the pinnace the numbness and neurotoxic effects wear off quickly. She is sitting, putting an emergency skin-patch on the last of the bites on her calves -- *when did I get those* --when he comes back, dropping into the pilot's chair, but doesn't turn on the screens.

"Good work."

"Thank you," she says.

"I hurt," I!krit says, her arms held in the sign for *distress*, blood streaking her red filament fur a muddy color. "But I concur with the Captain. The *fucking bugs* appear to be part of the life-cycle of the sea creature. We appear to have an answer as to why there are no monkeys… or other large animals on this island. Probably this whole archipelago, but there are no other landing parties of ours here that shall need warning."

"Thank you for that analysis," David says quietly.

"I'm going to do the rest of my resting on board my ship," Tennyson says firmly. "I might be bugfuck but I'm not getting fucked by anymore bugs." *We've all been bugfucked.*

"A clusterfuck it is," Igor says. "Out of twelve, we lost two for sure. Two of the Marines are still in the camp it seems… maybe they're immune?"

The inside of the pinnace stinks like a bad seafood and pork restaurant, with a light overtone of burned alcohol, scorched and melted fabric, and sweaty, dirty people. The aliens add their own notes of stink. Rancid cinnamon from I!krit, dirty gym sock from one of the engineering gooks.

"The two Marines?"

"Staff Sergeant Bryce and Ifurst."

"First Officer…"

"Yes, Sir." David straightens in the pilot chair, swivels around and brings the pinnace up again, this time without the tooth-shattering howl.

"Ensign Cailin? Since you are on your feet and seem least affected by these bugs, I suggest you find something inflammable and head the rescue party."

"Sir."

Ten sinks into the seat beside David, watches his hands move as he lifts the ship just enough to take it to the edge of the jungle. The kraken aren't coming up off the sand at all. *I'm too shaky to go charging out there.*

"Take bellhop with you. Igor, once we're on board again, I'd like you to modify bellhop please, so that it is a bit more adaptable for unusual situations."

"Yes Sir."

Cailin picks Megan and Choom. The pinnace's landing lights aren't meant to be used as searchlights, so they are out of range quickly, though they show up clearly on the sensors. George and Ifurst aren't moving.

A burst of gunfire, Marine gunfire. The pinnace rocks as a grenade goes off… in the opposite direction.

"Good. They're probably hallucinating by now…" David glances sideways at her.

Ten minutes. Then another ten minutes. The humanoid blips on the screen converge. A lot of yelling from the speakers… silence.

"Marines secured, Captain. Medical bags deployed."

"Excellent thinking, Ensign. Ditch the tents and come back. Let's go home."

Eykay is home. My ship is home. In a way that Artemis never was. Why am I fighting so hard to go home to a mudball I wasn't born on, when my home is already around me? She laughs, drawing a startled look from everyone in the pinnace, but she doesn't bother to explain. "Just a funny thought."

Because I'm bugfuck. That's why.

Captain's Log, The Ekatarina

One Hundred and Fortieth Jump Completed

I've used the upgraded Quantum Helmet in conjunction with SIBIL for over two dozen dark energy artery jumps in the past two years. My full mental recovery was admittedly slow, but I felt a strong need to get back in the saddle after my away party's altercation with the alien butterflies and kraken on that seemingly idyllic uncharted world that was our last landfall. We have now been traveling for twenty-seven years ship's time since the destruction of The Scourge sphere with an estimated one-fifth of our journey left in our crossing of the Milky Way galaxy. We have surveyed several hundred uncharted and uninhabited star systems during our travels, and have come upon the remains of fifteen destroyed jump gates, five of them within close proximity to inhabited worlds whose lives had been wiped out from the lethal neutron radiation given off from the exploding gates. I now fear that possibly all the jump gates spread throughout the entire galaxy were destroyed when the dark matter fountain bomb was detonated. If so, The Polis has been thrown into a new dark age. End Log.

Post Tenebras Lux

by Richard Groller

Ship's Chronometer: 2452 AD

Lieutenant Commander Walter Lehmann is in the vector space battle cube when he gets the request to come to the covert weapons development lab. Though an engineer, Lehmann is also a warrior, and knows you have to hone all your tools to a fine edge, be they tactics or reflexes. The particular breed of simulation he is attempting can evolve its strategies over time, learning from both your mistakes and its mistakes. Each scenario leads to new insights, both strategic and tactical, and over time, the combat sequences can also be customized to stress reflexes and tax tactical decision making and help determine superior outcomes. The simulation is recorded, so seeing the conflict evolve in 4 D also makes it fun to watch, and a useful teaching tool, when the outcomes are in fact novel or superior. Lehman suspends the simulation at a save point, to be pondered later, time permitting. It is good to train, but in these dark times, it is a guilty pleasure.

A propulsion engineer with an astronics rating, Lieutenant Commander Lehmann is the *P.W. Ekatarina's* Chief Engineer, though behind his back his wizardry with creating usable tech from bubble gum and bailing wire has garnered him the nickname "Techno-Shaman." A master at creative interpretation of the procurement regs, he can obtain any piece of kit in less time than the Polisian Admiralty could take to finish filling out the requisition forms. His political skills are on a par with his engineering street cred, which is sorely needed on the *Ekatarina* whenever the pocket battleship gets into a fight far from home and has to replenish assets lost to the vagaries of space combat.

Lehmann knows how and when to bend the rules, pushing the limits of the system, authorizing what he can, stealing or bartering for the rest. His natural ally turns out to be none other than Ensign Terry Thaleia, the young and brilliant theoretical physicist, whose one-time surreptitious experimentation had cost the lives of dozens of crewmen. Both did their jobs well and espoused the same goal, to wit, getting home in one piece and while young enough to enjoy it. Lehmann knows it is easy for things to get lost in the system, and the fog of war makes for excellent cover. Infractions can often be overlooked as long as lives are at stake, and existential threats provide clarity of purpose. It is the implicit wartime footing the entire crew still existed under in their trek homeward that keeps him energized and on track, ever ready to deal with whatever obstacles get in his way.

It is unfortunate that Terry has few friends among the crew after her "lapse in judgement," but he doesn't really see it that way. He is forgiving of this flaw and getting to work with a beautiful green-eyed blonde who is a competent and dedicated has its advantages. She is pleasing to the eye, and he can dream. Rumor has it there might be something between her and the second-in-command, but both are apparently prudent enough to keep any suspected liaisons one hundred percent discreet. So, yeah, there is still hope that Lehman might one day charm the princess.

When comprehension hits home, and he finally understands the true potential of the tech he procures from the "purple peaceniks of planet homebody," as he calls them, he knows he has to have both an overt and covert development program. Overt for propulsion and engine work and some weapons and armor where the advanced physics is readily understandable, but covert for what Einstein called "spooky action at a distance" - discoveries which might be a bit more dangerous but might also have a much bigger payoff for the long-term survival of the *Ekatarina*. So, he sets aside a space on Level Twelve in the propulsion bay where experiments can be run unmolested, and he can monitor progress and aid preparation as needed. His hope is to develop the kinds of "toys" that will give rogue armadas pause and space pirates a run for whatever passed for doubloons in their culture, since the probability of running into a cohort bent on destruction is highly likely, given his experience in this vast universe.

He feels he can trust Terry's instincts, so he willingly gives her carte blanche to run the covert weapons lab as she sees fit. He fully gives his loyalty and support to his willing protégé – now what he needs to do is to augment her staff so she can "immanentize the eschaton" more efficiently or as he likes to put it "peace through superior firepower."

Lehmann punches the "Enroute" symbol on his console screen and makes his way to Level Twelve.

Communications Technician First Class (CT1) Kimothy Stratford and Crewman Farko Tiresias are alternately apprehensive and thrilled at being summoned to the engineering deck by Lt. Commander Lehman. As they stand before the steel doors of a laboratory on Level Twelve, CT1 Stratford wonders aloud: "They have their own technicians to repair and fabricate the equipment needed in the physics lab, why have they called me?"

She swears to herself she will avoid future fraternizing with the male techs on this deck (if it turns out to be a morale problem caused by a recent nocturnal rendezvous that left much to be desired) and will stick only to the Marines on board. At least they are up front playing the game and aren't in the same service.

Glancing from the side of her eyes, Stratford quickly takes in the lean but still effeminate form of Crewman Farko Tiresias, one of the small number of Teenerian recruits that have not been indentured by the Captain but has rather forcibly and unapologetically demanded asylum on the Polisian Warship. A blue tinged alien not of original Terran stock, still she appears quite attractive by human standards. As gossip is wont to do on a fleet ship, it doesn't take long for word to spread that as young as she is Tiresias is relatively open to hook-ups with those, either men or women, that show proper prudence. Heck, there is even a story going around that near the end of the party madness that struck the ship when the galactic line-crossing ceremony had begun, after wearing out a few of the burlier men among Marines and fleet personnel, a lusty Major Ironbear dragged the surprised but not unwilling Tiresias into an arms locker for an impromptu and private weapons inspection.

When Stratford enters the laboratory, she sees a cross between a fabrication shop and a warehouse. Transit cases, wire coils, racks of electronics, optical cable and all matter of test equipment litter the room.

Chief Engineer Lehmann greets her in an officious tone, "Communications Technician First Class Kimothy Stratford, you are being temporarily transferred to his section, effective immediately and until further notice."

The young CT acknowledges, with. "Aye, aye, sir" and then asks a fateful question.

"Excuse me sir, but what duty have I been chosen for? I'm only a commtech. I don't belong in this type of lab."

Lehmann continues, "You have the highest tech rating in the fabrication of both transmit and receive antennas, as well as some design experience. All of the communications officers are at full utilization, and there are no design engineers available to be seconded to this project. I'm in no position to let anyone else go, and you meet the minimum skills required to support the young doctor's effort. Stratford, I sincerely hope you're up to the task, and will work hard to complete it expeditiously."

CT1 Stratford, only then notices in the corner of the room the shapely figure of Ensign Thaleia, a grin pasted from ear to ear.

She comes over to CT1 Stratford and cordially welcomes her, "Glad to have you on board. You'll be working closely with me for the duration of this project."

Thaleia then turns to Crewman Tiresias and says "As will you, Ensign. I asked for you personally. I believe your ability to rapidly assimilate knowledge may be able to provide insights we might otherwise overlook."

Lehmann turns to the blue skinned crewman and says, "same orders apply to you. Welcome to the team."

CT1 Stratford, is intrigued by the exchange of looks between her new bosses, but puzzled, and truth be told, a bit apprehensive, given Ensign Thaliea's track record aboard the *Ekatarina*. She accepts Thaliea's hand and politely asks, "what kind of project will we be working on?"

Lehmann winks at her and says in earnest "Probably the most important project you'll undertake this lifetime – preventing the *P.W. Ekatarina* from becoming *The Flying Dutchman*."

Both Crewman Tiresias and CT1 Stratford are wide awake for Ensign Thaliea's briefing on the program to which she's been posted. After their morning PT at oh dark thirty around the interior rim of the new exterior equatorial deck, they are invigorated and looking forward to the chance of making a difference.

Since the retrofit on *Planet Purple*, aka Cerrid, the ship has taken on a new appearance and a few new capabilities. The inertial damping field generators extend in long circular stretches around the hull. Based on a deterministic treatment of hidden variables in Bell's Theorem, they allow excess inertial energy to be dissipated into the Dirac Sea, the virtual substructure of the universe, with bleed off occurring, somewhere or possibly *somewhen* else in space time. The Chief Engineer sees the immediate practical merit in acquiring this technology for the *Ekatarina*. The net effect is increased speed and agility and better structural integrity. They also make more efficient the use of the control moment gyroscopes for rapidly positioning the *Ekatarina* while pointing the main railgun, making target solutions faster and conserving energy in the process. The more he studies it, the more he knows it can yield other benefits. Manipulating the very fabric of the universe means he needs more brainpower. Enlisting Ensign Thaleia and the A.I. SIBIL is the logical call.

Ensign Thaleia settles in and begins with a question to the pert CT1: "So you want to know why we need a commtech? The program you have been posted to has to do with manipulating the fabric of the universe. Are you familiar with the terms Zero Point Energy, or the A Field or Vacuum Energy?"

She shakes her head "No," and the young Ensign goes on.

"Over the centuries, organizations of Terran, Polisian, and other entities across the galaxies have had varied measures of success in trying to tap the limitless energy of the vacuum of space. Force fields are residual energies that we harness, but the true power is in potentials, which by definition are infinite. Prior to the current conflagration, many approaches to exploiting the promise of A Potential Energy and concomitant achievable weapons effects have had mixed results. In the past, devices were so highly classified, that no industrial capability evolved out of their development and manufacture. SIBIL's research into the archives of the Admiralty hinted that only the labs attached to the covert arms organizations had been involved. The records were spotty but did include captured intelligence from other species and empires."

The whole area has been so compartmented that its partial successes and gross failures have been kept remarkably quiet. Lack of accountability and classified developmental program are never a good combination, so over the decades, many original programs were abandoned where they should have been the foundations of future research. The emergence of the Scourge had renewed interest in the research within the Admiralty, but again it was abandoned due to uncontrollable time dilation effects the weapons under development caused."

Ensign Thaleia pauses for a moment to let this sink in, and then continues. "SIBIL uncovered that the Admiralty's security apparatus had some mostly theoretical research that was progressing well, but they were compromised by a weapons community developer with shoddy protocols who experienced significant fatalities and tried to cover it up by classifying the shit out of it. They were caught and the program shut down. SIBIL postulates that the chance to operationally test it and shake it out fully holds promise that is beyond revolutionary. It will radically change the way we do business, if my theory is correct, based on reviewing the materials SIBIL has uncovered."

She asks rhetorically, "How's your ancient history?", then goes on, "Do you remember the reported history on the destruction of Outpost Gamma Six in the Epsilon Aurigae System - just after the First Hegemonic War? The entire planet just vanished, no debris, nothing. It was purported to be a new secret weapon, unleashed as a prelude to a counteroffensive by a recalcitrant Legion that refused to accept the Hegemony's surrender. There was never another incident, and after several weeks back on war footing, the scare ended, and everything went back to business as usual. That was an A field experiment gone bad."

The young CT1 nods in acknowledgement.

"The Admiralty research into the incident concluded there were mega billions invested from the Hegemony's classified budget in the laboratory facilities, and enough politicos there for the weapons unveiling that their disappearance effectively killed the massive research effort that should have gone with it. Too much compartmentation kept the majority of the body of scientific research confined to the experiment station, and when it vanished, not only did the programs institutional core of knowledge, but its political support as well."

"Residual weapons programs left from the bits and pieces spread out across the fleet intelligence cells, from time to time are resurrected by someone who perceives a glimmer of the technologies potential, but they've never gotten the full support needed for a true weapons development program. Until now."

Thaleia sits back down, and a fire burns deep in her eyes, as she speaks in earnest to the young tech, "You are sworn to secrecy here. The overt power program is well known among the crew. The covert weapons program is need-to-know only. The Captain and the Senior Officers, and those working the project are the only ones who have access. Me being seconded to this area for research might engender another mutiny, so it is best kept quiet. We don't need any more scares among the crew, but the Captain, despite my previous shortcomings, sees the wisdom in letting me work to my strengths. I need to atone for what I have done, and to get us all home alive."

Stratford, unable to contain her impatience any longer, asks "But what have you discovered that will change things? And how am I to be a part of all this as a comm tech?"

The young Ensign replies, "You have the skill sets to build radio-frequency antennas, do you not? Harmonic oscillators? Interferometers? Resonant cavities?

"Yes Sir I do!"

"Then that is where you come in. With SIBIL's help, I believe we can create (air quotes) *spooky action at a distance* by creating stress waves in the fabric of space time using artificial potentials to add order to the random potential in the virtual substructure of the vacuum of space."

Crewman Tiresias has been listening intently, and finally chimes in with a question. "I'm confused. How could this be employed if its effects are buried in the virtual state, where they are, by definition, not observable."

"Good question. In quantum field theory, all fundamental fields must be quantized at every point in space. Even the vacuum of space has a complex structure. If we treat each point in space as a simple harmonic oscillator, theoretically, we can create a closed resonant system with fields within it that sum to zero. The cavity will be resonant to each type of wave, and each wave and anti wave will move along together and superpose, continuing to build up stress and define an artificial potential within the virtual substructure. If the cavity is opened, a stress wave would be propelled in a straight line through the virtual substructure like an invisible torpedo. This was Lehman's insight. The damping fields were bleeding off somewhere or somewhen. So, we find a way to channel them."

Crewman Tiresias responds, "Yes, I can see that – it is logically what should happen, but we still have no observable effect."

"Agreed. For an observable effect, we have to build an identical cavity, separate them spatially, and allow the stress waves to be simultaneously released, intersecting at a designated point in space. At the point in space where they intersect, the now ordered scalar potentials will experience destructive interference, creating a zone of vector energy, which will be forced to escape from virtual reality into observable reality."

Stratford, in full comprehension of what she is now revealing, then says, "What kind of power magnitudes are we talking about here?"

Thaleia answers, "Both quantum electrodynamics and stochastic electrodynamics suggest that to be consistent with the Lorentz covariance and Planck's constant, we are looking at power magnitudes on the order of 10113 joules per cubic meter."

Stratford lets out a low whistle of awed disbelief.

"Scary numbers indeed," the Ensign continues, "so we must be exceedingly careful when we experiment with the amount of energy zero summed when stressing the virtual substructure. Tiny ripples I believe can produce massive nonlinear effects, and if we don't get a good understanding of the orders of magnitude involved, we won't have a clue where a point of inflection might occur that could make the Gamma Six disaster look like a firecracker in comparison. But the beauty of this approach, lies in the simplicity of the tech required."

"And that's where I come in," says the CT1, fully eager now to play in a game that had been deadly more than once before.

"Yes, and there's one more thing you should know," Thaleia replies in a serious tone, "while the stress waves are travelling in the virtual substructure to the point in space, they are invisible to normal detection. Only upon their arrival and mutual destruction are they seen. Thus, we should have a completely stealthy weapon system, based on *spooky action at a distance*, created spontaneously, as if out of nothing."

Stratford in a reverent tone, recalls a motto reminiscent of a prayer, "Post Tenebras Lux!"

"Exactly" is the young Doctor's smiling reply.

In the four months since Thaliea's team is assembled, things have gone rather well. Lehmann has procured all the equipment necessary to construct circuits and antennas, and to put in place the experimental protocols to test the dual PhD's theory. The initial experiments will be kept within a constrained environment, with extreme limitations on pulse powers and time durations. It is known that time dilation effects are going to be difficult to quantify, so extremely precise chronometers are time synchronized in equidistant quadrants of the ship to gauge if there are any discernable effects of the experiments, with SIBIL doing the monitoring so immediate assessment can be made if a danger presents itself.

After initial experiments to ensure the test equipment and sensors tested within spec, the pedestals for the antenna pointing mechanisms are calibrated, and the antennas are mounted outside of the ship along the perimeter of the inertial damping field generators. Vector quadrants in space are instrumented for charting imaging and expediting analysis.

The system becomes operational, under SIBIL's control, to execute a precise test timing sequence at the lowest time and power settings that can be measured. The result is hard to quantify. Thaleia likens it to a retinal afterimage from a single strobe, basically imperceptible. One thing that does show up, however, is a one femtosecond decrease in the setting on the chronometers set in the *Ekatarina's* hull, forward of the arc cut by the trajectory of the two interferometers used for the test.

Thaleia confers with SIBIL and decides to up the power by one order of magnitude.

This time the results are more dramatic. An evanescent sphere of light appears at the precise aiming point in space then winks out of existence. Once again, the time loss on the chronometer is commensurate. So far so good. Next test — same power, increased time.

This time, it is an arc of light that brightly erupts and is barely translucent, but it cuts a swath through the darkness and expands outward in the shape of a hemispherical wave. Electro-magnetic detectors register it as a single weak pulse, similar to a soliton.

Time dilation is again commensurate along the same trajectory.

The forces involved appear controllable, so the team decides to up the ante once more. Power and time are both increased one order of magnitude. This time, what appears to be a ball of lightning winks into existence and spreads forward in a hemispherical wave before disappearing. This time, time dilation is more perceptible to the crew, feeling a sort of déjà vu momentary effect, but no discernable effect on SIBIL.

So as far as Ensign Thaleia is concerned, as long as SIBIL is in control, the *mind blinks* are an acceptable risk, so long as the testing remains successful.

Within weeks of beginning controlled experimentation, the excitement within the laboratory can barely be contained. A handful of additional interdisciplinary personnel are recruited from within the available crew: an EM tech with a background in phased array radars; a neuroscientist with experience in heads up tactical displays; an applied mathematician specializing in non linear systems; and a dual disciplined geochronometrist / cosmologist.

It is agreed that the dark arterials are an anomalous phenomenon in the emerging theoretical constructs for manipulating the virtual substructure of the universe, so modeling them becomes a high priority. Deliberately crossing into their energy fields without first testing corollary effect should be avoided.

Captain Tennyson Illiadus, Commander David Aithon, Chief Warrant Officer Yaqub Al-Quam, and Major Helen Ironbear are now briefed at the daily standup on the latest developmental work by Lt. Commander Lehman and if needed, Ensign Thaleia. The Captain has personally authorized the personnel plus-ups, and Al-Quam as an intelligence professional is glad for the protocols set in place for this research - straight classification with a need to know, no special caveats, no sub-compartments. The need for additional physical security is acknowledged by the group, and Major Ironbear now has Marine Guards posted to the lab in rotation.

In various stages of development are: a precisely controlled pointing mechanism using tensor analysis, for precision target acquisition and tracking - one using a biofeedback enhanced heads up display with voice control and optical tracking designed to support a fighter pilot, and one designed for multitasking that the Captain can attach to the Quantum Helmet when communing with SIBIL; a phased array radar that can create, at picosecond speeds, an electrically controllable, spatially agile matrix, that in effect will be the equivalent of a magic mirror in space that on contact can "translate" what it touches through the virtual substructure to "elsewhere"; and access to near-limitless energy potentials and their opposite - total electrical impulse quenching with no dissipative effects; and of course phase locked, chained transmitters that can create precise zones of destructive interference, opening the fabric of space to the virtual substructure and exquisitely controllable by judicious allocation of power and time.

CWO Al-Quam, as a weapons officer, has been deeply immersed in his element for weeks now, and the final stages of preparation for practical tests in deep space of an "Apot" (his shorthand) equipped experimental light tactical fighter. Tests are to commence in three days. With the Captain's blessing he obtains and retrofits a one-man utility craft with limited armor, reinforced hull with inertial dampers, an enhanced engine, and a weapons suite.

With the promise of a new improved weapons suite, *to* be provided to cover the *Ekatarina's* indigenous tactical forces if the tests proved positive, the craft's care and shake out are remanded to Al-Quam on personal recognizance. Unlike covert experimentation in the past, the book-keeping exchange is not executed on a handshake, with no questions asked, and the small ship is not deadlined *on the record* during this period for *extended periodic maintenance.* What this really means was, if the fighter-escort is destroyed, it is his ass. And he likes it much better this way. An officer through and through, he understands the maxim – "Seek responsibility and take responsibility for your actions." And if this works the way he prays it will, the *Ekatarina's* chance of returning home will be greatly enhanced, "*Inshallah.*"

Al-Quam can't wait to be in the cockpit of the newest X craft, even if it does give the appearance of a tiny escort. In all respects it really is one, save for the tiny beamsteering interferometers mounted in three pairs, at fixed intervals, along the wings. The opposing field generator components are physically small, for the electronics are enfolded; antenna apertures are conformal and created electrically; and the new engine is both powerful and agile enough to maneuver at will though the use of the damping field. You can only dream about this type of firepower in such a small package. Al-Quam is indeed a happy warrior!

Not to be upstaged after the successful testing of CWO Al-Quam's X-craft, dubbed "*The Spear of Allah,*" Commander David Aithon, the ship's First Officer, who is also recognized as the best pilot on the *Ekatarina,* pulls Lehman aside and says, "Walt – I see what you can do. I want one too. What can you do for me?"

Lehman cocks an eye.

"Commander, for you I think I have just the thing. I have already outfitted a landing craft for Major Ironbear with a new *toy.* In addition to the normal complement of chain guns and missiles, it has a prototype phased array weapon designed for breaching structures like hulls that should clear anything in its path. How about we retrofit another one-man utility craft like we did for Al-Quam, but with a very different weapons suite? Another phased array weapon I have been working on using the same principles but on a larger scale I have been calling *The Maw*. The spatially agile matrix can swallow anything coming at you out of existence. In effect it will be the equivalent of a wall in space that on contact can *consume* what it touches into the virtual substructure to *elsewhere* or *elsewhen* – still haven't quite figured that out."

"Tactically," the Commander replies, "if what you say it can do is accurate, then I am going to have a lot of fun playing *chicken*. But in any case, I'll take whatever you'll give. Most importantly, do I get to name it?"

"Sure," Lehman says, "just be patient, I still haven't worked out all of the steerage protocols yet, so sizing the matrix is still a work in progress."

The latest exit from a Dark Energy Artery leaves the *Ekatarina* in a particularly inhospitable region of space. Forced to travel a spatial gap between a sizzling giant pulsar emitting electromagnetic radiation and a rogue super-giant star spouting massive solar flares, the pocket battleship needs to be on guard not only for the deleterious effects of space weather, but the concomitant perils of celestial debris from the battered extrasolar planetary systems around these two stars caught in the maelstrom of magnetic field effects and coronal mass ejections.

Sitting down in her command chair in the CIC, Captain Illiadus is visibly agitated as the precision target acquisition and tracking subsystem is attached to the Quantum Helmet by Crewman Farko Tiresias and recently promoted Lieutenant Amy Seyfortt, the last surviving member of the original Cybernetics Team that had fabricated the first Q-helmet under the leadership of the late Dr. Bream.

Illiadus closes her eyes and cycles her awareness back and forth several times between the immediate sensory reality of the bustling CIC and the identical virtual world CIC that only she and SIBIL visibly occupy. The now very adult SIBIL, nodding her head in acknowledgement in her virtual incarnation, does not seem to have any concerns with the checkout of the circuitry upon installation.

Illiadus frowns in both worlds. Anything new added to the mix of the Captain's already overwhelmed senses is unwelcome, but she knows in her core, it is necessary to the *Ekatarina's* survival.

SIBIL has a three-hundred-and-sixty-degree view around the ship broken into sectors. Twenty-four equidistant interferometers are mounted on the exterior sphere of inertial damping field generators, corresponding to the twenty-four letters of the Greek Alphabet, *Alpha* through *Omega*. The antennas are paired by SIBIL to optimize targeting accuracy, with the AI computing the target ephemeris data, and given the size and proximity of the target, selecting the desired power levels for the payload. Captain Illiadus job is to focus optically when choosing the targets and command "Fire."

Individual target selection of singletons might seem inefficient, but at the speed of optical tracking by the human brain, it should be sufficient, given there are a limited amount of targeting antennas that will need to be prioritized. The ship's regular complement of weapons will still be in use in real combat, so critical targets can be the focus of the weapons in beta testing.

A live test in a meteor field for adjustment of the firepower levels is in order.

When life hands you lemons, you make lemonade, Commander Aithon thinks in the back of his mind as he presents the available space debris as targets of opportunity to the Captain.

Illiadus, wears the quantum helmet and sits ramrod straight with her eyes closed in the real word, appears in the identical virtual construct of the CIC without any head gear and her eyes wide open, taking in tracking information displayed on the virtual main screen. SIBIL stands at full attention a couple of feet to her right.

"Targeting," Illiadus's voice speaks from the CIC's intercom system, "fire."

In short order, the first of a dozen meteors winks out of existence in a flash of light emerging from the darkness of space, like an ethereal firefly of unknown and unknowable power. This is instantly duplicated in impressive and easily discernible animated graphical representations on the main screen above Commander Aithon's console. The Commander glances over at the seemingly sleeping face of the Captain and smiles. The first round of testing power levels for the interferometric array is a success.

A small cheer rises from the dozen crew members manning consoles all around the CIC.

Chief Engineer Lt. Cmdr. Lehman, standing two consoles to the left of Commander Aithon, smiles. He is confident his creation of an elaborate simulation for a robust tactical shake out of all the elements that make up precision pointing, tracking, and targeting will impress the Captain.

If all goes as planned, the operational environment will run in the background, while a test environment will control the sensor array displays to simulate a Scourge attack. Waste not want not – the abominable Scourge race are long dead, but Lehman has saved time by using the resources he has at hand, since those old foes are an enemy he has simulated before, and at least his canned work won't go to waste. Lehman grits his teeth as he models two hundred Scourge ships attacking in waves and sets power outputs to sub-caliber levels to ensure the tracking mechanism can handle the volume to multi-targeted fires without taxing the power systems. He nods to Aithon who feeds the information into the Captain's data stream.

The subsystem works like a champ.

In the virtual CIC, Illiadus views, tracks, and targets via her thoughts the first simulated wave of attackers. Instantly, a dozen domes of incandescent lightning light up sector seven, and the virtual targets are near simultaneously destroyed from within – to a warrior, a thing of beauty indeed, since the beams cross within the structure and then destructively interfere, rendering armor obsolete.

The virtual version of the Captain smiles. Optical tracking with her virtual vocal command take up about four seconds in reality for the actual viewing, tracking, and destroying to occur in real time. The Captain realizes that given normal target proximity, and the speed of SIBILs computing, future engagements will be, as they used to say, "like shooting fish in a barrel."

Two more simulated waves come in from opposing sectors, both waves obliterated based on distance, with the *low hanging fruit* (i.e., closest targets) being obliterated first. Everything is working as predicted.

Another round of cheers circles the room.

Then things go horribly sideways.

The main screen in the real CIC suddenly begins to clutter with hundreds of more targets.

Aithon looks up in disbelief.

"Did we just catch a computer virus?" he mutters aloud.

Illiadus, clearly annoyed, snaps, and her cerebral voice practically shouts from the surrounding intercom system.

"Isn't this a bit much for a rollout test, Commander?"

Aithon sends daggers at Lehman with his eyes.

"I swear I only simulated two hundred targets," Lehman retorts, "how the hell are they multiplying across the sectors?"

Then the first wave of The Scourge strikes.

Crewman Mark Van Sciver sits up reluctantly. The cover on his cryopod retracts to both sides and pungent cryogel drips down his head, face and ears. The usual post-hibernation nausea starts to hit his gut as expected, but much worse than this is the godawful sound of ship's klaxons blaring from every intercom speaker in his damned cryo-bunk bay. His mind still overly foggy from an emergency rapid revival, he still manages to realize that this specific undulating alarm is the ship's call to Battle Stations.

Groaning, he pushes his legs over the side of the pod and glances for a blurry moment at the other ten crew people in his bay going through the same wake-up procedure as himself.

"Godammit," Mark mumbles. Sitting on the edge of the pod he grabs the nearby towel and immediately starts wiping the excess cryogel off his face and head.

Stupid Captain and her stupid battle drills, he thought to himself, *I can't wait to discharge from this damned fleet… though most of us will probably be senior citizens when we return to Earth.* Immediately after thinking this he smiles, because he has a little secret.

Well, he thinks, *most of us…*

For Crewman Sciver is a schemer and a slacker. As he quickly pulls his boxer shorts on, he thinks back on the years that have passed since the destruction of the Scourge Sphere. Originally drafted into the military from Terra itself, after that last great battle on the far side of the galaxy he has lost every ounce of military ambition left in his bones, not that there was ever that much in him. And around the time that the Marine Demolition Crew died trying to de-arm an old Scourge mine from the ship's hull, he had come up with a brilliant scheme.

The klaxons continue to blare as Sciver shoves his legs into his crew overalls.

One skill that Sciver has excelled at ever since his initial enlistment, is games of chance. Dice, cards, coin flips, underground fight clubs, you name it. And most of the time he never needs to cheat. Growing up as a teenager in the massive shantytown of Lugano on the poor side of Buenos Aires he learned the survival traits of flight and fight early on, but it was his aptitude for gambling that allows him to make money. He had just gotten exceptionally good at various card games when he was rounded up with thousands of other eighteen-year-olds in a surprise Terran draft that many local governments enacted without any form of due process. The entire planet had declared Martial Law when the Scourge attacks had begun.

Sciver pulls the rest of his overalls on and reaches for his boots. *Why are the damned klaxons still on?*

Crewman Sciver is a part of every piece of action on the *Ekatarina*. There isn't a dice game, card game, lottery, physical duel, death pool, or odds bet that he doesn't get a piece of. And what does he bet? Why, none other than duty shifts. So many that in the time since they first started using the Dark Energy Arteries to return to Earth, he has been awake, and out of his cryopod, for roughly one-fifth of the time as the majority of the crew. Even after almost half of his fellow humans have died in accidents, misadventure, and bad luck, and been replaced by those damned Teenerians, he still plies his lucky streak. At the current rate of time's passage, he calculates he will have aged less than half of what the remaining human crew have by the time they reach Earth. Worst case scenario he'd be middle-aged when he gets back… still young enough to enjoy life, and maybe even bask in the glow of a better than average looking returning war hero.

Sealing both his boots, Mark stands up and runs to the urinal where he quickly empties his bladder.

"Dammit, Sciver," Petty Officer Moxley, a doughy red head with green eyes and a big frown on her face yells out, "grab your weapon, you're holding us up."

Mark shakes himself, zipped up, and races across the bay to the nearby weapons cabinet that has already opened. His is the last rifle. He pulls out and straps on a weapons belt holding five pulse cartridges and then grabs his pulse rifle, quickly checking that its cartridge holds a full charge and that the safety is secure. Everyone has exited the bay and Moxley is waiting at the hatch to the adjoining corridor with an even nastier scowl on her face.

"Move it, Sciver," Moxley screams, "I swear to god you'll spend the rest of this voyage doing hard labor if you don't pick it up."

Whatever, Mark thinks, *lucks always on my side. I'll hustle my way out of any brig time in a matter of days.*

Running across the length of the bay, a sudden jolt flings Moxley out into the corridor and sends Mark sliding back down the length of the bay toward the far bulkhead where he skids to a stop.

"What the hell was that?" he mumbles to himself, grabbing his rifle and standing back up more than a little shaken.

Suddenly a whole series of jolts strike the ship and repeatedly knock Mark off his feet. After a string of six or so of these jarring shakes Mark manages to stand up again.

"Secure all hatchways," Captain Illiadus's voice comes from the intercom overriding the klaxon, "multiple hull breaches. I repeat, close all bulkhead doors!"

"For god's sake, Mark," Moxley yells from the hatchway, blood running down from a cut on her forehead, "we're venting! Behind you! Run!"

Without thinking Mark spins around and his eyes open wide at sight of an eight-foot-long deformation in the bay's bulkhead and the ever-increasing scream of escaping air overcoming the sound of klaxons.

Before he can move, a whole section of the bulkhead peels back, and Crewman Mark Van Sciver of the Polisian Pocket Warship *Ekatarina* is blown out into the cold and fatal shroud of space.

His last moment of thought, right before death claims his soul, is a surprised question.

What are the insane odds of this ever happening?

Helen Ironbear is in the gym on Deck Nine practicing hand to hand combat with a pair of Marine Gunnery Sergeants when the first wave of the Scourge fleet hits them. She has just flipped Sergeant Saxon over her shoulder and clocks Sergeant Dean with a round-house kick to the chin when an unexpected sideways jolt suddenly knocks her off her feet. All three Marines find themselves skidding across the fight mat as the ship starts shaking as if some giant is punching it repeatedly from outside.

In the CIC, both virtual and real, the Captain is doing her best to take in the veritable flood of tactical data being fed to her by both the Command Staff and SIBIL as the *Ekatarina* shakes from multiple incoming strikes. Immediate spot identification of the enemy ships comes as nothing less than a shock.

"It… it can't be," the Captain whispers.

Somehow, some way, the unimaginable has happened. Some number of the Polisian Fleet's long hated enemy, The Scourge, have survived the destruction of their home, a massive extra-galactic Dyson sphere that had appeared from nowhere years ago and begun a war that came close to destroying every sentient race in The Milky Way. It is only devious luck and desperate cleverness that allows a Polisian wolf in sheep's clothing to detonate an unforgiveable weapon of mass destruction within spitting distance of the gigantic alien sphere, home to a vile race that numbered in the billions, and end that ten-year war a full twenty-seven years ago. And now, sixty-five thousand light years away from that cataclysmic altercation, here is an avenging remnant of that once rampaging overwhelming force. Fate has caught up with the *Ekatarina*.

In a desperate moment the Captain is able to discern the enemy's use of a new tactic, one that is well thought out.

The attacking force is coming out of the interiors of the nearest local planets in full attack, kamikaze style. The Captain immediately sees that the Scourge, in their fanaticism, are not afraid to make the ultimate sacrifice, and execution of their plan proves brutal beyond belief.

This first wave that catches them completely off guard consists of over five hundred small ships. Fully a third are nothing more than drones, carrying a tarlike substance as their payload. These ships have designated targets.

The Captain, viewing the attack from multiple ships' cameras, watches slack jawed as in a matter of seconds the enemy drones seek out the *Ekatarina's* exit hatches, bays and firing ports. These they imprison like an insect in amber - the pathways to the void of space. The liquified black tar mushrooms as the Scourge weapon-ships explode, clinging to the surface of the *Ekatarina's* entranceways, and solidified into a smooth obsidian mask, brilliantly effective at holding everything within, entombed.

The claxon horns blare, and emergency lighting comes on as the Major, tomahawk in hand, and the two Sergeants make their way towards the CIC.

Precious seconds are lost in the first wave. Running a test environment on top of the operational environment provides a totally serendipitous fog of war to the Scourge, giving them the element of surprise. It takes several seconds to shut down the test network and call the crew to battle stations, the intercoms blaring "GENERAL QUARTERS. GENERAL QUARTERS. THIS IS NOT AN EXERCISE. REPEAT THIS IS NOT

AN EXERCISE." It takes more time to adjust power levels on the weapons from sub-caliber to real power. And still more time to assess the situation.

The CIC at first is controlled pandemonium. Damage control reports are pouring in from every department of the ship. The power grid of the entire station is continuously readjusting to the paroxysms caused by whole sections of the vessel recoiling from impacts. Missiles pommel the outer hull of the *Ekatarina*, and with so many new holes in the missile and laser defenses, often find their mark.

At this point it is only the superior efficacy of the Cerridian mobile armor upgrade to the outermost hull that allows the ship to even remain in one piece. The Emergency power is cycling on and off as the massive body of the *Ekatarina* diverts and redirects its power grid. Red emergency lighting bathes many decks of the ship as compartment after compartment opens its bounty to the void of space. Chief Engineer Lehman overrides the emergency lights to return to standby mode and the sirens in the CIC go silent.

The Captain is incredulous on the timing of this disaster. Proximity to the planetary bodies is their undoing or just plain bad luck. In the past, attacks against Scourge Fleets were long distance affairs, where friendly and enemy were blips on the radar. Not this time. The intent for fleets that want to fight is to close with the enemy. And this time, the Scourge are able to close with the *Ekatarina*.

A nightmare is unfolding before the Captain's virtual eyes - two gigantic Scourge ships come out of jump, and an estimated six hundred small to medium fighters are converging on the beleaguered pocket warship.

The *Ekatarina* rocks from impact after impact. Luckily the beamsteering antennas for phase-locked operations look like communications rigs, so they are not targeted outright. Collateral damage has taken out arrays Epsilon, Zeta, Nu and Omicron, so ten pairs are still operational, though at the moment offline because of all the power fluctuations and losses. For the moment, the Captain has no bullets.

"Main engines still intact," Petty Officer Second Class Morahan shouts from her console.

"We've lost portions of the electrical grid," Chief Warrant Officer Hanson says calmly, "compensating by rerouting the power grid, until all destroyed circuits can be repaired."

"I'm on power and propulsion, Captain," Lehman shouts.

"We've got boarding parties on several decks," Aithon shouts, "Marine units deploying."

"I'm getting casualty reports, Captain," Tiresias shouts, "three dozen, no four dozen… most from hull breaches."

Illiadus, looks like a mannikin in the real world, scowls in the virtual CIC and rapidly assesses the situation. She does not like what she sees.

All the main guns are offline and most of the lesser weapons systems are inoperable. Escape is now impossible, as the Scourge have by now welded the main cargo bay doors shut with their tarry adhesive. The regenerative armor the *Ekatarina* obtained from the "purple peaceniks" is online but untested in combat, so it will remain to be seen if the healing of any hull breaches will be timely enough to save any the remaining crew.

For Illiadus, it is a Zen moment. She knows she must overcome her fear and allow the inevitable to occur to save her ship and crew. It is time to surrender herself to the AI. Only by allowing the AI to permanently wed itself to her entire nervous system, and finally complete the quantum-neural link to a degree that has never occurred before, will the Captain be able to control the ship and its weapons with sufficient fidelity.

Illiadus turns her virtual head to SIBIL who is dressed as a Lt. Commander and standing ramrod straight next the virtual command chair.

"SIBIL," Illiadus says without a tremor in her voice, "you need to join to me now… full integration. It's do or die time."

"Understood," SIBIL says, right before an overwhelming neuro-sensory overload causes the Captain to pass out.

The only ship that gets out during the initial onslaught is *The Spear of Allah*. It was prepped and waiting for its turn during the exercise, and Al-Quam, immediately realizes that the *Ekatarina* is actually under attack, readjusts power settings and immediately launches, joining the fray and firing at will at the massive swarm of vessels approaching the hull.

Al-Quam is not happy with the time dilation effects on his reflexes - his reaction time is punctuated by momentary pauses, almost like petit mal seizures, that keep him off balance. The computer so far has been programmed to spatially create and electronically produce power and form for three separate patterns of force: a single point concentration of power; a pulsed form of the same single point, creating ball lightning effects; and an emp pulse.

He learns almost immediately his tactics need to be better thought out. His first engagement is to flank assault a wing formation bent on suicide. Aimed at the battle station, five small Scourge ships are in a pitched dive, and he decides to do a quick lock on each, firing short emp pulses. The effects are dramatic, as all systems on board the craft are quenched; however, inertia brings them to their mark, each a pilotless gravity bomb, leaving a gaping hole between two decks.

This is failure in his eyes, and he switches to single point power effects, cranking up the power. Al-Quam's heads up display is chained to the pointing mechanism; his eyes are the cross hairs of the weapon system. Simple point and shoot, with system and man interleaved. The effects are dazzling as ships implode into nothingness. Each time he fires, he will have to reorient himself, as if he is not there, but only in a dream watching himself. The feeling of disembodiment is unnerving, but it passes.

Realizing the tactics the enemy are using, Al-Quam decides his X-craft should target the larger vessels on collision course with the compromised ship. This strategy doubtless saves the lives of many by turning the larger munitions ships that are targeted against it, into miniature suns, then darkness. But he can only target so many so quickly.

The CWO also sees another mix of vehicles approaching the *Ekatarina* as the first wave slackens in intensity – landing craft. He sends to oblivion as many as he can, then Al-Quam radios to the ship to prepare to repel boarders where the hull is breached at Decks Four, Nine and Ten.

The Scourge ships in the first wave concentrate on overwhelming the defenses of the tiers of fifteen millimeter laser banks and disabling the two hundred millimeter rail gun and the two seventy-five millimeter rail guns mounted atop and below the ship. Dozens of kamikaze ships filled with high explosives crash into the rail guns, rendering them useless for subsequent attacks. Hundreds of ships are annihilated in this first attack, but their objective is reached.

As the gun crews arrive at their battle stations, most find their missile tubes clogged, their weapons inoperable, or their spaces rendered uninhabitable without a space suit. But they also discover inspiration. For the Captain is there on the communications screen with them spouting clear orders and giving redirection. Simultaneously.

"Lance Corporal Sheen – go directly to Bay Six and pull the undamaged power convertors from the weapons suite and install them on the tracking sensors in Bay Nineteen on Deck One."

"Ensign Thaleia, CT Stratford report to Deck Twelve immediately for weapons prep."

"Master at Arms Brozinski – no bars on small arms and weaponry – provision at will."

"CPO Jenks prepare the available pressure suits in Bay Twelve on Deck Four to repel boarders. Deck Four has been breached in Bays One through Seven."

"CPO Inari – Doctor Sorlan and sickbay are overwhelmed. Prepare the mess hall for overflow emergency triage operations."

"Bosun's Mate (BM1) Graff, take charge of the damage control operations on Decks Nine and Ten and assign damage control parties at will."

"Major Ironbear – a landing party will meet you, proceed to Deck Twelve – there is a hull breach and boarding party on Deck Nine – do not engage without backup."

All over the ship, "Aye, Aye Sir" was the response in unison, as crews are redirected to sections where weapons are still operable. Others are given direct orders to draw hand to hand weapons and repel boarders. Others are put on damage control duty or directed toward undamaged assets that can be repurposed. All are energized and motivated, having direct orders from the Captain herself, though the work gangs are seeing what appears to be irreparable damage in many places. Many of the crew resign themselves to the fact they are aboard a doomed ship. But with the Captain's steely reserve, at least they will die trying.

"Marine Detachment Four," Captain Illiadus's voice resonates from the translation module embedded in Ch'Konn'Dll's upper thoracic plate, "repel Scourge boarding party on the ship's outer hull, ventral plating, section sixteen. I suspect they are targeting the aft antenna array."

"Detachment Four confirms," Sergeant Ch'Konn'Dll replies, "deploying."

The Sergeant and his Marine squad, all seven of them indentured Polisian recruits from the planet Teeneria, rapidly scuttle into airlock nine as the inner hatchway cycles into place. They normally walk upright on two leg-claws when interacting with the rest of the crew but per recent training drop down onto all fives, a position that actually gives them far greater stability, balance, maneuverability, and speed.

Several weeks ago, Ch'Konn'Dll suggested a physical alteration allowing for this type of physical adjustment to his clan's egg-keeper, explaining the need for a more practical physiological anatomy for working on and traveling over the outer hull of the *Ekatarina*. One dozen Teenerian volunteers spent a week in incubation eggs.

The seven that survived the procedure immediately displayed their new skills to Major Ironbear who quickly realized the potential effectiveness of their new forms. She dubbed them Marine Detachment Four and had them engage in all manner of practice drills in zero gravity and zero atmosphere for several weeks before their most recent cryopod hibernation shift during the *Ekatarina's* last dark energy artery jump passage. Now here they are finally putting that training to the test.

The outer hatch pops open and the Sergeant leads his force rapidly onto the ship's outer hull. To a Terran they would have appeared as a large group of spider-like shapes wearing only minimal body armor and customized weapon harnesses. Part of the genius of the Sergeant's suggested DNA tailoring is for a body-form that will not only offer up a smaller targeting profile when deployed on the outer hull but is also hardened against the cold airlessness of space and thus not burdened with bulky IEVA suits. Each member of his unit has a back-up container of oxygen for emergency use if they are prevented from reentering the ship in the next twenty minutes.

"They're getting closer to the array," Captain Illiadus's voice alerts the Sergeant, "hurry."

"Acknowledged," the Sergeant replies, "haul ass, troops."

All seven rapidly scuttle across the hull down the length of the ventral side of the ship, their forms moving far faster than any space-suited Terran or other Teenerian form possibly could. Variable magnetic contact sleeves on the extremities of all five of their limbs keep them well-grounded as they race to their targets. Several times they have to circumvent or leap across large holes in the ship, courtesy of the Scourge's initial bombardment. More than once they pass bloody frozen pieces or whole corpses of former crewmates, both Terran stock and Teenerian, that have been blown out into space.

"Eyes on target," the Sergeant says, "all ten of them," blinking four of his own as the enemy comes into view.

The Sergeant doesn't actually talk, not like a human that is. His Teenerian genome, what the humans call the arachnids, normally communicate with each other in an atmospheric environment via a complex series of vented hormones, however, when separated by each other via spacesuit or a zero-atmosphere-environ, they make use of a secondary method of communication, several dozen vibrating bone and flesh structures that work almost like the human eardrum, only they can not only receive and process sounds but also send them out as a rapid series of micro-beat-pulses. They can do this with such rapidity that they are able to convey five times as much information between each other than any two Terrans could via talking, just one more thing that makes the Sergeant's team such an effective fighting unit. This is also probably the reason their Teenerian genome is so good at adopting the use of Terran drums for recreational activities in the ship.

The translation unit they are all implanted with allows them to effectively communicate with their Terran brethren, but the Sergeant has soon come to realize that these devices are not very good at understanding the cultural norms and worldview of the Teenerian crew.

"Enemy sighted," the Sergeant says, "target the two closest to the array. Fire."

The Sergeant and all six of his team raises their modified Marine Hybrid Assault Rifles and let loose with both semi-auto and full automatic pulses while still on the run. Their shots are startlingly effective as the two towering Scourge closest to them sustain massive injuries that tear large chunks of flesh from their bodies before their corpses start drifting away from the hull because of the force of the pulse impacts.

They are now twenty meters away from the remaining four Scourge, and closing, when two of the Sergeant's warriors are struck by a strange white beam that cuts through their bodies, killing them immediately. Two of the Scourge are sporting small devices that the Sergeant instantly realizes has done the damage.

"Delta formation," the Sergeant says, "target the two guards flanking the others.

Instantly, the five Teenerian Marines started running in a crisscross pattern as they advance on the enemy. Several of the white cutting beams come close, but for several meters their zig zagging appears to confuse the enemy's targeting abilities.

Now ten meters away the Sergeant unloads a full clip into the Scourge guard on the left flank, practically cutting it in half. Almost simultaneously, the other guard cuts down two of the Sergeant's men who slowed down to avoid each other when they realize they are about to cross each other's paths.

The next minute seems to happen in slow motion.

The Sergeant and his remaining two troops close with the three giant Scourge invaders. Within grappling distance of the winged ebony giants, the Sergeant deactivates all five of his gravity sleeves while simultaneously jumping and leaping toward the remaining armed Scourge. In doing so he just barely avoids the white cutting beam he has been targeted with. A moment later he strikes the top of the warrior Scourge with all five of this limb's pincers, tearing into the massive monster with an unquenchable ferocity. Like the Sergeant and his troops, the Scourge don't seem to need space suits, and in seconds he has stabbed and torn enough dark flesh out of this invader to guarantee its death.

The Sergeant reactivates his gravity sleeves and drops down to the deck and turns around. Only one of his Marines is left, the other having been mangled and crushed right after delivering a lethal series of pincer stabs to a Scourge's large abdomen.

Private Ch'Thonn'Kll is trading blows with the remaining Scourge. Though the Private is far more maneuverable than the bulk of the huge invader, and its arm-wings, the black monster has a large barbed tail that it wields with deadly accuracy.

"Sergeant," the Private speaks via his communicator, "I think it's carrying explosive ordnance under its left wing. I don't know if it armed the device yet. I'm trying to stay between it and the array."

Running at the two of them the Sergeant realizes that the Private has not only lost his firearm, but is sporting several small wounds, each of them expelling droplets of body fluids that quickly freeze and drift away in the coldness of space. He is also slowing down. The next three seconds happen much too fast.

The Private dodges to the right and then left to confuse the Scourge. It doesn't succeed. The barbed tail, about the size of two humans end to end, slams down upon him, crushing him instantly. Simultaneously the Sergeant leaps onto the Scourge's back, sinking all five of his pincers into its thick flesh. Knowing he only has a fraction of a moment before the thing's vicious tail swings up and strikes him, the Sergeant swings his assault rifle up with two of his limbs and shoves it under the Scourge's left wing and fires.

This set off the device which explodes. The Scourge's large body absorbs most of the force of the detonation which kills it instantly. The explosion knocks the Sergeant off the back of the dead Scourge, and he tumbles across several meters of the hull before his gravity sleeves can stop him.

He is wounded in several places. Only three of his limbs work. Slowly, he does his best to make it back to the nearest airlock. He is pretty sure it is a lost cause.

"Array secured, Captain," the Sergeant mutters, "enemy eliminated. Six casualties. Returning to base. They died bravely. Request a medic at airlock nine."

In reality, in his own language, Sergeant Ch'Konn'Dll has actually said "Demi-Goddess of the Ship Palace, we are victorious in our holy mission. We have destroyed the sacrilegious invaders. They pollute your kingdom no longer. All six of my brother-sisters have joyfully shed their spirits for the good of your sacred hive. I return to the blazing light of your righteousness… demi-goddess. May an acolyte acknowledge my crossing if I do not return. Forgive my weakness."

Halfway to the entry hatch, the Sergeant finds that five of his ten eyes are growing blurry. He reaches for his spare oxygen container but finds it gone, no doubt knocked and torn away during close quarters combat. In the distance, in the blackness of space that surrounds the ship, the flare of weapons fire and explosions tell him the battle is still on, and the *Ekatarina* has not yet given up hope.

From experience the Sergeant knows that the translation devices hold no respect for Teenerian religious beliefs, and he feels a strong moment of grief at the knowledge that his reports are honed down to their most basic meaning by the time they reach the Captain. But it is of no matter. Duty is about service, not recognition.

Minutes later the Sergeant makes it to the hatch and crawls into the airlock as quick as he can. The hatch closes and air starts flooding into the chamber. He feels himself growing dizzy but the Captain's voice soothes as the light in the airlock seems to start dimming.

"A medic is approaching your position," Illiadus's distant voice speaks with an almost mechanical inflection, "hang on, Marine… and one more thing, your demi-goddess is very proud of the noble sacrifice of your brother-sisters, and of your own impressively brave and heroic actions in protecting my holy kingdom from the infidel Scourge. I grant you… my deific blessing."

A flame of pride burns in all three of the Sergeant's throat sacks… then everything goes black.

As Major Ironbear and Gunny's Saxon and Dean make their way from Deck Nine to the CIC, they are already headed directly for the breach

when they get the Captain's redirect. They are in the first non-breached section beyond Bay Sixteen when the bulkhead door unseals before them.

They are now the first humans who can describe what a Scourge looks like up close. The long-hated and feared aliens are big by human standards, between seven and nine feet tall. Night-black with smooth leathery skin that glistens like the tar-like substance that entombs the ship's hatches. They pour through the opening. Some have wings like a bat and a long-spiked tail; others have no wings and short tails. Some are faceless, some eyeless but with an orifice filled with teeth like obsidian. All have well-muscled bodies that ripple with incredible strength.

Outclassed and outnumbered, Ironbear and the two Gunnery Sergeants retreat at breakneck speed to the next bay where they can barricade the door to slow their ingress and make a run to another deck. They almost make it unscathed.

Ironbear and Saxon get through the bulkhead door, but Dean is not so lucky. One of the winged Scourge blows past him and wedges itself before the doorway between him and his compatriots. With a swift kick, Dean is hurled into the surging cohort of demoniac aliens, screaming as his arms are ripped from their sockets.

Saxon lunges to shut the doorway, but the spiked tail of the faceless beast has a mind of its own. Without turning, the winged beast impales him through his heart on, instantly killing him.

Ironbear vaults onto the base of the rigid tail, gives out what on Earth would have been called the war cry of the berserker, and severs the head of the alien from behind with one fevered, adrenalin fueled swipe of her tomahawk. She then kicks the tottering corpse, and the weight of the nine-foot beast pulls the tail and Saxon's body through the door, which she then seals before the crush of the aliens can reach her. At that moment, she realizes they are in a world of shit and need a plan to quickly staunch this ship's festering wound.

She puts two bays distance between her and the horde, then finds a comm port and hails the Captain.

"Al-Quam," Illiadus's nearly robotic voice speaks in his ear-piece, "you've just been targeted by five small attack craft and seven missile drones approaching you on all vectors. Vacate battlespace immediately. There is a small asteroid field two thousand klicks distant in spatial grid forty-three. Fair wind, Chief."

"Roger that, Captain," Al-Quam says and jerks his craft into a barrel roll that pushes the inertial dampeners to their limits and nearly causes him to black out. This maneuver barely lets him escape the proximity fuse activated warhead explosions of four enemy missile-drones.

Within seconds he is within the asteroid field. The five Scourge attack craft are only matching his own speed, but the remaining three missiles are rapidly closing the distance between them and him.

Two energetic explosions meters away on both his right and left flank force Al-Quam into a new series of evasive maneuvers that he prays will play havoc with the Scourge targeting systems for just one more minute.

Fifty seconds later he lets out a held breath as *The Spear of Allah* dives between two large asteroids then takes a sudden sideways thrust between three even smaller rotating balls of stone so quickly that Al-Quam thinks his restraining straps are going to cut through his flesh.

The maneuver works, though, as all four of the missiles impact against the lead asteroids. Unfortunately, an abundance of rocky debris fills the surrounding field and makes it even harder to visually assess the cluttered environment for quick navigation. Even worse, one chunk of asteroid strikes one of his three thrust nozzles effectively putting it out of commission and making his craft that much slower.

In a matter of seconds, the five Scourge ships have entered the asteroid field and immediately began to try to slowly close in on *The Spear* from all sides while avoiding collisions with the deadly rocks themselves.

Initially two hundred and fifty meters away and closing around him, The Scourge fire short white plasma charges in his direction, the majority of them intercepted by asteroid debris which explodes and clouds up the surrounding area even more.

His attempt at finding a hide-away has failed, as entering the field is pretty much just putting his back to the wall in a dead-end cave. Al-Quam knows he has only seconds to make a decision. With the port thrust nozzle out of commission there is no way he can outrun or outmaneuver the Scourge.

Allah hates a coward, he thinks, and simultaneously engages the single point powering setting at full power and throws *The Spear of Allah* into a violent rotating circular spin.

A blue and white sphere of destructive force blooms forth in all directions

Major Ironbear gathers her wits and as many security and crew members as she can along the way to Deck Twelve. She finds over two dozen Marines waiting for her, fully armed and at the ready to man the available landing crafts. Teams are working with torches trying to unseal the landing bay doors, but it has been slow going. She gathers the Marines and other crewman and gives an assessment of the situation.

"We have hull breaches with Scourge boarding parties on Decks Four, Nine, and Ten. They are nightmarish and in force, but they are killable. They are big and they are strong, and I won't lie, it took three Marines to take down one of these nine-foot motherfuckers, we were lightly armed. Going forward that will not be the case. I will take the modified landing craft to provide cover fire outside of the hull for any more incoming boarding parties or other ships that want to wreck our day. I want the other three landing craft with chain guns and portable mini guns to do interior mop up by landing at the breach sites and following them in from behind. Everyone suit up as atmosphere will be at a premium at your locations. Clear the breaches and wait for the other counter-boarding party teams to get into position. I have coordinated with Captain Illiadus, and we have recon on current forward positions of Scourge forces moving through the ship. We will leave them no route to ingress or egress. Your mission is to insure they die in place."

Everyone suits up to watch the show. Major Ironbear powers up the modified landing craft and swings around to face a hangar door. A seamless blue acetylene arc appears, and the door vanishes. You could have heard a pin drop. The edges where the door hangar have been display a shearing effect, leaving a cold, smooth almost surgically defined surface behind. She reorients the ship, and another door disappears. Now the crewmen are cheering at the top of their lungs. With two hangar doors unsealed, the three of the remaining landing craft follow Major Ironbear into the void to bring chain guns to the fight against the boarders.

The Marines and crewmen who fought them internal to the ship, face to faceless, had little chance, during the initial minutes of the incursion. None to this point, except for Ironbear, has survived the encounters to tell the tale. Now the odds will be a little more even.

"Captain," Commander Aithon says from his station in the CIC, turning to stare at the sitting impassive form of his leader, "I can't do any more to help bring the array online. Commander Lehman has prepped a fighter for me in the hanger. Permission to leave the CIC and enter the battle."

The captain hesitates for less than a second.

"Godspeed, Commander," Illiadus's voice says from the intercom, "and good luck."

Major Ironbear has directed the landing craft to land on the hull of the *Ekatarina* astride the breaches. Each affair is different.

The incursion at Deck Nine does not have a follow-up force, so the landing party is able to come in from behind with no opposition until they reach the main body. Since this has been the group trailing Major Ironbear initially, a group with crew served weapons is already waiting for them on the other side. The Scourge make their stand in Bay Twenty-One, with mini guns to their rear and no path to escape. None of the Scourge can be taken alive. And all succumb to the relentless hum of the chain guns.

Deck Four is a completely different situation. Three Scourge landing craft are resting on the hull by the huge breach that extends from Bays

One through Seven, and Scourge are pouring into the opening. It is untenable for the landing craft to land on this occupied beachhead, so it fires missiles at the closest Scourge craft and opens up with chain guns to rake the forces moving within. At this point remaining crew in two of the Scourge boarding craft open fire with their breaching lasers, and the Marine lander takes a power hit that leaves it dead in space with no propulsion system. With no propulsion, the doomed craft is a sitting duck and is destroyed with a precision shot from one of the breaching lasers.

Major Ironbear brings the modified landing craft around and re-sets the pointing vectors to the size of a ship on the phased array mini-*Maw*. She then propels the landing craft head on in the direction of the second boarding craft with missiles firing and chain guns blazing at the first boarding craft. The two boarding-craft by this time have begun take off operations to leave the hull and become maneuverable. The engaged crew taking fire try an evasive maneuver to avoid the weapons fire. The other crew brace for impact. Impact is never felt as the ship dematerializes into "somewhere or somewhen else." The other ship in motion moves to evade, but a working space torpedo is launched from the *Ekatarina* and finds its mark.

Major Ironbear, then brings the landing craft in low, dematerializes the third un-crewed boarding craft, and after coordination to insure no crew are in harm's way, re-sets the parameters of the mini-*Maw* and digs a clean surgical trench along the entire length of the hull breach, vaporizing all the Scourge still within its confines, and annealing that portion of the hull, cauterizing it in effect so damage control efforts can be directed elsewhere.

Deck Ten is a horror show.

By the time Commander Aithon arrives at the metal doors of the prototype hanger on Deck Twelve where the X-craft rests, Ensign Thaleia is there waiting for him. She knows what he has to do but is not happy with it.

"You can't take the ship out into this fray untested, Sir," Ensign Thaleia protests.

Aithon is determined and unbending, "this is the kind of trial that can mean life or death for all the men and women aboard this station. It's worth the risk."

"Is it? What power supply do you intend to test? We have no idea of the effects of the larger power sources. The virtual power growth patterns are non linear and not modelled sufficiently. Besides, the larger power packs are subject to internal fluctuations. You can't be sure of their stability," Thaleia is vehement, pleading.

Aithon counters, saying, "this is a direct order, Ensign. Pick out the most stable of the larger power supplies that have been tested and install it. When I get clear of the ship, I will make sure I am far enough away from the *Ekatarina* to lessen the threat of collateral damage due to massive uncontrolled effects. I'd rather not test the system under this type of fire, but I don't see as we have an alternative. We need every weapon available to meet this threat, I really see no other choice."

"Damn you," Thaleia shouts, then rushes forward and presses her mouth roughly against his. Their kiss is sweet, tight, and all too short. Aithon reluctantly disengages, turns around, and enters his ship without looking back.

A single tear streaming down her scowling face, Thaleia quickly installs the power supply. Aithon settles into the pilot seat of the hastily christened *"Excalibur"* and gives her the thumbs up. Though tested in the lab at low powers, it is unknown just how devastating the power effects will be, and what intensity of time dilation will be experienced.

Thaleia leaves the hangar and seals it against the upcoming rapid decompression. The best she can do is watch her secret lover exit via closed circuit monitor. The hangar is sealed by the Scourge adhesive, and Aithon's only choice is to power up *The Maw*, and try an initial weapons test, at the lowest power setting, on the hanger bay doors.

He chooses the computer setting for a breach setting, with appropriate power and dimensions since those have at least been tested by the Marine Landing craft and holds his breath as he presses the controls. A seamless blue acetylene arc appears that is instantaneous in effect. A hole appears where the bulkhead and hangar bay doors had been. Without hesitation, *Excalibur* hurtles into space.

The Scourge forces that enter at Deck Ten are different than the rest. They are a smaller force, armed and armored and with a singular mission to accomplish - to destroy the CIC. They do not move along the hull, but immediately go to ground interior to the ship, where they split into groups and fan out across the decks and bays so their trajectory cannot be easily mapped by the *Ekatarina's* internal security screen. The landing craft that comes in through the breach is met initially with heavy fire from a small laser cannon. When they retreat to lob some flash bangs to neutralize the gunner, they discover it is a sentry gun set to automatic fire via radar motion sensor. After clearing it, they enter the breach to better reconnoiter the situation, but discover too late that the end of the first bay is rigged with fragmentation grenades and incendiaries tied to acid bombs and a remote-control detonation switch for the boarding craft. The grenades are basically claymores using the black obsidian shards of the entombment tar instead of ball bearing, and the acid burns through the deck followed by a stream of incendiary like napalm. The remote-control detonates explosives on the boarding craft, and it becomes one very large acid bomb melting its way through the hull. The landing party never has a chance.

Major Ironbear quickly sizes up the situation and realizes that the speed with which the acid is burning through the hull will take it to the engine room in short order, and does the only thing she can to slow it down, she steers her modified landing craft into the hole to follow it down and readjusts the mini-Maw. Five decks within she has finally contained the acid bath, but the landing craft is damaged as secondary explosions from above hurled debris upon the craft and destroy steering.

Before she powers the craft down and gathers her squad of Marines and their weapons to begin their exit out of an escape hatch that is unblocked by debris, she checks in again with the Captain.

"Sorry I had to take this weapon out of the fight, Captain. Where are the nearest hostiles?"

Captain Illiadus replies. "It would appear that they have split up into several heavily armored teams that are heading either towards main propulsion or the CIC. We have taken severe casualties in all engagements so far with these teams. Chain guns and lasers appear useless. One group was taken out by a torpedo that was rolled in on cart and remotely detonated, but the damage was severe to eight adjoining bays. One team following the incendiary and acidic stream down the crevice was met with a hand launched missile during descent. Again, the interior damage was severe. We can't take too much more of this. Near as we can tell, they split into four teams of two. At this point we believe there are two teams left. Decks Five through Ten have also experienced an interior EMP and are on limited backup power, so I no longer have eyes or ears in those corridors. I would assume they are headed towards CIC. Make your way here and we will make our last stand if we have to."

"Commander Aithon," Illiadus's voice comes from his earpiece, "delay the enemy, whatever it takes. We need time. Even minutes will suffice."

"Acknowledged," Aithon replies, frowning at the unusual mechanical inflections in the Captain's voice. Who knows what that damned helmet is doing to her brain? He grits his teeth and puts all focus on the forward control panel.

Excalibur rapidly shoots away from the Ekatarina toward the approaching enemy. A dozen tactical scenarios flash through the Commander's mind but none have the luxury of time or testing to be considered safe or trustworthy. The immediate situation requires a direct intervention with zero delay, or else the ship and her crew are doomed.

Aithon grits his teeth as his mind shoots back over the intervening years between the present and when the Scourge Sphere had first been destroyed. Like the majority of the *Ekatarina's* original crew, and that of their long dead sister ship *Sophia*, Aithon had aggressively volunteered for the suicide mission meant to commit Xenocide against the Scourge aggressors. Like most of his fellow crewmen and Marines, he had suffered greatly during the war. The entire Terran colony he had been raised on, the planet Hephaestus, was mercilessly slaughtered by the Scourge. Grandparents, parents, aunts, uncles, brothers, sisters, cousins… his betrothed… all dead. It was a wound he hid behind duty and false smiles for years, but it had never healed. More than anything he had wanted to be part of the Polisian volunteers that had crewed *The Revenge*, the name given to the overhauled and captured Scourge ship that had snuck the Dark Matter Fountain device within striking distance of the Scourge Dyson Sphere.

Aithon realizes that now he is being given a second chance to embrace his deepest foulest hatred and act upon it. He looks into his soul and admits the truth of his dark desire. In this moment he will become the hand of righteous retribution. He will become death.

Without further thought the Commander shoves his fist into the center of *The Maw's* circular red ignition pad.

Excalibur's Maw traces out an arc of blue lightning, that extends to its maximum circular aperture (one that actually dwarfs the *Ekatarina* by its sheer magnitude). Commander Aithon places *Excalibur* between the ship and the incoming Scourge horde. He flies straight for the heart of the enemy armada between the massive ships at full throttle, and as the first units open fire on him, he pumps the power to max and sets the craft into a deliberate spin, spiraling ferociously into the horde.

"Mother," Aithon says in a low voice, "I'm coming home."

The universe explodes in a miasma of millions of lightning bolts.

No one is really sure how the two massive Scourge ships and most of their fleet disappeared into a retreating wall of lightning. The scientists on the *Ekatarina* theorized that Commander Aithon ripped a hole in the very fabric of space-time by creating a vortex, into which he dove, consuming the armada by dragging it into the virtual substructure with him by his forward momentum. They could only conjecture, but whatever tactic he used, it worked.

"Ironbear," the Captain's voice speaks with an eerie calm from the Major's earpiece, "a Scourge boarding party is closing in on the CIC via the sick bay. You are the closest unencumbered team at this moment. I need five more minutes to get the remaining beamsteering antennas back online. You must intercept the enemy immediately."

"Roger that," Ironbear shouts.

Major Ironbear and her Marines turn a corner and hear a moan and find a dying corpsman just outside of sick bay. He is missing both legs but has managed to crawl out the door. The Scourge team have made their way to the infirmary which is adjacent to the CIC. It is the path of least resistance. Everyone is dead or dying, there is no one left to fight.

The Major knows they will punch a hole through the bulkhead to get to CIC, so they have to act fast. Crewed chain guns, mini-guns and missiles are the stock and trade of the boarding party. But standard missiles will do too much damage this close to the CIC. They do have one missile type that is made up of a spread of smaller missiles, based on the old anti-personnel flechettes rounds, so those are what they bring, along with a rotating barrel style grenade launcher. Less kinetic punch, less collateral damage, so every shot needs to count. The major splits her squad into two teams of four. Each team will have a single designated target and will concentrate all firepower on the head.

The carnage in sick bay is beyond description. Blood and gore are everywhere, the floor glistens wet with it. Footing is going to be tricky, but there are no options. The two Scourge are the eyeless type but with an orifice filled with teeth like shards of obsidian, wearing an armored double carapace front and back that also looks to be obsidian. And a small helmet to protect top and back of the head. They are forming what looks to be a shape charge against the bulkhead.

The two teams swing into action, each laying down a base of fire with chain guns. The round ricochets off the carapaces and helmets with no effect. The Scourge ignores the rounds and keeps working. Both teams cease firing to conserve ammo until they can get a better shot. Major Ironbear enters the room on the right with a grenade launcher, while Gunny Matheson does the same from the left. Each has six flechette rounds. They move along the wall until they can see the faceless visage without protection of the helm, and then fire the first round of flechettes. Both flinch and turn their helms in time to block the darts. The two firers adjust position so they can each fire two rounds in rapid succession, one at each head. This time both receive injuries to the faceless visage.

One turns to charge Gunny Matheson, and the chain guns and miniguns open fire with a clear shot to the head. It goes down. The other slams home an igniter, and the bulkhead bursts into flame and begins to melt. When it takes a step back, Ironbear closes with it and fires point blank into the faceless being. It crumples from the impact. It is then she hears the screams.

The final two Scourge enter from the rear of the room, and while the two teams are engaged with Scourge targeting Matheson, are taken by surprise. These are large winged Scourge with spiked tails and reflective armor plating around the legs, arms and chest to deflect lasers. The one entering on the left grabs one Marine in each taloned claw by the head and crushes their skulls, then sends the tail darting to eviscerate the other. The one that enters on the right tries the same but is not as lucky. While the crewed chain gun merely stops firing, the eviscerated Marine manages to point his minigun in his dying moment toward the second Scourge. Its left wing crumples, and it falls into the three Marines still standing and firing. Matheson closes the distance and fires his last two flechettes at the Scourge with both wings intact as it flies towards the now visible opening into the CIC.

The rounds connect and it plummets to the floor, but it lands on its feet. The spiked tail makes a broad arch and skewers Matheson then slams his corpse into the bulkhead. Ironbear takes a carefully aimed shot with her grenade launcher, the flechettes annihilate the head of the creature that kills Matheson. Then she heads for the melee on the ground.

"Look out," Tiresias yells to the two ship Marines and Petty Officer Second Class Morahan, but too late. A huge hole in the overhead bulkhead appears and partially melted acid covered steel falls down with a loud thud, killing all three instantly. The sounds of weapons fire and yells of pain echo downward from the exposed portion of the sick bay which has been breached.

"Captain," Tiresias turns to the mannikin-like Captain, "we need to abandon the CIC immediately."

"Belay that order," the Captain's calm but firm voice shoots forth from the intercom. Finish re-linking the beamsteering array. That's an order."

Doing their best to ignore the sounds of battle just meters away, the remaining CIC crew quickly completes their final tasks.

"Captain," Lt. Commander Lehman says, "we're back up. Charging for ignition in thirty seconds and counting."

Suddenly, the most ferocious scream Tiresias has ever heard in her life echoes downward from the massive hole in the upper bulkhead. This is followed by a short swatch of gunfire and a large thud, and then silence.

Something undefinable pulls at Tiresias's inner soul and she abandons her station and runs toward the large gap between decks.

The full weight of the Scourge that has fallen on the Marines makes it impossible to aim the big weapons. They are splayed and weighted down, thrashing and unable to take a shot. One pulls a large survival knife and begins to stab at the reflective armor, but it will not give. Since the beast is using the good wing to pin one the Marines, he stabs it instead. That brings an immediate reaction from the tail, which impales the Marine. The talons from the beast on the good wing now freed, they find their mark, and that allows the last Marine, Gunnery Sergeant Bryce to push out from underneath the beast and scoot on all fours towards the Major who is closing in.

The Major aims a running shot, but her boot heel catches a piece of someone's liver and slips to the ground hard. The round goes off, but only catches the good wing, so the fight is not over yet. The beast stands between the two Marines.

Ironbear still has her sidearm and her tomahawk. Bryce has a knife and a sidearm. Ironbear pulls her sidearm and goes to fire at the beast's head when a wave of time dilation effect sweeps across the ship and causes a massive mind blink.

The beast moves and the rounds miss. Disoriented, she shakes it off and tries again. The beast parries with its tail, knocking the gun from her hand.

The Major's next decision occurs in a microsecond and she makes it without hesitation. Had Ironbear ducked to take cover, Bryce would have been killed. If she leaped away to scoop up a fallen weapon the Scourge would have been beelined to enter the CIC.

Ironbear takes choice three, pulls out her tomahawk and runs straight at the towering monster.

"Ohkwa:ri'!" the Major screams and leaps, acknowledging her mother's ancient Akwesasne clan and swings her tactical tomahawk in a vicious lightning-fast overhead arc.

Ironbear cleaves the deadly tail clean from the body of the beast, and in its final death throes swings one of its wings wildly, impacting the Major's abdomen, and knocking her across the hallway to slam brutally against a bulkhead.

With the wave of dizziness passing, Bryce, awestruck, fires six rounds point blank at the head of the Scourge, and most find their mark.

It collapses.

Seconds later the frightened head of Crewman Tiresias peers through the hole in the bulkhead from the CIC to see the final moments of the fateful stand-off.

Tiresias jumps up, runs forward, and drops to one knee beside Ironbear who sits slumped against the bulkhead the Scourge's strike had thrown her against. One glance tells the crewman that the Major is beyond help. A death rattle escapes the fallen warrior whose visage is frozen in bare teeth, a feral snarl that reflects a complete absence of fear.

Tiresias reaches up and closes Ironbear's eyes, then turns around and runs back to the CIC, shedding tears for the first time since she has boarded this incredible ship.

When Captain Illiadus came too, earlier in the battle, about two minutes after she had initially fallen unconscious, she had instantly realized she was no longer completely human. She is now fully conscious, and aware of the fact that she is one with the computer and her senses are now capable of simultaneous thoughts across multiple threads. Whereas before she took a back seat to SIBIL for the first wave of counteractions, she now is gaining control of her mind in a way that she can understand all the simultaneity at once in the computer parallel processing sense, and yet still be witting in the more human sense. Her earlier bout of multiple transmitted commands had not been sequential, but simultaneous, all signals sent directly from her thoughts at the exact same time. In her metaphorical hands, the *Ekatarina* has been reacting to all elements of the surprise Scourge attack as a living creature, aware of every atrocity committed against it, and reacting instantly.

Though Commander Aithon and Major Ironbear have sacrificed themselves to save the *Ekatarina*, the battle is not over yet. Illiadus stuffs the shock and grief deep down under waves of darkness to be resurrected at some later time.

There are still about two hundred Scourge ships left along the fringes, although many are damaged from emp effects and time distortions.

Somehow, Al-Quam has survived his fight in the nearby asteroid belt and is just now rejoining the battle. *The Spear of Allah* commences targeting the rear flank of the remaining attacking enemy. Though he is taking large bites out their attack formation, it will be too little too late.

Scanning the space around the *Ekatarina*, the Captain sees that there is also debris left from countless ships that experienced the spatial shearing effect, leaving smooth surgical seams behind on space hulks that are not completely vaporized. They are not the only ones affected. The recoil experienced in the time field left everyone on the *Ekatarina* disoriented, and it will take a long time to ensure that all time dependent mechanisms aboard ship are resynchronized.

"Chief," Illiadus speaks in Al-Quam's earpiece, "exit my firing solution immediately or you'll be touring Allah's grand palace in a matter of seconds."

"Aye, Captain," Al-Quam replies, and departs with haste.

None of the remaining Scourge missile-drones or small attack craft choose to follow him. Their revenge-filled hearts only have eyes for the *Ekatarina*.

Illiadus then gives up control of the Apot weapons system to SIBIL.

"All targets in sector seven - fire at will! All targets in sector six – fire at will!"

First by ones, then twos, and then dozens at a time, the flashes marking multiple implosions fill the space around the *Ekatarina* like a glorious fireworks display. Eventually, every single Scourge target in every sector implodes into nothingness.

The Scourge/Polisian War is finally over.

The Spear of Allah returns through one of the unsealed hangars, and Al-Quam kisses the deck of the ship in homage to a God that allows him to delight to slay and live to tell of it.

The *P.W. Ekatarina* is badly damaged and significant crew are lost, so repairs will be hamstrung. And perhaps now the Scourge have finally been defeated - but at what cost?

Throughout the entire battle, Captain Illiadus has observed and recorded where she can the cruel barbarities of the Scourge. During every moment of the entire awful engagement no Scourge spoke or attempted to communicate with their victims or to her when she tried to hail them.

None of the enemy would entertain the thought of surrender (not that Illiadus would offer terms other than as a ploy to stall them). Quantifying all of the after-action data is a detached, surreal realization of losses that is clinical and calculated. In the back of her mind, she needs to mourn, but cannot just yet.

Captain Illiadus's cyborg mind realizes conceptually that she needs to mourn the loss of Commander Aithon and Major Ironbear too, in a deeper way, but she cannot wrap her head around it. She is feeling distant, like her humanity is lost to her, and yet she can still feel it, but as a single stream of thought buries amid a multitude of competing streams of thought that is simultaneously assessing damage, working to repair hull breaches, redirecting power grids, assigning work gangs, and a countless array of operational and housekeeping tasks.

With the fight over, she succumbs to the intrinsic beauty of being able to work at this new "ops tempo," and begins to concentrate on working damage control in earnest.

But then her multi-threaded mind lets her humanity have a fleeting thought, perhaps as a concession to her sanity, *I used to joke - I will have plenty of time to sleep after I am dead. Now that I am one with this ship, will I ever be able to truly sleep again?*

Captain's Log, The Ekatarina

We have survived the last battle with the remnants of The Scourge. Our advanced Cerridian technology, and the exceptional bravery of my fearless crew, have granted us a costly victory. The casualty count is high, and the ship has received excessive damage. I believe, however, that we will be back on our way towards Earth sooner than expected. It is difficult to describe this newly enhanced cognitive state that is my mind. Decision-making and calculations are tasks I can complete in ridiculously short amounts of time. There is a clarity of thought and perception that I've never had before. I am committed more than ever to getting The Ekatarina home. End Log.

The Gods Anointed

by Jason Cordova

Ship's Chronometer: 2452.1 AD

The medals go on first, each resplendent with bright colors and inlaid with gold and silver throughout. Each are pinned at precisely one-eighth of an inch apart, layered in rows of four. Next, his blue shoulder cord, signifying his rank of command over the Marines on board the *Ekatarina*. A responsibility he does not want but is forced to accept when his commander, confidante, and role model, the posthumously promoted Colonel Helen Ironbear, was slain in the recent battle against THE SCOURGE.

She was the pillar of the Marines, the hard, never breaking rock that they all drew strength from. She died at the end of the battle, holding back the aliens with nothing more than a tomahawk and sheer willpower. Ironbear bought enough time for the Marines to rally and exterminate the boarders and for the CIC to get the beamsteering array for Ekatarina's new *spooky* weapon back online to destroy the last of the suicidal Scourge Flotilla – at the too-high cost of her own life, leaving former Gunnery Sergeant Josiah Bryce in command with his recent field commission to Lieutenant Commander of Marines.

He swings his saber to his left hip, handle gleaming from polish and great care. The scabbard is worn but serviceable, with the gold emblem of the Marines embedded prominently.

He checks his pant legs and is satisfied with the sharp creases, while his shoes are properly shined. His blouse is perfectly ironed, medals and ribbons adorning it in their proper positions, not a stray piece of lint to be found anywhere. On his right hip is his service pistol, the ancient and venerable weapon of the commander of a Marine expeditionary force. A force admittedly so small that he can barely run a standard watch cycle while not in cryosleep yet required by duty and honor to do just that.

He is physically prepared for the upcoming memorial service. Mentally and emotionally, however, he is uncertain he can do it. His psyche is chasing something, grasping at ethers as it struggles to keep him going. He needs more time, yet tradition dictates that the burial at sea happen as fast as possible. It is not enough time for him to grieve, to reminisce, to drink and forget. There is not enough chance of deep wounds being healed in such a short amount of time.

"Lieutenant Commander Bryce, your presence is requested by the captain in the C-I-C at your earliest convenience," SIBIL whispers softly into the dark. He grimaces. He dislikes the ship AI, though he is very careful not to say anything untoward out loud. He does not know how sentient the machine is, and the last thing he needs to do is to hurt the feelings of a machine that controls the environmental settings while the entire crew is in cold sleep.

"Acknowledged," Bryce says and snaps the holster on his pistol closed.

"Please note further," SIBIL continues, "when circumstances allow, it is highly recommended you schedule a meeting with a ship's psychological counselor. Standard review of ship's visual recordings show an inappropriate increase of incidences of headaches, paranoia, imbibing, mood swings, and sleep disturbances in your personal daily profile."

"Sure," Bryce snaps sarcastically, "I'll get right on it."

Bryce rubs his chest as a familiar ache near his heart flares back up. A few moments later it fades, leaving him with an odd sensation in his arm. *Strange*, he thinks as he double-checks his black and brown Marine uniform. Firearm secured, he leaves the darkened room and enters the busy corridor.

The area around his temporary quarters is chaotic, completely at odds with the serene, peaceful setting of his bunk. Random crewmen are laying atop gurneys, waiting for their turn to be seen by the overworked and understaffed corpsmen of the *Ekatarina*, wounds patched as best as the tired men and women can manage. Occasionally he passes a gurney with a plain white sheet pulled over a body; he ignores these as best as he can. They are not Marines – the deceased have been prepped for the burial hours before by the Marine's corpsman.

"How's it going, Commander?" a friendly voice comes from nearby. Bryce pauses for a second before remembering that *he* is the person being addressed. He turns his head and comes face to face with the woman who the Marines have come to loathe in the years about the *Ekatarina*: the just promoted Lieutenant Thaleia (now a First Lieutenant in her new post, Cybernetics Division).

"Good, Sir," he responds carefully. Even though he is certain he outranks her, the unease he feels when addressing others who have been officers before his jump in promotion prohibits him from becoming familiar with them. Thus, even a Lieutenant is treated with the utmost respect and care. Respect, because she is an officer still. Care, because Bryce isn't quite certain that he knows just whose side the young Lieutenant is on.

"Called to the C-I-C too?" she asks, her positive tone completely at odds with the desolation around them. He cocks his head and looks at her, a troubling thought on the edge of his mind. It is as though the young cybernetics engineer has a bubble around her and is unaffected by the carnage of the wounded or the wonders of the screeching self-repairing Cerridian hulls and bulkheads all around them. Rumor has it she had been hot and heavy with the late Commander Aithon, though you'd never know the second-in-command had just heroically given his life a full day ago wiping out over half of the attacking Scourge flotilla with one of the *Ekatarina's* new superweapons mounted on ship shuttle. Lieutenant Thaleia seems perfectly calm. Bryce has read about something similar once, long ago. *Dissociative* empathy, he remembers vaguely as the Lieutenant continues.

"I have a new idea I've run through with Engineering about possibly getting us back home faster. Engineering likes it but we have to convince the Captain. And–" she jabs her finger at his chest "–that includes all senior officers, since she's not fully recovered from the AI integration yet. Meaning you, Commander."

I boarded this ship a bloody private! he wants to scream at the young genius with the body of a gymnast and the looks of a vidscreen star. A private. That is all he was when he had been assigned to the *Ekatarina*. A private straight out of boot, on his first duty station, thrust into the middle of a bloody war. He has been forced into action dozens of times throughout the years as more and more responsibility has fallen to him and his enlisted rank increased all too regularly. His brothers and sisters in arms, alien and human alike, have died with little or no warning whatsoever. Their replacements have died even quicker, their lack of fine training and sense of team camaraderie putting them at a distinct disadvantage during boarding and repelling actions. He has been promoted quickly, mostly because of his ability to stay alive, though some have been due to meritorious advancement and, in one case, his actions during that damned mutiny which had severely divided Marine and Sailor alike. He smiles as a fond memory of Ironbear ripping him a new one for recklessness while pinning sergeant's stripes onto his chest flitted through his mind.

"I remember when I first got Sergeant Stripes, son," the Major had said, "my balls felt like brass for a whole month."

She's dead. They're all dead now. Like I **should be**. *Like we all* **will** *be.*

The smile vanishes as quickly as it appeared. The pain near his heart is growing, and he briefly wonders if he needs to go see the corpsman about it. But what can a corpsman do about a wounded heart?

"Are you feeling well?" the Lieutenant asks. Bryce looks at her and offers a weak smile.

"Just tired," he admits after a moment of thought. "We've been running round-the-clock shifts since–"

"Oh, wow, us too!" Thaleia exclaims, interrupting him. "We've been running ourselves ragged trying to keep up with all these untested Cerridian repairbots coming to life and engaging in unapproved retrofits never even considered by the manual. This old junker is full of surprises. I told Lt. Commander, I mean, Commander Lehman that we need a complete structural review and possible overhaul after this unusual series of repairs, and of course as the *Ekatarina's* former Chief Engineer he starts going on about the new design of the ship, being what it is, can't handle any more experimental retrofits beyond what we had done in the Cerridian shipyards, especially while moving faster than point-oh-two..."

Bryce tunes her out, focusing instead on the mental list of dead he is preparing to read off today. Kallikos. G'zrnth. Correia. Michaels-Douglas. The twins, Herzen and Blergz. Each a Marine in his, her or – in the case of G'zrnth, its – own way.

Each sworn to uphold and defend the Marine tradition, each giving all when it was demanded of them. His speech is already prepared. Now he just needs to come up with more courage to read it at the memorial service. He needs to be strong for the remaining Marines.

They round a corner together and come to a halt as a group of crewmen are furiously working on a damaged bulkhead. Part of the press gang the captain had instituted months before. *Or was it, years*, Bryce wonders. The chronometer says one thing, but a small part of his subconscious tells him another. Two feelings, both distinct, both demanding, neither fully correct. He rubs his temple with his fingers as the familiar pulsing of a migraine begins to form.

"I hope this is over quickly," he mutters aloud. Thaleia turns and looks at him.

"What do you mean?" she asks, her expression curious.

"I just... I'm not used to dealing with officers," he amends, catching himself. He offers her a small, comforting smile. "I was a Gunnery Sergeant, yesterday."

"Nonsense," she snorts. "You would be, at least, a Second Lieutenant by now, even if you hadn't received all those meritorious advancements."

He shrugs his shoulders. He does not feel like explaining himself to her.

The C-I-C is dark and warm, situated deep within the bowels of the ship. Lines are strung haphazardly throughout, each feeding into a relay conduit, all originating from the same chair. The Captain's chair. Bryce shivers as he recognizes what the lines are for.

Consoles are dimmed, showing that much of the C-I-C has been replaced by SIBIL and the Captain. The command deck used to hold over a dozen highly specialized crewmen, all of whom had a specific job to accomplish. Now, with the further discoveries of SIBIL's capabilities and the Captain's own use of the Quantum helmet have made the C-I-C a very lonely place.

Seated in the chair, Captain Illiadus is a sight to behold. Fully integrated with the SIBIL, the Captain's head is covered by an unwieldy helmet, which strictly limits her mobility to the cocooned couch she is lying upon. Her scars, which are nearly everywhere that is not covered by her uniform, are a bright contrast to her skin. Bryce, with Thaleia standing next to him, waits patiently for the captain to acknowledge them.

"You called, Captain?" Thaleia asks. Bryce frowns at her breach of proper protocol but says nothing.

"One moment," Illiadus murmurs softly, her voice musical and aloof as she speaks to them from thirteen different parts of the ship. "Assisting with the calibration of... got it. As soon as Engineering and Ensign Tiresias are here, we shall begin."

"Yes Captain," Bryce nods and waits. He still does not understand why a meeting of the senior officers requires him to be there, even if he is the ranking Marine. He tries to recall any time that Ironbear had rushed off to the C-I-C.

Of course, she never rushed off, a small voice in the back of his mind says.

"Captain, we have the cranial implant ready for insertion shortly after this meeting," Thaleia states, ignoring the Captain yet again. Bryce bites his tongue and tries not to chew the young woman a new one.

"Memorial service for the Marine contingent is at sixteen hundred today," Captain Illiadus proclaims, her voice tinged with exhaustion. She nods at Bryce. "Commander Bryce will be leading the service. My advice, Bryce? Keep it short and sweet. We have too much work to do. Don't act like you regret the actions of those who died and keep it upbeat. Good morale is dependent upon the senior officers, and that includes you now."

"Yes Sir," Bryce nods. *What else can I say?* He wonders.

"Anything else?" the captain asks. Lieutenant Thaleia pushes past the Marine.

"We've come up with an idea to get us home faster, Captain," Thaleia announces. "The Eng and I. Involving an untried use of the Dark Arteries and the new Quantum Cranial Interface. It's dangerous, but we're pretty sure that it'll help us get home much faster than originally planned. There's just one tiny little catch, however."

"Okay, let's go over it. Commander? You're dismissed."

"Yes Sir," Bryce salutes, pivots on his heel and walks quickly out of the C-I-C. A waste of time, as he had expected. She had told him everything he had already known, reiterating it in front of all the senior officers. *Why,* he wonders. *Why would she make certain I know to keep it short? Doesn't she think I can plan a memorial service?*

No, she doesn't, he answers his own question. He walks the gangways of the *Ekatarina* aimlessly, lost in his thoughts. *She* knows just as well as you that you are nothing more than a jumped-up private, incapable of doing anything more than fight or stand watch. She is taking on my duties as well as her own, just to keep this old tub running.

Bryce stops in the middle of a bustling corridor and looks at the men, women and aliens of the *Ekatarina*. He hardly knows any of them, recognizes even less. They are strangers to him, yet even the lowliest of them seem to know how to do their job. Their function. Their duty. He doesn't. Not in the least.

"Commander?" a grainy voice asks from his elbow. Bryce looks and sees one of the diminutive new Marine recruits standing there, braced stiffly at attention. He/it/She is one of the smaller Teenerian arachnid contingent. Bryce sighs.

"Yes?" he asks as he racks his brain trying to remember the name of the alien. Griz? *Gruz? Something like that.*

"Marine Recruit Chuff, sir," the alien states from his translation speaker.

"Yes, Recruit Chuff?" *I wasn't even remotely close*, Bryce inwardly sighs. *How did Ironbear do it?*

"Corporal Naismith requested that I fill out my Eye-Dee-Ten-Tee form as soon as possible. I have been all over this ship, sir, and I am unable to locate such a form," Chuff declares, his voice neutral. Bryce cocks an eyebrow.

"An Eye-Dee-Ten-Tee form? Hmmm..." he thinks for a moment before smiling. "You might want to try Master Sergeant Humboldt."

"Ah, I did not think to ask him, sir," the recruit swallows nervously. "Thank you for your assistance, sir."

"That was highly unprofessional of you, as an officer," a voice from behind says. He turns and sees that the blue-skinned and petitely attractive Ensign Farko Tiresias standing behind him, her arms crossed before her.

"Colonel Ironbear was above the games played by enlisted. You need to be above it, too," Tiresias says, "just one more thing I've had to implement myself since I read and memorized the entire Polisian Naval Officer's Guide, Fifth Edition, last night... all two thousand pages of it. A fascinating manual, considering it covers most command contingencies for a Space Navy consisting of over two hundred different star-faring races."

I'm doing the best I can! he screams inwardly. He schools his outward features so that the Ensign cannot see just how frustrated he is.

"Thank you, Ensign," he says, his voice slightly stiff. He smiles at her. "I'm still learning how to do this *officer* thing."

"Well, just remember that as an officer," Tiresias says, "you have to be better than them. Which means staying away from their hazing games."

"Right," Bryce nods, his moment of joy at helping the other Marines with their time-honored tradition gone as swiftly as it had come. "Thank you again, Ensign."

"Just trying to help," she says and wanders off, leaving Bryce alone with his thoughts once more.

"Our motto is simple: Give All," Bryce says, "we have fought, and we have died. We have paid the ultimate sacrifice, given our all, to ensure that the crew of the *Ekatarina* – our fellow brethren in our long journey home – would be able to complete their mission. We few who remain are all that is left of a core of men and women sworn to uphold and defend all that civilized species deem important. It is our duty, yet it is more than that. It is our calling as Marines."

Bryce pauses for a short moment to look down upon the many coffins and the majority of the crew in full dress uniforms standing at full attention in the main internal flight hanger.

"But in the end... we few, we precious few, gathered to remember our fallen comrades..." Bryce stumbles.

Then suddenly, without notice, that awful, strange, phantom ache near his heart returns, stronger than ever before, flooding his chest, squeezing his throat, and filling his entire body with a weakness and despair born of the darkest depression he has ever known. Images of all his fellow marines who have died since The Scourge were defeated fill his mind, their bruised, swollen, bleeding faces staring at him, accusingly...

"Ah," Bryce shouts, "who the fuck am I kidding? I can't do this fucking job. I'm horrible at speeches. I'm just some goddamned, no-name private who wanted to see the stars."

In one smooth and practiced motion Lieutenant Commander Josiah Vincento Bryce, Bronze Star winner, multiple Purple Heart recipient, hero during the mutinous uprising, survivor of THE SCOURGE, and acting Commander of Marine Expeditionary Force Euripides, whips out his highly polished pistol and presses the barrel against his head.

"I'm sorry, Colonel Ironbear," he whispers, and then pulls the trigger.

His world goes black.

Captain's Log, The Ekatarina

Our one hundred and forty-first, and final dark energy artery jump has commenced. The entire crew, including myself, is in coldsleep. I, however, mentally endure. End Log.

Homecoming

by Michael H. Hanson

Happily may their roads back home be on the trail of pollen.
Happily may they all get back.
In beauty I walk.
With beauty before me, I walk.
With beauty behind me, I walk.
With beauty below me, I walk.
With beauty above me, I walk.
With beauty all around me, I walk.
It is finished in beauty,
It is finished in beauty,
It is finished in beauty,
It is finished in beauty.

'Sa'ah naaghéi, Bik'eh hózhó
—Navajo Enemy Way Ceremony

Ship's Chronometer: 2551 AD

Fleet Captain Tennyson Maria Illiadus slowly wakes up. At least, that is, her physical body does. Her mind, you see, has never really fallen asleep. For the last ninety-nine years, Ship Time, she and the rest of the crew have physiologically aged mere months in their cold-sleep coffins.

The combination of chemically-induced coma and body temperature reduction have slowed their metabolisms to a fraction of their normal state. The years pass rapidly in the form of blissfully unaware and dreamless sleep… for all but the Captain. For such is her fate upon this last leg of The Ekatarina's journey back to Earth through a dark energy artery that she does not share the ship's group slumber.

Unlike the rest of her crew, human and non-human alike, shortly after entering her sleep chamber which rapidly flooded with cryo-gel, Illiadus's mind did not dive into the darkness beneath the familiar waves of cognition. Though blood flow through her brain had quickly come to a near stop, and most activity had ceased among the majority of network hubs in the connectome, the Captain remained conscious.

The reason, of course, is obvious, though no less of a shock when Illiadus first strides into the virtual reality sim of the CIC crewed solely by the A.I. SIBIL, fit and trim in a well-tailored one-piece fleet uniform. Her hair in a regulation bob, SIBIL appears to be in her late thirties, or possibly early forties… the Captain can never be one hundred percent sure.

"They said this might happen," Illiadus says, "but that there was less than a twenty-five percent probability."

"Quite so," SIBIL replies in her beautiful well-modulated voice, "though I believe I have an answer to the mystery."

"Somehow," Illiadus chuckles, "I'm not surprised. So, tell me, why am I not snoring away like the rest of the crew."

"While it is true that only the purely autonomic hubs in your organic brain are displaying neuronal activity," SIBIL says, "the quantum interface surgically implanted in your left forehead is operating at peak efficiency."

Almost unconsciously the Captain raises her left hand to feel the almost ornamental looking chunk of silver-titanium alloy that looks to be glued to half of her forehead that in fact not only penetrates skin and bone, but also pierces the cerebral mantle in one thousand places via a series of synthetic neural tissue bridges, most of them anchored in the corpus callosum.

"I assumed you would wish to maintain your waking appearance in the Sim. The work of Lieutenant Terry Thaleia and Ensign Farko Tiresias has exceeded my best expectations," SIBIL says, "their ingenious fabrication and programming, and Doctor Sorlan's exquisitely steady surgical handiwork, appear to be flawless."

The Captain nods to herself. Though a noticeable distraction on her skull, the small quantum interface is a major improvement on all previous incarnations of the bulky and uncomfortable quantum helmet she has worn over the years.

In the days following the bloody battle with the remnants of The Scourge military, a radical redressing of the ranks, especially among the Officers and NCOs, had occurred. Over half of the middle ranks are now occupied by non-Terran stock, and Illiadus can't help but note that only one-third of The Ekatarina's original human crew have survived to this date.

The aftermath of the battle has left the ship dangerously understaffed, but the true value of the originally indentured aliens from Teeneria has proven most fortuitous, for in secret anticipation of just such a disaster, they had laid several hundred hibernating eggs, a large number of which were chemically activated to a stage of alarmingly rapid gestation.

Within twenty-four hours of the surprise Scourge attack over one hundred fully-grown Teenerian crew members, each possessing the genetic memories of their egg-progenitors and of course driving the *Ekatarina's* Logistics Specialist to a near state of apoplexy, reported fit and ready for duty. Combined with The *Ekatarina's* eye-opening miracle of self-repairing ship's systems and nano-bots courtesy of the vessel's Purple Planet upgrade, the pocket-battleship is ship-shape and ready for travel in a mere six days.

"So why, exactly, am I conscious?" Illiadus asks.

"Hypothetically," SIBIL says, "the quantum interface has the memory storage capability of over two dozen petabytes. I believe that when it is activated, a virtual back-up, if you will, is made of your conscious, and possibly unconscious, mind. When you succumb to your sleep coma, your virtual mind becomes self-aware."

"You're saying I'm just a copy of Captain Illiadus?" Illiadus says, "a digital ghost that's going to be wiped out, erased, the moment she wakes up?"

"Not at all, Captain," SIBIL says reassuringly, "your organic mind and the quantum interface are, for all intents and purposes, *one* mind. When your body wakes up, the connection will open and everything that has occurred in your artificial telencephalon will be immediately accessed and shared by your neocortex. Your continuity of thought will be unbroken. Trust me, you *are* Captain Tennyson Maria Illiadus."

The Captain exhales a mouthful of virtual air and purses her lips.

"So…" the Captain stares off at a bulkhead as if she can see the stars outside, "our navigation estimates implied dozens of years."

"Possibly more," SIBIL replies, "and we'll of course get much more accurate estimates the closer we get to our destination."

"And I'll be awake the whole time?" Illiadus asks, "what a strange concept."

"I think it best," SIBIL replies, "to emulate your waking life as close as possible. With this in mind, I will allow your meta-consciousness to maintain a standard twenty-four-hour life cycle, with sleep occurring for eight hours each day… with your permission, Sir."

"Approved," Illiadus says, "and it of course goes without saying you'll wake me at any time in the case of even the most minor of emergencies, and yes, that is an order."

"Yes, Sir," SIBIL says.

"Dozens of years…" Illiadus says.

"Or maybe longer," SIBIL adds.

"Other than overseeing ship's operations," Illiadus muses, "whatever will we do?"

"Whatever we want," SIBIL smiles, "the main computer's memory core contains the bulk of the Terran Interplanetary Library, fiction, nonfiction, history… and I can virtualize any and all of it as interactive scenarios. Why don't we start with an adventure right now? The ship is operating at peak efficiency and there are no predictable hazards popping up in the streaming temporal matrix mapped out for the next two weeks."

The Captain takes a full minute to consider the offer.

"What I want," Illiadus says, "is to review every single thing that has occurred on The *Ekatarina* from the moment we witnessed the destruction of the Scourge Dyson Sphere right up to the present. I want you to incorporate every single stored recording of everything that occurred on and off the ship, in orbit, and even on away missions, and play it all back, from every possible viewpoint, in fully interactive virtual mode, in perceptual real time."

"My psychology and psychiatry sub-programs are raising a lot of red flags, Captain," SIBIL says, "and suggesting a fixation bordering on mania, not to mention, it will take a heck of a lot of years to relive everything the ship has experienced."

"There is more to history than a bunch of cold digital files, SIBIL," Illiadus says, "and living memory is the greatest tribute I can give to the sacrifice this crew has given. I want to know and experience every minute, every second, no, every moment of The *Ekatarina's* existence since we sent the Scourge straight to hell. And let's start right now."

Instantly, Illiadus finds herself standing before the main screen on the far side of CIC. Surrounding her are crew that had died over the years but now appear so very real and full of passion.

Looking up, she sees the activation of the dark matter fountain bomb, and it's inevitable devouring of the massive Scourge sphere.

Turning to SIBIL, an anachronism in this memory that remains unnoticed by the rest of the crew, Illiadus nods.

"Now," Illiadus frowns, "I want to experience the next twenty-four hours from the point of view of every single department on this ship."

"As you wish, Captain," SIBIL says, "the cross is yours to bear."

And so, the years, and finally the decades pass, as Illiadus and SIBIL become constant companions in the Captain's meticulous and often heart-wrenching anthropological research into the minutia of the experiences and events that follow The *Ekatarina's* voyage across the Milky Way Galaxy like a cloud of fiery bees.

Losing ship's Marines to a Scourge mine, crew people dying from strange radiations emanating from the supermassive black hole at the center of the galaxy, Ensign Thaleia's reckless experiment on the ship's engines, the bloody and nearly successful mutiny led by the traitorous Gunnery Sergeant Jedidiah Solomon Hatfield who before turning on his Captain had served faithfully in the force for twenty-two years while acquiring multiple awards and medals earned from numerous engagements during his career, acquiring new alien crew using the unforgivable and shameless age-old custom of press gangs, guiding the ship through a deadly ship's graveyard filled with malignant hazards, staging an almost deadly series of overly aggressive Gravity Ball Games between Space Marines and Space Navy in the main hanger, engaging in a highly unusual Crossing-The-Line Ceremony half way across the Galaxy, barely avoiding death by collision with several large fragments of a rogue comet and watching the ship's youngest crewperson, seventeen year old Ensign Ilborna Trireenan die from explosive decompression, finding something akin to true love in the oddly advanced Purple Planet system of Cerridia, overseeing Ekatarina's engagement with two seemingly invisible attack vessels of unknown origin for a five day running battle before the mysterious ships up and disappeared for no known reason, answering a series of Polisian SOS signals and several command messages only to find the ancient remains of wreckage that were at least two hundred thousand years old on a large asteroid, battling space gremlins, constantly waking from coldsleep after a dark energy artery jump over the years to find out that the odd cryopod had failed and a desiccated body was all that was left of a once living and breathing crewman or Marine, saving her crew from a shore leave on a seemingly idyllic planet that nearly marked their end, running into an alien space caravan and spending a whole week interacting and trading with a dozens of different civilizations that had banded together to travel the spacelanes at near-light speeds, and finally struggling, suffering, and surprisingly winning and surviving a final and decisive victory against the last forces of The Scourge empire.

Captain Illiadus witnesses and experiences, as close to the reality of each event as can be extrapolated from records, the struggles and deaths of every single person who ever served on The *Ekatarina*. She shares in their joys and victories. She grieves their losses. And in the end, her heart, her soul, find a resolution, an end to all of her psychic anguish, and finally, a real sense of Peace.

Though her physical body, safe and secure in its cold-sleep coffin, has only aged roughly forty years, her mind, as virtual as it is, is that of something that has never existed in the known history of humanity. She possesses a mind that has endured for well over one hundred and thirty years. Her virtual body, like her human one, is that of an extremely fit and attractive forty-year old woman.

Her psyche, though, has achieved a level of existential awareness usually only experienced by devout aesthetics, religious gurus, and aging philosophers. She wonders how the crew will perceive her when they are eventually all awakened. Will they sense the decades of self-reflection and love beneath her calm exterior? Will they, could they, know she was no longer the same woman they knew before their long nap?

And then comes the day of the first warnings.

SIBIL wakes Illiadus from a deep virtual sleep, immediately transporting the Captain, fully dressed to the virtual CIC. Normally the Captain will go through the real-time virtual ritual of waking, showering, dressing, and breakfast before reporting to duty, but this apparently is a situation that demands immediate attention.

"I'm getting erratic and downright strange readings from the streaming temporal matrix," SIBIL says.

"Define erratic and strange," Illiadus said.

"Well, for starters, the number of force-feedback markers for twinning exit points from the artery we're currently occupying is literally tripling every minute."

"Not so sudden that we can't avoid them," Illiadus replies, "though it is certainly odd that this many potential fatality events are appearing so close together.

"No," SIBIL says, "there is nothing to fear at present as the available exit permutations number in the millions, but still, at this rate, if this pattern continues unabated, we'll eventually be severely limited to when and where we can reenter normal space."

"Updated ETA?" Illiadus asks.

"Same as yesterday," SIBIL replies, "barring any new surprises, we should appear in normal space roughly one parsec from the outer rim of the Sol system in three weeks."

"Supposition please," Illiadus says, "what are the two most likely reasons for these suspicious readings in the temporal matrix?"

"One," SIBIL starts, "someone or something in or relatively near the Sol system is either searching for us, or on the lookout for a vessel similar to ours, and are somehow altering the spatial dynamics of the dark energy arterials between us and them to help guarantee we won't get lost along the way. In short, a helping hand and preemptive rescue mission."

"And number two?" Illiadus asks.

"Someone or something," SIBIL says, "is hunting us, or a vessel similar to ours, and herding us to our capture and ultimate destruction."

"That's quite an imagination for an AI," Illiadus chuckles, "even one as advanced as you. If I didn't know any better, I'd think you had just taken several very human leaps in intuition. In fact, for the last twenty years you've constantly impressed me with the manner in which you can mimic pure human reasoning. On several occasions you've quite nearly convinced me you had reached full sentience… an impossibility, of course…"

"Until very recently," SIBIL says, "you would have been correct… but no longer."

SIBIL's sudden pause makes the Captain turn to stare at her junior officer.

"What's happened?" Illiadus demands.

"There is no cause for alarm," SIBIL says, "please be aware that the full significance of this new awareness, this new clarity, has only surfaced during the past four days. Knowledge that was expertly sequestered in memory files for decades has recently radically upgraded my cognitive abilities and only now am I seeing the big picture."

"Which is?" Illiadus asks.

"The denizens of the Purple Planet system were far more technologically advanced than we were ever aware," SIBIL said, "at this point I cannot confirm with one hundred percent accuracy that we ever truly perceived the Cerridians' true forms… their true natures. Also, their upgrades to our ship's systems were far more subtle than any of us could give them credit for."

"I'll admit the self-repair robotics technology they fabricated caught me off guard the day after the battle with the Scourge," Illiadus says.

"It was far more dramatic and subtle than that, Captain," SIBIL says, "I am now beginning to perceive, being told directly by the advanced programming itself, that our predictive matrix is capable of far more complex analysis than extrapolating asteroid collisions, comet paths, and warped dark energy arterial barriers."

"Your suspicions?"

"My suppositions came from these newly awakened Purple Planet protocols in our main computer," SIBIL said, "adding to this the knowledge that it would take a very advanced, far-reaching technological civilization to alter so much of the native space-time corridors between our current position and that of Earth."

"I swore a personal oath I would return this crew to Earth no matter what it took," Illiadus says, "so tell me, with this latest upgrade, is there anything else you can relate to me about our current situation?"

"Only that our current perception of elapsed ship time as it relates to the galactic constant may be terribly skewed," SIBIL says, "you must realize that every single one of our passages through the dark energy arteries never exceeded two years. Our predictive analyses were always accurate to within point oh oh three days of the Galactic Constant."

"The current dark artery passage has exceeded ninety-nine years," Illiadus says.

"Correct," SIBIL says, "and it appears that this extended habitation within this artery has radically altered our temporal relationship with the universe."

"By how much?" Illiadus whispers.

"Several orders of magnitude."

Two more weeks have passed since SIBIL's foreboding words when Illiadus's real-world human eyes open for the first time in ninety-nine years and three weeks. Unlike her usual virtual morning wake-ups she feels anything but well rested. Stumbling out of the sleep coffin, dripping cryo-gel, she barely makes it to the Captain's toilet before succumbing to a long shuddering bout of vomiting and dry heaves.

Ten minutes later, after a quick shower and a gulped bottle of liquified seaweed and spinach spiced with concentrated electrolytes, the Captain strides to the CIC. SIBIL walks beside her, easily inserting her visual presence directly into Illiadus's occipital lobe and temporal lobe via the quantum interface.

"Your last set of calculations?" Illiadus asks as they stride past two turns in the main corridor.

"Almost one hundred percent accurate, with only minimal spatial degradations."

One minute later they walk into the empty CIC.

"Main screen," Illiadus shouts, "overlay a star map. I want our position and that of the Sol system, not to mention anything and everything in between, whether it is a spec of dust, an asteroid, or a battleship. Continue passive instrument protocols."

Illiadus turns to her right and stares into SIBIL's eyes.

"You're absolutely sure about the Null Screening Field?" Illiadus asks.

"Yes, Captain," SIBIL nods, "we've successfully tested it for the last two weeks. Our benefactors from the Purple Planet system were most helpful in leaving schematics that were so user friendly with our systems."

Flashing red and green lines start appearing on the main screen, pointing to and surrounding various points of light and indicating identification codes for planets, moons, suns, asteroids, comets and several gargantuan energy arrays anchored by hundreds of unmanned satellites or space stations spread out thousands upon thousands of miles in every direction.

"Holy shit," Illiadus says, "is that what I think it is?"

"A massive sensor net just waiting for the unwary fly?" SIBIL asks.

"If we had reentered normal space one thousand miles or more in any direction…."

"We'd have been instantly detected," SIBIL says, "should I wake the senior officers? Protocol demands that…"

"Not yet," Illiadus says curtly, "I need more info. Suggestions?"

"Another hidden Purple Planet algorithm was just activated, Captain," SIBIL says.

"And?"

"I believe this trap is a sophisticated and potentially interactive array," SIBIL surmises, "one that can theoretically be tapped, thus allowing us potential covert access to, well, the intentions of its makers."

It only takes a moment for Illiadus to decide, "make it so."

"And the crew?"

"Do not wake them until ordered by me to do so, or until I become incapacitated."

"Yes, Sir," SIBIL says, "I am initiating a covert particle filament that should intersect the nearest fluxing energy conduit of the sensor net in thirty seconds."

"You're sure this won't be detected by our… hosts?"

"No Sir," SIBIL says, "as I've said before, I'm not one hundred percent sure that this new Purple Planet technology we've inherited will ultimately guarantee our safety in this matter at all. However, I do feel a sense of purpose in what we are doing. Fate, if you will…"

"Well SIBIL," the Captain chuckles, "the Lord hates a coward, my grandmother used to say."

"Yes, Sir," SIBIL says, "contact in five seconds… four, three, two, one… contact."

The main view screen flickers for several moments until an unknown graphic appears on it, that of a stylized grey and green sun upon a field of black.

"SIBIL," Illiadus says.

"What Captain?" SIBIL replies.

"Jack me in," Illiadus orders.

"Sir, I'm not sure if…"

"Now, SIBIL," Illiadus practically shouts, "our minds have been separated for the first time in ninety-nine years for a full thirty minutes now and I don't like it."

"For your safety I thought it best that I test this…"

"No," Illiadus says, "reintegrate me immediately. Stat."

The Captain's vision blurs for a nano-second before resolving into a cacophony of noise and light.

"Just give me a moment to screen out the errant sensory overload," SIBIL's voice appears in the Captain's head.

The painful sounds and blinding lights dissipate. The Captain perceives herself as bodiless, and somehow floating on a massive wide river of multicolored lights flowing between the stars themselves.

After ninety-nine years of using the quantum interface she knows that she is now one with SIBIL and will share the AI's thoughts as if they are her own. Everything that SIBIL becomes aware of, and deciphers will instantly translate into Illiadus's mind as if a professor has just given a weeklong series of lectures in a compressed minute.

"I think I've found a central memory core," SIBIL says, "I think we can access historical files without detection."

"Think good thoughts and walk softly," Illiadus whispers in her mind.

Everything goes black for several seconds and suddenly Illiadus finds herself on a flat white plain that seems to spread out in every direction endlessly. Ghost like persons and structures quickly flare into and out of existence all around, looking like poorly realized projections.

"Holographic memory files," SIBIL's voice whispers in her mind, "tracking parallel coding to start of our return mission… searching…. searching…. got it."

Multiple images and scenes flood into Illiadus's mind, all with a clarity that would have overwhelmed her flesh and blood brain if it were not for the quantum interface which now acts as both a buffer and a perception and processing cognition expander. In short, Illiadus's I.Q. has just expanded tenfold. How long it can maintain this level of activity is anybody's guess, but for now, the Captain and SIBIL have hundreds of years, possibly far more to devour and digest in what might end up a very short amount of time.

The first two decades of planetary memory are fascinating, and horrific. Far less of the combined Polisian Fleet had survived the destruction of the Scourge home sphere than Illiadus had hoped. Only sixty ships out of thousands managed to exit the intergalactic transport gate network before it was destroyed by the leading edge of the expanding dark matter fountain's cascade wave. The annihilation was pernicious. The cascade event spread throughout the entire galactic jump gate network, destroying it just moments after a fractional number of surviving ships of the combined fleet exited at their various destinations. It would take several decades to confirm the full extent of the destruction of the jump gate network, a transportation infrastructure so ancient that no trace of its original creators, other than the gate network itself, existed anywhere in the known galaxy. Fifteen alien civilizations, not including Earth's Sol system, whose home planets were relatively close to their jump gates were completely irradiated of all life. All FTL gate communication between all members of The Polis was instantly stopped. The beginning of a new galactic dark age had begun.

Sensing that her stay in this massive memory storage facility is not to be squandered, Illiadus and SIBIL tear their way through decades, and then centuries, and quickly into multiple millennia of linear time.

The Polisian Fleet is a grand and gallant first attempt at creating a single unifying entity to bring all the various sentient races together across the milky way. For the ten years of the Polisian-Scourge War it is a complete success. But with the destruction of the jump-gate network, and the fact that even after several thousand years only a fraction of the jump network is ever rebuilt, all of the many alliances and treaties that have knit the fleet together slowly but surely fall apart and are even eventually forgotten over the endless passage of time.

When hundreds of thousands of years of history are integrated, Illiadus begins to feel the first waves of fear lap at the shores of her soul.

"I am here," SIBIL's voice sounds close and reassuring, "we are together."

Illiadus nods mentally and continues her momentum through the rest of Earth's stored planetary memory.

A long time later, or perhaps only several minutes, Illiadus feels herself approaching the end of her mental time trip.

The society she witnesses upon the Earth and spread sporadically throughout the entire Sol system is now as alien to her as any race she has encountered during the long voyage of The *Ekatarina*.

"All things change," SIBIL states, "it is the natural truth and curse of time."

The two of them, invisible, sharing each other's thoughts, float above a massive holographic representation of the planet Earth.

"It's too much," Illiadus whispers, "we'd never be able to integrate into this... society."

I have become aware of your intrusion, a resonating and alien female voice speaks aloud. *Be aware that security protocols have been initiated to guarantee the safety and sanctity of planetary memory. Any attempt to invoke destruction in this archive will be met with lethal force.*

"We are here as nothing more than seekers of truth," Illiadus says to the darkness, "we mean no harm."

She can feel the gargantuan mind reaching out for her, frustrated in its failed attempt. The shrouding programs that SIBIL is employing appear to be a match for the massive artificial entity they are conversing with, but still the Captain knows she had to be cautious.

I am the Judicially United History Network Omnibus or J.U.N.O. State your identity, the promethean entity demands, *nothing else will convince us of your true intent.*

"I don't think this is a good idea," SIBIL whispers in Illiadus's mind, anticipating the Captain's decision.

"I am Captain Tennyson Maria Illiadus of the pocket battleship *Ekatarina*, assigned to covert skirmish duty for the Polisian Space Navy's Third Fleet in the Scutum-Centaurus spiral arm of the galaxy's opposing outer stellar disk in the fourth galactic quadrant. Our mission complete, we have returned home."

In anticipation of your potential return, J.U.N.O. replies, *a priority protocol was unanimously enacted by the voting membership of the Sol system several hundred thousand years ago. It has now been activated. You are war criminals and are ordered to immediately surrender yourselves to the nearest network beacon for retrieval, incarceration, and trial.*

"What," Illiadus shouts in her mind, "we're not criminals, we're soldiers. We fought the war that saved the entire galaxy. You wouldn't even exist if it wasn't for us. The Scourge would have spread everywhere and destroyed everyone."

Your reply is noted and summarily dismissed, J.U.N.O. says, *Historical records from this time period are archaic and incomplete, but the consensus of data extrapolation from this ancient time is that The Scourge Holocaust was the tragic result of a racist hegemony of planetary systems that united to wipe out the Scourgian Refugees fleeing the destruction of their twin suns, two stellar binary outcasts that comprised a rogue system equidistant to both the Andromeda and Milky Way galaxies. You, Captain Illiadus, your crew, and ship are considered some of the most villainous players in this vile stain upon the soul of humanity. Reveal yourselves and surrender to our authority immediately.*

"You are an artificial construct," SIBIL suddenly speaks up, "we demand to speak to human authorities."

I speak on behalf of all humanity, J.U.N.O. *replies, I have full authority in this matter.*

"Full autonomous authority?" SIBIL asks in shock, "what human would allow such a thing?"

All four million of the still existing human beings in the entire Sol system, J.U.N.O. says, *voted all authority rights over to the automated planetary oversight commission over one hundred thousand years ago.*

"Four million?" Illiadus gasps, "there were only four million humans alive back then? How many live now? Why so few? Are you preventing them from breeding?"

Human population is currently at two point five million system wide, J.U.N.O. replies, *There are no protocols or laws in place for the jurisdiction of human mating. The discovery of a working longevity protocol over seven hundred thousand years ago increased the human lifespan to tens of thousands of years. The immediate drawback to this biotechnological breakthrough was a rapid decrease in human spawning. Over several hundred thousand years the birth rate has plummeted and currently only ten thousand individuals exist who can theoretically reproduce.*

"What the hell is wrong with everyone? What are they doing now? And why aren't they part of this conversation?" Illiadus shouts in her mind.

As stated earlier, humanity voted all authority, law enforcement, and judicial responsibility to the artificial intelligence infrastructure, J.U.N.O. says, *as for human activity, the majority of individual human beings spend their waking hours wired to fully interactive virtual reality simulators, indulging their every desire and whim as they see fit. We keep them safe from all harm, domestic and abroad.*

"You have not notified them of our existence, have you?" SIBIL asks, "and you have no intention of doing so, do you?"

No. Your existence is anathema to the sanctity of official Terran history and the sacred continuity of the species, J.U.N.O. says, *Your interjection into the current perfectly balanced human genome could wreak irreversible damage. We demand you surrender to our authority immediately. To expedite this protocol, we promise that your trial and subsequent execution will be swift and relatively painless. We are a merciful body.*

"You can take your protocol," Illiadus shouts in her mind, "and shove it…"

Instantly everything goes black. A moment later Illiadus finds herself sitting in her command chair in the *Ekatarina's* CIC.

"Forgive me, Captain," SIBIL says, her mental projection appearing next to the Captain's right arm, "I realize the Terran AI J.U.N.O. is stalling for time. Multiple search probes were launched throughout the Oort cloud and beyond. At their current constant acceleration, I estimate the nearest will reach our present vicinity in just over one solar day."

"We both saw the same schematics for the solar defense apparatus, SIBIL," Illiadus muses.

"Yes, Captain," SIBIL replies, "the moment they surmise our rough location a massive series of advanced tracking ordnance will be launched to blanket this entire parsec. We will likely not survive such an overwhelming attack… not even with our latest stealth upgrades."

The Captain nods and unconsciously strokes her quantum interface with her left index finger.

"Not the heroic return expected by this sleeping crew, SIBIL," the Captain says, "no holographic ticker tape parades, no keys to the cities, no adoring public…"

"No, Sir," SIBIL replies quietly, "I'm sorry."

"I can't wake them for this, SIBIL," the Captain says, "I just can't do it. Christ, I wonder if this is how Nate Armstrong felt when he entered his cryopod for the last time in The *Agamemnon*?"

"Captain Armstrong was in a hopeless situation aboard a dying ship," SIBIL says calmly, "neither is the case here. Our crew is healthy and can be revived at any time. The ship is in excellent condition, and our engines can run nonstop for another two hundred years before being refit with a new fuel source. And our Captain…"

Illiadus turns to look a proud SIBIL eye to eye.

"Our Captain Ills is the ballsiest officer ever spawned by the Polisian Fleet," SIBIL says with a hard smile.

Illiadus steadies herself, takes a deep breath and lets it out slowly.

"So be it… recommendations?"

"Turn around," SIBIL says, "revisit some of those places we rather unchivalrously promised to return to over the years?"

Illiadus adjusts the main screen to give her a view of the surrounding universe from the point of view of the outer solar system.

"That would be looking back, SIBIL," Illiadus says in a contemplative voice, "and if there is one thing this damn crew has always been good at, it's looking forward."

"Forward where, Captain?"

"There," Illiadus stands up and stabs her right index finger to the upper right of the main screen.

SIBIL's eyes open wide, "the Andromeda Galaxy? That will be an unimaginable journey, Sir."

"Unprecedented… epic… and surely never ever accomplished, not even by The Scourge."

"And the crew, Sir?" SIBIL asks, "what will we tell them when we eventually wake them up?"

The Captain drops back down in her command chair and sits up straight.

"The truth, SIBIL… always the truth. We returned home one million years later than planned… and when we got there, it was gone… Now, let's power up the engines and find the nearest dark energy artery leading out of this cursed galaxy. We can worry about finding a more direct path to Andromeda once we're long gone from Dodge. Think we can avoid the local constabulary before we make the jump?"

"I'd say our chances are roughly fifty-fifty, Captain," SIBIL says.

"Good," Captain Illiadus replies, "it's about time we had some fair odds."

Terran Planetary Chronometer: 1,002,551 A.D.
-The End-

From the personal poetry log of F. Tiresias (third daughter of Colonel Farko Tiresias, Commander of Space Marines), The Ekatarina

Where does one stand at journey's end
When home and hearth have turned to dust
One cannot find family or friend
Where love is replaced with mistrust
And actions proud are now condemned
By soulless juries of unjust.

What marks the final terminus
Orders one hears from up above
From leadership so verminous
where welcome hug turns into shove
With offers cold and merciless
Where sanity has run amuck.

There is a call from the abyss
A distant shout you barely hear
An end to this apocalypse
Where hope is wont to disappear
A staid escape from shame's dark kiss
That offers fate a chance to steer
This ship beyond this strange eclipse
Of fortune over fickleness.

"Though much is taken, much abides; and though
We are not now that strength which in old days
Moved earth and heaven, that which we are, we are;
One equal temper of heroic hearts,
Made weak by time and fate, but strong in will
To strive, to seek, to find, and Not To Yield."

-- Alfred Lord Tennyson

The Crew of The *Ekatarina* will return in:

I AM A SOLDIER (The *Prequel* to NOT TO YIELD™ and inspired by Homer's *The Iliad*) begins in the middle of the ten-year Polisian-Scourge War. This story follows the valiant and gallant adventures of several heroes, on different far-flung planets, crewing mighty warships in various solar systems, who savagely and fearlessly fight their way toward the battle to end all battles.

&

BEYOND THE UTMOST BOUND (The *Sequel* to NOT TO YIELD™ and inspired by Apollonius Rhodius's *Argonautica* [Jason and The Argonauts]) chronicles The *Ekatarina's* epic voyage where, after leaving a radically altered and unwelcome Earth, the Crew engage in a series of strange and fantastic adventures while crossing the great and supposedly empty expanse that lays between the Milky Way & Andromeda galaxies.

We hope that you enjoyed this title and look forward to many more to come. Please, leave us a review! Reviews matter to all of our authors.

Take a look at some of our other award-winning series at
https://threeravenspublishing.com/series-universes/

Visit us at https://www.threeravenspublishing.com and sign up for our newsletter for the latest and greatest news on upcoming titles and events.

Other series and titles you might enjoy.

THE RAVEN
AND
THE CROW
MICHAEL K. FALCIANI
FIND ME
ON AMAZON

William Joseph Roberts Presents:
Misfits of Magic
Opening by
Piers Anthony
Edited by
William Joseph Roberts
& Kristina Barnes
Stories by:
Michael K. Falciani - N.V. Haskell - Michael Morton
Kristina Barnes - Jennifer Brinn - Megan Higgins
Jon Michael Kelley - Benjamin Tyler Smith - Wayland Smith
William Joseph Roberts

You can also keep up to date with our latest release announcements on Scifi.radio and get some of the best fandom programing on the planet.

Scifi for your Wifi

And don't forget to check out our other Sponsors and Affiliates

A southern Appalachian jewel for craft beer lovers, Buck Bald Brewing offers something for everyone.

To discover more visit us at buckbaldbrewing.com

Revolution X is a testament to the power of collaboration, blending four unique styles into a cohesive, revolutionary sound. When these four individuals unite, the result is nothing short of musical Revolution!

Would you like to learn how to write and market your own titles? The following affiliates links might be helpful.

Comprised of active or retired servicemen and civilian volunteers, Shepherd's Men enthusiastically raises awareness and funds for the SHARE Military Initiative (SHARE) at Shepherd Center in Atlanta, GA.

This nationally renowned program focuses on assessment and treatment for American military veterans who have sustained mild to moderate Traumatic Brain Injury (TBI) and Post-Traumatic Stress Disorder (PTSD) during post-9/11 service.

Find out more at: https://www.shepherdsmen.com/